JOHN LYNCH

ZAPPA'S MAM'S A SLAPPER

Published by Mandrill Press www.mandrillpress.com

ISBN 978-1-910194-11-9

Author picture by Ruth Jenkinson Photography

To Tara, who showed me how to turn the book
I'd written into the one I'd wanted to write

And Ayisha, who kept my nose to the grindstone
until it was done

And to Helen, the best proofreader a writer could hope for

Also By John Lynch

Sharon Wright: Butterfly

As R J Lynch:

The James Blakiston Series set in northeast England in the 1760s

Book 1: A Just and Upright Man

Book 2: Poor Law

Non Fiction

The International Sales Handbook

CHAPTER 1

All I'd said was, I wouldn't mind seeing her in her knickers. I wouldn't have thought, being honest, that that merited a showdown with her brothers.

I tried to explain. She's a bit on the chubby side, Kathleen, which I like. Not a grotesque fatty; just a bit of a plumper. Real fatties, I don't care for. I've got a pic I took of a thumper sitting on one chair when three would not have been too many. I took it from behind, which is the only way you could really bring yourself to look at her. Great blue denim bulges hanging down on each side. You'd wonder how anyone could let herself get like that.

Jessica made me leave that one out of the exhibition. 'It's an interesting eye you have, Billy,' she said, 'but it wouldn't please everyone.'

I said, 'That's not what the instructor told us in Young Offenders. He said you should nurture your own unique vision.'

Jessica's eye twitched. She didn't like being argued with, and she had this ambivalence towards my time inside – it was what made me a celeb but she said it was her job to publicise it and not mine. Which is all very well, but if I hadn't been in Young Offenders I'd never have got into taking pics. They'd run this course on digital photography (and how stupid is that? To do digital photography you need a digital camera and how did anyone think a Young Offender was going to get one of those once he was back on the street?) and I'd signed up to deal with the tension of not knowing whether I'd get out. I'd loved it.

No, with Kathleen I'd pictured her sitting on a bed in nothing but a pair of those knickers Marks & Sparks had in their adverts when they were going after the smart young people who wouldn't be seen dead in Marks, you might as well ask them to shop in Milletts. Everyone remembers those knickers. Every man, anyway. Lot of lezzies, too, I should think. The ones coming a couple of inches down the leg and cut square. Nice patterns, interesting colours and a dark edge to waist and leg. And the models they used hadn't exactly been short-changed in the upper body department.

Lovely. Kathleen would be sitting on the bed in these and nothing else, one leg pointing straight out in front and the other drawn up under her, arms crossed at the elbow and hands clasped so that you saw nothing more revealing than a bit of flesh squeezed each side of the arms. And she'd be looking straight at the camera and smiling. That's one of the things I liked about Kathleen – that she was always smiling. That and not being skinny. She had a lovely smile, Kathleen.

Jessica said I had a fantastic eye for a pic, 'a real intuitive grasp for composition,' which was exactly what the instructor at Young Offenders had said.

And that's all it was.

But I'd said it out loud and some mischief-making twat had told Kathleen's brothers and they were offended. Or pretended they were. They wanted me to explain myself. I suppose they thought, being two of them, they could take me on. Big mistake. I'd tried to leave my reputation behind when I'd been brought to this street. 'Make a new start,' the Education Officer had said. But you can't always do that. People won't always let you. It was 2004, I was sixteen years old and at the start of what I hoped was going to be a different life from the one I'd been living up to then, and here I was trying to talk myself out of trouble – a route I'd never taken in the past.

I told the brothers I'd just been thinking about a pic, didn't have any designs on their sister's luscious body. I suppose I can't keep calling them the brothers, you don't know who I'm talking about. Harry and Tommy Doyle, they were. First generation English, the father a copper who'd lived here since he was six but the Doyle boys still came on like they were born in Tipperary. My foster parents were called Howard, but PC Doyle knew I had an Irish surname so he'd stop me in the street and talk about Ireland, what a grand place it was and did I know where my family came from? Which I didn't. My grandparents were born here so if the call had ever come from Lansdowne Road I'd have had to say I wasn't qualified but if you've got an Irish name the Paddies always want to co-opt you. He was all right, Mister Doyle. He even asked the Howards if they wanted him to take me to Mass with his family when they went on Sundays. The Howards said they'd leave it to me, I didn't have to go but I could if I wanted to but if I didn't I needn't.

Which I didn't.

I've never been to Mass in my life.

Or any other kind of religious service, far as I know.

(Except in Young Offenders, of course, where you went to anything that was going just to get out of your cell.)

But I liked it that he'd thought enough of me to ask.

You'd wonder sometimes why, when the father's all right, the son has to be a dickhead.

(Another thing you'd sometimes wonder; if Ireland is such a grand place, why do so many Irish people come over here and never go back?)

Harry said, 'You keep your hands off our sister.' He stuck his finger in my chest as he said it. I've always hated it when people do that. Even then we could still all three of us have walked away, no harm done. That's certainly what I wanted. I said, 'I told you. I was just imagining a pic.' And then I told them the stuff about liking to see a girl who wasn't as thin as a rake, smiling. And about how I'd compose the pic.

Harry said, 'You calling our sister fat?' He had an English accent, same as I did, not a touch of the Paddy about him, but it takes at least a generation and usually two to get people to realise that they're English and not Irish. (If they're American, they never seem to grasp it.) We had about four Irish families in the street. They'd all troop off to Mass on Sundays and they didn't do their socialising locally but in the Hibernian Club downtown. Didn't have as much as they'd have liked but intended their children should have more. The aspirational working class, I learned to call them in Sociology. The English version has disappeared, apparently. Anyone who aspired has made it and those who are left have given up. Live off the State and what you can nick. Like my mother and the Creep. But there's still plenty of immigrants who aspire.

Christian Brothers did the teaching at Saint Simeon's, which is where the boys went, and they were known for their discipline. Maybe the treatment they handed out was what made the Catholic kids think they were so hard. It was a mistake, but most of them made it. Either that or it's just part of the Culture for Paddies to prance around pretending to be hard. They told us in Sociology never to underestimate the power of the Culture. Capital C.

'No,' I said. 'I'm not saying your sister is fat. I'm saying she'd make a lovely picture.'

I think I'd realised by now that Harry was determined to bring this to a fight and nothing I did was going to change that. But, I had to try. When you're in jail for an offence like mine, you never actually do your time. The best you can hope for, and this is what had happened to me, is that you're released on licence. What that means is that if you commit any kind of offence they can take you back inside to finish your original sentence. Even if the new offence is shoplifting a Snickers bar and the original sentence was life imprisonment, they can still take you back to serve it. And as it happens my original sentence was life imprisonment, because that's mandatory in this country for the offence I'd been found guilty of. Although, because of my age, they didn't call it that, they called it detention at the pleasure of Her Majesty. But life imprisonment is what that means, at least in my case. The judge made that clear when he sentenced me. And I wouldn't be going back to Young Offenders. I was an adult now, and it would be adult jail I went to, and I'd had some of that already and I hadn't liked it. At all. So I wanted to stay out of trouble if I could and if that meant seeming to back down in front of the Doyle boys, back down is what I'd have to do.

There are limits, though. Which Harry Doyle overstepped when he called my foster mother an ugly cow. I dropped him.

He went down with a satisfying thump and didn't move. I looked at Tommy. 'You can have one, too,' I said. 'But you don't have to. It's up to you.'

Tommy was younger than Harry, younger than me in fact, and he was looking seriously nervous. All the bombast he'd got from standing beside his big and rather stupid brother had left him.

'Do you think he's all right?' he asked.

'He went down a bit hard.'

'Maybe we should get help.'

'Maybe *you* should get help,' I said. 'I didn't want this in the first place.'

'Me neither,' said Tommy. 'He makes me go along. If I don't do what he wants, he beats me up.'

'So,' I said. 'That's what they teach you at Catholic school, is it?'

Harry had started to make noises. He rolled over and tried to sit up. It took him three goes.

'Our dad likes you,' Tommy said. 'Our sister likes you, too.'

'Does she?'

'I doubt she'll let you see her in her knickers, though.' He grinned at me. 'That's not what they teach you at Catholic school.'

Mister Doyle stopped me in the street the next day. 'Harry's concussed,' he said. 'He's going to miss a few days' college.'

'I'm sorry. It wasn't my fault.'

'I know whose fault it was. I've heard the whole story. They won't trouble you again.' He looked as though he was going to move on, but didn't. 'They have a youth club,' he said. 'At the Hibernian. Dancing on Saturday nights.'

'Yes?'

'Kathleen goes there.' He looked at me closely. 'Well,' he said. 'Just a thought.' He looked back as he walked way. 'Harry told Kathleen you said she was fat.'

'I didn't say that.'

'I wouldn't be talking to you if I thought you had. Tommy told her what you said. I think she's flattered. You can forget glamour photos, though. Her mother would kill her. And then she'd kill you.'

* * *

He'd talked to my foster parents, too. Mister Howard asked me into their sitting room when I got home. You only got there by special invitation.

'Billy,' he said. 'Why do you always refer to us as your foster parents?'

I didn't answer.

'We're not your foster parents, Billy. And this isn't your foster home. This is a hostel, and Missus Howard and I are wardens.'

They had a wooden clock with a little plate on the front. There was an engraved message on it, but I couldn't read what the message said. I sat and listened to the tick.

'It's no good staring at your hands, Billy. We need to talk about this.'

As far as I could remember, we hadn't had a clock at home. There was a digital on the video, of course, and another on the microwave. The one on the video was always right because it came off the television signal. That clock ticking in a quiet room was the most comforting sound I could think of.

When they'd been doing their tests, I was asked to write down the three nicest words I could think of. I'd put "comforting" at the top.

Missus Howard made one of those little gestures at Mister Howard, and he shut up. 'Billy,' said Missus Howard. 'When you first came here, you said you liked trees, and gardens, and parks. Do you remember saying that?'

I nodded.

'There's an arboretum near here. Do you know what an arboretum is, Billy?'

I shook my head.

'It's a tree place. Like a zoo, only where zoos have animals, an arboretum has trees. I like to go there sometimes. I'm thinking of going on Saturday. Would you like to come with me?'

I nodded.

'We could take a picnic. So we didn't have to hurry back. Would you like that?'

I nodded.

'Are you still collecting five new words a day, Billy?'

'Yes.' I had to say it twice because it came out a bit too quiet the first time.

'Well, that can be one of today's five. Arboretum. A tree collection.'

'Thank you.'

'All right, Billy. Why don't you go and wash now, and get ready for dinner?'

I went to my room. I'd heard from some of the others who had been there longer than me that the Howards had a daughter who sometimes came to visit and stayed for dinner. Some people had a mother like Missus Howard. And I had one like mine. It didn't seem fair, somehow.

But life isn't. Fair, I mean. All you can do is keep slugging away until you see a chance. Then take it.

CHAPTER 2

Number: 27619   *Name: Billy McErlane*   *Date: 2 September 2002*

My Ideal Life

Question: Write an essay (not less than 1,000 words) describing the life
you would most like to live. Don't worry about money or what is possible
– just tell the reader how you would like to live if you could.

In my ideal life, I live alone. I'm in a big flat in a building that's a bit old
overlooking a park. There is a garden belonging to the building and I'm
allowed to go in it, but my flat is on the second floor. I have a big sitting
room and a bedroom and my own kitchen and bathroom and toilet.
There's a TV and a radio and a CD player for when I want them, but I
don't usually unless there's something I'm really interested in like an
important rugby game or maybe athletics. In athletics I specially like to
watch the longer races where each person is on their own and has lots of
time to think about things while they're running. When I was younger I
used to run to school and I'd pretend I was in a big important cross
country race and I'd think about all sorts of important stuff while I was
running. Running does that to you.

I never watch boxing in my ideal life. Boxers set out to hurt each other
and it should be stopped. And I don't watch stuff like Rebus, where
people do horrible things to other people. I might watch Midsomer
Murders sometimes, or repeats of Inspector Morse, or those things with

Miss Marple. Or Poirot. People do unkind things to other people there, too, but you don't see it. And they don't shout and scream at people.

In my ideal life I never watch stuff like Big Brother because people are always shouting and saying nasty things to each other and I don't like it when people do that. And the people are always stupid. And I don't watch comedy shows because they're always trying to make themselves look big by making other people look small. But if there's a repeat of Morecambe and Wise or The Two Ronnies I watch that.

There would be lots of books in my sitting room in my ideal life and a great big window, one of those windows that stick out from the house, I forget what they're called. It's very quiet in the room and I sit at the window and watch people in the park. There are lots of families in the park. In fact, it's almost all families. And the families are happy and don't shout or hit each other. There's a father and a mother and a boy and a girl and that's it. Only two children. Two is enough. But sometimes there's also a dog. And the father and the mother have their arms round each other's waists and talk to each other as they walk along and you can see they like each other a lot. And the boy throws sticks for the dog, and the girl twirls around on the path, watching her skirt be like a Catherine wheel. But it never gets so high that you can see her underwear.

And sometimes there's a girl on her own in the park. She's wearing nice clothes, maybe a uniform from a nice school where children are taught to be polite and not make other people feel small. And I know if I went down into the park I could sit down on the bench with the girl and have a nice conversation about what she's going to do one day and what I'm going to do one day. And it wouldn't feel as though we were in competition. With each other or anyone else. But we don't ever talk about rude things, or make hints about the stuff that makes boys and girls different. And she tells me about her brother, and her mother and father who sometimes walk in the park with their arms round each other's waists, and who really like each other and never ever shout at each other in front of the children. And they have a dog. I don't actually go down into the park and have this conversation. But I know I could do, and one day I will. Probably.

When it gets too dark for people to walk in the park, I open one of the books and read. And I learn my five new words a day.

One of the best parts of my ideal life is food. Buying it and cooking it and eating it. I go shopping every day, and I have enough money to buy what I want, and I've learned to cook from reading books and watching TV. And I make my own bread.

For breakfast I have poached egg on my own bread, toasted.

In the middle of the morning I have a mug of hot chocolate with more milk than water in it and a biscuit.

In the middle of the day I sometimes have soup with my own bread, toasted. Sometimes sardines on my own bread, toasted. Sometimes cold chicken or ham. Or a pork pie with cheese and HP Sauce.

At four in the afternoon I have a mug of tea and a biscuit. Or maybe sometimes a cream cake. Chocolate éclairs are nice.

And then in the evening I have stew, or roast beef with Yorkshire Pudding, or fish. I like fish. Proper fish, not fish fingers and stuff. And it's quiet when I eat.

And then I go to bed, and because I'm at the back of a big house overlooking a park, there isn't any noise.

I'm sorry, I know that's not 1,000 words, but it's all I can think of.

Except that sometimes in my ideal life someone would come in and hug me. Just hug me, nothing else, and they wouldn't say anything, and after a while they'd leave. But I'd remember that I'd been hugged, and how it felt. I don't know who it would be that hugged me.

CHAPTER 3

After I was sentenced I was transported two hundred and fifty miles south, to a Young Offenders Institution west of London. While I was there the Chief Inspector of Prisons issued a report that said accommodation standards in the place were poor, cells were dirty, offenders could not have a shower every day and there was far too little for the young men to do. I couldn't argue with any of that. What I took in first was a big Victorian building of red brick with dirty sandstone above the windows. Get inside and you became aware of the portable cabin additions, which were probably only twenty years old but were already more run down than the original structure.

I started in the induction wing and went from there to the young persons' development wing which was a reminder of the big gap there can be between what people say they're going to do and what actually happens. This wing was an anti-bullying unit. In theory. In practice, it was run by six long-term prisoners who really should have been moved on by now but who held sway over the young guys. The ringleader decided to show me on my first day who was in charge (them) and who had to do what he was told (the rest of us) so I smacked him. When his nose broke he was moaning like a little boy and none of the others came to help him. After that incident I was moved to a general wing. I'd thought I might be in trouble, but no-one said a word to me.

When I finished doing their tests, they told me I had an IQ of 143.

'Do you know what that means, Billy?' the psychiatrist asked.

14

Honestly. I just stared at her. She tells me I'm forty-three per cent more intelligent than the average person and then asks if I know what it means.

'What do you think you'd like to do?' she said. 'When you get out of here?'

I looked at my feet.

'Billy?'

'You've fallen through the net a bit,' she said when she realised I wasn't going to speak. 'The Government says local authorities have to arrange for the education of young people in care, but the fact is that it doesn't happen. And then, of course, your mother... Strangely enough, coming into this place has probably given you a boost. You can start your A levels in here. In fact, if we can convince the Parole Board, you can probably go out to the Sixth Form College to do them. If the college says yes, of course.'

I was shaking. My heart was banging and I felt as though I was going to be sick.

'Shall I tell you what you're doing, Billy?' the psychiatrist asked.

I didn't say anything.

'It's called magical thinking,' she said. 'You think it's unlucky to talk about what you'll do when you get out of here. Don't you?'

I nodded.

'You think if you talk about it, you won't get out.'

I nodded again.

'That's magical thinking, Billy. You'll either get out of here or you won't, but talking about it won't stop it happening. And if you don't talk about it, think about it, plan it, you won't make a success of it if it happens. Which means you'll end up coming back here.'

'Everybody comes back,' I said.

'No, Billy, they don't. A lot of people come back, that's true, but some make it on the outside. You have the brains to be one of them. If that's what you want. Is it what you want?'

I nodded.

'Say it, Billy. I want to hear you say it.'

'I want to get out,' I said through the tears. 'I want to make it.'

'I have a big say in whether you get out, Billy. But only one person can decide whether you stay there. And that's you.'

I worked in the kitchen. That's what they had for us. The glossy pamphlets for visitors talked about A levels, but the education you could actually get was stuff like *Introduction to Literacy* and *Introduction to Life Skills*, both of which bored me to tears, and the work skills they wanted to teach you were things like veg prep.

Juvie and Young Offenders are based on the idea that everyone in them is as thick as pigshit and in my experience that isn't true. But learning how to slice a carrot was better than sitting in the cellblock listening to people fantasizing about girls they'd done it with and whether Crystal Palace would be relegated, or get into Europe, or whatever it was Crystal Palace were supposed to be in line for that year, and so I stuck with it.

There was one guy in there who claimed to have banged all the female instructors who came in to teach stuff. Every single one. Whatever name came up, he'd say 'I've had her. Fucked her on the table in Reception' or 'Shagged her rotten in Classroom Three. Mad for it, she is. Nympho'. There was one woman who hadn't even been in yet, we'd just heard about her coming when they were looking to sign people up for her course, and Woolf claimed he'd had her.

And when they talked about girls, they always talked about them as if they were the enemy and you had to hurt them and they expected you to and liked it. Which I was sure couldn't be right. I'd only ever had one girlfriend but that's what I'd wanted her to be. A girl who was a friend.

So that's what I got away from when I went to the kitchen.

Which is where I was when the Governor sent for me.

I'd been to the Governor twice before. Once in 2002 when I'd first come in and he'd wanted to make sure I understood what was expected of me and wouldn't feel overwhelmed by being in a prison for young adult males when I was only fourteen. What I think he wanted to know was: was I likely to top myself? And the second time was six months later after I stopped a couple of lads from doing Williams.

Williams was seventeen but he had the brain of a ten-year-old. He was the sort of inmate *Introduction to Literacy* was meant for, except it was too advanced for him. I don't think he ever learned to read. He didn't wash or clean his teeth unless someone made him, so a couple of guys used to march him down to the showers once a week and make sure he got clean, which I thought was fair enough. We had to live with him. He used to breathe through his mouth, which was always open. He wouldn't hurt anyone, though. A big softy. Sat in his cell and cried a lot. When it got a bit noisy people would tell him to shut it and it would all die away to a whimper.

I came back onto the wing one day and these two had got Williams backed into his cell. They'd hung a shirt over the CCTV camera so the screws couldn't see what they were doing. In theory, the moment that happened there should have been two guards at the door checking it out, but we all knew that never happened. Let the boys police themselves was what the screws thought. They never said it but they thought it.

They'd got Williams's pants off and Leroy had his dick out. His own dick, that is. There wasn't much doubt what they were going to do, and if there had been, the way Leroy was humping his hips in Williams's direction would have removed it.

There were some other people on the wing. Some of them had clearly come in while this was going on. They'd all made themselves scarce.

Williams was terrified. He may not have been able to read *Mister Messy* but he knew when two men bigger than him (and Leroy was a monster) were planning to do a nasty thing to him and he didn't like the idea.

I stepped between them. 'Leave him alone,' I said, sounding a lot more confident than I felt. I looked at some of the other cells. I had this idea that people might come out to help me. Some hope.

Leroy turned in amazement. 'What the fuck do you think you're doing?'

The other one, Denzil, said, 'He wants it for himself, Leroy.'

He was the easy one, if you could call either of them easy, so I did him first.

Most people get it wrong when they try to kick someone in the balls. Here's a short primer in case you ever find yourself in this position. First, be quick. As quick coming out as you are going in. If he catches your ankle and holds on to it, you've got trouble. Especially if someone the size of Leroy is adjacent. Second, and possibly most important, *don't aim for the front*. On the other hand, don't aim too far back, either. Get him just underneath the hanging sac, so you ram his squelchy soft goolies up into his body where the hard bones are. Third, use maximum force. You're not trying to cause him a little difficulty, you're out to inflict serious damage. Do him before he does you. Splitting the skin of the sac is your priority objective. Wrecking the whole package is the outcome most positively wished.

We were out in the corridor now, with Denzil rolling on the floor and screaming. I leapt for the shirt and tugged it off the camera. I knew I couldn't take Leroy, even on his own, and I could see he was seriously angry. Angry enough to want to kill, or at least maim. And he'd killed before, had Leroy. In my case I knew I never wanted to be near a dead body ever again, but with Leroy you got the feeling that the first one was the difficult one and after that it wouldn't grieve him to do another. He probably should have been in Broadmoor, not Young Offenders.

I can't say the screws got there any faster than they had to. By the time they pulled him off me, hitting him over the head with their sticks, his hands on my throat had caused me to stop seeing and, pretty well, to stop breathing.

All three of us ended up in hospital, with a screw sitting by the bed we were handcuffed to. Denzil while they patched up his manhood; Leroy while he recovered from having his skull smashed and they waited to see if he'd regain the power of speech; and me because I'd nearly been asphyxiated and there were bruises on the back of my head.

I got out first.

They took me straight to the Governor's office. He wasn't very happy with me.

'This has to go down on your record as a racist incident, McErlane.'

I just stared at him. Racist incident?

'You attacked two black prisoners. Not just assault, but racially motivated assault. Do you have anything to say for yourself?'

I shook my head.

'Is this a refusal to say anything to incriminate another inmate, McErlane? Or do you really have no defence to offer?'

I stared at a spot just above the Governor's forehead. He relaxed. 'Very well. In recognition of your willingness not to complicate matters by saying something that would require an investigation of a most sensitive matter, I'm going to go easy on you. Fifteen days loss of privileges. Suspended for three months.' He leaned forward. 'Stay out of trouble for thirteen weeks and the whole thing's forgotten. Think you can do that?'

I nodded.

'Very well. Take him back, Chief. And, McErlane. Leave the other races alone. All right?'

He placed a finger vertically against the side of his nose. He wasn't a nice man, the Governor. But then, I suppose he couldn't be.

So that was the Governor I was going to discuss my educational future with. To be fair, the business with Leroy didn't seem to be an issue any longer.

'You want to do A levels, McErlane.'

'Yes, sir.'

'Why?'

I hadn't expected that one. "So I can get a good job" didn't seem too brilliant if he came back with "In your dreams. You're doing life, sonny. Where's this job going to be? In the prison library?" I decided to play it straight. 'To keep my brain working, sir.'

His face was a blank. It was like he was waiting for me to add something. But maybe what I added would damn me. I'd seen that before, and not just in here. I kept silent. He opened the file on his desk. It had my name on it.

CHAPTER 4

Number: 27619　　　*Name: Billy McErlane*　　　*Date: 9 September 2002*

What I'd do differently

Question: Take a frank look at the life you're leading now and what brought you to this point. Then imagine you have a time machine that can take you back as far as you like (but only in your own lifetime). Write an essay (not less than 1,000 words) saying how far back you'd go, what you'd do differently when you got there, and why.

I suppose the easy thing to say is that I'd go all the way back to when I was born and make sure I wasn't. That would save a lot of trouble. Or maybe if that isn't allowed I could scream without stopping until she decided she couldn't take me home and handed me over to another mother. One who came with a father attached. What I'd have liked would have been to find a family with a father who went out to work every day and brought his money home and didn't drink and never hit anyone, and a mother who didn't take drugs and dressed like a mother and kept her knickers on except when she was with her husband and out of sight of the children and who knew how to cook and kept the house clean and one other child, a daughter, five years older than me, who worked hard at school and kept an eye on me. That would have been ideal. Although the daughter could also have been five years younger than me, and I'd have kept an eye on her. That would have worked, too. I think if I'd had that I'd have been prepared to do my bit to make them proud of me.

Or if I couldn't do those things I might go back to when I was six and the social workers came with the police and this time I'd tell the truth instead of lying to protect that bastard and they'd take me away and put me in a nice foster family that would take care of me.

Or of course I could go back to when I was nine and they did take me away and put me with a foster family and this time I'd behave nicely so I could stay there and not end up being in a home. Because if there's one thing a home is not it's a home.

And even after that I could go back to when I was twelve and my mother was making such a fuss about getting me back and promising she was going to be a proper mother from now on and her new man who she called my new father, which he wasn't and never was going to be, would help her provide a loving safe home for all her children. (Except the two with serious learning difficulties. She said she didn't want them back. She said it wasn't possible to love them. Not even for such a wonderful mother as she was going to be.) And this time when the social worker said it was my wishes that counted, and if I didn't want to go back I didn't have to, and then later when the judge in the family court said the same thing, instead of saying yes, I want to go home with my mother and this creep she's teamed up with I'd have told the truth and said, no, that's the last thing I want. I'd even rather stay in the home with the rest of the deadlegs, but really I'd like to be back in a nice foster home with a foster mother and a foster father and only one other child and if you could only get me into one of those I promise this time I'd be good and not mess it up so they couldn't manage me. That would be a very good change I could make.

But I know what I'm really supposed to say here. I'm supposed to say I'd go back to the time just before I did the thing I did that brought me in here and this time I wouldn't do it. So that's what I'm going to say. That's the change I'd make. I wouldn't do the thing I did that brought me in here.

I'm sorry, I know it isn't 1,000 words but I can't write any more.

Oh, except that you asked me to say Why and I haven't. Why is because I don't like being here and I don't want to be here and there's nothing I wouldn't do to be somewhere else. Nothing. Everyone says when you start going to prison you just keep on going to prison and I'm sure that's true for a lot of people but it isn't true for me. If I ever get out of here I will NEVER do anything that means I have to come back. I hate it here. No offence.

CHAPTER 5

'You and I have something in common, McErlane,' the Governor said.

'Yes, sir?'

'According to this piece you wrote about what you'd have done differently if you had the time over, you wouldn't do what you did do that brought you in here.'

'No, sir.'

'Neither would I, McErlane. Neither would I.'

He was silent so long I felt obliged to say, 'No, sir?'

'I graduated in Sociology, McErlane. I was brought up in a nice liberal family. The sort of family I think you dream about.'

'Yes, sir?'

'I wanted to do something to help my fellow man. I thought the Prison Service might offer that opportunity.'

'Yes, sir?'

'It doesn't.'

This was like pulling teeth. 'No, sir?' I said again.

'Most of the time I find myself watching over people who were never going to live their lives anywhere but in prison and still aren't. Whatever we may attempt to do for them. And sometimes I have to rule on someone like you. I don't know which is worse.'

'No, sir?'

'Stop doing that, McErlane. We both know how bright you are and I'm not impressed.'

'No, sir.'

He looked at me, eyebrow raised.

'Sorry, sir.'

'Do you remember Myra Hindley, McErlane?'

'I know who she was, sir. I never met her.'

'Fortunately for you. Did you ever wonder why she never got out of prison? She had enough well-placed people on her side, in all conscience.'

'No, sir.' Personally, I couldn't see any reason why someone who had done what Myra Hindley had done should expect to get out of prison – ever – but I wasn't going to say that till the Governor had declared his own position.

'I'll tell you. In theory, the Home Secretary is the only person who could decide. To keep her in jail or let her go. The Parole Board had their say, Loony Longford had his say, every nutcase writing letters to the Press had their say. The poor tormented woman has done her time. She's a changed being. Let her out. And, on the other side, our wonderful tabloid press was braying for Old Testament vengeance. Keep her in. Keeping her in meant doing nothing. Which is always the easier option. But only the Home Secretary could say, yes, let the poor cow out. You understand?'

'Yes, sir.' I don't think I really needed to say anything. This was all flowing out like something the Governor had said many times before. I've noticed that. Usually when people talk you get lots of "ums" and "ers" while they compose their thoughts, but sometimes it all just flows out without interruption. That's because this is something the person has said many times before and they know it by heart. Sometimes that's a warning signal because the person has become a bore on this subject, but if the Governor was leading up to something to do with me I thought I'd better pay attention.

'What the Home Secretary does in cases like that, McErlane, is he talks to a psychiatrist. More than one, I should imagine.

And what he's asking is: will she do it again? Am I safe in letting her out? Or will I go down in history as the stupid berk who let a mass murderer out of jail so she could mass murder all over again? Because if I do that, I think my political career could be at an end. And possibly I'll be burned in effigy at *The Sun's* annual staff barbecue. Do you see the point here, McErlane?'

'I think so, sir.'

'And the problem with this, McErlane, is that in the last resort the psychiatrist only has one answer. Which is: that the only guide we have to how someone will act in the future is how they acted in the past. We can say all we like about change and redemption and the power of the Lord and seeing the light and rehabilitation and remorse and everything else that gets bandied around in this connection. But in the last resort, the only guide we have to how someone will act in the future is how they acted in the past. Do you see how that might have related to Myra Hindley, McErlane?'

'Yes, sir.'

'Good. And do you see how it might relate to you?'

You get that a lot in prison. Screws (and some inmates) are in a position where they can play head games with you, and sometimes they do.

That's what the Governor was doing. He was playing games with my head. He was telling me: you may get out of here to do your A levels and lead a normal life. Or you may not. And it isn't you that'll decide. It's us.

I knew people doing my sentence sometimes got out early. Even before they'd graduated to adult prison. And I knew people sometimes didn't. What the Governor knew was that I was desperate to be one of the ones who did. And that gave him scope to play his games, the sadistic bastard.

I was dismissed then. He said he'd think about my situation and we'd talk again. Then he let me stew for three weeks. Twenty-one days is a lot longer in prison than it is on the street.

When I was called back, I heard no more about Myra Hindley. He was as nice as pie.

'You know it isn't me that decides, McErlane.'

'Yes, sir.'

'It's the Parole Board. They'll listen to what I say, on behalf of the staff here. They'll listen to what the psychiatrist says. They'll listen to what the probation people say. But they'll make up their own minds.' Then he threw in a bit of his head game stuff. 'If we say no, it's almost certain the Parole Board will also say no. But if we say yes, there's no guarantee they'll agree with us.'

'No, sir.'

'There's a good chance they will, though.'

'Yes, sir.'

He stared at me. He let the silence go on. And on. He knew what it was doing to me. Then he said, 'I've talked it through with the staff here, as you can imagine. I have it in mind to recommend to the Parole Board that they say yes.'

I can't remember when I had last cried before then. When I was about three, probably. Before I realised that crying didn't get you anywhere. Probably made things worse, in fact. Crying makes people think you're weak, and they'll try to take advantage. He lapped it up, though. Of course he couldn't talk to me while I was crying. Couldn't wait for me to stop, either. Far too busy. So I was dismissed again. This time with instructions to wait till the Education Officer asked to see me.

CHAPTER 6

Missus Howard packed the picnic and my camera equipment into the boot of their Toyota and drove us to the arboretum. It took about an hour and a half to get there.

'What were yesterday's five words?' she asked as we left the outskirts of town.

'Cerebration,' I said.

'Celebration?'

'No. Cerebration. It means thinking.'

She smiled. People always seem to think you won't notice that sort of smile, but people like me do. Whatever people like me are. We see every gesture, every bit of body language. We hear the things no-one says. Melanie said I'd have made a good salesman. Her ex used to say that's what the best salespeople do. They hear the words no-one speaks.

'Pedagogue,' I said. 'Mentor. Cathar. Buzoc.'

'Buzoc? What's a buzoc?'

'It's an Arabic musical instrument. Like a mandolin.'

'Might be a bit difficult to use that one in conversation.'

Yes. Well. Using the words in conversation isn't really the point.

We didn't say much the rest of the way. When we got there, Missus Howard bought two tickets and we went in. I carried the rucksack with the picnic in it. I'd slung my camera round my neck. The 200 mil lens and the tripod were in the rucksack with the food.

'So,' she said when we'd walked about a mile. 'What do you think of it?'

'It's brilliant.'

'Brilliant?'

'So peaceful. So quiet. Just the wind in the trees. And the birds.'

'That's what I enjoy about it. You like it quiet?'

I nodded. She was waiting for more. 'My mother had too many children,' I said. 'I had three sisters and two brothers.'

'Had?'

'I suppose I still have them.'

'You never show any interest in seeing them.'

'No.'

I could sense that wasn't enough. Obviously. I said, 'It was always noisy. You couldn't hear yourself think. And if you tried to read a book they jumped on you.'

'But you must have been used to it. It must have seemed normal.'

'Yes. Until they took me away.'

I began to understand how good Missus Howard was at leaving you with a silence you had to do something to fill. 'That was seven years ago,' I said. 'I was nine.'

'That must have been scary. Going away from your family at that age.'

'My foster parents were lovely. But I was horrible to them. So they sent me away and I was put in a home. Then I realised what I'd lost. But at least at the home when I went to big school they gave me a uniform and made sure I did my homework. They had a quiet room where you could read. And books. They had books. But there was fighting all the time. And you had to defend yourself or your life wouldn't be worth living.'

'Did you like fighting?'

'No. But I was good at it. To be able to fight, you don't have to be big. You have to not care about getting hurt.'

'No fighting in the foster home?'

'No. They were good to me. They used to read with me. I couldn't really read properly when I went there. They taught me.'

There were sandwiches, cake and a pork pie. The pie was just for me. And there were crisps for me, and a bottle of orange squash Missus Howard had made up at home. She had coffee and a bottle of water. She didn't eat any cake, either. We ate sitting on the grass beside an enormous tree. There was a board on it that said it came from the west coast of America.

I put the zoom lens on the camera, mounted it on the tripod and started taking pictures. Missus Howard wanted to know what I was shooting, and why. I explained that I used this lens to take people. After a while I'd swap it for the shorter focal length lens and shoot trees. 'I'll use the tree shots for project work at college. Sharpening lines and clarifying detail in Photoshop. The mugshots are for me.'

'Any people are a long way away.'

'Not to this lens, they're not.'

'Show me.'

I focussed on a man in a brown jacket sitting about half a mile away with a cigarette hanging from the corner of his mouth, then moved away so she could get her eye to the viewfinder. 'That's amazing,' she said.

'What I most like doing is photographing people who don't know they're being photographed. So I get them as they are and not as they'd like us to think they are.'

'Isn't that a bit sneaky?'

I shrugged. I'd got enough shots for now. I swapped lenses and folded up the tripod.

'When you call our place your foster home it's because you miss the foster home you did have.'

I nodded.

'Mister Howard doesn't mean to be unkind when he says you mustn't call it that.'

I stared at my feet.

'We have to help you face up to the world, Billy. Not as you'd like it to be. As it is. One of the things that means is calling things what they are.'

She went on a bit longer before she realised I'd stopped listening.

'Do you find this hurtful, Billy?'

'No.'

'You don't find it hurtful. But you don't want to talk about it.'

I can do silence, too, Missus Howard. I'd turned to watch a family. There was a man, a woman and a little girl. The little girl had what my mother would have called "a mind of her own". This mother didn't seem to be reacting like mine would. She was kneeling beside the child, holding onto the pushchair the child so obviously wanted to push instead of get into, and she was talking gently.

'Would you like to have children of your own some day, Billy?'

I shook my head. 'No. Yes. Maybe.'

'Well, there's lots of time before you have to make up your mind. Do you think you should use the toilet before we go back?'

We were quiet in the car. Then Missus Howard said, 'Constable Doyle says he suggested you should go to the Hibernian Club. Get to know more people your own age. Apart from the ones at college, I mean. Do you think you will?'

'I might. I haven't decided yet.' I had, of course. A place like that, you'd have to be nice to people you didn't feel like being nice to, or they'd shut you out of their circle. I didn't want Kathleen Doyle to see that happen to me.

CHAPTER 7

Psychiatrists get on my tits. They go back over everything you've ever said and everything you've ever written and tell you it means stuff.

Like:

'Billy. When you wrote your essay about what you'd change if you could go back in time, you said, "I'd go back to the time just before I did the thing I did that brought me in here and this time I wouldn't do it. That's the change I'd make. I wouldn't do the thing I did that brought me in here." Do you remember writing that?'

'Yes.'

'What was the thing you did, Billy?'

'Doesn't it tell you in my file?'

'I know what you did, Billy. I want to hear you say it.'

'Why?'

'Because I have to tell the Parole Board whether I think you show enough remorse to be let back into the community.'

That made me think. I didn't want to say it. This seemed to me to be a game we were playing; not just a game but a game within a game, of which she knew the rules and I didn't. But I said it. 'I killed my stepfather.'

I felt really cold when I said that. Cold and sad. But you don't hug yourself when a psych is watching. God knows what they'd make of it if you did that.

And then there was: 'Billy. You're by no means the only child who ever fantasised about being a changeling. Many children imagine they've been spirited away from their real parents by people of less intelligence, or nobility, or culture.'

I heard that from every psych I ever had. The ones who'd cottoned onto my love for reading would tell me it's a staple of folk fiction, especially fairy tales. I'm sure that's true. But what about when your mother herself can't really be sure who your father is? What about that? When she's been with so many men for money she hasn't a clue whose sperm it was that broke into the egg? *What about people like me?*

'Tell me about your sister.'

'I've got three.'

'I'm talking about Chantal. Tell me about Chantal.'

'What do you want to know about her?'

'Come on, Billy.'

'Chantal is three years older than me. When they took me home...'

'Clarify for me. "They"?'

'When I'd been in the home and then my mother and her new man went to the Family Court and said they wanted four of her children back, Chantal was fifteen. If she did herself up you could think she was twenty-something. She used to go out in the evenings with my mother. Looking for men.'

'Didn't your stepfather object?'

'He'd get angry if he thought the men hadn't given them enough money.'

'What did your stepfather do while your mother and your sister were picking up men?'

'I wasn't there. I suppose he watched. Times when it was too cold for standing up against the back of the pub and the men had nowhere to take them, he'd come rushing back to ours and get us all out. Take us up to my gran's for the night.'

'She didn't mind?'

'Not usually. Once or twice she wasn't in and we had to use the shed in her back garden to sleep.'

CHAPTER 8

I chose the name Billy when I was eleven. It was 1999, I'd had eleven years of answering to the one my stupid mother gave me and I wasn't going to do it any more. You can imagine the stuff I got.

"Zappa's on the crapper." "Zappa's mam's a slapper." You can probably make your own up and I'm telling you, I'll have heard it.

Zappa McErlane. I ask you.

People home in on stupid names. People in authority. Every time I changed class or we got a new teacher I could see her eye going down the register and she'd be thinking, "Oh, yes. Zappa. He'll be the one. I'll have trouble with him." And if they think they will, they do.

And then my mother started with the cuckoo in the nest stuff.

'Always got your head in a book. I'm sure you're not one of ours.'

'You'd know if I'm one of yours. I'm not one of *his*.'

'Don't be rude to your stepfather.'

'He's not my stepfather. He's not any kind of father to me.'

And then the slap round the head, from one of them or the other. Both, sometimes. When he wasn't too pissed to stand.

We did anger management in Young Offenders. There wasn't much anger management in our house.

What you're supposed to do, you're supposed to learn to recognise the signs that you're getting angry. And in times when you weren't angry, you'd already have analysed what it is that makes you angry and worked out strategies for dealing with it. Non-violent strategies. Things like confronting the person whose behaviours are causing you trouble and suggesting they change them. Behaviours is always plural. Normal people don't say behaviours when they mean behaviour but that's what psychs and social workers say.

We used to role play this stuff. So, for example, I'd say to Lee, "I don't like it when you fart in my face when you know I'm trying to concentrate on my book. It makes me lose my temper. I wish you'd stop it." And Lee would say, "I'm really sorry, Billy. I'll try to remember how you feel and not do it. And I'd like to say that it irritates me when you're always reading and I'd like you to spend some time talking to me."

So then whoever was in charge of this role play would say, "Let's unpick this a little. Billy, why do you get angry when Lee breaks wind in your face?" And I'd say, "Because it spoils my concentration. Reading is my best time because it's when I feel I'm somewhere else and not here. Or I'm learning stuff and I want to be able to take it in." Then whoever it was would say, "I'm sure Lee can understand that, can't you, Lee?" Lee, of course, would nod as though he really, really cared about why I was pissed off. "So do you think you'll be more understanding next time you see Billy reading?" More enthusiastic nods from Lee. And then it would be his turn. "Lee, why do you feel irritated when you see Billy reading?" The truth would have been for Lee to say, "Because I can't read and he can and he thinks he's better than me," but stuff gets handed down about what's okay to say in role plays and what isn't, and something like that isn't. So Lee, lying through his yellow teeth, would say, "Because I respect Billy and I'd like him to be my friend. I know he likes to read, but sometimes I'd like him to take a bit of time out to talk to me." And then it would be, "Well, Billy. Do you think that's a reasonable request Lee is making of you there? Do you think you could be expected to give up a little of your quiet time to chat with Lee?"

Now, the honest answer to that would be, "Oh, yes? And what are we going to talk about, me and Lee? Because he's only got one topic of conversation and that's girls and what he's done to them in the past and what he'd like to do to them again as soon as he gets out of here." But I can't say that, because that would be ratting Lee out and ratting out breaks every rule prisoners in YOI have. So I'd say, "Yes." And then we'd have a nice solemn negotiation over how much time it would be reasonable for me to give Lee during these matey conversations we were going to have. They like you to negotiate, because when you're negotiating you're learning to use social skills instead of just blowing your top.

And next day I'd be reading something I was totally absorbed in and Lee would come sneaking up behind me and when he was right on top of me he'd scream "Geronimo" or something and lift his leg and let a real rasper go right in my face, and I'd smack him and we'd be rolling around on the floor each trying to get the killer blow in and the screws would wander up and stick us both in the cooler for a couple of hours.

Anyway, there wasn't any anger management in sight when my mother woke up half way through the morning with a hangover and not enough money to show for the previous night's whoring. I'd probably had to run three miles to school without any breakfast because I hadn't got to sleep till three with all the noise and I'd slept in and I had no money for the bus and there was no food in the house but she'd still be steaming when I walked home in the afternoon.

'What good do you think school's going to do? There's no jobs for the likes of you. You'd have a better future if you helped your stepfather with some of his bits and pieces.'

'He is not my stepfather. And what am I going to help him with? Pimping my mother and sister? Breaking into the neighbours' houses when he knows they're out? Flogging dodgy videos in pubs?'

And then the slaps and the stuff about being a cuckoo in the nest and an unnatural son and, 'Better not think you're going to have the table to do your homework on, *because you're not*. Chantal got her best top torn last night and I'm going to have to mend it.'

Sometimes they needed me to read the stuff from the Council and the DSS and fill out forms. They dreamed up this idea that they should be rehoused, that because they had four children and only three bedrooms they had some kind of right to a bigger house. They were big on rights.

Then it would be, 'Billy, love, just give us a hand with this, will you?'

My mother would pace around the floor with a fag in her hand dictating what she wanted to say. I'd suggest I needed to write a rough draft first, like with a school essay, and the Creep would say, 'John Smith's. That's a draught, but it's not rough,' and they'd both cackle like Paul Merton had just walked through the room and my mother would tell one of the younger ones to bring them two cans of Harp out of the fridge. She said she thought better with a drink and a fag in her hand.

The Creep said you had to start this sort of letter with "Whereas". God knows where he got that from.

CHAPTER 9

Statement in support of appeal

18 October 2000

Whereas we have been informed that our request for larger living accommodation has been turned down on the grounds that the provision made for us is already higher than the standards required by Law and that the council does not have any suitable houses that could be made available to us.

We feel that the council has not fully understood our position. When the man came to inspect us he said that our house is better than we are entitled to. How is that possible? We have four children, a girl of 16, a boy of 13, a girl of 11 and a boy of 8. For all of these and ourselves we have three bedrooms. Sir, a girl of 16 is a woman and must have her own room. Husband and wife must have their own room. In a loving family home things go on between them that it is not right for the children to know about. That means the three other children must all share one room. Children grow up too quickly these days in any case and although we try to protect them from bad influences they are exposed to things they see on television and videos. Also, some of the children at school do not come from the same kind of loving family homes and they talk about things. The youngest girl is growing fast and begins to look like a woman. Is it right to leave her and our oldest boy prey to temptation through sleeping in the same room? They are good children and we have done our best to raise them to know right from wrong but human nature is human nature. Also, the youngest girl has already started with her monthly periods and it is not right that she should have to deal with these matters that are sensitive for a properly brought up girl in a room with two boys. They are good boys but you know what boys are.

Also, there is studying. We both want our children to have better opportunities in life than we had and that means they must work hard at school. The oldest boy already has lots of homework every night and we try to make sure he does it properly. The youngest girl will move to the comprehensive this year and she will have the same amounts of homework. How can they both do this in one room? When there is also a younger boy there who needs room and space to play with his toys?

Also, our family is a big family. The government wants to encourage extended families and ours is a great support to us in bringing our children up right, but we have nowhere an aunt or an uncle can stay the night.

Your inspector made a big fuss about the fact that when he came my oldest daughter's uncle was sharing her room with her. He even threatened to report us to the social services. Sir, what else were we to do? Put him in a small room with three children? It is not possible and I want to say that I was really insulted by his suggestions. I can assure you that her uncle would not dream of taking advantage of his niece. Also, nine o'clock is far too early to make a visit like that without warning and I would like you to instruct your inspectors not to come before the afternoon. And they should tell us when they are coming. Of course the place looked a mess. This is a loving family home and I am sure you know how untidy young children can be.

Sir, we need a house with six bedrooms. That is one for us, one for each child and one for family members who visit and need somewhere to stay. We understand that you do not have a six bedroom house available but you do have more than one three bedroom house and what we need is for you to knock down the walls between two of them to make a single home suitable for our needs. Also we need help to buy furniture for the extra rooms and I hope you will put in a good word for us with the social services. And we would like the new house to be in a better area than the one we live in now. Ask yourself if you could raise a family as you would like if you were surrounded by the sort of riffraff we have around us.

Sir, now that you understand our true position and the kind of family we really are I know that you will tell your housing officers to put us at the top of the list for the sort of place we must have. We don't want to have to take this to the newspapers because that is not the kind of trouble makers we are.

CHAPTER 10

I told them what I thought of this letter. As far as it affected me personally, the most objectionable bit was the suggestion that I might be tempted by sleeping in the same room as Leanne. My mother wanted to know who the hell I thought I was. My sister was turning into the sort of young woman any man would give his right arm to get to know, and there she was in my room every night, and what better way for us both to grow up a bit than by cuddling up together in the dark? And even if we ended up giving them more mouths to feed that wouldn't be a problem because more mouths meant more money.

Then Chantal weighed in with, 'Kylie fancies Billy.'

I snorted and I'd like to pretend this didn't touch me but they weren't fooled. I've never really understood what made Kylie hang around with Chantal. Chantal was smiling that horrible grin she has when she knows she's hit the target.

The reference to riffraff was a real mistake. I told them it would be but they refused to listen. They didn't even admit I was right when a brick came through the window at two in the morning after someone at the Council leaked their letter to the local paper.

They said they'd had no idea how the neighbours felt about us until they saw the letters. If they'd had to go to the local school and listen to what the kids there said they would have. I did. Even I was surprised, though, that the paper printed some of the letters. I hadn't worked out then how important it was for local newspapers to get a bit of trouble going. That became clearer after I went to court.

Dear Sir

I would like to thank you for your public service in publicising the disgraceful letter from the trollop McErlane and the man she has the impertinence to describe as her husband. It isn't the McErlanes who have to worry about bad influences on their children. It's us. If they think we're happy to have our children educated alongside the children of the family from Hell, they've got another think coming.

Name and address withheld.

Dear Sir

Will "Mrs" McErlane please explain why honest taxpayers who work for their money should have to subsidise people who sponge off the state and have more children than they can possibly hope to afford because they can't get their minds out of their underwear and now their children can't either?

Name and address withheld.

Dear Sir

Myself and my husband were really sad to hear about the poverty-stricken lives the McErlane family have to lead because of our meanness in not giving them houses far bigger than anything we could afford for ourselves. I know I speak for the whole community when I say that we would all be happy to go without the holidays and treats we might stupidly have thought our hard work in paid employment entitled us to so that these people can live like kings and queens without doing a hand's turn.

Name and address withheld.

There was more. The paper got a whole week's controversy out of it by letting them out a few each day. My mother said she was going down to the Council offices to find out who had leaked her letter and rearrange their faces for them. Then she was going to the newspaper to demand they print an interview setting the story straight. And after that she was going to see our MP to get him to intervene and stick us up to the top of the housing list. But she never did. You have to be organised to do stuff like that.

When all the bragging was going on in Young Offenders I could have told them about Kylie, but I didn't. I probably still had a soft spot for her.

And then there was what she gave me. The sort of thing you don't get from nice girls. "Getting shankered" the YOIs used to call it. Like it was some kind of medal. Although to be fair to Kylie it was nothing like as bad as chancre. That's really nasty, from what I heard at Young Offenders. And whatever it was, someone must have given it to her first. Obviously.

Chantal met me from school, which she'd never done before, and told me we had to go to my grandmother's. I'd been planning to go to the library, which is where I usually went when I had a really important essay to finish, but Chantal said my mother said to go to my granny's and at least there was more quiet there than there was at home.

While we walked along I asked Chantal what we were going for but she said our mother had said to and she didn't know why. Maybe I'd be able to do whatever it was my grandmother needed and then she'd feed me and then I'd get down to work on her table. That had happened before. I'd been working on this essay for six days and I only had tomorrow night before the deadline. I wanted it to be the most perfect thing I'd ever done.

Chantal said, 'You've been at the library every night this week. Is that really where you go?'

I said, 'Of course. What do you think?' and she did that eye-rolling thing that says, "I don't need to tell you what I think. It's too obvious."

When we got there, the door was locked and no-one was in. I thought my mother hadn't understood what our granny had said, but Chantal said no, she was probably in the shed down the back garden where we'd had to sleep a couple of times when the Creep had brought us up here in a hurry and my grandmother had been out.

'She's not going to be down there,' I said, but Chantal said to go and look because you never knew. So I did, just for the peace although it was obviously a waste of time. Chantal stayed back at the house. And I was right. My granny wasn't there.

But Kylie was.

We did it on the little Z-bed the Creep had slept on while the rest of us lay on the floor. I wasn't going to at first but Kylie said she really wanted to and if I'm honest I did, too. She put this really serious look on, the kind I've seen since then on the faces of psychs, and asked me if I was gay. Said if I was she'd understand. I didn't want her thinking that. It would be all over by morning. God knows what Chantal would have done with it. Or the Creep. So I told her, no, I wasn't gay, and she said, no, she didn't think I was. Then she said I didn't need to be scared. 'I've been on the pill since I was thirteen. And I'm older than you, so if anyone lands in trouble it'll be me.'

And all this time she was doing girl things. Running the tip of her tongue round her lips. Moving forwards and backwards. Touching my arms with her hands. Like that. Girl things, as I said. And she looked so good, sweet almost, although sweet was never a word you'd apply to a friend of Chantal's, with her little breasts pushing forward and the way her short skirt flared out across her bottom. Then she leaned forward and kissed me. I liked her warm lips and her tongue pushing into my mouth but gentle, no aggression in it. Sort of like asking a question with a kiss. But also telling me. Saying, "This is what we do, and this is how we do it." In charge.

That's something I've never really understood about girls. All the time they're growing up it's like they're the ones in charge, they're the ones who know things, they're the ones who decide. And then, suddenly, they've got a baby and they're tied and there's some boy, some man, and now he's the one in charge, he's the one who decides and if the girl even suggests she might want something else, like him to come home and hand over some money so they can eat together and she can get something for the kid, his kid, he gives her a slapping. It's always been like that, all the time I've been alive, and I don't understand it. How does it change so fast?

I'm not saying that's what's happened to Kylie, not necessarily, because I haven't seen her since I went to prison and maybe it isn't. But probably it is.

The first time was a disaster, because it was over before it started and I was really embarrassed and I wanted to cry but Kylie wiped the mess off her stomach with my Y-fronts and then she hugged me and said we'd be able to do it again in a minute and it would be fine the second time, I'd see.

And it was.

Chantal kept dancing round me and jabbing my arm and laughing while we walked home. She wanted to know if I'd enjoyed it, which I had, and what I thought about Kylie and whether we'd arranged to meet again. For a while it was like we really were brother and sister and not two people who lived in the same house and didn't like each other.

When we got home it was obvious they'd all been in on it. My mother gave Chantal one of those looks that ask a question and Chantal said, 'Twice, the little monkey,' and my mother started to laugh and said, 'My little boy's a man now.' It was only later that I wondered if Chantal had been outside the shed, watching.

We had shepherd's pie for dinner because my gran was there and she always made proper pan and oven meals and not the sort of stuff my mother gave us and we had cabbage and carrots with it instead of just frozen peas and oven chips or a carryout. All through the meal I was trying to pretend I didn't see them nudging each other and looking at me and sniggering. Then I said I had to write an essay. My mother said, 'He's a man, but he's still a little boy in some things.'

My gran said, 'Let him get on with it. You never know where he might end up.'

And the Creep said, 'He can look after us in our old age.'

When I said I'd had a girlfriend, I didn't mean Kylie. Obviously I went looking for her because I'd enjoyed the thing on the Z-bed, the second time, anyway, and I would have been very happy to do it again. Also I'd been thinking about this business of girls being in charge and then not being in charge after they had their baby and being with people who gave them a slapping and I was sort of thinking maybe Kylie and I could do it differently. Make decisions together and be in charge jointly, sort of thing. And nobody slap anybody. Be friends as well as the other thing. Because she really was nice, Kylie. In her way.

But Kylie said she didn't want people to think she was a baby-snatcher. She said she'd really enjoyed it, and I was a real sweetie, and I'd make some girl really happy, but it really couldn't be her. Not just then. Maybe when I was older and the age difference wasn't so really obvious I could be her toy boy.

At that time in my life I just accepted what happened. It was strange, this Life thing, and I didn't really understand it. I knew that mothers didn't usually arrange for their sons to be deflowered, that was a father's job if it was anyone's and if the father did it he did it out of sight of the mother, but if I thought about it at all I suppose I thought they were just amusing themselves. Then a couple of nights later Leanne slid into my bed. I said, 'What do you think you're doing?' and she said, 'Mam told me to. She says you know what to do now and you can teach me. Shall I take my nightie off?' I said, 'No, and you can get out of my bed and back into your own and stay there.' She didn't argue. She pretended to be insulted but really I think she was pleased.

I didn't find out about the little present Kylie had given me until Young Offenders Reception when they gave me a medical and the doctor wanted to know about what she said was an unusual discharge so she took a sample to do some tests. It was a woman doctor and when she came back to give me the news she said she'd be more embarrassed than I was. She was wrong about that.

She also said I should think myself lucky it wasn't AIDS and I needed to be more careful what kind of girls I went with.

I didn't get angry with Kylie, though. I had nice memories of her. Still have, really. I hope she's doing okay.

CHAPTER 11

There was a lot of trouble about the essay I finally finished in the library the night Kylie and I did it on the Z-bed. It was an essay I hadn't had to write, but I did because I wanted to. Maybe I did a better job than usual because of what I'd done with Kylie earlier. I don't know.

The point was that it wasn't for the English teacher. If it had been, I know what would have happened. She'd have scrawled "C" on the bottom of it in red ink and given it back to me without a word. That's what happened to all my essays. No matter how hard I worked on them. And then, when she talked about that week's essays in class, if I'd said anything about mine it would almost have seemed as if she hadn't read it. However much effort I'd put in, I could never hit the target.

Getting a "C" wasn't such a big problem, because it was enough to scrape a pass and get through the tests, but I'd have liked something better and I tried hard but somehow I couldn't seem to get up there.

But this essay was for the regional heats of a national competition and I wanted to do well. Miss Maguire had made it clear that no-one was forced to write an essay but she really hoped her regular "A" essay students would try. She suggested that anyone who didn't usually get an A probably needn't bother but they could if they wanted, just for the experience, because ambition was a good thing even if you didn't really have the talent to go with it. She also made it clear that she wouldn't read the essays, she'd just put them all in a big padded envelope and send them off to the organisers.

There were only three regular "A" students. Katherine, Claire and Virginia. I don't know what their fathers did but they all drove nice cars when they dropped their daughters outside school. I did know they lived in some very nice houses that didn't really belong in our part of town but had been built when they were hoping to get posher people, people with good jobs and more money, to come and live there and smarten the place up. The houses had high walls with broken glass on the top and gates and burglar alarms and CCTV cameras. I didn't at that time understand why they sent their daughters to our school instead of paying to send them to the Royal Grammar or Church High or somewhere. Later, when I did Sociology, I realised the girls were probably suffering from having small "l" liberal parents. If my mother had had that kind of money, I certainly wouldn't have wanted to go to our school.

Time went by and then Miss Maguire stalked into the classroom, barely glanced at Miss Taggart who taught Maths, shook her head and shouted at me from the front of the room. 'Billy McErlane. Come with me. Now.' She had an envelope tucked under her arm.

She didn't say a word to me as we walked along the corridor. When we got to the Head's office she banged on the door and walked straight in. She told me to stand in front of the Head's desk. He was sitting down but Miss Maguire stayed on her feet. She took the envelope from under her arm and opened it, staring at me all the time. Her eyes glinted like angry stones. She took something out of the envelope and held it between her fingertips. 'Do you recognise this, Billy McErlane?'

Of course I did. I'd sweated blood over it, and I could see my careful double underlining beneath the header.

'Yes, Miss.'

'Would you like to tell us where you got it?'

'Got it? I wrote it, Miss.'

She gave a huge sigh. 'Listen to me, Billy McErlane. You are attempting to make this school *and me* a laughing stock and I will not allow you to do that. You have only managed a C for every essay you have written for me and now you expect us to believe that you have written the very best essay for under fourteens in the north of England. I give you one last chance. Where did you get it?'

I was stunned. Overwhelmed. I couldn't answer her and I didn't care about answering her. I had won the regional heats. I had written the best essay. I felt as though I would fall over.

The Head was watching me carefully. 'Sit down, Billy,' he said.

Miss Maguire started to speak but one look from him and she snapped her mouth tight shut. He held out his hand towards her. 'May I?'

Watching her hand it over, I was amazed she didn't stamp her foot. The Head said, 'You wrote it by hand, Billy? You don't have a computer at home?'

'No, sir.'

'No Google? How do you do your research?'

'Out of books, sir.'

Miss Maguire turned purple then and I really did think she might explode. 'You have *books* in your house, do you?'

'No, Miss.' I took the library card out of my pocket and held it up. 'I use this.'

I'd seen that look so many times on other people but I never expected to see it on a teacher. It said, "Just you wait. I'll get you for this."

The Head began to read my essay. After a while, he looked up at me. 'This is important, Billy. If you don't tell the truth now, it will be difficult to put right later. Do you understand?'

'Yes, sir.'

'Very well. I will ask you once only. Did you write this essay?'

'Yes, sir.'

He nodded. Then he looked at Miss Maguire. 'These others. The ones he got only Cs for. May I see them?'

'He has them back.' It was like she was spitting the words out.

'Billy?'

'They're in my locker, sir.'

'Would you bring them for me?'

And so I did. When I got back to his office, it was like it sometimes was at home when my mother was really angry with someone, even angrier than she always was anyway. You couldn't hear it, because no-one was speaking, but you could feel it.

The Head told me to sit down again. Then he started reading the first few paragraphs of my essays. After a while, he said, 'You mark hard, Diana.'

She said nothing. The Head pushed the essays back towards me. 'I think we might review the marking of those, Billy. However, we still need to see something that will satisfy both of us that you really are the author.' I noticed that he emphasised "both of us". Miss Maguire looked as though she'd been eating lemons. The Head passed me a pad of lined paper and a pen. 'I want you to write an essay for me now, Billy. I want you to do it sitting there where I can see you.'

'Yes, sir. What about, sir?'

'Do you know what the word "injustice" means, Billy?'

I heard Miss Maguire breathe in really sharply. 'Yes, sir,' I said.

'Write me an essay about injustice. Start now. Finish in your own time. I'll make things right for you with your other teachers.'

A week later, my picture was in the local paper. No Katherine, no Claire, no Virginia. Just me and Miss Maguire.

And that probably sounds much nastier than was justified, because Katherine, Claire and Virginia could not have been nicer. They congratulated me on my win in a way that suggested they really meant it. Katherine's mother's four-by-four stopped by me the evening my photograph appeared and Katherine called me over to shake her mother's hand. The paper had printed my essay in full and she had read it. I had an immense talent, she said. Had I thought of journalism? Did I think I might become a novelist? Would I like a lift home?

I was quick to say, No thank you. I didn't want Katherine seeing my home. My mother never came to school open days, which suited me fine.

I walked home in a daze of happiness. It ended when I opened the door.

My mother has various levels of angry, from crabby snapping after just getting up hung over and needing a cigarette to full-on, incandescent, burn-anyone-in-your-path rage.

Tonight she was maxed out. Waving a Harp in one hand and a cigarette in the other and yelling at anyone in range. When I came through the door she put the cigarette in her mouth to give herself room to hold the paper. She waved it in my face. It was open at the picture of me and Miss Maguire.

'What is this?' she screamed. 'What...the...fuck...is...this?'

The Creep and Chantal were watching with unconcealed pleasure. Clearly they'd been getting it in the ear before I turned up to take the heat. Leanne and Tyler were sitting in front of the huge wall-mounted TV the Creep had brought home from somewhere and shushing their mother. What happened on screen was far more real than anything in their home.

'It's the paper,' I said. Stupid, I know, and asking for trouble but the best I could come up with.

My mother dropped the paper on the floor so that she could take the fag out of her mouth. 'I...know...it's...the...paper,' she said. 'Do you think I'm stupid? Is that why this fucking woman, whoever she is, can take the credit for my genius son? Because I'm stupid?'

Ah. Of course. 'She's my English teacher,' I said.

'And how long has she been your English teacher?'

'This is the second year.'

'Two years. And how long have I been your mother?'

'Altogether, do you mean? Or minus the bits when you weren't?'

She swung one of her haymakers but she was drunk and I was ready for it. I ducked underneath and let her swinging hand go all the way round. This was the hand with the can in it and lager sprayed over the Creep, who leapt out of his seat swearing and smacked her so hard she went down in a heap and stayed there.

I stepped forward. 'You do that to my mother again, I'll drop you.'

He laughed and lit a cigarette.

Chantal said, 'A reporter came round two days ago for an interview. He had a photographer with him. She thought it was about the house stuff. She told him to eff off.'

Katherine, Claire and Virginia didn't show up at the start of next term. What I expect happened was that their parents got together and discussed the situation and agreed they'd made a mistake sending their daughters to that school and they needed to go somewhere their parents' money could afford. That's what I think happened.

But I can tell you Miss Diana Maguire held me responsible.

CHAPTER 12

Dear Editor

There is no need for us to draw your attention to our sons imense sucess in the recent essay writing contest because you have already writen about it. Though we wish you had said more about the parents and loving sister whose care broght our yong jenius to this sucess and less to the teacher who has seen him for such a short time. Some peeple jump on evry band wagen. What we hope now is that the peeple who wrot the nasty leters about us when we wanted the new house feel ashamd of theirselvs. If our children do this well with no room think wat they wuld do with more.

Yours sincerely

Alice McErlane (Mrs)

I refused to write this letter, so she got Chantal to do it. I thought it was cheap of the paper's editor to print it exactly as Chantal wrote it. I saw the joke, though, and I don't doubt a lot of other people did, too.

One bad result of the letter was that people who had not previously connected me with the family everyone reviled in the press now did.

A better one was that the reporter came again with his photographer, and this time they got their interview with my mother and their picture. The television was in the shot, complete with the strange and very individual mark that the Creep had never been able to explain. Next day, the police

58

came knocking on the door. They took the Creep away in a car and the television in a van. Leanne and Tyler were inconsolable. For me it was a double whammy, only in reverse. Two things that caused me bother had both gone.

CHAPTER *13*

The Education Officer took her time asking to see me, but eventually it happened. She went through my file slowly. 'When you were thirteen, you won an essay writing contest.'

'Yes, Miss.'

'You don't need to call me Miss. You won the regional heat, and then you went on to come third in the national competition.'

'Yes, Miss. Sorry, Miss. Yes, I mean.'

'The first two prizes went to girls from public schools. And then you.'

'Yes.'

'How did you feel about that?'

'It was the best time of my life.'

'Coming third after two rich kids?'

You get a lot of this.

People have their own agendas (that was one of my five words one day and it's a beauty when you're dealing with employees of the state). If your future happiness depends on someone else's decision, you need to see very early where that someone else is coming from and talk as though you agree.

'I loved it. I was the top working class person to win a prize. In my book, if you took away the privilege and started everyone equal, that meant I'd come first.'

I didn't actually give a toss about that, hadn't even thought about it but it was the right thing to say because she was nodding her approval.

'The next six people after me were from public schools, too. All their privilege and I'd beaten them.'

61

She was smiling at me now. 'It must have seemed as though the world was opening up for you.'

I nodded.

'Tell me what your dreams were.'

Oh, well. I could go on for quite a while here, bore her to tears probably, because I did a lot of dreaming around that time. What I had to be careful of, though, was only giving her the bits of the dream she'd approve of. What I'd dreamed about most often was going to Oxford, that centre of equality and the common man, and then becoming a famous novelist and living in a big house on all the money I'd be making. I'd marry someone like Katherine and on the top floor I'd have my study where I wrote the famous novels that publishers all over the world were clamouring to get their hands on. Katherine and I would be enough for each other.

When we passed in the corridors of the big house we'd pause and hug. Dinner would be in the evening, not in the middle of the day, because then we'd be having lunch. And while we ate we'd have conversations where we used five words words. Words like "picayune". It would be good to have conversations with your wife where you used words like "picayune".

And if we had any children, we'd send them to expensive schools where the teachers cared and the other children wanted to learn, and not to the sort of dump I'd gone to and Katherine had spent her miserable and unwise year in. But maybe instead we'd give scholarships to deserving children. Secretly, without anyone knowing.

I could see some flaws in this dream if I told it to the Education Officer. From her point of view it might look a bit elitist (another five words word) and I didn't think she'd be very fond of elitist dreams. But what's a writer if not someone who can invent?

'I dreamed about being a teacher,' I told her. 'I dreamed about going back to an inner city school like the one I was at and helping children like me to overcome their disadvantages, the way I had. Because you can't do it on your own.'

Her eyes were shining now. I thought she could have cried quite easily at this point. I thought if I'd gone on and said, 'I dreamed about finding a sensitive Education Officer and giving her a seeing to,' she'd have been lying back over the table and lifting her skirt and inviting me to help myself. But probably she wouldn't, and not only because she was wearing jeans. You have to be careful not to get carried away. You have to keep a grip on what's reality and what's possible and what's just fantasy. It's very easy to confuse those things when you're in prison.

And, anyway, I didn't fancy doing that with the Education Officer at all. Kylie had been nice, I'd enjoyed that and at the time I'd have liked to do it again but a grown up woman? I didn't think so. Though I have to say, the Education Officer looked quite neat in her jeans and blouse and jacket nipped at the waist and her hair cropped close. *Gamine* was a five words word once, and it suited her down to the ground.

But I wasn't ready for that. Not then.

'I'd have written stories in my spare time,' I said.

'Tell me what sort of stories you'd have written.'

That bit was easy, because I could tell the truth. 'Stories like Annie Proulx and Alice Munro and Margaret Atwood and Sean O'Faolain and William Trevor and VS Naipaul write,' I said, careful to put the women first.

'Why them?'

'When you read their books you get the feeling that they're stopping you in the street and saying, 'Let me tell you a story.' I love that. A bit like the *Ancient Mariner* except that with them you actually want to hear the story.'

'Well, Billy. I think we should do everything we can to help you achieve that dream. I think we should get you out of this place and into college. And as soon as possible.'

'Thank you, Miss.' I said a while ago that I never cried, but when she said that I did let a few tears come. Not a whole flood. Just a couple to dampen my cheek. It would make me look grateful. Which is fine, because I was.

CHAPTER 14

That day when the Education Officer said they needed to get me out of there and into education was also the day I signed up for digital photography. I was fifteen by then and that course is what really changed my life.

There were only ten places on the course. The Education Officer said that a photograph was, in the last resort, telling a story and photographers had to make sense of what they were looking at before they shot it, so anyone who wanted to be chosen had to submit a single page describing the place they came from and another describing a person. She said it was surprising how many people looked at things without actually seeing them and there was no point giving anyone like that a camera.

The person I wrote about was Leroy and there's already a description of him in this book so I won't put it here. The other piece I submitted was this:

I grew up on The Lotus Estate in Newcastle, close to the Tyne. People who don't know Newcastle might be surprised how nice some of it is. The Town Moor is close to the city centre, and it's a heck of a thing for a city centre to have. Nearly a thousand acres of common land, bigger than Hyde Park and Hampstead Heath put together. There are some nice houses in Newcastle. The ones on The Lotus aren't the best, but actually they aren't bad. When Newcastle started rehousing the people who lived in condemned slums, they didn't put up an endless chain of high rises the way some places did. Most of the rebuilding in

Newcastle is two and three storey, brick built, and they introduced two things the old back-to-backs didn't have. One is large areas of open space dotted around all over the place where you can play anything you want or just walk, sit, meet, talk. The other is gardens. The eighteenth and nineteenth century houses in Byker had little stone backyards with a netty in them but they didn't have gardens. Ours do. Some people have made quite a show of them, and some haven't, but the place is okay. It isn't buildings that make a place a dump. It's people.

When the Education Officer read that, she pursed her lips and said she thought I needed some re-education on social studies, but I was clearly the most creative person applying and she was going to give me a place. 'What's a netty?' she asked.

'It's an outdoor lav.'

'Oh. Of course.'

Months later, when our relationship had changed somewhat, the Education Officer put a piece of paper in my hands and said, 'What do you think of that?' It was a description of me, written by an inmate called Stephen whose last name I can't now remember.

Billy McErlane

Billy is the kind of person you want to have as a frend but he doesnt make frends easily. His eye's are the most interesting thing about him. There blue and they seem to look at you like anyone elses eye's but there watching you like police eye's or judge eye's. Billy is my height about five ten and has wavy brown hare and a pale skin and when he smiles I wish he would be my frend but he looks like someone who can handle himself and I know he can and I don't want to take chances with him. He looks like a sport man and you can see him playing rugby or football.

I passed it back to her without comment except to say, 'Terrible spelling.' She shouldn't have shown it to me. I had known Stephen wanted to be my friend but I hadn't wanted to encourage him. He didn't make it onto the course. But I did.

* * *

There are two aspects to digital photography; composition and processing. They're both important. And, right from the start, I was good at them.

I said before that education and training in Juvie and Young Offenders are based on the idea that we're all as thick as pigshit, which my experience says isn't true. Nevertheless, most inmates act on the principle that it *is* true, because they've been told so often and for so long that they're as thick as a Ghurkha's foreskin that they've come to believe it. (If a Ghurkha reads this, let me say that I've never seen a Ghurkha's foreskin (and don't want to, thank you very much) and I've no idea whether they're thicker than, say, mine or not. It's just an expression. No offence intended.) Anyway, the impression you get inside is of a whole bunch of people with not a gorm between them. Mister and Missus Head had a son and they called him Richard. Whatever the underlying reality may be. Which matters when it comes to processing, because there are a few theoretical concepts and prisoners tend to switch off. They've been told they won't understand anything theoretical, so they don't.

So to start with I may not have been any better than the other nine at composition, because you can either see a picture or you can't, but simply because I accepted I had a brain I was down the road and out of sight when it came to using Photoshop to turn the pic I had into the one I really wanted to have taken.

That meant I was picked out by the instructor for special praise. And *that* meant that the small gap in performance and achievement between me and the next best person on the course started to grow. When the ten weeks of the course were up, it had become a big gap.

We spent the first seven weeks of the course in prison, photographing people and stuff there. On one day of each of the last three weeks we were allowed out into the town. We had to wear tags on our ankles, we were divided into two groups of five and there were two screws with each group but, even so, it was a taste of freedom. On the last day, the instructor stood us all a pizza and a Coke. We had to eat them outside because the manager of the restaurant saw our prison uniforms for what they were and he wouldn't let us in but that was the best pizza I ever ate.

The instructor said something after five weeks or so that I hadn't noticed but which, when he pointed it out, I saw was spot on. He said, 'You like photographing people. But that doesn't mean you have to like the people you're photographing.'

We both studied the pic he'd been looking at. It was a head-and-shoulders portrait of Leroy, but Leroy hadn't been very co-operative about having his photograph taken so I'd shot him through a crowd and then in Photoshop I'd cut away everything I didn't want until I was left with what I did.

I loved that about digital photography. The old film-based stuff would have left me with a horrible grainy effect if I'd cut away a pic and then blown it up that much, but Photoshop puts in lots of extra pixels that are exactly the colour and shade they need to be. And if you use PhotoZoom as well you can blow a pic up to seven hundred dots to the inch without damaging it at all, and seven hundred dpi is what you need if you want a print bigger than a little holiday snap.

That's called interpolation. Interpolation wasn't a five words word because I heard it after I'd already got my five for the day, but it's one I use all the time now.

And the instructor was right. After I'd cut away everything around Leroy, all the other people and the tables and chairs and stuff, I'd got a picture of just Leroy. Well, obviously. Except that that's not what I mean. When I say I'd got "just" Leroy, I mean I'd got essence of Leroy. Leroy as barmy king-sized scumbag, which is what he was. Anyone looking at it would have said, "What a turd that man must be. What a full-blown shithead. And by no means sane."

We had this conversation looking at the screen, the instructor and me. We didn't print any of the pics, not then, because there wasn't the budget. Photographic paper and ink are expensive. And I wasn't sorry, because I wouldn't have wanted Leroy to see himself as I saw him. He might have objected, and Leroy's objections tended towards the physical. And it didn't stop with him. When I looked at the pics, I didn't want any of the subjects to see what I'd made of them. There wasn't anyone in the prison that I cared for.

CHAPTER 15

It would be months before I found out whether the Parole Board was going to let me out, and a while after that before I'd go. Meanwhile, any trouble I got into would count against me. Melanie called it the Valley of Death.

Melanie was what I now knew the Education Officer was called, although I was only allowed to call her that when no-one was listening. She'd been married to a man who sold computers, great big ones not little PCs like I processed my pics on, and she'd got that expression from him. When you were waiting for an order you were in the Valley of Death.

I got to know a lot about Melanie's ex. One of the things she said quite early on was that his attitude to computers was like his attitude to life. He was stuck on mainframes and couldn't see that they weren't the thing any more. Mainframes were where computing had begun, but networks had taken their place. You had to see mainframes as great big dinosaurs, thumping through the world on their own knocking down trees people depended on for clothing and food and crushing the little shelters they'd built to stay warm and dry. Whereas networks were lots of people, huge numbers, all the people in the world eventually, all co-operating with each other. Mainframes were bad, networks were good. But Melanie's ex referred to people who sold PCs and networks as "the white socks boys" and didn't want to know. He went to work in expensive suits, white shirts, silk ties. Which Melanie didn't seem to approve of but it sounded all right to me.

Her husband was the past, and so she had made him history. She said that sentence more than once. She found it funny. Obviously.

Although it seemed there must have been things she liked about him because she never actually bad-mouthed him and occasionally she'd get a faraway look and she'd start talking about him in a very different way. Like when she told me she'd never married again and probably never would, and then she said that vegan networking men were sweet and sensitive and caring but occasionally a woman needed a rampaging meat-eating dinosaur and nothing else would do. "Someone you can't just piss on any time you want" is what I thought, but I kept that to myself. 'Alpha males are better lovers,' she said. 'It's sad, but it's a fact and there's nothing anyone can do to change it.'

She saw him sometimes, the computer salesman, and he hadn't remarried either.

She made sure I understood that she didn't approve of his lifestyle, that he used too much of the world's resources, earned too much money and his car was too big and too polluting and his holidays in faraway places damaged other people's way of life, but I do know that sometimes they'd go to a posh restaurant where he knew the chef and had told him to be ready for a vegan guest. Melanie would pick at a curdburger or something while he ate rare beef with a softened goose liver on top sitting on slabs of potato and covered in rich and unctuous gravy ("I'm surprised it didn't kill him on the spot") followed by sticky toffee pudding ("It would sit on his stomach all night!") and then cheese ("The cholesterol!"). And they'd drink red wine that she said should have been stiff and bitter with tannin but wasn't because it had aged so long in the cellar, which was what you paid for in a wine of that quality. But with the pudding he'd drink a pudding wine and she'd join him in a glass of that, too, just to be sociable.

And there wasn't much doubt about what they did afterwards, and I have to say she was a good advertisement for it. That peevish air, like she'd lost something and was prepared to fight you for it, would depart for a few days after he'd had at her following a big meal.

'He still loves me, Billy,' she told me once. 'Even though he thinks I'm a mad woman, he still loves me.'

I spent a lot of time in Melanie's company. I had become her project. I was to be the bad 'un turned good, the proof she needed that her theories about crime and human nature were right. I'd pass my A levels, go to uni, get my degree and then go back and save kids from the sink estates I came from. In a pig's arse, but that's what she thought.

The police cause crime. If there weren't any police, there wouldn't be any crime. I don't know where she'd grown up, although I'm pretty sure it was nowhere near me or anyone like me. She spoke a bit like Princess Diana, but also like a politician doing the Estuary thing. If you put a "t" on the end of a word you got a black mark (except you couldn't call it that, because that was racist). I tried to enunciate (a five words word) so that people would understand what I was saying, and I could tell she didn't really approve of that. But she wasn't a Geordie. She didn't have people straining to understand her and looking at her like you would the village idiot.

Not that you could say village idiot. It would have been inappropriate. Lots of things were inappropriate.

She said university had radicalised her. Another thing she believed was that it's governments that produce inequality. People are naturally sharing, and if you leave them alone they'll make sure that everyone has enough and no-one has too much.

Larrff? I nearly pissed myself. Round our way, if you got a new pair of trainers or a mobile phone you'd better be able to fight or you wouldn't have them very long. If you couldn't defend yourself, people who already had more than you, because they were better thieves and bigger bullies and more organised, would focus on the little you had and take it.

I think even then she had ideas about additional services I could perform, but we'll come to that. Just looking at the official ones, she knew I'd struggle with my A levels if I didn't get some work in before I went to college. Assuming that the Parole Board were going to let me do that.

So Melanie went to the Governor and said I had to get out of the kitchen and start reading and then I had to talk about what I'd been reading. Not to Lee and Leroy and the rest of the gang. To her, and to the team of volunteers she was going to organise from among her teaching acquaintances.

And occasionally I had to be allowed out to go to a class or on a field trip.

I wasn't present at this conversation. The Governor would have been no match for Melanie on a mission. He was a pragmatist and she was a dogmatist. He didn't care all that much and she did.

From what I gathered afterwards, she hit him over the head with three hammers at the same time.

The first was government policy on education and training provision for Young Offenders. The Home Office's proud words bore no relation to what really happened, but nobody rocked the boat. She said she would. She'd get a campaign going to force Governors to live up to what the government promised. Obviously they wouldn't get any more money, because you don't, so if they had to start organising classes wholesale they'd be in trouble. Much easier to do it just for me, using volunteers who were as barmy as Melanie and didn't want to be paid because they were committed to the cause. They'd all get a mention when I became a famous academic, covered in honours, and wrote my memoirs.

The second was the Valley of Death I've already talked about. All the time I was mixing in general population, I was a walking invitation to other prisoners to see how far they could provoke me before I'd retaliate. Which Melanie knew would be a long way, because I had something to lose and they didn't, but she also knew I wasn't unbreakable. Did the Governor really want more publicity about bullying in his nick? This argument took on new power when Williams topped himself while I was out taking pics and eating the best pizza ever. Leroy had been at him and it seems he couldn't take it any more. The Governor couldn't prevent an autopsy and when she found out he had spunk in his back passage, Williams's mother went berserk and tabloids rode on her coattails. The Governor kept his job, but by a whisker. And I was sucked into it because, when I got back that evening and found out what had happened, I completely lost it. I called Leroy a murdering bastard and then I went for him right in front of his cell. If the screws hadn't intervened immediately, one of us would have been dead. Almost certainly me. That Leroy could do what he had to someone as inadequate and helpless as Williams was beyond my comprehension. Leroy jeered at me, but he did everything he could after that to stay out of my way. I don't think I'm a person who hates easily but I hated Leroy.

Melanie's third weapon to persuade the Governor was his share of glory from the success of the project. He'd be in my memoirs, too.

The Governor stopped me in the corridor shortly after this. 'McErlane. Do you really have any intention of teaching kids from sink estates?' Before I could think what to say, he did it for me. 'Don't answer. It's written all over your face.' He started off down the corridor. Then he turned back.

'Lead your own life, McErlane. Don't let that woman lead it for you.'

CHAPTER *16*

English, Sociology and Art & Design. That's what I was going to do my A levels in, if I did them, and that's what I was going to study while I was still in the nick. Melanie chose these subjects but I was happy with the choice. English because I was going to be a famous writer (though I still kept that from her). Sociology so that I wouldn't lose sight of where all this was supposed to lead me. And Art & Design because you could choose photography as a major and I was obviously good at that.

There was also the availability of volunteer instructors to consider. Melanie would teach me Sociology and make sure I got a sound ideological grounding. Art & Design because the photography instructor was keen to watch my progress and prepared to do it for nothing. And English because of Dave.

Dave Wilson wasn't a vegan because I saw him eat more than one pizza with pepperoni and everything else, but other than that he was exactly what Melanie wanted for me. A committed man of the left, an old style socialist who'd raised himself in just the way I was going to (except he'd missed out on the prison bit), and someone who would do what Melanie wanted. Dave fancied Melanie something rotten but he was never going to get anywhere. Nobody could have mistaken Dave for an alpha male. Melanie might have been happy to swap appropriate thoughts on literature and movies but when it came to a rodding she looked elsewhere. Later, when she had taken my deflowering by Kylie and built on it, she told me, 'There's no call for equality in bed. And no deferring. Take what you want and expect the other person to do the same.

Women don't want to be treated like virginal goddesses. They want you to save them from the foggy, foggy dew.'

A few years later, I was living in Norwich and joined a rugby club. One evening after a hard-fought defeat we were in the clubhouse, both teams together, and the singing started. I heard the words, 'She sighed, she cried, she damn near died, She said what shall I do? So I pulled her into bed and I covered up her head, Just to save her from the foggy, foggy dew.' When I heard that, I remembered that afternoon with Melanie. I bought a large scotch for me and another one for my opposite number, but I didn't tell anyone what I was smiling about.

It was six months into my A level preparation and the fifth time I'd been outside with the camera. The pattern we had was that Melanie would sign for me, escort me, take responsibility for my behaviour and for getting me back on time. Then I'd download the RAW images from the camera to the computer and when he next came in I'd show them to Mister Walker, who was the photography instructor and who never did invite me to call him by his first name (Joe). He'd make suggestions on how I might process the pics. Increasingly, though, he just commented on what I wanted to do, or had already done, and so I'd start work without waiting for him.

I always saved the untouched images anyway, so if he'd wanted me to go back to the start I could have.

It was early spring on the calendar, but you couldn't have told by looking. It didn't really get light, even right after midday, and everywhere was damp. By about two thirty I'd had enough. Melanie said we should go to her place to dry out and we'd have a meal before I went back. We'd done that before. The meals would be surprisingly tasty considering she was a vegan, but what she'd have done without mushrooms and potatoes and tomatoes I can't imagine. One time we had red peppers stuffed with fennel and I found myself thinking of her ex with his rare beef. I knew which I'd rather be eating.

When we got in, Melanie told me to go and have a shower to warm myself up. Inside the bathroom door she hung a dressing gown which I assumed her ex left there and told me to put my clothes outside and she'd shove them in the dryer for a few turns. I went to bolt the bathroom door but the lock wouldn't work. 'Oh,' she said, 'Don't worry about that. I keep meaning to get it fixed.'

I said, 'It's bent. Give me a screwdriver and I'll straighten it out for you.'

'Another time,' she said. 'There's only me here usually and I don't need to lock myself in.'

I knew it had worked last time I was there so I said, 'I wonder how it got like that,' but she didn't have any suggestions.

The shower had a really good motor to it and the water was nice and hot. I'd soaped myself and was sluicing it off when the door opened and Melanie walked in without a thing on. I was shocked, but she stepped straight into the tub and put her arms round me in a really strong hug and kissed me. I could feel her shaking and God knows I was as nervous as I could be.

Next thing, she was on her knees. Woolf had talked about this when he was going on about the women he was supposed to have had, but I never believed him. I mean, I never believed him about anything, but I believed him even less about this. Why on earth should a woman want to do that? Right in her mouth? And keep it there, right till the end, right till...well. I'm not going to spell it out.

And then, when that was done, she turned off the shower and handed me a towel and we both dried ourselves without saying a word. I thought I'd be getting the bum's rush now, but not a bit of it. She took my hand and we went into her bedroom. Still without speaking. She'd had the electric blanket on to warm the bed and when she bent over to turn it off I could see why a woman's bottom was something men got excited about.

She made sure I got between the sheets first and then she followed me.

Kylie had been about five foot two, little all over, and she'd been manageable. But Melanie, she was a grown woman. I've already said she was neat, *petite*, *gamine*. But there was still more of her than there had been of Kylie. Everywhere. And much more hair. Down there. All right, what I'm saying is I was scared. I didn't feel up to this. And what she called "your beautiful cock", that wasn't up for it, either.

Not at first.

But Melanie knew what she wanted and how to go about getting it and by the time we left that bed and went downstairs for supper in our dressing gowns I wasn't afraid of being with a grown woman any longer. I was stunned, astonished, grateful, but I wasn't scared. And neither was "your beautiful cock".

And supper was a nice surprise, because she was still having the mushrooms and grilled tomatoes but for me there was a pizza, everything on. And she had a bottle of red wine and I had two glasses of it. And then there was chocolate pudding for me.

When she dropped me back at Young Offenders, she said, 'You do know not to say anything about what we did?'

Oh, yes, Melanie. I knew not to say anything about what we did.

When Mister Walker saw the pics I'd taken that day, he sat and looked at them for a long time. Then he said, 'How would you describe your vision, Billy?'

Well, I didn't know how to answer that. I took pictures. I knew I took my own kind of picture that wasn't like the pictures other people might take of the same subjects, because I'd seen that during the original course, so I supposed I must have had my own vision, but what it was I couldn't have said. I saw the world and I shot it.

Mister Walker said, 'Would you like to know what I see when I look at these?'

I said, 'Yes.' Of course. I mean, I'd have said that anyway, obviously. But I did want to know.

He said, 'I see a sheet of glass.'

I didn't understand and it must have been obvious.

'Between me and your subject. I see a sheet of glass. Clean glass, clear glass, totally transparent glass but glass. Like the plate glass window on a department store.'

I said, because understanding was beginning to glimmer, 'Like a barrier, you mean?'

'Yes. Exactly like a barrier. I can see through it but I can't walk through it or put my hand through it. It doesn't matter whether you're photographing people or buildings or something totally abstract. You show us what you see, you hold it up to the light, you say, "See this child; see this old woman; see this cornice; see this pattern," and we do see it, with perfect clarity. But we see it at a distance. We see it, but we see it on the other side of a barrier. Why do you think that is?'

I shook my head. 'I just take pics.'

He smiled. His unlit pipe was pointing straight at me. 'You just take pics. No, Billy. That's the last thing you do.'

CHAPTER 17

Dave Wilson said, 'Joe Walker says you're the most talented apprentice he's ever had.'

'Does he?'

'That's how he sees you. An apprentice. Someone to pass his art on to. He thinks you'll surpass him. He says you have what it takes to be famous. A famous photographer.'

I didn't know what to say.

'You're not the best pupil I've ever had,' Dave said.

'No?'

'I'm looking forward to teaching you in college, don't get me wrong. You're a good critic and by the time you get to university you'll be better than that. You understand what the author is saying. You draw parallels. You put things in context. But you don't create. You're an essayist, not a novelist. You look sad. Is that bad news?'

I nodded.

'Don't let it be. You *will* make a great photographer. Cultivate the gift you have, not the one you want.'

Melanie took Williams's death hard. She'd only known him through organising his Introduction to Literacy course and she knew he was pretty much a lost cause, educationally speaking, but he'd topped himself in a place she was connected with and it hurt her. Why had he done it, she wanted to know?

'I think he couldn't take it any longer. When you're always bullied there's going to come a time when you say "Enough".'

'They're not taking any action against Smith. The Governor thinks let well enough alone. Personally, I think he needs help. I think he needs to be made to confront what happened, and his part in it.'

Yes. That would really change Leroy's ways. Not. I said, 'I don't think he's bent.' She was looking at me. 'Leroy,' I said. 'He's straight enough on the street. This was just...'

'Bent? Straight? Do you think that kind of language is appropriate?'

Oh, dear. They're just words, Melanie. No value judgements are implied.

But I was forgiven. Her lips moved against my ear. 'I'm glad you're not bent.' She giggled, presumably at her daring.

I didn't tell her I was glad, too.

CHAPTER 18

It was somehow my fault that the police had removed the Creep and the television. Had I not won the essay prize, these things would not have happened.

That's how my mother saw things, anyway.

The Creep was back within a day. The television never returned.

And Chantal was also gone. I didn't get the blame for that.

I had mixed feelings about this child my sister was going to have. On the one hand, it meant the council provided her with living accommodation which freed up a room for Leanne to have her monthlies in without the embarrassment of being watched by her two brothers. Although the embarrassment was actually ours, because she was always trying to tell us about it and we were always trying to shut her up. On the other...well, Chantal could no more identify young Tyrone's father for certain than my mother could mine, and I knew what that could do to you. She claimed the fatal seed had been planted by Kevin Chung, but only because she was attached to him around the time of the birth and he'd have given her a fat lip if she'd admitted that anyone else had got close enough to father a child on her. It didn't help. He gave her plenty of fat lips anyway.

As it turned out, the child wasn't called Tyrone. All the time she was carrying him he was going to be Tyrone, as long as he wasn't a girl, in which case he was going to be Paige. But when he was born Chantal had to stay in hospital with him for a couple of days and she got my mother to go and register the birth. She didn't see the certificate until they let her out and she came round ours to show off her baby. She'd even got Kevin with her. I don't know whether he was casing the joint, checking out whether we had anything worth nicking. He'd never visited before. Reading not being her strong point, she went over the birth certificate several times before she accepted that what she thought she was seeing was what she actually *was* seeing.

'What the fuck's this?' she said.

It turned out my mother had recycled Zappa.

'Zappa Chung?' said the new mother in a rising cadence of disbelief.

My mother gestured at me. 'He won't use it. It's a nice name. It's got character.' She appealed to the Creep for support. 'Hasn't it?' But the Creep observed his right to remain silent, probably wisely, and went on breathing smoke and cigarette ash all over the kid.

'Anyway,' my mother said, 'Tyrone's a nignog's name.'

She didn't seem to understand what she'd said. She went on cooing over baby Zappa and giving him her own share of smoke and ash while the rest of us tried not to stare at Kevin. Oriental he might sound, but he was the colour of the old mahogany sideboard in my granny's front room. He claimed he was from Ethiopia, which didn't explain why he sounded pure Yardie. Or why his mother, when she took off for Jamaica, described the trip as "going home". I thought he might smack my mother. Or the Creep for being with her. Or me for being her son. But he just gave her the cold eye and lit a cigarette.

The Creep was getting itchy for a drink. When he mentioned it, my mother thought it was a great idea. They'd been oohing over this baby for minutes and how long is someone three days old supposed to hold your attention? The

Creep looked at Kevin, who said he preferred to drink somewhere else and left without a backward glance. Chantal glared at my mother. 'That's you. What did you have to say that about nignogs for?'

My mother shrugged. 'I didn't mean any harm. I'm not racist. He knows that.'

Chantal levered herself off the couch and held out the baby to me. 'You'll look after little Tyrone, won't you, Billy? While we're down the pub?'

'I'd love to, Chantal,' I said, 'but I have stuff I have to do.'

'Billy! This is your *nephew*!'

'And your son,' I said. 'And I think you mean little Zappa.' I left. As I shut the door, she was starting on Leanne and Tyler.

CHAPTER 19

Child Placed at Risk by Mother

Arrests after Brawl in Pub

Two women were ejected from a public house after they dragged another woman to the floor by her hair and assaulted her, a court heard.

Briony McCarthy needed medical and dental treatment after she was kicked and hit by Chantal Chung, 17, and her mother Alice McErlane, 33.

The court was told the violence began when McErlane's daughter Leanne, 11, and son Tyler, 9, entered the pub at 5. 30 to ask Chung to return to the house in which they had been looking after Chung's three day old child Zappa since noon. No arrangements had been made to feed the children or to clean and change the baby. Chung heard McCarthy laugh and believed that she was passing comment on her fitness as a mother.

Both women pleaded guilty to public order offences. More serious charges of assault were dropped.

Chung was given a 12-month supervision order and ordered to pay £60 costs and £250 compensation to the victim. The bench accepted that she had been the prime mover in the assault. McErlane was given a conditional discharge. Both mother and daughter were banned from all pubs within a three mile radius.

Martin Bepper, chair of the bench, told the women: "You had been drinking for more than five hours without making the most basic provision for children in your care. This court cannot and will not condone violent assaults carried out under the influence of drink."

The court heard that Social Services had taken the baby and both children into care.

Tracey Barnes, prosecuting, said: "While she goes under the name of Chung, after the man she alleges to be the father of her baby, she and Mister Chung are not married and Mister Chung does not appear to share accommodation with her and the baby." Chantal Chung, Leanne McErlane and Tyler Murphy, commonly known as Tyler McErlane, were all in care until less than a year ago, together with brother Billy McErlane who was not present at the time of the incident.

Catherine Walsh, mitigating, said Chung accepted that her behaviour had been unacceptable and had experienced feelings of shame and contrition since the incident. She had been discharged from hospital only that morning and felt that hormonal imbalances following Zappa's birth had triggered her reaction to what she saw as a slight on her as a woman and a mother. Both she and McErlane were suffering dreadful torments following the removal of their children. McErlane would suffer from being barred from public houses as much of her husband's business was conducted there and she liked to be present in order to assist him.

CHAPTER 20

Their being banned from pubs was my fault. If I'd done what any normal person would have done and looked after baby Zappa while his mother went on the piss, it would not have happened.

'What are you going to do to bring in money?' the Creep wanted to know.

'Me?'

'Yes, you. Your mother can't work now, can she? Thanks to you.'

'Put her on the street,' I said. 'There's plenty of slappers hanging about down the back of the bus station.'

He hit me so hard I went over the back of the settee. I put my hand to my mouth. When I looked at it there was blood on it.

I came round the settee slowly. He could see from my face he'd got trouble. My mother said, 'Billy! Don't, Billy!'

I got him with my toe on the inside of his knee, where I know it hurts. He yelped and put both hands down to grab the pain, which brought his head into range. I swung my fist with all my strength into his chin.

I was afraid the police would want to talk to me, but they didn't. When he went to the hospital he must have come up with some tale about how he got his jaw broken but he never told me what it was.

I also thought the social workers might come and talk to me after my mother had told them she couldn't after all cope with Leanne and Tyler and didn't want them back. Thought they might ask if I'd like to go into care, too. To which the answer would have been, "I'll go and pack. It won't take long – I don't have much."

But they didn't. She changed her mind about Leanne after a couple of months but so far as I know she never saw Tyler again.

I found out later, when Melanie cared to share a titbit out of my file with me, that my school record had swung it. I was the only one who turned up every day, didn't truant, handed in my homework on time.

According to whichever social worker compiled this report, that meant the others were being scapegoated by my mother and the Creep while I was some kind of golden bollocks in whom the family invested all its hopes and plans for the future.

I'd have liked the chance to put my side, but that was not to be.

When I got in from school a few weeks later, Chantal was there with the baby and a freshly gleaming black eye.

'Kevin?' I asked.

'The police were after him. He thought I might have told them where he was.'

'Had you?'

'How? I didn't know.'

'But he punched you anyway.'

'You're not getting the whole story,' my mother said.

I shrugged. If Kevin Chung was involved I didn't want any part of the story, so not getting all of it wasn't a problem. Chantal had other ideas.

'I'm entitled to have anybody I want come round.'

Oh. Yes. Right.

'Kevin only comes round when he feels like it.'

'When he wants a shag, you mean,' said the Creep.

'He never gives me any money. I told him, I don't love him any more and I don't want him round. I told him to take his stuff away.'

'Stuff?' I asked, getting involved in spite of myself. 'I thought he didn't live with you?'

'Not that kind of stuff.'

'Oh,' I said. 'Did this stuff have anything to do with why the police wanted him?'

'Not much,' said the Creep. My mother cackled.

'I love Regus now,' said Chantal. 'I told him so.'

Regus. *Regus.* 'Regus?' I said.

Regus was a legend locally. Ten years older than me, "Love" tattooed on the fingers of one hand, "Hate" on the other and the Newcastle united badge all over his chest. You could just see the red and grey flags and the lion's head among the black hairs curling out of the top of his shirt. He once broke all the fingers of a man who stole the handbag of a woman he was interested in.

When a youth, off his head on drugs and alcohol, tried to mug him, Regus beat him senseless and then forced the girl with him into the boot of his car. Six months later, a skeleton in Kielder Forest, fifty miles away, was identified as the girl from the clothes on the ground beside it.

Regus was arrested and charged with her murder, but the mugger was the only person who could put the two of them together. Friends of Regus took him away for a chat and when he came back he refused, from the wheelchair he would spend the rest of his life in, to give evidence and Regus walked free. If you had any sense, you steered clear of Regus Hunt. My sister was not known for having a lot of sense.

Chantal said to me, 'He's got some work for you.'

'Regus Hunt has work for me? He employs people now?'

'He needs someone to make deliveries for him. He says you'd be ideal, because you're a juvenile.'

'Chantal,' I said, 'you can go to hell. And you can take Regus with you.'

'Just a minute,' said the Creep. 'How much money are we talking about?'

I said, 'I don't care how much. I'm not doing it.'

'How much, Chantal?'

'Well, he wouldn't be paying Billy. He'd give the money to me, for the baby.'

'Oh.' The Creep had totally lost interest.

'I've got homework,' I said, making for the stairs.

'Please, Billy.'

'No.'

'But...'

'No.'

I'd hardly got my books spread out before there was a tap on the door and Chantal's face peered round it. 'Billy...'

'No.'

'Billy, please.'

'No.'

She was right in the room now. I put down my pen. 'Chantal, I have to have this in by tomorrow morning.'

She sat on the bed. 'I'm glad you're doing well at school, Billy. I hope it pays off for you.'

Baby Zappa was face down on her knee, utterly relaxed. He twitched as I looked at him, some dream image flitting through his mind. I said, 'You're getting the hang of motherhood.'

'Only when he's asleep,' she said. 'It's murder when he wakes up.' Her eyes filled. The mascara heavy under them had already been breached a few times. 'I thought he'd be someone to love who'd love me back,' she said. 'But he only thinks about himself. 'Cos he's a man, I suppose. Help me with Regus, Billy.'

'Sorry, Chantal.'

'You don't know what he's like when he doesn't get what he wants.'

'I can imagine. Why do you stay with him?'

'Who else is there that's better? You men, you're all the same.'

'Maybe you'd be better off on your own.'

'Oh, right. A woman on her own. Round here.' She shook her head, as though I was too dumb even to listen to. 'What do you think would happen to me?'

'Move away.'

'With what? How? Where?'

I picked up the pen again.

'Is that what you'll do, Billy? When you finish school? Move away?'

'As soon as I can.'

'Maybe I could go with you. Just you and me, Billy.'

I pointed at the bundle sleeping on her lap. 'What about him?'

'Oh, him too. Of course. You won't, though, will you? You'll go on your own.'

'I want to go to university, Chantal. I want to be a writer.' There. I'd never spoken the words before. Not even silently to myself. The dream was too big to expose to mockery. Even my own.

'I hope you don't end up disappointed, Billy. It isn't good to hope for too much.'

I got my head down and started on the first problem. I'd got used to working like this, with people trying to talk to me.

Chantal said, 'You'd like Regus if you gave him a chance.'

Areas of triangles. I'd been lost with this stuff but Miss Taggart had told me to stay behind one day after school and she'd gone through it, just her and me, and I'd got it.

Chantal hadn't moved. I said, 'Was it Kevin who gave you that black eye?'

She shook her head. 'He wouldn't dare. Not now I've got Regus.'

'So Regus gave it to you?'

'Yes.'

Had it not been too stupid even to think, I'd have said her expression at that moment was one of pride.

'He didn't mean it,' she said. 'He loves me.'

'He hit you.'

'He was jealous.'

'Of what?'

'He thought I'd been out with somebody.'

'Who?'

'Kevin. Someone. I don't know.'

'Had you?'

'No! Well. Only for work purposes. That doesn't count.'

'But he hit you.'

'I told you. He was jealous.' She stroked her hair. 'That means he loves me. That's how you can tell.'

'I didn't realise that.'

'He wouldn't be jealous about someone he didn't love, would he? Stands to reason.' She stood up, slung the baby over her shoulder and walked over to where I was sitting. 'What are you doing? Oh, geometry. I hated geometry.'

I said, 'Wouldn't you rather be with someone who showed he loved you without hitting you?'

She seemed to be considering that. Then she said, 'How would I know he really did? Love me?'

'If he said he did?'

She looked at me. Then she laughed. 'You're too good for this world, Billy.'

Chantal said I'd like Regus. I thought I wouldn't. A few years later I would see that he was a businessman, and the things he did were designed to help his business run smoothly. Maybe, behind the violence, he saw himself as a normal sort of guy. I've seen a few violent men who saw themselves as normal people. Normal people who run businesses, pay their taxes, get married, raise children, become governors of their local school. Normal people who confine previously healthy men to wheelchairs for the rest of their lives; normal people who drive to Kielder with a girl in the boot, have sex with her and then kill her. That sort of normal.

CHAPTER 21

Melanie bought a digital camera of her own. She already had a computer and now she loaded Photoshop onto it. She got the educational rate for the software but she still must have spent a few hundred quid, all told.

I was shocked when I found out what sort of pictures she wanted me to take.

Shocked and excited.

She knew what she wanted and she set it up. All I had to do was point the lens. The lens wasn't the only thing I was pointing.

She had on this lace and silk thing I hadn't seen before. I don't know what you'd call it. Not a sleep suit, I'm sure of that because sleeping was the last thing it was intended for. The person wearing it might doze off but not the person she was with. It was long enough to come half way down her thighs but because she'd pulled it up it didn't quite cover her bottom. I mentioned that before, didn't I? That when she'd bent over to turn the electric blanket off I'd had my little "Ahah" moment when I'd suddenly realised the power women's bottoms have to excite men. I've read about this and it seems that nature intends it. Girls have flat bottoms just like boys, but when they get to puberty their hips flare out as a signal to men that they're ready to mate. I don't know how that worked for cavemen but it does a hell of a job on me.

And, let's face it, there are bottoms and bottoms. And Melanie had a *bottom*, no doubt about that. She was built to entice. As I don't doubt she knew. She could seem awfully prim when she felt like it but she had the power and she knew she had it.

Melanie. All fours. Her bottom, uncovered and facing me. The camera in my hands. Oh, God.

When I'd got all the exposures I thought were necessary, Melanie wanted to go straight into another pose but that had to wait. I put my hand on the place where the silk stopped and the gorgeous pink flesh began. I just couldn't stop myself. I pushed gently down and Melanie let herself be pressed onto the bed.

It was an hour or so before we were ready to get back to work.

We got dressed and Melanie sat beside me and watched as I processed the pics. I was still learning at that time and some of what I did was a bit crude if you set it against the methods I have now but it worked. Starting out with a picture of that wonderful bum, I cropped everything I could that wasn't part of it and put what background I couldn't cut in the softest focus imaginable. Over Melanie I applied a glow fading from inside to out. I adjusted the flesh tones so they gave a hint of warmth, perhaps of activity just ended, and I raised the contrast between the soft flesh and the blue silk. Then I created a duplicate layer, selected the image and applied a High Pass filter at six per cent. The whole screen went grey, with just a few scratch-like blotches, and I felt Melanie stiffen. 'What have you done?'

'Wait,' I said. I set the blender to Hard Light, full on, and dragged opacity down almost to zero. Then I flattened the two layers into one image.

As I say, it was fairly crude by my standards today but it astonished Melanie. This approach was one I'd learned to use when I wanted to sharpen woodland pics I'd taken because it separates lines, however small, and makes them stand out from each other. Even in a fairly distant shot of tree foliage, you can pick out individual twigs. You can imagine what it does to a close-up view of the sort we were looking at. Especially when you remember the surrounding nest of hair.

Melanie held her breath for a long time, then let it out slowly. She reached out a finger and placed it on the screen – delicately, because she knew how I hated to have to work through smudged or dirty glass. 'What do you call that?' she asked.

I looked at her. Honestly, she'd embarrass anyone.

'Why are you blushing?' she said. She started to laugh. 'You are *so* bashful! I don't believe you, Billy! You've just been down there with your fingers, your nose, your tongue, your lips, quite apart from your utterly beautiful cock, and now you don't want to tell me what you call it! See? I call yours a cock. What do you call mine?'

'Melanie, please.'

'Never mind Melanie, please. We have to deal with this, Billy. Do you know what the Victorians used to call it? A pudendum. Do you know what pudendum means, Billy?'

I shook my head.

'Shame. It means shame. The Victorians called a woman's vulva her shame. Can you believe that? Do you think I should be ashamed of mine? Louder, Billy. I didn't hear you.'

'No,' I said. 'No. I don't think you should be ashamed of it.'

'Then why are you ashamed to put a name to it?'

I really didn't have an answer to that.

'Vulva, Billy,' she said. 'That's one word, isn't it? The correct Latin word, really. A lot of people think it's vagina, but they're different. Here.' She took my hand and placed it between her legs. I'd thought she'd got dressed, but she hadn't put any knickers on. 'That's my vulva,' she said. 'And this,' she said,

97

extending my index finger and slipping it inside her, 'is my vagina. See? Oh, Billy! You've gone bright red!'

Well, who wouldn't? And then she had to get into this thing of making me list all the words I knew for it. Well. Trying to make me.

'Mott,' she said. 'Do you know that one?'

I nodded.

'It's an Irish word, mott. Or at least it's the Irish who use it. It means mound, so you can see the point, can't you?'

I knew all about that because there's a William Trevor story where this travelling salesman is in a strange town and he gives offence to a local man by rolling down his car window and shouting out, "Any chance of a mott, would you know?" And William Trevor is Irish, of course, and so is his travelling salesman.

She got me to admit I knew pussy, and box. And fanny, obviously. I knew where she was trying to take me and I refused to go there. She kept pressing me.

'Blit,' I said.

'What?!'

'Blit,' I repeated, even more quietly.

'Well. I never heard that one. But come on, Billy. You're not trying.'

'I'm not going to say it.'

'Not going to say what, Billy?'

'The word you want me to say. I'm not going to say it.'

'What word do I want you to say, Billy?'

'I've told you. I'm not going to say it.'

'What does it begin with, Billy? What letter?'

I could feel my skin burning with embarrassment. I said, 'You know what letter it begins with.'

She was almost giggling, bobbing up and down in excitement, her skin pink, her eyes gleaming. She was like a little girl. A very grown-up little girl. 'Come on, Billy. Tell me what letter it begins with. Or I'll take you straight back to prison. And I might not come for you again.'

'That's not fair.'

'Tell me?'

'C.'

'What?'

'C,' I shouted. 'It begins with c.'

'And what does it end with?'

'Stop it, Melanie.'

'Tell me?'

'*Cunt*, Melanie. The word is cunt. All right?'

She threw her arms round me and hugged me. 'Oh, Billy. Why did you find that so hard?'

'Because it's a filthy word.'

'It is not a filthy word, Billy. It's a beautiful word. Men have used it for filthy purposes, but it remains a beautiful word for a beautiful thing and it's time women took it back. I want you to use it when you talk to me. All right? All right, Billy?'

'All right, Melanie. But it's not a subject I want to talk about, so I won't be using it very often.'

She kissed me on the lips. 'Oh, Billy. If I didn't know what a stupid thing it would be to do, I could fall head over heels in love with you. Follow me, please.'

She walked from there into the bedroom. When I got there she was already taking off her clothes once more. I followed suit.

Later, lying naked by her side, I said, 'Fadge.'

'What?'

'That's another word for it. In Newcastle. They sometimes say fadge.'

'Fadge!'

'It's also the name of a round flat loaf. Of bread.'

She had her hand over her mouth and her eyes were streaming tears. 'Oh, Billy,' she said. 'You're priceless.'

CHAPTER 22

I was still inside when Jessica first saw my work, but she didn't know that and at least now I knew the Parole Board's decision. As long as I stayed out of trouble for three of the four weeks before the new term started, I'd be released on licence. I'd have a week to sort out somewhere to live and then I'd start at college. Probation would have to approve the somewhere to live, but Melanie said she knew just the place and she'd see to it for me. She'd already organised funding from a charity that helped disadvantaged people get an education, and the local authority would pay for my accommodation. They weren't very happy, according to Melanie, because I hadn't grown up there but they were going to do it.

Mister Walker had suggested putting some of my pics forward for a photography competition, Melanie had agreed and the Governor had given permission. The exhibition was in London, it was going to be open to the public but before that happened there was judging by a panel of experts. Jessica owned a gallery that sometimes showed paintings, sometimes sculpture and sometimes photographs and she was one of the experts.

Mister Walker said the standard would be high and I shouldn't expect to win any of the prizes but if I placed high enough, which he thought I might, I'd get a professional critique of my work. He said I'd find that valuable.

Fourteen hundred people had entered the Under 18 Section. Two hundred were longlisted. In the end, ten photographers were chosen to have their pictures exhibited. There was one third prize. One second prize. And one first prize.

The winner of the first prize was me.

The timing could not have been better. Prizes would be awarded in London on the second day of my first week of freedom, so I could present myself as an A level student and not a prisoner in a Young Offenders Institution. What's more, I'd be able to keep the prize, which amounted to a cheque for two thousand pounds, a digital camera body worth eight hundred pounds, my choice of lenses up to two thousand pounds in value, a computer with Photoshop loaded and a printer.

My last day in Young Offenders was agony. I had decided to stay in my cell as much as possible because I'd seen the expressions on the other inmates' faces and I knew there was nothing some of them would like more than to get me embroiled in a fight that would see my licence revoked before it had even begun.

It started around three in the afternoon when Denzil pissed through my door, catching my bed, my books and me. Leroy and a few others were right behind him, baying for me to come out and avenge myself. It ended ninety seconds later when six screws raced onto the wing. Four of them grabbed Denzil and Leroy and rushed them downstairs to Solitary. The other two stood guard outside my cell and told me to scoop up all of my possessions and follow them.

'I haven't done anything,' I screamed. I was shaking with rage. I just couldn't stop myself. The sheer injustice made me want to kill somebody. Everything I wanted was in my grasp and it was being snatched away.

'We know that,' said one of the screws.

The other one said, 'Just get your stuff. You're not in trouble. We're taking you where you'll be safe till tomorrow.'

As they were marching me down the corridor, one of them said, 'We knew they'd try to get you today. We were just waiting for it to kick off. The Governor told us to make sure you stayed out of trouble.'

'The Governor?'

No answer. I said, 'Where are you taking me?'

'You'll find out.'

In Reception a Chief Officer (they're the ones in white shirts) was waiting for us. He told me to go into a holding cell. It was empty except for some civilian clothes and a Nike bag. *My* clothes and *my* bag.

'What's going on?' I asked.

'You're going out a few hours early. Get changed.'

I looked vaguely ridiculous when I had done that, because in the two years I'd been inside I'd grown several inches and the clothes I'd brought in with me no longer fitted. The Governor came in looking more jovial than I had ever seen him. 'She's on her way,' he said. She? Not my mother, surely? I hadn't even told her I was getting out.

The Governor turned to me. 'We don't treat many people like this, McErlane. You've been a model prisoner and you're getting your reward. What you have to do in return is stay out of trouble for the rest of your life. I don't want to see you back here and I don't want to hear you're banged up somewhere else. Got it?'

'Yes, sir.'

'See you take notice. I've rung the Brown woman and she's coming to collect you. Your hostel room won't be available till tomorrow, so you'll stay with Miss Brown tonight. She has a spare room and she's prepared to let you use it. Don't take advantage of her hospitality and don't cause her any bother. You're on licence. Got that?'

'Yes, sir.'

He held out his hand and I shook it. 'We don't get many like you through here, McErlane,' he said. 'You've earned your shot at freedom. Take it. Good luck. And for God's sake get yourself some clothes that fit.'

'Yes, sir. Thank you, sir.'

A screw walked with me to the gate. When it opened, Melanie was waiting in the space between that and the main gate. She smiled at me distantly, as though I was a damn nuisance she'd got herself stuck with and she was just going to have to make the best of it. The screw locked the gate we'd just walked through and then unlocked the outside gate. He grinned as I stepped through with Melanie. 'Best of luck, Billy, lad. Stay out of trouble, eh?'

Then the gate swung shut behind us.

Melanie's cold, professional manner disappeared the moment we turned the corner and got into her car. 'All night,' she laughed. 'We've got *all night!*'

I said, 'The Governor says you've got a spare room.'

'Oh, I have, Billy. I have. And you're not going anywhere near it.'

CHAPTER 23

On the way back to her place we stopped at Marks & Spencer and Melanie bought Beef Wellington, which I had never eaten before. 'It's supposed to be enough for two,' she said. 'But you'll have to eat it all yourself.' She got garlicky mushrooms to start, which we shared, and a berry pudding with cream for me afterwards. I was allowed two glasses of wine.

Then she loaded the dishwasher and we walked hand in hand into the sitting room.

'Will you do something for me?' she asked.

'Of course.'

'I'd like you to undress me.'

I don't think there's much doubt that that was the happiest night of my life. Certainly to that point and probably since then, too. I had other nights, nights when I was with a woman I loved and who loved me, but nothing will ever quite match that first night out of jail.

I woke at three to find Melanie wrapped tightly round me. I dozed off and when I woke again at seven she was on top of me. It was nine when we got up, showered and dressed.

Melanie looked at me and laughed. She said, 'This is madness.'

'What is?'

'You. Me. Do you know how much older than you I am?'

I shook my head.

'No,' she said. 'You don't. And I think I'm not going to tell you.'

We enjoyed a lazy morning together. We had lunch – smoked salmon and salad in a baguette for me; pea soup for her. Then we went into town and I bought a jacket, a pair of chinos, a shirt and a tie for the prize ceremony. I say I bought them but in fact Melanie paid and we agreed that I would give her the money back when I had collected my prize and cleared the cheque.

And then she took me to the hostel, my new home, and I met the Howards.

The moment I arrived I knew what I was looking at. The place I'd had in mind when I was writing about what I'd do differently and I said, really I'd like to be back in a nice foster home with a foster mother and a foster father and only one other child and if you could only get me into one of those I promise this time I'd be good and not mess it up so they couldn't manage me. Here it was. This was the foster father and this was the foster mother.

Of course, there was more than one other child here because this was a hostel for young adults who'd been children in trouble. The Howards got paid for looking after us and it wouldn't have worked for them if there'd only been me and one other. In the time I was at the hostel there were never fewer than five residents and sometimes as many as eight.

This was the street with the aspiring Irish families in it. There were also aspiring Indian families there and I was always impressed by how clean and well turned out their children were when they went to school because it was obvious these people didn't have much money, but what they did have went on the family and the children and cooking proper meals to eat together and school uniforms and books and field trips and stuff like that. Not cigarettes and lager and tattoos and eating rubbish fast food in front of the television when they felt like it and stupid leisure clothes for people who never did any leisure activities.

The houses were council houses which were built fifty or so years ago, but some of them have been bought by the people who live in them. I've mentioned the Paddies and the Indians but there are also some white English people, most of whom have lived there quite a while and are getting on a bit. Their children have moved out but they come to visit and bring their own children. Some of the cars they drive are quite expensive, so I guess it's worked for those families. And sometimes they come and take the old people away for a holiday for a week or two.

In the middle of the street is a great big house and that's the hostel. Mister Howard told me this house is about two hundred years old and originally it stood in the middle of its own huge park, but the land has mostly been sold off and now there's just a fairly big garden. Two men come once a week in summer with a ride-on mower to cut the grass and other men turn up sometimes to trim the shrubs and spray weeds. Missus Howard puts in bedding plants every spring and some of them, which are called biennials, in the autumn and I became quite good at telling snapdragons from marigolds and like that. There are also plants like lupins and anemones and a thing called Bear's Breeches and a few others. Those are herbaceous plants.

One of the best things about living in the hostel was coming back in the evening knowing what I'd find and that it wouldn't be mayhem. This wasn't a hostel where everybody just came and went. It was trying to give experience of home life to people who hadn't had that. One of the rules of the house was, unless there was a very good reason not to, we ate together in the evening. That's all the residents and Mister and Missus Howard. Missus Howard didn't cook, a woman came in every day to do that, but she ran the place. And the Howards watched us, how we ate, what our manners were like. They didn't allow any ragging to go on at meal times. And they insisted that everyone join in the conversation. They could make you feel quite isolated if you didn't.

Not all of us had been in prison but none of us came from what you would call a stable background. Except Guy, maybe, and something had obviously gone wrong there, too. Mostly we were used to eating alone, when we felt like it, watching television or walking down the street. And what we ate would be a pie or a burger or chicken nuggets or a pizza or something like that. And always with chips. Even the pizza would be with chips. In the hostel we ate at one big table with no television in the room. You couldn't read there, either, and the ones who smoked couldn't. And no alcohol.

There were almost never chips in the hostel. Maybe once a week, tops. We had roast meat on Sundays, lamb or beef but never pork because occasionally we'd have a Jewish or a Moslem resident staying for a while. Not often. If we had someone who wouldn't eat meat (that didn't happen often, either) that person would have fish. We never had a vegetarian or a vegan so I don't know what would have happened then. Other days of the week we'd have shepherd's pie, cottage pie, lasagne, spaghetti bolognese. Big filling meals. Fish pie, sometimes, which I'd never come across before and I loved because it wasn't really a pie, just like cottage pie and shepherd's pie aren't, and it had layers of smoked fish and white fish and salmon with slices of tomato between the layers and sometimes spinach and some olive paste which had a special name that I've forgotten. But it was very tasty. And always two or three different vegetables.

Afterwards there'd be cake, if you wanted it.

Breakfast would be porridge or corn flakes or you could have a boiled egg but you had to ask for it the night before.

If you were there at lunchtime Missus Howard put out things so you could make your own sandwich. Tomatoes for slicing, and lettuce. Sweet red onion. Crusty bread and mayonnaise and mustard and sliced ham or corned beef. Tuna sometimes. Or pilchards. Although if it was pilchards I liked to make toast and spread the pilchards on that.

You could make yourself a cup of tea or coffee any time and we were encouraged to drink a lot of water but fizzy drinks of any kind were absolutely banned. Some people have brains that can't handle fizzy drinks.

Missus Howard told us if we ate properly our brains would work better and so would our bodies and we'd feel better. And she was right.

So that's the place I was introduced to that afternoon. I shook hands with the Howards and they introduced me to the residents who were there at the time. Melanie was very formal, as though she was my guardian or something and she was glad to be getting rid of me. She explained about the photography prize and how she would be taking me to London tomorrow to collect it and I wouldn't be back until the next day.

The Howards were very impressed by the photography prize and even more so when Melanie told them about the essay prize I'd won before I went inside. 'Billy's very modest,' she said. 'He would never tell you about that himself.' Then Mister Howard said it was good to be modest in public as long as that didn't mean you weren't proud of yourself. If you'd really achieved something, like winning a regional prize for essay writing and then coming third nationally, then it was good if you didn't go around showing off like the Great I Am but at the same time it was vitally important that you gave yourself full marks for talent and ability and hard work and you were allowed to pat yourself on the back.

Missus Howard said, 'Photography and writing, Billy. You're a really creative person.'

After Melanie had left, Missus Howard took me on a tour of the house. First we went to my room, so that I could leave my stuff there. I had a corner room which was about three times the size of the one I'd shared with Leanne and Tyler and several times as big as the cell I'd just left. It had windows on two sides and both of them looked out onto the garden. There was a bed, a wardrobe and a washbasin. Best of all, there was a big desk with a chair. There were two other chairs, both easy chairs, and there was a bookshelf, which was empty. The floor was covered with a proper carpet, wall to wall.

The next best room to this was the library. There was a table in the middle of the floor with six chairs around it and all the walls had bookshelves against them. The shelves were full of books. I picked one out. It was *She*, by H Ryder Haggard.

Missus Howard said, 'Do you like books, Billy?'

'Yes,' I said. 'I do.'

She showed me an exercise book on the table. 'You can take any book you like to your room, but you need to write in this register the name of the book and the date you take it out. When you bring it back, put the date in the last column. See?'

There was a quiet room, where no-one was allowed to take a mobile phone or play music. And there was a television room and a games room with a full size snooker table at one end and table tennis at the other. The place we all ate was a big dining room right next to the kitchen.

After the tour, I took *She* to my room. Then I went for a walk in the garden. One of the residents, Guy, followed me out. I'd never met anyone called Guy, although I'd seen the name in books. Nor had I ever met anyone who talked like him. He sounded like someone off the news programmes. Which wasn't so far out, because he told me his father was a big wheel in television. He offered me a cigarette.

'No thanks,' I said. 'I don't.'

'Oh. I assumed that's why you'd come outside. To have a smoke. It's why most people come out here.'

'I wanted to see the garden,' I said. Guy lit his cigarette and let me know that this garden was nothing compared to the one his parents had. That was two acres, apparently, on the banks of the Thames in Oxfordshire. He said this one was more than two acres, probably, but land here wasn't anything like as expensive as where his parents lived, because that area was so much more desirable. He didn't say why he wasn't living there, and I didn't ask. I'd learned in Young Offenders that questions like that could bring information you'd really prefer to be without. Guy had no such inhibitions.

'I looked you up on Google News,' he said. 'I'm not sure we've had a killer here before.'

I didn't say anything.

'What's it like?'

I turned to look at him. 'What's what like?'

'You know. Having killed someone.'

I went on looking at him. Then I turned and walked away. He caught up with me by the pond. It was quite a grand pond. There were tall iris flags with the seed heads still intact (though I didn't know then that that's what they were) and a water lily covering half the surface. Big silvery-gold fish came to the surface and then sank again.

'The fish are koi,' Guy said.

'I'm quite shy myself.'

When he didn't say anything I looked at him again. He was bubbling with quiet mirth. 'That's brilliant,' he said.

'Thank you.' I said that calmly, but inside I was shaking. I'd made puns before, and jokes that depended on wordplay, but people had always looked at me like I was some kind of idiot. This was the first time, the very first time, I'd made one and the person I made it to had laughed. Laughed properly and not all ho-ho-ho sarcastic.

(I made another one a few days later and there's no way I could fit it into this story so I'm just going to tell it anyway. Because it did have an effect on me. We were having dinner together in the dining room and Missus Howard said something about having to get some people in to do a special cleaning job. And she said, 'Beeswax is so expensive.' And I said, 'Well, it would have to be, wouldn't it? Bees have such tiny ears.' And they all laughed, even the ones who hadn't a clue what beeswax was, and Mister Howard was beaming but I just kept this straight face like I'd seen on chat shows and sitcoms and let it look like I couldn't imagine what people were laughing at. Which turned out to be the right thing to do because I started to get a reputation as a dry wit. And that's important because it influenced the mask, the persona as I would one day learn to call it, that I adopted to deal with the world. Everybody has one. We all make a mask and try it out and if we like it we make it ours and then we wear it so regularly we forget we ever did make it and we think it's us, the real us. My mask could have been made of violence, like Regus's. That wouldn't have come as a surprise. But I made that joke about koi, and then the one about beeswax and pretty soon I was on my way to another persona altogether. One that would open doors that would have stayed locked and bolted against a violent one.)

Guy said, 'I didn't mean to give offence. When I asked what it's like.'

What I wanted to say was that I wouldn't mean to give offence, either, when I ripped his head off and shoved it up his arse. But that would be going right against the "make a new start" advice Melanie had given me, so I didn't. What I did say was that I hadn't been offended. I just wanted to put it all behind me.

'Understood, old man.' Old man! They'd had Greyfriars books in Young Offenders, tatty old things that were falling to pieces like many of the books there and although I hadn't understood half the time what they were going on about I'd read them just as I read everything on offer in that place. "Old man" was the sort of thing Bob Cherry said. Though not to the Fat Owl of the Remove.

Guy must have had some inkling of what I was thinking because he said, 'I was at Shrewsbury before I came here.'

'Is that like this place?'

He smirked. 'Not exactly. More like where you've just been, I should think. The food's better here, I'd have to say that. Do you want to take a walk down the road and back?'

And so that's what we did, and Guy pointed out the various houses in the street and told me who lived there. Including: 'That's where Kathleen Doyle lives. She's an absolute corker. But she has two warlike brothers to contend with and her pa's a policeman.'

CHAPTER 24

Melanie collected me next day and we took the train to London. 'Your hotel's paid for by the organisers,' she said. 'People might wonder why I'm sharing your room so I've booked one of my own.'

We had coffee on the train and took the Tube to the hotel, where we checked in.

Then back onto the street and Melanie introduced me to Pret a Manger sandwiches. She had something filled with bell peppers and I had an All Day Breakfast sandwich, which was delicious. Then I had a brownie and after that I had carrot cake. Melanie said, 'God bless your stomach,' but she was smiling.

I was sitting on a high stool with Melanie on another beside me and I was staring out of the window. Pavements thronged with people. In the road cars, buses and taxis, millions of them it felt like, all jumbled up together and cyclists threading their way through them. Even when I'd got caught up in the Saturday crowds in their black and white shirts streaming towards St James's Park I'd never seen so much movement, so many people and I didn't like it. Then a man came right up to the window and stared in at us. At *us*. In fact, at me. My stomach churned; I felt like I was going to be sick.

'Billy? Billy! Billy, what on earth is the matter with you?'

The man was dressed in dark blue; dark blue chinos; dark blue shirt; dark blue jacket; dark blue wide-brimmed hat. A wide tie in flaming golden yellow. Black hair. A sallow, greasy complexion. And his eyes…his eyes were palest blue, and bloodshot. And staring. At me.

Melanie looked from me to the man; from the man to me; and back again. She raised a hand and on the hand she raised a finger. The man laughed. He turned and walked away. I sat on my high stool, shaking.

Melanie put an arm round me. 'What was that about, Billy?'

'He knows. He knows who I am.' Even as I said it, I felt how stupid it was. And not just stupid; childish. And yet it was how I had felt.

Melanie hugged me. 'He doesn't know the first thing about you, Billy. There are far more mad people walking around than ever get locked up, and most of them are in London. He saw you and he stared at you. It didn't mean anything. Come on; let's get out among all these people.'

We walked through the streets for a while. Up Regent Street, along Oxford Street, down Charing Cross Road and back to the hotel. It took about two hours. I'd never seen London before and I was fascinated. The noise, the people, the babble of so many languages. And the buildings.

Photographers don't look at buildings the way I imagine other people do. We don't look at shop windows and what's in them, for example; what we see is the whole building and the way it matches or doesn't match the ones on either side. Then we look at individual details. Pediments. Cornices. The material the builders used and the changes older buildings have undergone.

Take Oxford Street. Most of the big names have stores there. Selfridge's for example has a beautiful building and I knew I wanted to come back some time and photograph it. It's a steel frame construction but you'd never know that because the steelwork is hidden by fluted stone columns and there's a lovely art deco main entrance with a statue of the Queen of Time over it. In one way it's just a shop, a place to buy and sell things, but the impression you get is one of power and capability.

After a bit of this, Melanie said, 'I'm exhausted. It's time for a cup of tea.' I had a chocolate éclair with mine. And then it came back, just hit me, right out of the blue, and down I went. I didn't need a man in dark blue with a golden yellow tie; all I needed was to be surrounded, hemmed in, by all those people. I was catatonic. I couldn't speak. Could hardly move. I didn't know what was happening to me, but I knew I'd never in all my life felt this bad.

Melanie paid the bill, dragged me outside and flagged down a taxi. She didn't speak on the way back to the hotel, and I just sat there, cold and shaking. We went straight to my room and she told me to take my clothes off and get into bed. Then she sat beside me, stroking my forehead. She said, 'Do you want to talk about it?'

I said, 'All those people, looking at me. Like they know who I am, what I was in for.'

'They weren't looking at you, Billy. This is all in your head.'

'And being able to do what I want. Walk in somewhere and buy a cup of tea and a chocolate éclair, just because I want one. I've got used to being told what to do.'

'Billy. Go to sleep. We'll talk about it when you're rested.'

I'd have said I couldn't do that, but I passed out in moments, so deep that Melanie had to wake me. She did that by getting into bed with me, as naked as I was, and taking me in her mouth. When we were done, she said, 'Feel better now?'

I nodded. Whatever it was that had flattened me seemed to have passed. For now, at least.

'We'd better both take a shower,' she said. 'Don't want to stink the gallery out with pheromones.'

'What are pheromones?'

'What we give off after sex. And before sex, for that matter. The smell of lust.'

The prize-giving was at seven, but I had to be at the gallery by six. Melanie went with me. Jessica met us at the door.

I'd never met a gusher before and I suppose at first I took it at face value. Later on I realised it was the same for everyone; that when she turned her attention full on you and told you you were the most important artist since Michelangelo (in so many words, she didn't actually say that) you went down under the weight of her charm. Whoever you were. I've seen her pull the same stunt on the Arts Minister and it worked on her as well as it did on me.

She took us into the main room in the gallery and showed us where the speeches would be, where to stand while I was waiting and where to move to when my name was called. We rehearsed the handing over of the prize cheque and she explained that I could either take the other prizes with me or they'd be delivered to my home address. She read that out and of course it was Melanie's address because that was what we'd put on the form. I hadn't wanted to put down HMYOI. Melanie explained that I had just moved home and I gave Jessica the hostel address. I said I'd take the camera body and the 15 to 85 lens with me but they could send the rest, please.

Then Jessica said, 'Before you get the cheque and shake hands, move here to the microphone to make your acceptance speech.' She caught my look of panic. 'You do have an acceptance speech?'

I looked at Melanie.

'Jessica,' Melanie said. 'Billy is very young.'

'I can see that. The other nine finalists are two years older than him.'

'Billy is very talented,' said Melanie.

'Yes, yes.'

'But he's still what you might call a naïf artist. He knows what he does but not why he does it.'

'We're not asking for his artistic credo, for God's sake. And please, Billy, no political statements. The public's had enough of that, bless them. Just thank the people who got you started in photography. Your parents, was it? Well, whoever. A teacher at school, maybe. You don't have to name him, no-one here's going to care who the fuck he is.'

I couldn't help being shocked. I'd never heard a woman who spoke and dressed like this one use that word. I'd thought it was a white trash thing. What in Sociology I'd learnt to call the underclass.

'Then thank the sponsors and the people who gave the prizes. That's very important. Don't forget the sponsors. Even gran dma Moses could manage that.'

I nodded. I was an essay prize winner, after all. Surely I could write a short thank you speech?

Melanie took me into a corner to put some words on paper. 'Who is gran dma Moses?' I asked her.

'Never mind about that. What are you going to say?'

After I'd written down the shortest set of words we thought I could get away with, we walked round the gallery looking at the photographs. Some of them were quite brilliant, even in the Under 18 section, and I began to wonder what I was doing here, but I overheard one or two people who seemed to know what they were talking about and they didn't seem to think the judges had given the prize to the wrong person. I felt quite good listening to those people.

Melanie said, 'Are you feeling nervous?' and I had to admit I was. I said, 'I've never given a speech before.' She said, 'Put it out of your mind. Think about something else.' Like what? 'I'll tell you what,' she said. 'Let's take another look at the three prize winners in the Open Section. See what you can learn from them.'

That turned out to be a good idea, because I got so bound up in studying the techniques these more experienced photographers had used that I completely forgot about the task coming up and suddenly we were being called to stand near Jessica because the prize giving was about to start.

The third and second prize winners gave their speeches and accepted their prizes to polite applause and then it was my turn. I said, 'I want to thank Joe Walker, who taught me how to take photographs and how to process them, and I especially want to thank my mentor Melanie Brown who is with me today and without whose help and encouragement I would never have entered this competition.'

Melanie had put the second half of that sentence into my speech and she smiled graciously at everyone in the room as I said it. I went on, 'I want to say a special thank you to the sponsors who made the contest possible and who have provided such a wonderful prize, for which I am more grateful than I can say.' Now it was Jessica's turn to beam. 'Finally,' I said, 'I must say thank you to the judges who placed my pics first. Though I have to say, having seen the work of the other entrants, I think they have made the wrong decision.' There was clapping and laughter at that, and I heard a woman say, 'He's very gracious isn't he? For such a young man,' and the man beside her said, 'You mean, for a Geordie pleb.'

That should have been that. I'd said my bit and I turned towards the chief judge as Jessica had instructed in order to receive my cheque. But a man stepped forward and, in a loud voice, he said, 'Jeff Thomson, Fleet Street Press. For the benefit of our readers, how does it feel for a convicted murderer who just got out of jail to be receiving a prize like this?' A photographer had appeared beside him and he was shooting me.

I was stopped in my tracks. I felt as though I was going to be sick. Jessica was looking at me, the chief judge was looking at me, the whole room was looking at me. I was shown up, not just as a Geordie pleb, which the man's voice had made clear was bad enough, but as a fraud and a killer as well. I stepped forward, pushing my way through the people. If I didn't get out of here I'd hurt someone. The photographer was still shooting and the reporter was trying to bar my way but I pushed past him. I wanted to drop him but I couldn't. If I hit someone it would be assault and I'd be back inside, my licence revoked.

Melanie was calling out to me but I didn't listen. I went through the door and onto the street. I could hear the excitement behind me but I had to get away. I had to.

CHAPTER 25

I didn't go straight back to the hotel. Mostly because I wanted to walk, but also because I couldn't remember what it was called and I didn't know how to get there. Melanie had been in charge of all that and I certainly didn't want to go back to the gallery and ask her.

My head was full of noise and my heart was full of panic. I don't know how many people I bumped into; I didn't care. When I get like that I can't bear to be sitting still. I'd had nights in Young Offenders, especially when I was waiting to be told whether I'd get out or not, when having to be in my cell was agony. I'd walk up and down. It's a tiny area, a cell floor, and that made it worse. I'd known that when I graduated to adult nick you're at least doubled up there, sometimes three people in a cell built for one, and what were the others going to say when I got up at two in the morning and started walking the floor?

Although I had heard that lifers were likely to have a cell to themselves, which wouldn't be quite so bad.

All those feelings came back to me now, not knowing what was going to happen but knowing it wasn't in my control and someone else was going to decide. And the panic was multiplied by the feelings I already had that I shouldn't be out; that people were looking at me; that everyone knew where I'd been until so recently. Which, of course, thanks to Jeff Thomson and Fleet Street Press, they did. I don't know how other people handle those feelings but in my case my head fills up and the dread and the thoughts follow each other so fast I can't get hold of them and if I'm not able to walk I feel like I'm going to die, and that dying would be the best thing.

But if I can walk then I slowly get on top of it. I don't know how it happens but it does. I think it may be the breathing you have to do when you're walking hard. The panic subsides and the noise in my head goes away and I start to be able to think. And I realise that the end hasn't come yet, and there *are* better things than dying, which in any case would come low on my list of things I want to do.

I could run on at great length here, which is interesting because, now that I really put my mind to it, that's what I'm doing when I'm walking. It isn't the breathing. Or it is, but it isn't just the breathing. My head is processing all sorts of stuff, random thoughts that I pursue or don't, and as it does that it's calming down. While I'm working through all the twaddle I lose sight of the big thing that's worrying me and when I come back to it it's still a worry but it isn't such a mountain any more. It's become sort of climbable.

Nowadays, I'd probably think about histograms and how to set the parameters of a pic I was processing to get the result I wanted. Maybe I'd apply different forms of light in my head and imagine the effect on this particular pic. But I don't seem to get panic attacks any more.

As I calmed down, I walked more slowly. As I walked more slowly, I took more notice of where I was. I looked at my watch. It was after eight. There was to be a reception after the prize-giving, which I gathered meant people standing around talking and having what Melanie had said would be bad wine and dry snacks. She said the sticks the snacks were on would have more life in them than the snacks themselves. Melanie might have stayed for the reception, but I began to think she was more likely to have gone back to the hotel. What would have been the point in staying? She'd gone there to watch me get a prize. They weren't going to give it to me now, were they? It had seemed so easy, to clamber out of the world I'd been born into and into the one I wanted to join. I should have known. I'd been told enough times. I remembered Chantal, in my room trying to get me to help her with Regus. When I was still at school. Before I'd started working with him; before I'd had any money for the Creep to steal; before I had to choose between Regus and the judge. 'I hope you don't end up disappointed, Billy. It isn't good to hope for too much.' Well, she'd been right.

But what was I going to do? Melanie had said I should have a mobile phone, all students had them, they were de rigueur whatever that meant, but I hadn't got round to it yet. And I still couldn't remember where I was staying.

I took the room key out of my pocket and looked at it. It was a plastic thing that worked by some kind of magnetism so far as I'd been able to tell. It was in a card folder and it took me a couple of minutes to realise that the hotel's name, address and telephone number were printed on the folder. When I did realise it, I laughed.

Two policemen told me how to get there. It took twenty minutes of hard walking.

Melanie was frantic by the time she saw me. I don't know how well our pretence that we weren't an item stood up in front of the desk staff when she threw herself on me.

(Actually, I don't suppose it stood up at all, even before that. Jessica told me, ages later, that she'd known there was something between me and Melanie the moment she clapped eyes on us. 'Anybody would have known.' I was aghast. 'Anybody?' 'Well, perhaps not anybody. Just every woman over the age of ten.' And when I asked how she'd felt about that she said, 'Hey. Each to his own, you know? Sixteen year old boy, woman of thirty? If that's what turns your crank, go for it. Great for the boy, I'd say.' Then she'd thought a bit and added, 'Though I think I'd wonder about the maturity of the thirty year old woman.' There were times I wished we'd had that bit of the conversation a little earlier.)

We went straight upstairs, no messing. Melanie said, 'Tomorrow we buy you a mobile.' She wrapped her arms round me. 'You're covered in sweat,' she said. 'You're freezing. You're shaking. Get your clothes off. I'll run you a bath.' So that's what we did. She followed me into the bathroom and started washing me like a baby, and I let her. 'Look at this chap,' she said. 'He never forgets what he likes, does he?'

There was a dressing gown in the bathroom and she told me to put it on. I said, 'How did it end? Who did they give my prize to? The guy who came second, I suppose.'

Melanie was staring at me. I said, 'Were they horrible to you?'

She took my face in her hands and kissed me, a long and lingering kiss on the lips. Then she pointed at the shelf that ran along the room's side wall. The camera body and the lens were standing on it.

I said, 'I don't understand. How could they still give it to me? After what happened?' Melanie reached into her bag, took out a cheque and waved it at me. 'Of course they gave it to you. My dear, you are the talk of the town.'

'How could that man do that?'

'You're joking, of course. It's the best thing that could have happened. You were just another photographer trying to get a start. Now you're a celebrity.'

I put the body and lens together and set the battery to charge. 'That's not what I want.'

'Billy, love. You've got a criminal record. It's in the public domain. You can't bury it. And walking out like that was a stroke of genius. I'm surprised you had the presence of mind. Give me your room key.'

She went next door and brought back the dressing gown from my room. Then she took her clothes off and got into it. I loved watching her undress, seeing all those adorable bits coming into view and knowing they were for me. Only this time she didn't undress totally, because she'd put some special things on for this evening. Things I hadn't seen before. 'These are French knickers,' she said. Under them she had a suspender belt and she was wearing old-fashioned stockings with seams up the back. I decided I liked French knickers. I said, 'I didn't walk out for effect. I thought they'd all hate me.'

'Oh, Billy. You have so much to learn about people.' She rang room service and ordered a meal. Steak and chips and a bread roll for me, some veggie thing for her. Chocolate brownie and ice cream for me. Coffee. A bottle of white wine. When the waiter knocked on the door, she made me go into the bathroom and keep quiet until he'd gone.

There was only one wine glass, so I drank mine out of a tumbler. There was only one coffee cup, too, but that didn't matter as there were two more in the room, with the kettle and tea bags they provided.

'What does Jessica think?' I asked.

'She's ecstatic. She thinks you'll be the biggest draw in her stable. For professional purposes, you're not Billy any more. She's renamed you BL McErlane. I've got an agency agreement you have to sign and send back to her. She's keeping your photos. She'll exhibit them in her gallery. Any she sells, she takes fifteen per cent.'

'Sells?'

'She sold five tonight, my poppet.'

I was amazed. 'How much for?'

'She's pricing them between fifty pounds and three hundred. Colin Maraine the art critic was there tonight. He bought one of the three hundred pound ones.'

'Three hundred? Pounds?'

'It was the one of the old woman with all her belongings in a supermarket trolley. She says she'll deduct the cost of matting and framing and then take her fifteen percent out of what's left. She says you need to learn to do your own matting and framing but she'll talk to you about that. I assume you know what matting is?'

'Sort of. Well, no.'

'Find out. And the reporter? He'll be here at ten tomorrow morning for an interview.'

'Melanie, I *can't…*'

'Billy, you *must*. You cannot walk away from a chance like this. Thomson will be good to you. He'll write a piece that will have everyone wanting a BL McErlane hanging on their wall. You're on the very first rung of the celebrity ladder. When you get closer to the top the Press will do everything they can to knock you off it, but first they have to help you get up there. Symbiosis, Billy. They need you and you need them.'

Euphoria had replaced fear. Melanie told me to put the finished room service trolley outside the door. When I came back, she'd dropped the dressing gown on the floor and was sitting on the bed with her shoulders back, hands resting on the bed behind her, breasts thrust out. 'Do you like this, my love?'

I said, 'You're beautiful.' Which wasn't just a line, but what I truly thought.

'And you're very sweet. How would you like to take these knickers off me and place your wonderful warm lips between my thighs?'

Which is what I did.

When I woke, the clock on the television said it was three in the morning. A green light on the charger told me the camera battery was ready to go. I got up, careful not to wake Melanie, and slipped the battery into the camera. Melanie was draped over the bed, her stockings and suspender belt still in place, a sheet winding in and out of her legs. On her sleeping face was a look of both abandonment and fulfilment.

I took about forty shots. I played with focal length, exposure, film speed. I framed her close-up and distant, wide angle and something close to macro. Then I got back into bed.

CHAPTER 26

Jeff Thomson turned up next morning on the dot of ten. He had his photographer with him. I'd been thinking about this and I knew there was one thing I had to get straight.

'We'll do the interview,' I said. 'I'll give you everything I can. But there's a condition.'

Thomson nodded in the direction of Melanie, who was sitting in a chair she'd placed against the wall. 'She told us,' he said.

How could she have told them? I hadn't discussed it with her. Melanie said, 'They can write anything they like about where you came from. They can say you're at college. But they must not say where you did your time, where you live now or where the college is.'

I was stunned. That had been exactly what I had been going to say, but how could Melanie possibly have known that? We hadn't talked about it.

She inspected her nails. 'It's obvious, Billy. We don't want your mother or one of your sisters turning up, do we? They could wreck the show before it's properly on the road.'

As it turned out, that wasn't Melanie's only contribution to the interview. But I didn't mind. Happier now, I turned to Thomson and started answering his questions.

On the train home, Melanie asked if I was looking forward to trying out my new camera.

'I already did.' I switched it on and showed her how to play back pictures on the little screen. I suppose I was half afraid she'd be angry, but her reaction was one of delight. She went

128

through the pics several times. 'I want to see these on my proper screen at home.'

'I'll load them for you.'

'They'd better not go on your computer when you get it.'

'Of course not.'

Did I know when I said that that I was lying? I don't know. Since it became clear that I could make a living by taking photographs and that people regarded me as an artist, I've read a lot about what people think that means – that business of being an artist. Artists don't have to play by the same rules as everyone else. In my early days of artistry, if that's what I was, I suppose I went along with this idea. I was different from other people. They had to play by rules but I didn't. What a glorious invitation.

But perhaps I'm making too much of this. Perhaps I just lied. Knew I was going to have those pics for myself but pretended I wasn't for a bit of peace.

When we got off the train, we went to Melanie's place and I put the pics on her hard disk. 'There,' I said. 'I've deleted them from the camera.' The lie came out so easily. What harm could it do?

I'd planned to go to the hostel next, just for the pleasure of being there, but that was not yet to be. There were more pics Melanie wanted for her computer. Both of us had to be in them, which meant I got to try out the timer function on the camera. It worked very well.

Those pics led naturally to other activities and it was dinner time when I finally reached home.

That evening was special, because the Howards' daughter came to visit. We were always polite at the dinner table because the

Howards insisted on it, but with Ann there we were even more so.

One of the other residents, Neil, was getting a name as an athlete and whenever he could he'd be at the local athletics club, training. He'd competed that day and come first in the 3,000 metres. Missus Howard insisted he put his medal and his certificate on the table so that we could all admire it, and she told him how proud we all were of him. Mister Howard said, 'Have you told your parents yet?' and Neil said no, he hadn't, and Mister Howard said, 'You must. Get Billy to take a photo of you with your medal and send it to them.' So I went to my room for my camera and took Neil's photograph while everyone stood around and grinned. I needn't have bothered, as it happened, because the Press photographer had already done it and when the evening paper arrived Neil was on the back page. Mister Howard told him to go out and buy two copies, one to send to his parents and one to keep himself for ever, so that he'd always remember his big triumph.

After dinner I went into the garden to enjoy the pleasant evening and Ann followed me out for a smoke. She said, 'I was watching you.'

'Oh, yes?'

'They're good at what they do, aren't they? My mum and dad?'

I said, yes, they were. The Howards were very good at running a hostel.

She said, 'I see a lot of people like you here. Just remember, they only have one child and it's me.'

I didn't know what she was talking about.

She said, 'Lots of people who stay here end up wishing my mother was their mother, too. But she isn't. She's only mine.'

I'd started to go red. I don't like it when I do that. I said, 'I wouldn't want her to be my mother. My mother is horrible,' and Ann said, 'Just as long as you don't confuse the two.' Then she said, 'They often wish they hadn't got into this business.'

'Oh?'

'They find the bunch of you a pain. When they started they were full of ideals, but reality kills dreams and they've had about as much reality as they can stand. They get some choice specimens here.'

'Yes,' I said, 'I suppose they do.'

'You're a murderer, aren't you? I'm surprised you're free. My parents think you should still be locked up.' When I didn't answer, she said, 'Well. I've finished my ciggy. Don't forget what I've told you.' Then she went back into the house. Guy had been watching all this from a little distance away and now he came to where I was standing. 'Don't listen to her,' he said. 'She talks like that to everyone. She's jealous of her parents' interest in us. I'm sure they've never said a word against you.'

It was nice to have Guy's opinion to set against Ann's, but one of them was clearly wrong. Which, I didn't know. Still don't.

CHAPTER 27

From Sink Estate Killer to Prize Winning Artist

Yesterday witnessed one of the most satisfying events we have ever been called on to report. BL McErlane, who only four years ago was sentenced as Zappa McErlane to what amounted to life imprisonment for the lust-fuelled murder of his stepfather, was last night crowned Young Photographer of the Year at the Jessica Robinson Gallery. In an exclusive interview with Jeff Thomson for this paper, the artist talked about his journey and named the people without whom he could not have made it.

Chief among these were Melanie Brown, Education Officer at the prison where he served his time, and Joe Walker who taught him the basics of digital photography. Billy also found time to praise the Prison Governor as having had a pivotal influence on his life. Perhaps strongest of all were the words he had for Miss Taggart, the schoolteacher who taught him maths and gave him self-respect.

One person who did not merit a mention was Billy's mother. Billy refused to say anything bad about her, but he clearly isn't willing to speak on her behalf, either. Does he resent the things she had to say about him after he was sentenced? It seems he probably does, but getting Billy actually to talk about his family proved impossible. What he did say was that prison had been the making of him. If he hadn't been inside, he would never have discovered his gift – what Melanie Brown, his mentor,

132

called his unique vision – and the only way he would ever have been inside the four star hotel where he had stayed the night and we conducted this interview would have been as a cleaner. 'Or veg prep,' he added. 'Or maybe picking pockets.' He said that without the trace of a smile.

Melanie Brown told us that Billy's goal after college and university is to return to a school on the sort of sink estate he grew up in and work there as a teacher to help others climb out of the same pit as the one he was himself born into. 'Billy's a very modest person.' She said. 'If you didn't know what his plans are, he'd never tell you.'

Well, maybe. But a star was born yesterday and the unique vision we heard of is just that. This reporter has already bought a BL McErlane print to hang on his wall. If you want one, we suggest you get it now. In a couple of years, McErlanes may be out of the ordinary person's price bracket.

CHAPTER 28

I was in Guy's room once and I picked up a book I saw lying there. Inside was a plate that said the book had been awarded as a prize "for contributions to the corporate life and ethos of the school". The name of the prize winner was not Guy's, as I pointed out to him.

'Oh, that,' he said in his languid way. 'Quite right, William. I transferred ownership to myself.'

'You mean you nicked it.'

'Such an unpleasant word, Billy. I did not wish him to possess it, so I deprived him of it.'

'Did you want it yourself?'

He looked at me, astounded. 'A book about French history? What should I want with such a thing?'

I could, of course, have pursued this conversation but experience told me I would end up no better informed. What matters is that our school – the school I went to when I was eleven; the school I was at when I won the essay prize and when I went to prison – also had a corporate ethos. In our case, it would not have been advanced by offering a book as a prize.

There were many offences against our school's corporate ethos, but working hard (or even wishing to work hard, because there were many effective barriers against actually doing it) was probably the worst. It was an offence against group solidarity and it was punished ruthlessly.

If you had been born where I had to a family like mine, you were intended to grow up poor and ignorant. This was not government policy; it was the dictate of those around you who

134

were meant to be as poor and ignorant as you. Those who aspired had gone. There was to be no more aspiring.

Available career choices were limited and meant to be limited. If you were a boy, you could thieve, rob, mug, deal drugs or simply (the majority choice) live on benefit. You could even have a portfolio career, freelancing in part-time thieving and mugging and selling stolen goods as opportunities arose while never giving up the safety net of benefit. If you were a girl, you could think about shop-lifting, thieving and part-time prostitution – still with the constant security of the benefit. Ideally, you would hope to accumulate children so that the amount of benefit increased. This would also get you subsidised accommodation and that in its turn would ensure that you never lacked for a man of your own. The fact that you had a bed on which he could have you when the feeling took him and under which he could hide anything he wished to keep secret would act as an irresistible magnet.

Would you want a man of your own, when he would often treat you as a punch bag? Yes, actually, you would. Why? Because you'd be a damn sight worse off without one. When Chantal had asked what I thought would happen to her on her own we had both known the answer. Regus was not just the man who hit her – he was also her designated protector. Without one of those she'd have been prey to any man on the prowl with a skinful of beer inside him. And when he left, the next one would already be in line, unzipping.

Most of our teachers went along with the group fatwa on anyone wanting to learn. It made life easier and, anyway, they'd long since given up. If we were ignorant that was our fault, not theirs. We were unsalvageable. Miss Taggart came out of a different bottle. She was nearly sixty and she'd be retiring soon, but until she went she was going to go on doing what she'd done all her life. Providing opportunities to people who didn't have any.

I took the opportunities and so I had to take the fights. Sometimes I won. Sometimes I fought them to a standstill. Sometimes I had to run. And sometimes there were just so many of them that I took a kicking.

The first time I landed in hospital, nothing happened. The police came, I refused to grass anyone up, the police went. The second time was much the same. The third time, I got the police equivalent of Miss Taggart. Sergeant Dane.

'You'll end up dead, Billy. You know that? Dead or so maimed you'd be better off dead. Is that what you want?'

'I can't grass, Mister Dane. You know that.'

He sighed. 'We don't need you to grass, Billy. We know who's doing it. What we need you to do is testify.'

I couldn't do that, either. I knew it and he knew it.

I reviewed my options. As far as I could see, I only had the one. I knew what I was getting into. The alternative was worse. I could give up all my ambitions, which I wasn't prepared to do. I could get myself kicked into a coma and maybe be a cripple for the rest of my life, which I also wasn't prepared to do. Or I could work for Regus, which I'd said I wouldn't do but which was now looking like the least bad choice. If you ask me, that's what they call a no-brainer.

I got the warning a few days after I was back at school, still with my wrist bandaged and with the cuts over my eye and on my cheek not wholly mended. If I didn't desist, next day I'd get the kicking of a life time. They were determined to bring me into line.

I stopped at Chantal's place on my way home and told her about it. That night I did my homework and next day I made a big production out of handing it in. I made sure everyone knew I'd defied my instructions.

I'd got about a mile from the school gates when it kicked off. Within thirty seconds, a black BMW screeched to a halt beside us. Regus Hunt and three men I didn't know came out of it, baseball bats swinging.

It took about three minutes. Afterwards, the police swarmed all over the place. I didn't say a word to them, and nor did anyone else.

Rattigan was outside school next day. He was waiting for me at the gate. 'Hey, man! Why didn't you say you were on Regus Hunt's crew? Nobody knew.'

'You fucking know now,' I said. I didn't like using words like that because they didn't feel like me, they made me more like them (and I hadn't yet heard posh Jessica in full flow), but I was really pissed off about what they'd forced me to do. Because I was in it now. I'd called in a favour, a big favour and I'd have to deliver. I'd made a pact with the Devil and the Devil collects.

It wasn't all bad. Not only was I left alone to get on with whatever studies I wanted to, I also had respect and position on the street that I hadn't had before.

Poppy Cannon was an example of that.

Poppy was another who really wanted to learn, but she'd crumpled soon after coming to this school at the age of eleven. Her father had walked out years before, her half-sisters and half-brothers were grown up and gone, her mother had committed some fraud or other against the DSS. Lots of people did that, but Poppy's mother was caught and now she found it very difficult to get benefit as well as having to pay back what she'd stolen. That meant she worked long hours as a cleaner and a waitress to pay the rent and put food on the table. Poppy had no protectors. For her it was conform or die.

She sidled up to me as I was leaving school on the first day of my new life. Day One, Year One in the post-Regus epoch. The approach was direct. 'Can I be your girlfriend?'

'What? Why do you want to be my girlfriend?'

'Then people will leave me alone. I can do what I want to do.'

I stopped and looked at her. She wasn't bad-looking, Poppy.

Unlike most of the girls there she stuck to the school uniform, wore shapeless trousers instead of short skirts and you never saw a trace of make-up on her face. She had blonde hair which she styled severely with a parting on the left and a hairclip and she kept it cut short.

I started walking again and she walked with me. 'What is it you want to do?'

She snorted. 'How much time have you got?' Then she told me, at length. She wanted an education, she wanted to get out of the dump we were in, she wanted a good job a long way from there.

All the time she was telling me this she was waving her hands around and she kept looking up at me as if she was checking what I thought and I knew why she was doing that because it was how I'd seen other girls talking to their boyfriends and she wanted people to think that's really what we were.

'Okay. You can be my girlfriend.'

'Hold my hand. Let people see us together.'

Now I was a protector. Because that's what she really wanted. This was a transaction she was entering into. But we could both pretend it wasn't.

It felt strange, walking along the pavement holding someone's hand. Strange but nice. Her hand was warm and dry. I said, 'Do you ever get hugged?'

She stared sideways at me. 'Hugged? Yes. Of course.'

'Who by?'

'Me mam, of course. Who else?'

'What's it like? Being hugged?'

She was laughing. She stopped walking, put her bag down and turned to face me. My bag was slung over my shoulder and she signalled to me to remove it. Then she raised her arms, wrapped them around me and held me tight. She said, 'It's like this.' We stayed like that for minutes, with people passing. I couldn't remember ever feeling so close to another person. As though I really was important to her. After a while she said, 'You can kiss us if you like.'

When we got to her door she said, 'Come in for a while.'

'I don't want to make...'

'My mother won't be home for hours. There'll just be me and you. If I'm really your girlfriend, you'll come in. People know that.'

We went in. Poppy took her coat off and made tea. She put some biscuits on a plate. We sat down. We looked at each other, two people unsure what to do next. Then she looked down. 'Do you want to go upstairs with me?'

I remembered Kylie in my grandmother's shed. How incompetent I'd felt, and glad that Kylie knew what to do. I didn't think Poppy would know what to do and I was sure I didn't. I said, 'Do you?'

'I want to do what you want to do, Billy. Have you got a condom?'

'No.'

'Billy, I don't want to end up pushing a kid down to the Social. I won't get to college like that.'

I nodded. 'Okay. We'd better not go upstairs, then.'

That expression on her face was relief. I couldn't deny that. But I didn't mind. I said, 'I'm not saying I won't want to go upstairs some time. We just won't do it now.'

'Okay, Billy.' Then she said, 'I'll go up and draw my bedroom curtains, though. So people will think we have.'

When she came down, I opened my bag. 'Do you understand these equations we're supposed to hand in tomorrow?'

'No. I don't.'

'Miss Taggart explained them to me after school once. Do you want me to show you how to do them?'

When I left a couple of hours later, she followed me out onto the pavement and turned up her face to be kissed. I had a lot to learn about this girlfriend business.

I know the story is supposed to just unfold, but I'll jump ahead a bit here and say that Poppy and I never did go upstairs. She was my girlfriend for a few months, until I was arrested in fact, and I spent a lot of time at her house with the upstairs curtains drawn, doing my homework there instead of at the library, and I really came to like her a lot and I bought a packet of condoms and carried them around, just in case, so we could have gone to bed together. I was physically excited a few times before we were done but we never did it.

I was sure she'd go with me and do it any time I asked, partly because that was the deal and partly, later, because she liked me as much as I liked her. I think. I'm sure she did. She said she did.

I remember one afternoon, for example. We were at her place. She never came to mine, I wouldn't have allowed it. We'd finished reading the set bit from Joseph Conrad and now we were on the sofa. We had our arms tight round each other and we were hugging and kissing and feeling very hot. And she said, 'How much do you love me?'

I didn't know how to answer that, so I just said, 'Lots,' which was true. But she said, 'Is that all you can say?'

And I said, 'What do you want me to say? How much do you love me?'

And she said, 'Up to the sky and down again, a million times.'

I thought that was lovely and I was kissing her face, just little kisses all over, and she was trying to catch my lips with hers as they went past, and then I started kissing her on the throat, and she was stroking the back of my neck, and my hand stroked her breast, not her bare breast, it was through her blouse and the soft little bra she wore, which it had done quite often before if I'm honest, but then I stroked her hip and my hand went down to her knee and I was getting pretty warmed up. And she said, 'Billy,' and I said, 'Yes?' and she said, 'You know I will if you want me to, don't you?'

I took my hand away then and sat up and looked at her. My thing, my beautiful cock as Melanie would say later on, was standing up really hard and I really wanted to do it with her. If I'd felt as strongly for her at the very beginning as I did now then we'd have gone upstairs together a lot earlier and that would have been that. I said, 'What do you want to do?'

And she said, 'I want to make you happy.'

And I said, 'You do.'

And she said, 'You'd really like to be inside me, wouldn't you?'

And I said, 'What do you want?'

And she said, 'Really, if I could have anything I wanted, I'd like to wait until we're married, and it's the night of our

141

wedding day, the first day of our life together. And I'd like to do it for the first time then. But, if you want to do it now, we will.'

Now, I know what's going on here. Some people are thinking, 'Aaah, how romantic,' and some are thinking, 'Aaah, I'm going to be sick. She's got him on a string and she's leading him by the nose like a donkey. Why doesn't he just put her on her back and give her one?' I know that's what's going on because, if I'm honest here, both of those thoughts were in my mind. Was she playing straight with me, or was she having me over?

And the fact is that it didn't matter. Because the point wasn't what was in her mind, it was what was in mine. And I loved her and I didn't want to be nasty to her or do anything to her that she didn't absolutely, truly, heart-of-hearts want me to do. And if she was ready to give in to my wishes I knew it was at least partly because I was bigger and stronger than her and there was no-one else in the house and if I wanted to I could just force her. And I didn't want to be the sort of man who forced women.

So we got up and went out for a walk to cool down, and then I went home.

And, looking back, I'm glad that Poppy and I never did it, because Kylie had already given me a dose although I didn't know it then and if Poppy and I had done it I'd have given a dose to her and I'd really have hated that, knowing I'd given the pox to Poppy when I felt about her the way I did.

As well as Poppy, now that I was on Regus Hunt's crew Kylie put herself back on the menu.

When I got home from Poppy's that first night, Kylie was there with Chantal and baby Zappa. They'd got carry-out fish and chips and they were sitting round the table with my mother and the Creep, tucking in. Chantal was letting the baby suck the occasional chip. It was quite convivial and domestic, for my family. They'd even buttered some bread and made a pot of tea, although Chantal was drinking Sprite and my mother and the Creep both had Harp cans in front of them. Chantal said, 'Yours is in the oven, keeping warm, Billy.'

And she looked at Kylie and Kylie nudged her and they both giggled.

I knew at once what was going on. I say that because Melanie sometimes accused me of being innocent (and so did Jessica, when I think about it. And a few others) and I want to make it clear that I'm not always as slow on the uptake as some people think I am. Now that Regus had intervened on my behalf I had weight. Respect. I was someone to take note of. What else had it been with Rattigan and Poppy? Kylie wouldn't be a baby-snatcher if she went with me now. She'd be a moll.

But I didn't want her. Three hours earlier, I'd have gone with her wherever she suggested, but now I had Poppy. And while I might not know Poppy very well yet, I knew she was in a different class from Kylie. Kylie had been sweet when she'd relieved me of my cherry but she wasn't what I wanted any more. Poppy didn't do any of those girl things like running the tip of her tongue round her lips, but Poppy had what I wanted and Kylie didn't. And that's just how it was.

So, when Kylie made her offer with Chantal giggling and my mother backing her up, I said no thank you.

Kylie was a bit taken aback, to be honest. But Chantal. Chantal was going on like I'd insulted her best friend, the finest person on the planet. It was so embarrassing even Kylie tried to shut her up. She was saying, 'No, no, it's all right, Chantal.' And, 'I understand. Honestly.' But she didn't.

Then Chantal got into her offensive stride and demanded to know if I really went to the library every evening or if I was seeing a girl. Or, worse still, a boy. 'Tonight,' she said. 'School let out three hours ago. Where have you been since then?'

'I've been with Poppy,' I said.

'Poppy? Poppy Cannon?'

'Yes,' I said.

'You prefer *Poppy Cannon* to my mate?'

Kylie stood up. 'Stop it, Chantal.' She stood in front of me. 'A little while ago it was you chasing me. Now you can have what you wanted and you don't want it. What gives?'

I shook my head. 'I'm sorry.'

'Oh,' she said. 'Don't say sorry to me. I won't go without, you can bet your life on that. I just hope you don't.'

Sometimes you read in a book, "Her eyes were blazing" and you think, how can eyes blaze? Eyes don't blaze. Well, Kylie's eyes were blazing. She slapped me across the cheek. I'd like to say it was a light slap, but it wasn't. She said, 'Poppy's a wimp. She'll be perfect for you.'

And then she flounced out.

After Kylie had left, my mother and Chantal got started on me and Poppy. Had we done it was what they wanted to know.

No, I said, we hadn't.

Chantal said, 'And you'd rather be with a girl who won't than Kylie, would you? Kylie who would and has?'

'She isn't a girl who won't,' I said.

'Was she on the rag?' said my mother. 'Was that it?'

'I've no idea,' I said. 'I didn't ask.'

'No need to be huffy. I'm just trying to see how it is.'

'I like her. Can't you understand that? I'm trying to treat her like I'd want to be treated if I was a girl. Which thank God I'm not. Not around here.'

Quietly, my mother said, 'You're being a gentleman. That's what you're telling us.'

'If you like. Yes, I suppose I am. I'm being a gentleman.'

'I don't know,' she said. She was looking at the Creep and speaking very softly. 'I don't know where we got you from. You don't belong round here. Not at all.'

Then the Creep said, 'Is he going to want those fish and chips? Or shall I have them?'

CHAPTER *29*

Regus gave me a bike. Not in person, he wasn't that stupid. This was a youth who'd been working for Regus, doing what I was going to be doing, and now he was taking a step up. He'd been riding this bike and now he was eighteen and he was going to sit inside one of the BMWs and if he did everything right then after a while he'd have a BMW of his own.

He didn't look anything like Regus. His head wasn't shaved, he didn't have tattoos, there wasn't any gold on view when he opened his mouth. He looked like he might have done a fair bit of weightlifting, but he could have been an athlete or a rugby player. Or a weightlifter, come to that. And his clothes were what I've come to think of as preppy, now that I've done some men's fashion photography.

He had some instructions for me that made everything clear. Apparently, Regus regretted the look he'd chosen for himself when he was too young to have any sense and he didn't want anyone who worked for him to look like that. So we were all to look like this guy. And always be polite, to the police or anyone else. Never make enemies. Never get people against us. Never steal or shoplift. If we found anything lying in the street, hand it in at the police station. Help old ladies across the road. Intervene if we saw a mugging and put a stop to it. If a copper asked us anything it was to be "Yes, sir" or "Yes, officer" and give every possible help. (Without grassing anyone up or saying anything that could be even remotely useful to the law. Obviously.)

He said his name was Marcus and he showed me the bike. It was black, without any maker's name on it. 'It's a Thorn,' he said. 'A Raven Catalyst. Very expensive.'

'Expensive?'

'Don't worry. No-one's going to steal it. I've been riding this bike for two years and everybody knows who it belongs to. We gave it that crappy paint job so it wouldn't look like what it is and the police won't ask how you came by it. And it's got a tracker in the frame. But I suggest you ride it round the turf a bit. Let people know it's yours now.'

'A tracker?'

'Sure. Just like the BMWs have. Anyone steals this bike, we'll find it. And then God help the person who took it.'

'Can I ride it to school?'

'Of course you can ride it to school. In fact, you should.'

The bike had wide tyres, like a BMX or a mountain bike, but they were smooth. And the gears were in the hub and not a derailleur.

'Slicks,' Marcus said when I mentioned the tyres. 'Nobblies are for kids. Unless you're planning to ride down muddy hills, which you're not. These tyres have almost no rolling resistance. All your energy goes into moving forward. You'll go faster with these and there'll be times when you need to go fast.'

Then he explained the gears. 'Much better than derailleurs. They don't need adjusting, they won't slip off the cogs and the chain is always in line so you don't waste energy pushing across the grain.' He showed me how they worked.

'Look in the pannier.'

I did, and found a mobile phone.

'It's pay as you go. You don't use it for personal stuff, and you never make calls on it. Not ever. We'll change it from time to time. You'll get text messages on it. Don't reply to them. Sometimes there'll be a place and a time. Go to that place at that time. Sometimes there'll only be a place, which means you go there now. Whatever you're doing.'

'What if I'm in school?'

'Don't worry. The man knows how you feel about school. He wants you to get an education. He needs bright people. And that's what you call him. From now on, the name Regus never crosses your lips. He's The Man. And my name isn't Marcus, except to you. If you ever mention Marcus, no-one will know who you're talking about. But we'll know you said it, and we won't be happy, Billy. The Man won't, and I won't. You don't want that.'

He explained the system of signals they had, so when I got where I'd been sent I'd know whether I should stop there until someone approached me or ride on because I had a tail, or the person I was supposed to meet was being watched.

'Things will be put in the pannier, Billy. You don't want to know what they are and you won't ever look.'

'Okay.'

'If you're stopped, a lawyer will try to get you out. If he can't, you'll just have to take it on the chin. Say nothing, except that you didn't know whatever it is was there, you don't know who put it there and you think you're being framed. It won't have your fingerprints on because you won't have touched it. Take whatever's coming to you. You're a juvenile, so it won't be much. And you'll be looked after.'

'Okay.'

'Any questions?'

'No.'

'Good.'

And he was gone.

The first text came on Saturday morning. I'd been planning to spend the day with Poppy, reading a set book and writing an essay about it. Instead, I cycled to the community centre and stopped outside. There were no signals. Then a man came out, dropped something into the pannier, snapped it shut and walked on. I stayed where I was.

Three minutes later, I got another text. I rode to the place it told me, the open area outside a block of flats, and stopped. Once again, no signals. Two men came strolling over the concrete. One of them stopped to ask if I could give him a light. While I was telling him I didn't smoke, I felt a tug at the back of the bike. The two men walked on. Three more minutes and another text. "Free till five."

I cycled home. I was shaking, but not from nerves. What I felt was elated. Sheer excitement. Adrenalin pumping. I picked up my book, but it was ages before I could follow the words enough to take them in.

Marcus was right about the bike. Riding it was a joy. I've got a Raven Catalyst of my own now. Charcoal grey with blue decals. Marathon slicks. Fourteen speed Rohloff SpeedHub. Shimano XTRs. Mavic XC717 ceramic rims. Brooks saddle on titanium rails. Magura Odur fork. The works. I've toured on it in the Jura and the Perigord Noir and Burgundy. I've ridden it in the Brecon Beacons and the Lakes and Snowdonia (all on roads, obviously with those tyres). As soon as I get time I'm going to take it to Peru and tour it there. I love that bike.

CHAPTER 30

The computer and the extra lens were delivered to the hostel after three days. I set the computer up in my room.

The lens I'd chosen with Mister Walker's help was the 200mm f/2.8. I'd really have liked the 400mm, but they cost the thick end of five thousand pounds. Maybe one day. I walked into town to see if my cheque had cleared, which it had. I drew out five hundred pounds and found a camera shop where I bought a fixed lens digital camera small enough to hide in my hand. I also bought a tripod. The rest of the cash was for Melanie, to pay her back for the clothes she'd helped me buy. Guy went with me and he wanted to know why I needed the little camera when I'd got the beautiful big one.

I said, 'I can't carry an SLR and a big lens wherever I go. This one will fit in my pocket and I need never miss a shot.'

'You've got some beautiful gear.'

'I hope no-one gets ideas about transferring ownership.'

'If that's aimed at me,' he said, 'I want you to know I'm insulted. Never steal from your friends. That's the code I live by. That and never kiss a woman you wouldn't fuck.'

'I don't kiss my mother, either.'

'My dear chap. You presume too much on the love I bear you.'

You had to smile, listening to the flowery way Guy talked. And knowing not a word of it was meant.

When we got home, I set the compact's battery to charge. I mounted the new lens on the SLR and the SLR on the tripod and pointed it down the road. Distant things came into sharp close-up. I focussed on a door some distance away. Then I stood back and let Guy look through the lens.

'Kiss my puckered poo-hole,' he murmured. 'That is miraculous.'

'In a digital camera,' I said, 'you don't have any film. You have a sensor instead. The sensor is smaller than a frame of thirty-five mil film would be, and it's closer to the lens. What that means is that the focal length on a digital acts like it's a lot more than it would be with the same lens on a film camera. This two hundred mil lens is performing like an old style three fifty. What?'

'It's Greek to me, old man.'

'Never mind. You don't need to understand. Just look at the results.'

'My mind is boggled. Can you do the same with this little chap?' he asked, picking up the compact.

'No. Fixed lens digitals use digital zooming and not optical. It doesn't go anywhere near as high and it just crops the outer part of the sensor, so all it gives you is a closer view of the bit in the middle. But it can't give you any more pixels, so what you get is a lot of grain and no detail.'

'I'm going to take your word for that, Billy. That's the Doyle's front door, isn't it?'

'Is it?'

'It is. And the window directly above that front door is the delectable Kathleen's bedroom.'

'How do you know which bedroom is hers?'

He pressed his finger against his nose. 'I wonder if she draws her curtains when she gets ready for bed?'

'I should think so, wouldn't you? There's another house dead opposite. Anyway, we won't be looking. That's the code *I* live by.'

'Spoilsport. Fancy a game of snooker?'

'Sure. Why not?'

Later that evening, Mister Howard wrote down the serial numbers of the two cameras, both lenses and the computer. He said he was going to add them to the hostel's insurance cover. There'd be a cost, which I would be expected to pay, but that was better than losing the lot and not being able to replace them.

Then I texted Melanie on my new mobile and asked if I could bring her money the following day, which was Saturday. She texted back, "Not tomorrow. I'll text you when."

Looking back, it seems strange that it was only around now that I started wondering what had happened to Melanie's ex. It didn't then. Melanie and I were doing these lovely things together. Why should I think about the bit of her life, which was the majority, that she didn't spend with me?

Anyway, he turned out to be the reason I couldn't take her money to her that weekend.

On the Monday I started college. And a letter arrived at my foster home on the Tuesday, very formal.

Dear Mr McErlane

As you know, I need to see you twice weekly to discuss your progress so that I can submit a report to the Parole Board. I have checked with the college and they tell me that your timetable leaves you free on Tuesdays after two p. m. and all afternoon on Thursdays. Please report to me at my home at four p. m. on each of those days.

ZAPPA'S MAM'S A SLAPPER

You should advise the hostel wardens that you will not be in for dinner on Tuesday and Thursday evenings.

Yours sincerely

M Brown

I'd been afraid that I'd be behind the others at college, but I wasn't. The one-to-one tutoring I'd been getting from Melanie, Mister Walker and Dave Wilson turned out to have been a lot better than some people had had at school.

English was still Dave Wilson, and I was still good. In Art & Design I was The Man. The one the others turned to for advice and help. I also found I could draw, which came as a pleasant surprise.

Sociology was a bugger. Melanie wasn't my teacher now, and the one I had was even more bonkers than her. I was in danger of making a fool of myself when Wendy intervened.

'You mustn't let the nonsense get to you.'

I'd just collected a coffee and a chocolate muffin and sat at one of the outside tables to enjoy the September sunshine. Wendy sat down beside me with a bottle of water. She took a pack of cigarettes from her bag and lit one. 'You don't smoke, do you?'

I shook my head. Had this girl been watching me? Why?

She said, 'The Sociology drivel. I know some of what he says makes you want to laugh, but it's an easy course and we're going to need the grade if we want to get to uni. You do want to get to uni?'

'Of course.'

'Well, then. Keep your head down, smile at his jokes, turn in essays that agree with his point of view.'

'Even when I don't?'

'Especially then.'

'I'll try. It may not be easy.'

'It could mean the difference between Bristol and Luton.'

'Which one do I want?'

'Oh, Billy!'

She had that look on her face. The one that says, "Oh, look! A real proletarian! How too divine!"

And now she had that other one. The one that says, "Oh, dear. I've upset you. In fact, I've upset someone whose been known to kill people. But I'm going to pretend I don't know." She said, 'I saw your photographs in the Art and Design room.'

'Oh, yes?'

'You're really good. I wish I had that kind of creativity.'

'I just take pics,' I said.

'Yeah. Like Mozart just played music and Shakespeare just wrote sketches.'

I was saved from having to tell her how ludicrously over the top that was by the arrival of three more people from our year who plonked down their trays and, every one of them, lit cigarettes.

Wendy said, 'Billy and I were just talking about choice of uni.'

That started a general conversation, which is how I found out about the university pecking order. Which ones were really hard to get into and which would be a total waste of time if you did. It wasn't a conversation Melanie would have approved of (though she'd been to Durham, which I was interested to learn was "just below Oxbridge") and I don't think I ever told her about it. Me, I was used to compartmentalising my life.

And Wendy wasn't the only one to congratulate me on my pics. I was a hero. A genuine working class artist.

Of course, they already knew I'd been in jail, because my story had been in the papers the day after I walked out of the prize-giving. Melanie and Jessica had been right. It added to my appeal.

* * *

I heard about the caveman when I went to see Melanie. In accordance with a texted instruction, I had taken my camera which was now mounted on its tripod so that I could take pictures of our antics. Although it wasn't me that was taking them. Melanie had the remote shutter release and was pressing it whenever she wanted to record what we were doing.

'Tell me about being a man, Billy' she said when things had calmed down and we were lying side by side.

'What do you want to know? It's what I do. I'm a man. I don't think about being one. I just do it. If I said, tell me about being a woman, could you do it?'

'Not without making you blush, my cherub. When you're over the bombing zone…'

'When I'm *what?*'

'That's what my ex calls it. Being over the bombing zone. Then he lines up his missile and guides it right into the target.' She kissed me on the cheek. 'Just like you do, my love, with your nice pink Exocet. Oh, Billy! You *are* blushing.' She kissed me again. 'You're so sweet. Do you mind me talking about him?'

'We haven't.'

'You do mind.'

'No, I…'

'You mustn't be jealous, Billy. This you and me thing is lovely, but I can't give up what I have with him. Not completely.'

'I'm not jealous, Melanie.'

And I don't think I was. But that wasn't what she wanted to hear, so she didn't hear it.

She snuggled close to me. 'Were you cross when I wasn't available at the weekend?'

'A bit,' I said. I hadn't been cross at all, been quite pleased in fact, but I was beginning to get the hang of Melanie.

'What I get with you is lovely, Billy. But sometimes a woman just needs what he offers.' She giggled. 'A good hard seeing to. You know what they say. A hard man is good to find.' She nudged me in the ribs. 'See? Now I am telling you what it's like to be a woman.'

Mister Doyle was walking home. He wasn't in uniform but you still knew he was a copper. He had that slow, measured way of walking and his eyes were always scanning, taking everything in without seeming to. You got a nice, secure feeling walking with Mister Doyle.

'I rang Newcastle,' he said. 'Talked to Sergeant Walsh.'

'Oh, yes?' Walsh had been the detective who charged me.

'You can't blame me. Killer, out on licence, makes remarks about my daughter. I'm bound to take an interest.'

'I suppose so.'

'Walsh says there was something funny about your case.'

'I must have missed the laughs.'

'Did you take the rap for someone, Billy?'

'The jury didn't think so.'

'Juries have to go on the evidence you put in front of them.'

'He put it.'

'Did you give him any choice? He had a murder case, Billy. He had to have a culprit. The public doesn't like unsolved murders so us policemen, we don't like them, either. It's not really like *Frost* and *Morse*. We don't go on looking for someone just because we think the wrong person's in the frame.'

I didn't say anything.

'He told me about that, too. The way you clam up and look at your feet when you don't want to answer.'

I went on not saying anything.

'And your mother. And your sister. I heard all about that.'

We'd reached his house. He gestured towards his front door. 'This is where I live, Billy. If you ever want help, or just to talk to someone who knows you're no killer, knock on that door.'

'Thanks, Mister Doyle.' I felt a powerful urge to confide in him, tell him what happened. I didn't, though. That would have been a silly thing to do.

'I mean it, Billy. Any time.'

CHAPTER 31

I hadn't given a lot of thought to what it meant to be a celeb. Jessica spelled it out for me. She brought a photographer with her, as well as a PA and a car.

The first thing we did was go through the menswear shops. We bought four different shirts and two pairs of chinos. Then we went to a Costa. When I asked why I needed so many clothes, Jessica said, 'We're going to take your picture in different places and release the shots at different times. Do you want your public to think you only have one set of clothes?'

'Isn't that normal for students? Anyway, I don't want a public. When I dreamed about being a famous writer, I was going to be a recluse. Reclusive author Bill McErlane.'

'Of course you want a public. Who do you think's going to buy the product?'

I hated that word used in that way, but before I could speak she went on, 'A celeb can be a recluse. Playing hard to get makes you even more celebrated. It isn't the Nancy Dell'Olios of this world that journalists salivate over but the JD Salingers.' She took some printouts from the bag she carried and put one of them in front of me. 'Tell me what you think of this.' I read the bit someone had highlighted.

Madonna is plugging Global Warming activism on her tour. In a video interlude of her song "Get Stupid", she flashes several images of the planet being harmed – with slices of it slowly being taken away. There are even flashes of Al Gore on screen, along with those of Mahatma Gandhi, John Lennon, and Barack Obama. She also grouped John McCain in with a montage that features Hitler.

I said, 'You don't want me involved in stuff like this.'
She put down another sheet. 'How about this one?'

Over breakfast at a private club above the Electric Cinema in Notting Hill Gate, Paloma Faith orders scrambled eggs – and requests that olive oil is used instead of butter. Has this former magician's assistant from Hackney become a diva, complete with unnecessary dietary requirements and exclusive places to demand them in? "I have to say," she replies, when I put this to her, "I don't like it when people make a fuss about food because they're usually just doing it to be special, but I do feel much better since I stopped eating dairy."

'Talk about having it both ways. Jessica, this just isn't me.'
'That's right, Billy. It isn't. So here's what we're going to agree. You don't do interviews. If a journalist asks your opinion on something, you don't give it.'
'On anything?'
'On almost anything. If they ask how you like your steaks grilled, tell them. As long as you like them rare. Your favourite breakfast is a full English, with*out* baked beans, and your idea of Heaven is a warm beef sandwich with mustard and horseradish on rye or sourdough. That's enough personal information. If it's people, places, politics…you don't answer. We'll be issuing titbits from time to time to tell people what you think. Position you, if you like.'
'But you don't know what I think.'

'Yes, we do, Billy. And you will, too, once you read what we've said.'

The Governor's words came back to me. "Lead your own life, McErlane. Don't let that woman lead it for you." Jessica said, 'I know what you're thinking, Billy, but before you protest, have a look at this.' And she placed another printout in front of me.

Feeling a bit chilling? Catherine Tate cuddles up to her beau Adrian Chiles as they enjoy a romantic stroll

They went public with their romance in September after they were photographed cuddling up to each other during a holiday in America. And continuing to indulge in displays of public affection, Catherine Tate and Adrian Chiles were seen enjoying a romantic stroll last Friday evening. As they walked the streets of Santa Monica, the 45-year-old planted a kiss on Tate's forehead while she, 44, wrapped her arm around his waist.

Adrian and Catherine chatted away as they enjoyed their evening stroll whilst hand in hand.

Tate appeared to be wearing Adrian's blazer as it looked a few sizes too big for her frame. The make-up free flame-haired comedienne stepped out in a pair of slim tight jeans, a striped scarf, Ugg boots and a dark top. The presenter was seen trying to keep his lady warm as they rested their feet and sat on a set of concrete steps.

Chiles allowed Catherine to rest her head on his shoulder as he stroked her leg.

Dressed rather smart for the evening date, Adrian wore a striped pale blue shirt with a pair of jeans and black leather brogues. He also wore a pair of reading glasses as he held a white carrier bag in his hand. During the evening, the former One Show host treated Catherine to some frozen yoghurt. Chiles and Tate have both been spotted together on several occasions, and she also appeared on his popular topical news series That Sunday Night Show.

Adrian, who now presents ITV's football coverage, has been single since he split from his wife Jane Garvey in 2008. The couple married in 1998 and divorced in 2009 – and have two daughters together, 11-year-old Evelyn Katarina and Sian Mary, eight. Catherine split from her partner Twig Clark, a stage manager last year, and they have an eight-year-old daughter together, Erin.

The actress, who is a regular on the U. S. version of The Office, reportedly enjoyed a brief romance with Take That's Jason Orange in late 2011.

* * *

I said, 'Where's the story? There's no story.'

'The pics, Billy. What do you see? Apart from two ugly people?'

'Well. They're posed.'

'That's right. You're supposed to think you're looking at two people so wrapped up in each other they've been snapped without their knowledge, but actually they posed for the pics. Maybe they're just polite. More likely they did a deal: we'll give you your pics if you go away afterwards. And I'll be doing deals for you. Better deals, I hope, because the journalist who wrote this didn't play the game.'

161

I read it again. 'What do you mean?'

'The reference to slim tight jeans. There won't be a single person who reads that without remembering that Tate's arse wouldn't look out of place on a shire horse.'

'Why do women have to be so catty about other women? I think she has a nice bum.'

'Then you have plenty to admire. There's also the reference to his popular topical news programme, which was so popular it was axed. Just remember: no interviews. Right.' She turned to the photographer, 'First shot, please. Leave me out of it. Just Billy drinking his coffee and reading his text book.' And she placed a book in front of me. I'd never seen it before and I can't remember what it was. 'Open it, Billy. Look as though you're reading it.' She put an A4 notepad beside me and a pen in my hand.

There were a few other people in the coffee shop and I didn't find it as easy as Jessica to ignore them, but I did as I was told. When the photographer was happy with what he had, Jessica said. 'What are you working on in English, Billy?'

* * *

We shot a few more pics, but not until we'd driven thirty miles to another town because we didn't want any sharp-eyed busybody from my past working out where I lived. The first result appeared three days later in one of the redtops.

Work to be Done

Hot snapper BL McErlane was spotted today enjoying a coffee while he prepared an essay on the Romantic poets. A McErlane print is a must-have on fashionable walls and you'd be forgiven for supposing there'd be little time in his life for anything else, but Billy is set on completing his education. He clearly wanted to be getting on with his work instead of talking to me but, with a politeness refreshing in one so young and so well known, he put down his pen and closed his book and told me what he got from his studies. "The artists of the past have a lot to teach us. Coleridge defined good poetry as the spontaneous overflow of powerful feelings, but spontaneity can be overdone. Wordsworth was more in control of his work and that's what made him the better poet."

Students are known for their drinking, and so are artists, but McErlane had a tough childhood and he knows the slope alcohol can lead down. He prefers coffee; specifically, Costa's Flat White with an extra shot. "It keeps me alert," he smiled.

I was amazed when I read that, because I hadn't said a single word that was attributed to me. I looked forward to more surprising facts about myself.

Weekends and some evenings I started going for long walks with the compact in my pocket. Guy came with me once or twice, but there were places I ended up that he didn't want to be in, so he stopped.

'You'll get mugged,' he said. 'Knifed, probably.'

'It's like home,' I said.

'Your home wasn't anything like that. You don't fool me. That's a sink estate, Billy. You don't know what those people are like.'

I looked at him. Did he really think that wasn't what I came from? I said, 'And you do?'

'Junkies, Billy. Dolies. Tarts, probably. Rent boys. Pond life.'

'You take drugs.'

He looked astounded. 'I smoke a little recreational pot. I'm not a druggie, for fuck's sake. And don't say that out loud in the hostel. You'll get me kicked out.'

'You think the Howards don't know? You reek of it sometimes.'

'Oh, bloody hell. You don't really think they know?'

'Ask them. Anyway, I need pics for my project and I'm going to get them.'

'Is anyone else on your course going there?'

Not so I'd noticed, they weren't. Wendy had suggested she might come with me ("to help" – I'm not sure how) but she wasn't doing Art & Design and, anyway, I'd turned her down. When she made this offer she'd been wearing a skirt so short it barely covered her bottom, fishnet tights and a blouse open almost to the navel. Her mouth was a garish slash of red and she'd painted around her eyes with prominent black. The hair she normally tucked neatly behind her ears was draped over her cheeks. I said, 'You couldn't go there looking like that, anyway. You'd stand out a mile. A chav on a night out.'

She pouted. 'I bought this stuff specially, Billy. It's my sink estate look. What shall I do with it?'

'Isn't there a Fancy Dress Ball later this term?'

'Oh, yes. So there is. You're very clever, Billy.' She looked at me as if she was turning something over in her mind. Then, in a very quiet voice, she said, 'Do you have anyone to go to the Ball with?'

My heart didn't stop because hearts don't stop, whatever they may tell you in books, but it did a little flutter. Wendy was lovely. She wasn't skinny but you'd never call her fat. And she had the most beautiful heart-shaped face, and blue eyes, and when she let it down her blonde hair framed it nicely. I began to realise, what with Poppy and then Wendy, that maybe I was a blonde man. Melanie wasn't blonde, but I wasn't with her out of mutual attraction.

'No,' I said. 'I don't.'

'Would you like to go with me?'

I put out a hand and she took it. She stood on tiptoe, lips puckered. I hadn't kissed anyone like that since Poppy, and I liked it. I said, 'That would be lovely.'

She said, 'My grandmother always said that a girl should never ask a boy out under any circumstances. She should always wait to be asked. But I got the feeling I'd have waited a long time in your case and I've already waited long enough.'

'I'm sorry. I…'

'You do like me?'

'Of course I like you. I just thought you'd have someone else. Someone better.'

'How better?'

'Well. Someone who went to a good school and knows which knife to use.'

'I'm not going to shape my life around cutlery, Billy. When I go to bed at night, the face I dream of is yours.' She kissed me again.

So that's how Wendy and I became an item.

The others on my course were doing the sort of project their lives gave them access to. Life on a Farm. The Work of a Riding Stable. When they started to see the results, everyone agreed that mine was somehow more "authentic". It wasn't to me. They were showing what they knew. So was I.

Melanie, of course, was delighted.

What I wanted was the faces of the hopeless. The young, with no education and no attention span and nothing to interest them except the thrill of violence. The doped, drinking, smoking or injecting themselves towards an early release from a life they'd not even begun to get anything out of. The single mothers who'd thought like my sister that a baby would be someone to love who'd love them back and found out too late that motherhood wasn't like that. And the old (which meant anyone forty or over) who were so scared of the drug dealers and the muggers they barricaded themselves into their homes and only went out in daylight.

I had to photograph all these people. With the 200mm, I could have shot them from a distance – but I couldn't take a camera like that onto an estate where I wasn't known (and known as one of Regus's crew) and expect to have it with me when I left. That meant using the compact. And that, in its turn, meant getting closer to what I was shooting.

I was careful because I'd thought the young guys who were hooked on violence and not drugs wouldn't care to be photographed. I was wrong.

'You're that guy. In the paper. That guy who takes pictures. The killer.'

His name was Kevin and he was the leader of the gang. 'Why are you taking pictures of us?'

I said, 'I come from a place like this. I want to show what life is really like for people who live here.'

'Why don't you go home? Where they know you?'

'I'm on licence. I'm not allowed to leave here.'

I could hear the buzz. They were going to have their pictures taken. People were going to see them. They'd be famous. Go to parties with Harry and Wills.

Three of them got in a line, arms wrapped around each other's shoulders, and said, 'Take us.' I took out the camera and shot them, grinning and doing their hard looks at the same time which was really something to see.

And that's how it started.

CHAPTER 32

I began this story with Kathleen and the dream of seeing her in her knickers, which in fact I never did. I saw Wendy in hers, though.

They had a big house, the Murrays, not much smaller than my foster home, and what Wendy called her room was more like a sort of extra little house stuck on the side. Wendy said it had been built as a granny flat, which was an expression I hadn't heard before.

'Mummy wanted my gran near so she could keep an eye on her but gran wanted to be independent, so they built this place. She had her own kitchen and sitting room and bedroom and bathroom, so she could entertain friends or be on her own, but she used to come to us for Sunday lunch or just when she was lonely. But then she died anyway. Like old people do.' She sniffed back a tear. 'The place was empty for a while. Then, when I got to college, Mummy asked if I'd like to have it. So we moved my bed and stuff in and I did.'

Mister Murray did something important in advertising and Mummy did what Wendy called "charity work". They were a bit like richer versions of Katherine, Claire and Virginia's parents. You'd never have known that from looking at Wendy because she wore the uniform college girl's gear. Jeans that had rips in them but were always spotlessly clean and ironed, or knee-length skirts in muted colours – grey, brown, that sort of thing. Blouses that didn't reveal much, although they couldn't hide the fact that she was a girl and fully developed. She had a silver crucifix around her neck and she'd play with it while she talked to you. She explained once that her parents believed their

169

children should earn their own way in life and not wear the kind of clothes that showed off their parents' wealth.

Mister Murray had a flat in the Barbican where he sometimes stayed on weeknights, if he had a dinner to go to or things were really busy in the advertising business. Sometimes Missus Murray stayed there and they went to the theatre, or dinner, or both, or she helped him entertain clients. Wendy had an older brother called Richard who was at Oxford. I asked if they'd ever had a dog, but Wendy said no. She said, 'That's a strange question, Billy.'

I went to the Murrays' quite often in the evenings. Sometimes we stayed in the granny flat and Wendy made dinner, which was usually sausages or something on toast, and sometimes we went into the main part of the house for a much posher meal. That's where I learned about Pecorino, and how to tell the difference between the Tuscan and Roman kinds (though I never could. Still can't). And I learned about *boeuf en daube*, and *boeuf a la Bourgignonne*, which Missus Murray said meant beef as cooked by the women of Burgundy, and lots of other things. And wine. I started to learn about wine. The wine I had with Melanie was things like Lambrusco and cheap Chiantis and Riojas, which wasn't what Mister Murray served. He said the absolute rock bottom starting point for a bottle of wine in Britain was eight pounds and if it didn't cost at least that it wouldn't be worth drinking. One evening I was there and Missus Murray said he had to be sure to be home on time the next night because they were going to dinner at the Tallers and Mister Murray said, 'Oh, no. You know what rubbish we'll get there.' Missus Murray said, 'Bernice is a wonderful cook,' and Mister Murray said, 'I'm not talking about the food. Last time we went, he gave us Tesco own label.' Then Missus

Murray said, 'Well, I'm sorry. It's a duty visit and you'll just have to think of it as a three line whip.' Mister Murray said, 'I'd better open another bottle of this, then. Stoke up on the good stuff tonight.' And they all laughed.

Then Wendy took a cigarette out of her pack and her father said, as we had known he would, 'If you're planning to smoke that, you can go outside or back to your flat.'

Mister Murray thought of himself as a creative person, being in advertising, and he was very interested in my photography. Wendy told me he'd called me a "rough diamond". I asked if that was good or bad and she said, 'He likes you. Mummy likes you, too.'

'How do they feel about you going with a convicted murderer?'

She wouldn't look at me. 'Nothing.'

'I find that hard to believe.'

'Convicted, yes. Murderer, no. That's what Daddy says.' She took a cigarette from its pack and played with it, still not looking at me. 'And he's right.' She was waiting for me to speak but I didn't know what to say. 'Isn't he? Isn't he, Billy? You didn't kill anybody. You couldn't.'

'I'm sorry, Wendy. I can't talk about that.'

'You didn't, though. I know you didn't.' She'd fiddled with the unlit cigarette so long she'd broken off the tip, and she threw it away. Her look of disgust could have been about the wasted smoke, or it could have been about me. 'Honestly, Billy, I wish you'd be more open with me.'

I knew she wished that. I wished it, too. But I couldn't be.

* * *

Something had been going on since that first time Wendy and I held hands and kissed. I knew it was there; I knew it bothered her; what I didn't know was what to do about it. She was a girl and I was a boy; we were in love; so the thing was about sex. Obviously. Sex to me was something women let men do to them in return for money to feed themselves and their children, or out of fear of a bashing, or so that they'd get pregnant and be entitled to benefit. "Normal" people only had sex when they wanted to have children and I didn't think I would ever want a child. I'm not sure how I defined "normal", but Wendy's family were normal and mine were not. Normal women did not have sex for pleasure. Poppy had understood that, which was why she and I had never gone upstairs together. I wasn't sure that Wendy did, and I didn't want her to be disappointed. And certainly not by me.

And there was something else. Something I didn't – couldn't – discuss with Wendy. She almost tumbled to it, though. 'Is there someone else?' she said one evening. 'No,' I said. 'There isn't.' As I spoke the words I had the strongest possible sense of Poppy – Poppy looking sad; Poppy turning from me; Poppy walking away. Because there was someone else. There always would be.

The granny flat had its own outside entrance and you couldn't get to it through the house, which meant that anyone coming to see us would have to come round the path and we'd hear them on the gravel. A point Wendy made more than once. One evening she said, 'It's such an advantage not being in a bedroom upstairs from where my parents are sitting.' When I didn't answer, she went on, 'Actually, it isn't an advantage if we don't both want to make use of it.' Another pause and then, 'Mummy asks me really nosey things, but she does it in that delicate way she has.'

I still didn't say anything.

She said, 'I told her you were a perfect gentleman.' Then she said, 'Sometimes, Billy, your silences can be a little bit irritating.'

'I'm sorry. What do you want me to say?'

'Well, you could start by saying whether you find me attractive.'

'I think you're lovely, Wendy.'

'But not lovely like that,' she said.

'What do you want from me, Wendy?'

She looked at me for a long time. Then she stood up and began to undress.

When she was done she took me by the hand, led me into the bedroom and lay down on the bed. She said, 'You can touch as well as look, Billy. It's all right.'

There's a song that goes, "If you can't be with the one you love, love the one you're with" . When I lay down beside Wendy and started showing her what I'd learned with Melanie (not that I told her that, of course), I actually said those words to myself – that's how dishonest I was capable of being.

'I'm on the pill, darling,' she whispered. 'I've been on it for weeks now. While I...you know. Waited for you. But I think I'd better put a towel under me. Don't you? Why don't you get undressed while I fetch one?'

Which is what we did. It wasn't what I'd wanted to do because I was scared, terrified in fact. I knew I'd have to take the lead with Wendy and I'd never done that with a woman, didn't in fact know whether I could, which is why I'd been denying my hormones and ignoring her signals. And I knew for certain that she didn't really know what she was doing.

But I needn't have worried. And what I found out was: that everything I knew about women and sex was nonsense. Normal women love having sex, as long as they're having it with men they want to have it with.

I had a feeling that evening I'd never had before. I didn't recognise it for what it was, but it was a nice one to have. I enjoyed the feeling even more than I enjoyed the actual love-making, and I enjoyed that a lot. And so did Wendy. And what I found was that the song wasn't just a song. Was Poppy in my mind all through my love-making with Wendy? No, she wasn't.

There was a washer and dryer in the granny flat, but Wendy always took her laundry to the house for her mother's daily help to do. I think she washed that towel herself, though.

I'm not going to put in the F word every time it was used while I was taking pictures for my project. The gang I was with used it a lot, two or three times in a sentence sometimes, and it will get boring if I reproduce that here, and I don't want to be boring just in the interests of authenticity. So I'll only write it when it seems absolutely necessary, and readers can interpolate it into the conversation as often as they like. They won't imagine them using it more often than they did.

I was used to that because I was used to them, or people like them. But not everyone was.

When I started putting up the pictures I was getting now, there was unrest among the students. Some of them thought I was some kind of left wing agitator, showing people who didn't really exist.

Tom, who I liked and who Wendy and I both saw as a friend, said, 'Where did you take these? I've lived in this town all my life and I've never seen these people.' There was a murmur of agreement at that.

I said, 'You see them every day. They're all around you. They're the invisible people. You see them, but you don't see them. Because you don't want to.'

Tom jabbed his finger at a pic of Kevin. 'He looks about my age. I never saw him in my life before. Where did he go to school?'

'He didn't. Or not very much. But when he did, it wasn't where you went.'

Carol said, 'You do see them, Tom. Go into town, hang around the big mall. They're in there. Begging or just larking around.'

Sarah said, 'My little brother had his mobile stolen in the mall. He was scared to bits. My mother won't let him go there any more.'

Tom said, 'You should get him to come down here, look at these pictures. He'd probably be able to identify the thieves.'

Just what I needed. To be turned into a grass. I said, 'Not till I've finished my project, thanks.'

The ones that caused the most grief, making the boys angry and the girls tearful, were the pics of old people stepping onto the road to scurry past the youths blocking the pavement. I'd done a good job there. You could feel the fear in the old people's eyes.

That's how my fellow students seemed to me – as boys and girls. I'd never apply those words to the feral youths on the street even though they were the same age. Younger, some of them.

'Why don't they move?' someone wanted to know.

I said, 'They can't. They live in council housing. That means they live where the council tells them to live. They have no choice.'

'But surely, the council must see that decent people shouldn't be living with riffraff? They must try to put them where they'll be safe?'

'Ah, well, no,' I said. 'The council doesn't distinguish between good people and bad people. That would be judgemental, and being judgemental is against all the rules liberals live by. You're doing Sociology. You should know that.'

That brought silence. The students thought of themselves as liberal, and so did the parents of many of them, and not being judgemental was against their rules, too.

'You're not judgemental, Billy,' said Tom. 'You couldn't be or you wouldn't be taking these pictures.'

'Me?' I said. 'I'm very judgemental. I hate these people.'

'It doesn't show in the photographs.'

'It isn't supposed to.'

Later, when Wendy and I were alone, she wanted to talk about the pic of a young woman about her age with a baby in a stroller and a shining black eye. 'Who hit her, Billy?'

'Her boyfriend, probably.'

'But why?'

'Because he's a total loser with no education and no ambition. He's achieved nothing in his life and he isn't going to, but with her he can be the boss. And the only way he has of showing he's the boss is by hitting her.'

'How do you know all this, Billy?'

'Because I'm one of them. That's where I come from. An estate just like that one.'

'You have education and ambition.'

'I was lucky. More lucky than you can ever imagine.'

'And you wouldn't hit a woman. I know you wouldn't.'

'How do you know?'

'Because I know you. You're a gentle person. I could never have imagined any man making love with as much tenderness as you do.'

'I'm more tender than your other men, am I?'

She jabbed me smartly in the ribs. 'I never had a man before you. Not in that way. As you very well know, Billy McErlane.'

And that, of course, was it. That feeling I'd had that first time and every time since. I hadn't recognised it but Wendy had, no doubt because she'd encountered it before. It was tenderness.

I liked tenderness.

It was round about then that Jessica slipped out the second of my celeb stories.

Art for All

BL McErlane is fast developing as one of the big sellers among photographers. While he welcomes this (as who would not?) he sees the danger to an artist of his work becoming the preserve of the well-to-do.

'Shakespeare wrote for ordinary people,' he says. 'The rich loved his plays and there were seats on stage for the elite. They'd even join in, talking to the actors while the drama unfolded, which must have made for some interesting ad libs, but the ordinary people of the town thronged the Globe, eating oranges and drinking and chatting to each other. It was art for the common man and woman.

Today, art has too often become the preserve of the super-rich. It's comforting for the artist to have a public that can afford to pay any price for what it wants but it's also a trap. I want my work to be available to everyone.'

McErlane's agent, Jessica Robinson, has assembled a line of prints featuring some of the best of his recent portraits and is making them available through retail outlets at prices that mean no home need be without its McErlane. The example shown here, The Future, is one of these and is available, framed and ready to hang, at only £60.

The picture she'd chosen was one I was particularly pleased with. It showed a man on a hillside, back to the camera, looking into the distance. Nothing of his face was visible, and the idea you got was of someone staring towards what might be. He was wearing a hip-length red coat, black jeans, white trainers and a brown hat with an absolutely flat brim. Two dogs were close to his feet.

I had known nothing of this bargain-priced range Jessica was launching, and I certainly hadn't said any of the things she attributed to me (people sat on the stage during Shakespeare's plays and spoke to the actors? Could that possibly be true?) but I was pleased with the overall message. I was even more pleased when I learned that eight thousand prints sold in the first week, many of them outside Britain. Fifty per cent of the price went to the retailers, which meant that my take before Jessica's commission came out of it was almost a quarter of a million pounds. The tax man helped himself to about one hundred thousand of that, and a few weeks later Jessica released a follow-up.

BL McErlane plays fair on taxes

Photographer BL McErlane doesn't do interviews. The celebrity-who-isn't won't talk about his private life. Nevertheless, this paper has learned that McErlane refuses to do what almost every actor, singer and big-name journalist or writer does, which is to evade tax by channelling earnings through schemes that mean they don't suffer the high tax rates that people on ordinary incomes pay. McErlane pays tax as a UK-based person, just like most of us.

We have also learned that his pet charity is CentrePoint, which provides a safe home to young people from abused or deprived backgrounds. He pays them a monthly sum that covers the cost of rooms for two residents and funds bursaries so that they can go to college and enjoy a better life than their childhood expectations would have indicated.

When we rang the artist to get his views on tax and charities, he hung up on us.

I hadn't known about CentrePoint; Jessica had made the payments for me; but it was a good idea. The people I was helping were people like me. I asked Jessica whether she paid her own taxes direct or through a company and she told me to mind my own business.

CHAPTER 33

I did a lot of moving stuff around for Regus. The work was regular. You'd have to say that for it.

After a while, some of what I moved was money.

Then he started leaving stuff at Chantal's place and I'd get instructions on what to collect as well as where to take it. Having to know what to collect meant having to know what it was.

And then I became a bank. I'd collect money and instead of handing it over straight away sometimes I had to hold on to it for a few days until he told me to deliver it. They were small amounts at first, but they got bigger. Like he'd been testing me and decided to trust me.

Bit by bit, he was making me into a dealer. If I got caught, he knew I wasn't going to grass him up. I knew too well what would happen to me. I had over two thousand pounds hidden in a safe place in my room when it all turned to rat shit.

It was Thursday, right after school, and I was at Poppy's place when the text came. I was to take all the money I had and deliver it to the Community Centre.

The moment I went into my bedroom, I knew I was in trouble.

It wasn't that the place had been trashed. Just that I could tell someone had been in there. I went straight to my safe place.

It was empty. There wasn't a penny left.

I went back downstairs but there hadn't been anyone else in the house before and there wasn't anyone else in the house now. I got on my bike and cycled to the pub. I pushed open the door and peeped round it. My mother wasn't there and nor was

Chantal, because they weren't allowed to be, but the Creep was. He was surrounded by a mob of people, all crowding round him and slapping him on the back and saying what a great bloke he was, which must have been a new experience. Nobody thought the Creep was a great bloke. Not even the Creep.

I thought about what to do. There weren't many choices. Staying home wasn't an option. When I didn't turn up with his money, Regus would send someone to find me. I could run away or I could go to the Community Centre.

And if I ran away I couldn't take the bike because the tracker would tell them where it was and I'd have nothing to buy food with and I'd have to steal, which I'd never done, and sleep in bus shelters and the police would find me and Regus would never believe it wasn't me who stole his money.

I was going to grass the Creep up. If it had been Chantal who took the money I might have covered for her even if it meant being tortured before I was killed. Which is what it would mean. Even if it had been my mother, though in her case I'd have had to think about it. But the Creep? Not a chance. Sorry.

If I gave him up I'd still get killed, I didn't see any doubt about that because Regus would have to make an example of me, making an example was how he kept order, but I'd probably go quickly with no more pain than dying has to cause anyway.

So, when I thought about it, there weren't really any options at all. I had one course of action, which was to go to the Community Centre and grass the Creep up.

Regus was smiling when he came out of the Community Centre but the smile didn't last long when he saw my face. He said, 'Have you got my money?'

I shook my head.

He stared at me for a long time. I didn't say anything. Then he tapped a message into his mobile and a couple of minutes later a BMW came round the corner. Marcus got out of the passenger door. I didn't know the driver.

Regus said, 'Put the bike in the boot,' and Marcus did that. Then Regus said, 'Ride in the back with the kid.' He went round to the driver's side and spoke to him through the window. Then he walked away.

I wanted to cry but I didn't. I wouldn't. I was thirteen and I was being taken somewhere they could kill me and it seemed so unfair and I didn't want to die and it wasn't my fault and if I'd let myself I'd have cried and cried.

Marcus must have realised that because he said, 'Don't bubble, man.' Then he said, 'You want to tell us what happened?'

So I did. All of it. Marcus just sat and listened, and once he said, 'That piece of shit?' and later he said, 'That piece of shit' again but this time as a statement and not a question.

When we got to Whitley Bay we turned north and went through Cullercoats and kept on going till we got to Seaton Sluice. It's a great place for a holiday, a great big beach with sand dunes you could play games and get lost in. I could see why they'd bring someone here to kill them and, sure enough, the car slowed down and we turned off and parked. We went right down to the far end where there weren't any other cars. I sat there for half an hour during which Marcus and the driver got out and smoked cigarettes, two men with not a care in the world. Then another BMW parked alongside us. It was Regus and he didn't have anyone with him. He got out and spoke to

Marcus and our driver. Marcus was telling him something and they looked at me from time to time and twice Marcus looked at the driver as though he was asking him something and the driver nodded but didn't speak.

Then Regus said something and Marcus came over to the car I was in and opened the door. 'Come on, Billy,' he said. 'Out you get.'

Regus was looking at me with no expression on his face at all. He said, 'Do you like your stepfather?'

I said, 'He's not my stepfather.'

'But do you like him?'

'I hate him.'

'So you could have stolen my money and made up this story to blame it on him.'

'Yes,' I said. 'I could. But I didn't.'

He looked at me for a long time. Then he said, 'I believe you.' To Marcus he said, 'You know where the place is.'

Marcus said, yes, he did.

'We'll see you there then. Didn't they use to do good fish and chips up the road?'

'Still do, far as I know.'

'I could do with something to eat.'

Marcus nodded towards me. 'What about him?'

'He can come with me. You'd like some fish and chips, wouldn't you, Billy?'

I nodded.

'In the car, then. You two better get off. How much petrol have you got?'

'Quarter of a tank.'

'Fill up somewhere else. We don't want anything putting us down here.'

While we were driving to the chip shop, Regus asked me about school. How it was going, what sort of marks I was getting. Then he asked me about Poppy.

'Please leave her alone,' I said. 'She knows nothing about this.'

'Leave her alone?' He seemed genuinely aggrieved. 'I'm not going to touch her. She's like you, though, isn't she? Wants to get an education and move on?'

I nodded.

'It's the only way, Billy. One thing I've learned since I started making money, other people have a better life than you can round our way. Which is why I don't live there any more. Education, Billy. That's the idea. Get an education and there's no knowing where you'll finish but even if you end up stacking shelves you'll still be a bloody sight happier than the people you leave behind. What the bloody hell are you bubbling for, man?'

Because I was. I'd given in. I'd fought it and I'd lost. I had to squeeze out the words between sobs. 'What's...the point...of telling us...to get an education...when...when you're going to kill us?'

'When I...look at me, Billy. Billy, look at me.'

When I did, he handed me a tissue. 'Wipe your eyes.' He gave me another tissue. 'And your nose. God, man, you're like a snotty little kid. Now listen, Billy. Nobody's going to kill you.'

I looked at him. I would never have believed it, but there was kindness on his face. I hadn't seen kindness very often, and I never thought I'd see it from Regus, but that's what I was looking at now. 'I lost your money,' I stammered.

'Didn't steal it, though. Did you?'

I shook my head.

'There *is* something you're going to have to do for us, Billy, and it *will* hold up your education for a while. But dying isn't it. This is the place.'

He pulled in to the side of the road and handed me the box of tissues. 'Clean yourself up while I get the suppers.'

When he came out he put two polystyrene boxes on my knees. 'Hold them.' I could feel the warmth through my trousers. 'The gadgie says there's a Costa machine in a petrol station down here. I'll get us two coffees.'

There were two cup holders moulded into the car and when he came out of the petrol station he put a paper cup into each one. 'We'll go back down the front, shall we?'

It wasn't really a question and he didn't wait for an answer, but this time we parked near the other cars. Although, as it was getting dark, people were starting to leave for home. He took one of the suppers from me. 'I put sugar in your coffee,' he said. 'Was that right?'

'Yes, thank you.'

'Thank you. God, that's something I don't hear much.' He looked around. 'Know why we use this place?'

'Because it's lonely?'

'No, man. Because there's no CCTV. Not yet. There will be. It's getting harder and harder to stay away from the coppers.' He started to eat his fish and chips, so I did, too. Eat mine, I mean. 'They'll be able to trace us down the Coast Road and through Whitley Bay and Cullercoats but then they'll lose us. They'll still know we must have come here, though. So what we'll do, we'll do what we have to here and then we'll take the evidence and dump it somewhere else.'

'What's that? What you have to do?'

'Deal with your stepfather, man. Your stepfather who isn't your stepfather.' He swallowed a chip whole. 'I asked for plenty of salt and vinegar. I hope you like it like that.'

I nodded. 'Are you going to…' I couldn't use the word.

'Aye. We'll kill him. We'll get back whatever money he's still got and then we'll do him.' He bit off a chunk of fish. 'And I'm afraid you're going to have to take the blame, Billy. You'll go down for it.'

'Yes.'

'You're a juvenile. They'll still give you life because they don't have a choice, but you'll be out a lot sooner than I would. They'd call it a gangland killing and I'd get a twenty minimum. More, mebbes. But you…four years max, I'd say. I'll pay for a good brief for you. Have you got plenty you could tell him? Good reasons to kill the man?'

I nodded.

'I thought you would have. And there'll be a payoff when you get out.'

'You could give that to Chantal. She needs it more than me.'

'No, Billy, I couldn't. Chantal doesn't know how to keep her mouth shut. Which is fine when I want to stick my knob in it, but not so good when the police come calling.'

'Okay.'

'The police won't believe you did it, Billy. But you just keep saying you did.'

'Okay.'

'They'll know we moved the body, but you just keep denying it. You say you did him there where they found him and you don't know what they're talking about.'

'Okay.'

'When he's been dumped, you walk down to the police station and give yourself up.'

'Okay.'

'Better give me your mobile. We don't want the Law reading your messages.'

I handed it to him. It probably seems I was a bit passive about the news that I was going to jail for a murder I didn't commit, but a few minutes earlier I'd thought I was going to die. Compared with that, what Regus was telling me to do was a walk in the park. I was looking at a life sentence when I'd expected a death sentence. Something else that went through my mind at the time was to wonder whether what I'd seen on Regus's face really was kindness, or whether he was sweetening me up because he was going to commit a murder and he needed me to take the rap for it. It didn't matter, because I didn't have any choice, but I did wonder.

Regus finished his supper and took out a packet that said Wet Wipes on it. 'I got these in the filling station,' he said. That's when I realised he didn't do this often. We were eating in the car because he didn't want any witnesses putting us together in a café. There was less chance of being seen this way. He took one out and wiped his hands. When I'd finished eating, he gave me one and I wiped my own hands. He took a carrier bag and put both empty boxes in it. 'I'll drop one of those a long way from here,' he said. 'And the other even further. We don't want the police finding both our prints in the same litter bin.'

We sat and drank our coffee. Then Regus said, 'I need a piss. How about you?'

I nodded. We got out of the car and walked into the dunes. It felt strangely friendly, standing a few yards apart and emptying our bladders.

It was more than an hour before Regus got a text message. 'They're there,' he said. 'We'll give the little shit fifteen minutes to sweat and then we'll go and fix him up.'

CHAPTER 34

It was a garage, a warehouse, I don't know what it was or what you'd call it and it stood a bit off from anything else. It had thick walls that looked as though they'd been there a long time and a very strong wooden door that was new. Something was being stored under tarpaulins but I couldn't see what it was.

I said, 'How will you do it?'

He said, 'I'm going to beat him to death, Billy. No point using a gun. You couldn't explain where you got it. Anyway, guns and knives mean longer sentences. But the police will check your fists. They're going to expect scuffs and grazes. So you'll have to give him a few shots yourself. You know how to punch?'

I nodded.

'I'd like to cut him a bit before I do him, but that gives you the same problem. If you really want to know, I'd like to cut his balls off and listen to him scream.'

I winced.

'But, like I say, I can't do that.'

We parked round the back. The other car was already there. You wouldn't have been able to see it unless you were round the back, too, and I couldn't see how anyone would have reason to be there. There was another door in the back wall, smaller than the one in front, and that's the one we went in through.

The Creep didn't hear us at first. He was too busy gesticulating and talking to Marcus and the driver, neither of whom was paying him any attention. You could see he was scared. Terrified, in fact.

They'd switched on two lights where they were and when we stepped into the circle of light, that's when he saw us. He pointed at me. 'That's him.'

Regus looked at Marcus and Marcus said, 'He claims Billy gave it to him.'

'He's lying,' I shouted.

Regus said, 'I know he is, Billy.' To Marcus he said, 'He have any left?'

'Nineteen hundred quid,' said Marcus, handing it to him.

'I thought he couldn't have had time to spend much.'

The Creep was still looking at me. 'You little bastard,' he shouted. 'I was going to buy things for you. I was going to take us on a family holiday.'

'Were you,' said Regus. 'With my money.' (There's room to interpolate an F word there. That's an example of what I talked about earlier.)

I said, 'We're not a family.'

Regus looked at the money. Then he put it in his pocket. 'A couple of hours buying rounds,' he said. 'Not much to get yourself killed for, is it? Anyone see you take him out?'

Marcus shook his head. 'We got him in the lav. Bundled him out the back way.'

I'm not going to give a blow for blow. I didn't enjoy it then and I don't want to talk about it now. It was horrible. I stood over against the wall while the Creep pleaded for his life and then they killed him. Regus wore a big gold ring with a stone in it, but he took that off first. I didn't want to watch but Regus said I had to, so I'd be able to describe to the police all the places I'd hit him.

When it was over, Regus told me to punch the wall a few times in a place where there wasn't any paint. 'Don't break anything. Just scuff your knuckles up a bit. Both hands, Billy.' Then he said to punch the Creep's face a few times. 'Hard. Let their microscopes find traces of his skin.'

That was the first time I'd looked at the Creep since he'd been dead. He didn't look like the Creep any more. He looked like a sad old man in his forties. All the life had gone out of his face. I suppose that's what being dead means.

Then Marcus went out to the car and came back with a big sheet of thick polythene and he and the driver rolled the Creep into it. Regus said, 'Don't break any speed limits, but get him back as fast as you can before the body stiffens. I'll see you both later.'

Marcus gestured at me with his head. 'You straighten him out?'

Regus looked at me. Honestly, the kind look was there again. I know it seems ridiculous after what he just did, but it was. 'Billy's all right,' he said. 'You'll stand up, won't you, Billy?'

I nodded. I said, 'Will you do something for me, please?'

'Aye, Billy. If I can.'

'Will you look after Poppy? Make sure people leave her alone?'

'I will that, Billy lad.'

Then he got into his car and drove away towards the north, and we got into ours and set off for Newcastle.

They took my bike out and stood it against the wall. Then they heaved the Creep out and dumped him in a heap.

Marcus said, 'You know what you have to do?'

I nodded.

'Good lad. Tell them what you've done but don't answer questions till your brief arrives. Act confused. Shouldn't be hard.' Then they were back in the car and gone.

I got on my bike and rode to the police station. Naturally there was no-one in it, but they had a phone you could use to get attention. I picked it up and, when someone answered, I said, 'I've killed somebody.'

I heard something going on at the other end, maybe he was telling someone to pick up an extension or scribbling a note, and then he was back on as nice as pie and asking me my name. I said, 'You don't have to keep us talking. I'll stay here till you send someone,' and then I put the phone down. There weren't any chairs so I sat down on the floor and when a police car arrived I was fast asleep.

They woke me up and I took them to where the Creep's body was. I said, 'Don't forget me bike, it'll get nicked,' and one of the coppers said, 'You won't need a bike where you're going, sonny.' (Interpolation is possible again there, and I don't think the police should talk like that to a thirteen-year-old boy who isn't giving them any lip.)

I fell asleep again in the car on the way down town and they had such a job waking me they called a doctor who said I was in shock and I couldn't be questioned till I woke up of my own accord, so they put me in a cell to sleep. I found out about that later. Obviously.

By the time I did wake up there was a brief there called Mister Henry and he turned out to be the dog's bollocks. He told them who I was and they went to get my mother but the custody sergeant, who was a nice fat man, told me later that she'd said (more interpolation required. Four of them), 'If he's killed his stepdad he'll get no help from me. I wash my hands of him.' (The interpolations would go before killed, before stepdad, before help and before hands. It's easy when you know how.)

While he was being pally, the custody sergeant asked how Mister Henry had known I was there and who I was. I said I didn't know. I'm not an idiot. CID put him up to that.

They put me in an interview room where Mister Henry talked to me first and said walls had ears and there were some things and some people I mustn't mention even to him while I was in there and did I understand what he meant? And I said yes. You don't grow up where I did and not know how to conduct yourself in a police station.

Then he said I should just tell my story and if there was anything he didn't want me to say or any questions he didn't want me to answer he'd come bolt upright and that would let me know to shut up. I said all right. He also said not to gild the lily, which I didn't understand, so he said, 'Simple answers and short answers, Billy. Always the best. Don't add little embellishments. Don't say anything you don't have to. Don't fancy the story up.'

Then he went out and when he came back he had a Detective Inspector with him, whose name I don't remember, and Sergeant Walsh.

The Inspector said I should tell them everything just as it happened and so I did. Well, I didn't, obviously, but I told them what I was saying had happened. Mister Henry looked very pleased and both policemen listened in silence all the way through to the end. When I'd finished, the inspector said, 'I've never heard such a load of bollocks in my life.'

I didn't say anything to that. The two coppers stared at me for a while and then the inspector said, 'I can't be doing with this shite. You talk to him, Sergeant.'

Sergeant Walsh said, 'You work for Regus Hunt, don't you, Billy?'

I said, 'No, Mister Walsh. I'm still at school.'

He said yes I did, I'd been seen talking to Hunt and his known associates. I said, 'Regus is my sister's boyfriend, Mister Walsh. That's why I talk to him.'

Then the inspector said, 'Fuck this noise. He needs a bit more time in the cells to come to his senses.'

Sergeant Walsh said, 'Billy, if we accept your story you'll get a life sentence. You'll spend at least twenty years in jail. You'll be nearly forty when you get out. If you ever do get out.'

I didn't say anything. The inspector said, 'Right. I've had it with this. Let's go, Sergeant.'

Mister Henry said, 'If you're not charging my client, inspector, I'd like him released.'

The inspector looked at him as though he was an insect and said, 'Don't be ridiculous.' And they went out.

Mister Henry said, 'Well done, Billy. You know not to say anything while I'm not here?'

I just nodded, because the custody sergeant had come in to take me back to the cells.

Mister Henry patted me on the shoulder as I went out.

CHAPTER 35

They fed me and left me alone. I'd have liked something to read, but I got a good night's sleep.

Next day, Mister Henry was back and they were having another go. Well, Sergeant Walsh was. The inspector just sat there brooding. Like a vulture.

'Billy. If we let you take the rap for this, you'll go to jail. It'll be a high security Young Offenders prison, not some cushy juvenile place you may have heard of.'

I didn't say anything.

'You won't like some of the people you meet there, Billy.'

Still I didn't say anything. I hadn't liked some of the people I'd met while I was in care and I didn't like some of the people I met here, so not liking some of the people I'd meet inside didn't bother me. Anyway, I didn't have a choice. I had to take what was coming to me or Regus would do me like he'd done the Creep, kind looks or not.

'Isn't this a strange way of proceeding, Sergeant?' asked Mister Henry. 'The prisoner is telling you he's guilty and you're trying to persuade him he's innocent. Isn't that the opposite of the normal police strategy?'

That made the vulture unhook his beak from under his wing. 'You're a top drawer brief. Whose paying your fee?'

Mister Henry looked surprised, though I don't think he was. The more I watched him, the more I saw how lawyers are like actors. Policemen, too. Are like actors, I mean. I'm not saying policemen are like lawyers. Although they are all playing the same game, and it is a game, but only they know the rules. 'Legal aid, of course. Who else?'

'We could have got him the duty lawyer on legal aid.'

'And you know how useless they are,' Mister Henry said.

'He's going guilty. You said so yourself.'

'But it's afterwards the negotiations start. Manslaughter, thirteen years old…he could even get probation.'

'You mentioned manslaughter. We didn't.'

'Oh, come on. No premeditation, two years of provocation, deprived background, momentary but overpowering rage…it's obvious.'

'Not to me it isn't.'

'But it won't be you that decides, inspector.'

'For now it will. Charge him, Sergeant.'

Sergeant Walsh said, 'But we know he didn't do it.'

'He says he did. That'll do for me. Take his confession and charge him.'

'With manslaughter,' Mister Henry said.

'With murder,' said the inspector.

'We'll ask for bail.'

'We'll oppose it.'

The sergeant did charge me and it was with murder and I didn't get bail, so now I was on remand. In an adult jail. That was a bit scary. Adult jails are full of people like the Creep or even worse and I was afraid they wouldn't take to me, given what I'd done to one of theirs. And the food was rubbish. And nobody told you what you were supposed to do. You were just expected to know. Which most of them did, to be fair. I'd thought it would go to trial after that, but the next week I was in a prison interview room and the three of them were with me again.

Sergeant Walsh said, 'Various things have come to light, Billy. There's still time for you to change your statement and have the charges against you dropped.'

Mister Henry said, 'Do you want to change your statement, Billy?'

'No.'

The inspector grunted and said he'd told Sergeant Walsh they'd be wasting their time, but Sergeant Walsh said, 'Let's just run through some of the things that have come to light and we'll see whether you want to change your mind. First off, where did you get that nice bike you've been riding round on?'

I'd been wondering whether this would come up. I said, 'Someone left it round the back of ours. I used to have a bike but it was nicked, so I thought I'd just ride this one until whoever left it came for it and then they could have it back.'

'When was that, Billy?'

'Ages ago, Mister Walsh.'

'I see. You didn't think to come in to the station and report it? As lost property?'

'I did that, as a matter of fact, Mister Walsh.'

His eyebrows went up into his hair. 'You did? We've no record of that, Billy.'

'No,' I said, 'Well. There wasn't anyone there, Mister Walsh.'

Mister Henry was looking very pleased with life. Sergeant Walsh looked sideways at the inspector and grinned. Then he said, 'Did you know there was a tracking device in the frame, Billy?'

I said, 'A tracking device? What's that?'

'It's a little thing that lets the owner know where the bike is, Billy. At all times.'

'Oh,' I said. 'So they could have come back for it if they'd wanted it?'

He didn't say anything to that. Not directly. 'We took a bit of the paint off the frame. Did you know it was a very expensive bike?'

'I didn't, Mister Walsh, no. It was lovely to ride, though.'

'You see, Billy, I'm wondering why someone would just leave an expensive bike like that in your back garden and not collect it, even when they knew where it was?'

Mister Henry said, 'I'm sure Billy would help you if he could, Sergeant. But as he's already said, he can't. Isn't that right, Billy?'

I nodded.

Walsh said, 'You couldn't move the body on that bike, Billy. Could you?'

I said I didn't understand (though of course I did) and he said the Creep hadn't been killed where they found him, he'd been killed somewhere else and brought to that place and could I explain how that happened? I said, oh, no, Mister Walsh, I killed him right there.

'No you didn't, Billy,' Walsh said. 'But let's leave that for now. Poppy says you used to get text messages and when you did you'd leave her and go off somewhere on the bike.'

'Text messages, Mister Walsh?'

'On your mobile.'

'I haven't got a mobile, Mister Walsh.'

'Poppy says you have.'

Mister Henry said, 'I didn't see any mention of a mobile phone in the inventory of Billy's possessions when you took him in.'

Walsh ignored Mister Henry as though he hadn't been there. 'Why would Poppy say you had a phone if you didn't?'

'I don't know, Mister Walsh.'

Mister Henry said, 'Young girls fantasize, Sergeant,' but Walsh went on ignoring him. He said, 'Who did you give the phone to, Billy?'

'There wasn't a phone, Mister Walsh.'

'All right, Billy. When did you last see Regus Hunt?'

'Regus? I can't remember, Mister Walsh. He's my sister's boyfriend, like I told you. But she doesn't live with us, so we wouldn't see him very often.'

'Just to talk to casually when you saw him in the street.'

'That's right.'

'But that would have been quite often, because Regus was round your way a lot. Even though he lives in Gosforth now.'

'Does he?'

'He'd be there every day, in fact. But then he wasn't there.'

'Wasn't he?'

'Strangely enough, he stopped going there the very night you claim to have killed your stepfather. He stayed away for three days.'

'Did he?'

'And so did two of his henchmen.'

Mister Henry said, 'What have the activities of this Hunt to do with Billy?' and the inspector said, 'Why do you call him "this Hunt"? He's one of your clients, isn't he?' Mister Henry said come to think of it he thought he did remember the name and the inspector said, 'I should just think you do. It was Hunt who told you to go to the station and represent McErlane. Wasn't it?' and Mister Henry said that was a very improper question.

Sergeant Walsh said, 'Three days is about the time it would take for your hands to heal after you'd battered someone to death, Billy.'

I said, 'Yes, that's about how long it took mine.'

'But you hadn't beaten anyone to death, Billy.'

'I wish I hadn't, Mister Walsh. Honestly. But I did.'

'Regus Hunt killed your stepfather. Didn't he? And you're taking the rap for him.'

I said, 'Oh, no, Mister Walsh. That would be a stupid thing to do.'

He leaned forward on his chair. 'Yes, Billy, it would. Because we're going to send someone down for that murder. We'd like it to be Hunt, seeing as he really did it, but if you insist we'll make it you. Twenty years in jail, Billy. You've never been in trouble before. You sure you can handle it?'

I didn't say anything and Sergeant Walsh said, 'Poppy says you're one of Hunt's crew, Billy. She says that's why she let you be her boyfriend.'

'I'm not.'

'So why would she say that?'

'I don't know.'

I wanted this to be over so I pretended to start to cry. Mister Henry said he thought that was enough and the inspector said it was all bollocks and they weren't getting anywhere anyway and they should let the stupid kid go down if that's what he wanted and if it wasn't for this it would be for something else and why were they wasting their time?

Sergeant Walsh said, 'We're going to let you go back to your cell, Billy, and think about what's in front of you. We'll be back in a couple of days to see if you've changed your mind.'

But they didn't come back, probably having realised that the inspector was right and they really were wasting their time, and a few months later we went to trial.

* * *

The length of time from arrest to trial surprised me. They had me on a plate, I was the one who'd reported the murder and shown them where the body was and they had my confession. You'd have thought they could just take me in front of a judge and let him sentence me. But it doesn't work like that and I was on remand for months.

It doesn't take long when you're in prison before you start to look forward to visits. A visit gets you out of the cell and reminds you that the outside world hasn't gone away. I'd never seen myself as someone who liked gossip but I lapped up what people told me. I found myself asking questions about people I'd never cared about before I'd come in here. I also found I was interested in the answers. And there's a little store in the visiting room and your visitor can buy you coffee or tea or a soft drink, and something to eat. No cigarettes, though, and smoking is not allowed in the room, which a lot of prisoners objected to but I thought was just fine.

To visit, the person needs a Visiting Order, which is called a VO. I didn't send one to my mother because I was still furious about the lies she'd told and I didn't want to see her. I sent one each week to Chantal and she brought money every time she visited. She didn't just give it to me because you're not allowed to do that. She had to hand it to the screws and it was put in my account and I could draw on it to order things like toothpaste and biscuits from canteen. Remand prisoners have more freedom that way, because they're not convicted yet and you're innocent until proven guilty. That's the theory, anyway.

And prisoners can have stuff if they make application. That's what it's called. Making application. I knew nothing about that but Chantal explained it to me. Regus had explained it to her. Obviously. So, she'd say, 'Make application to receive any papers and magazines you want and I'll pay the money to the newsagent outside the prison and he'll send them in.' But I couldn't think of any papers or magazines I'd like to read. Chantal said, 'How about *GQ*? *Playboy*? *Penthouse*?' But I wasn't into any of that. I said, 'What about books?' and she said she'd find out and when she came back she said I could have books if I made application and as long as they were new and I should tell her what I wanted and they'd be sent in by WH Smith. She also said I could have small items of electronic equipment and did I want a Gameboy? I said, no, but a radio would be good. But it would have to have an earphone because I shared my cell with two other prisoners even though it was a cell built for one. So I made application and books started to arrive and a radio and life inside got a little bit better and I became less bored and less frustrated.

I said to Chantal, 'I hope it's not you paying for this out of your own pocket,' and she said, 'Don't be daft.'

I asked her how my mother was getting on without the Creep and she said, 'Oh, she's got someone else now. What did you think?' I asked what the new man was like and she said, 'He's an even bigger arsehole than the one you killed.'

Mister Henry came two or three times and later on Mister Mukherjee, who was going to be my barrister, came to talk to me about how he was going to present my case. Oh, yes – and a social worker came once. They counted as official visitors and didn't need me to send them a VO.

But the best visits were Poppy's. I'd sent her a VO but I didn't expect her to come and when a prison officer comes to your cell to say you have a visitor he doesn't say who it is so as I walked into the visiting room I was expecting to see Chantal. And I did. But she wasn't alone.

I came to a complete halt. Just stopped walking. When he crashed into me the prisoner behind swore, words I'm not going to repeat, and the prison officer escorting us glowered at me and said, 'What do you think you're doing, McErlane?' He thought I was putting on some kind of show. I wasn't, though. 'Which is your table?' I pointed to where Chantal and Poppy were sitting. 'Go and sit there, then.' And I did.

Most prisoners, and most prisoners' visitors, have done this before. You could say they were raised to it. They knew what being in prison meant and when they got into the visiting room a buzz of conversation started immediately. Poppy and I didn't have that, and we just sat and stared at each other. Chantal looked from one of us to the other and back, muttered under her breath and stood up. 'You want tea, Billy? Or coffee?'

'Tea, please.'

Poppy stretched both of her arms across the table and took my hands tightly in hers. Then Chantal came back carrying a tray and put a paper cup of tea in front of me and gave another to Poppy and gave me a KitKat, a mint Aero bar and a packet of bacon-flavoured crisps. I said, 'Thank you,' and Chantal said, 'I need a fag. I'll wait for you outside, Poppy.' Poppy said, 'Thanks, Chantal,' and then she and I were alone. Well, as alone as you can be in a room full of prisoners and their visitors (mostly wives with children) and screws walking up and down the aisles. I said, 'Thanks for coming. I didn't know whether you would.'

'I miss you.'

'I miss you, too. Tell me what's happening.'

'Well. Big adventures, actually. You know Jordan?'

I nodded. Jordan was one of the thickest of our class-mates.

'Well. The day you went away, he came banging on my door. I wouldn't open it. I knew what he wanted. He was shouting horrible things.'

'I'm sorry you had to put up with that.'

'Oh, I didn't. Not for long. Two men turned up in a lovely car and made him get into it. Next time I saw him he had a very bruised face and he wouldn't even look at me. And everyone's left me alone since then. And now I'm changing schools.'

'How did that happen?'

'Mister Hunt came to see my mother and offered her a job.'

'Mister Hunt? Regus Hunt?'

'Regus, yes. He looks like another Jordan but he's a lovely man. He's paying Mam more than she's been getting and he's given us a flat in Gosforth at a rent she can afford.'

Regus. A lovely man. Chantal had said much the same thing. I still didn't believe it.

'That's for you, isn't it?'

'Mm?'

'You asked him to look after me. Didn't you?' Her eyes were fixed on me. 'Yes,' she said when I didn't answer. 'I thought so. That's part of the deal. Isn't it? For owning up to a murder you didn't commit.'

'I can't talk about that, Poppy. I'll never be able to talk about it. And you must never, ever, say what you just said to anyone else.'

'Mister Hunt would look after me.' She squeezed my hands. 'Until you're out and then you can take over.'

I lowered my voice, scared of what might happen to both of us if anyone heard what we were saying. 'Poppy, I'm serious.'

'Okay. Okay, Billy. Billy…'

I smiled. 'You always say "Billy…" like that when you're going to ask me something.'

'Well, this time I'm not asking, I'm telling.'

She fell silent. I said, 'Go on, then. Tell me.'

'Yes. I'm a bit embarrassed, really.' She dropped her voice to a whisper. 'I'm sorry I never went to bed with you.'

'What?'

'I didn't want to end up with a baby. But we could have made sure that didn't happen. I could have told you to buy some condoms.'

'I did buy some. I've been carrying them around for ages. Just in case.'

'You never said.'

'I didn't think you wanted to.'

'Well. I didn't want to. I was scared.'

'Scared? Of me?'

'Not of you. Scared it would hurt. Scared I'd get pregnant. Scared of people saying bad things about me. But now I think about it all the time and I wish we had. We'd both have something to remember while we're apart.'

'We can't do it in here. The screws might object. And anyway, I had to leave the johnnies at the gate.'

'Billy!'

'You leave all your personal stuff there. It's called your property. I just hope they look after it. There's a lot of thieves in this place.'

'Please be serious.'

Please be serious. I wasn't sure I could be when she talked about this. And, once again, I know how it seems. Poppy was happy to talk about going to bed with me when we couldn't, but she'd been less forthcoming when we could have. But it still didn't matter, because if I'd just wanted a girl to have sex with I'd have gone with Kylie and that wasn't what I'd wanted – I'd wanted someone I could love. Forever. And that was Poppy.

I said, 'Gosforth's a nice place.'

'Yes. It is. I've seen the school I'll be going to and it's nothing like ours.' I could see she was excited about the changes in her life. 'I watched the kids coming out and they looked happy. No-one was being attacked.'

'It'll help you get what you want.'

'What I want?'

'A levels. College.'

'Oh. Yes.' She gave my hands an especially hard squeeze. 'What I really want is to take you home with me.'

Now I thought I might be the one to start crying. I freed my hands, opened the KitKat and pushed the Aero across the table. Poppy said, 'You eat that. It's yours,' and I said, 'I don't have time. We've only got a few minutes left.'

'Take them back to your cell.'

'We're not allowed to.'

'Not allowed to? You mean, people can come in here and buy you stuff and you can't take it out of this room?'

'That's right. So eat it. And then we'll share the crisps.'

She tore the wrapper off the chocolate. 'That's crazy.'

'Yes, it is. But don't say anything or they'll take it out on me.'

When Mister Henry came we met in a special room and not the ordinary visiting room and he'd tell me what they were doing to help me. He said I was to plead not guilty to murder but guilty to manslaughter. The jury would decide and so that's who Mister Mukherjee was going to be aiming at. If we got manslaughter, I wouldn't have to get mandatory life and I might even get a sentence short enough for them to be able to say I'd already served it while I was on remand and then the judge would say I had to be supervised for three or four years but I'd be able to go back to school and get on with my life. A lot would depend on Mister Mukherjee's speech in mitigation.

He said he had some good stuff from Miss Taggart and the headmaster. The judge would ask for reports before sentencing and that's where the social worker came in so I should make sure I gave her a big sob story about the terrible life I'd led with the Creep in the house.

Which reminds me that I'd completely forgotten about the psych. My first one ever was the one I saw while I was on remand. So that was another visitor.

Both of my cellies were men in their forties who'd been in and out of prison all their adult lives. One of them was called Joseph and he wouldn't take Joe. He explained that he was Jewish and Joseph was an important name in his religion. He said you never heard of Joe and his Technicolor Dream Coat, did you? Any more than you heard about God calling on Abe when he wanted him to go to the promised land. I hadn't a clue what he was talking about. Usually, if people I knew talked about the promised land it had to do with a woman and the place between her legs. But I liked him

The other one was a complete shit. Worse than the Creep. He got really aggressive when the books started to arrive. Reading enraged him for some reason and he said anyone who read was a poof. Books, that is. He had tabloid newspapers delivered and he was forever talking about people like Britney Spears and John Terry. Why they mattered to him, I don't know. I'm quite sure he never met any of them but he knew more about Wayne Rooney than Rooney's own mother could have. When he saw me with a book, he'd say I was going to be his tart and one of these nights he was going to…well, I'm not going to repeat what he said he was going to do. He was a big man, the Shit, and mean looking and he scared me.

Joseph talked to me one day when the Shit was at visits. I'd noticed that Joseph never had a visit, but I didn't say anything about that to him. You learn quickly what's all right to talk about and what isn't. And he told me not to worry about the Shit. He said there was a man on the outside who had made it known I was to be looked after and that man had a lot of clout and he, Joseph, would make sure I didn't come to harm but so would a few others in there. He said he'd thought of telling the Shit who my protector was but the Shit was probably a grass as well as his other drawbacks so he didn't want to. But he'd make sure I was okay.

I'm going to admit that this conversation caused me almost as much bother as it did reassurance. Mister Henry had warned me, in his oblique "Walls have ears" way, that it wasn't beyond the police to put someone in with me who would try to get me to say something I shouldn't and report it back to them. So, although I wanted to ask Joseph whether he was talking about Regus, I didn't.

When the Shit came back from visits he was worked up and going on about how he couldn't stand much more of this and if he didn't get his end away soon there was going to be trouble. And that night, when Joseph seemed to be asleep, he slid his hand under my blanket. 'Come on, pussy,' he said. 'Let the dog see the bone. And speaking of bones…'

Joseph wasn't asleep at all. He said, 'Leave the boy alone.'

The trouble with this sort of thing in prison is, once it starts, you can't back down. Joseph couldn't, and the Shit couldn't. They swapped a few words and then they swapped blows. I'd have thought the Shit was too big for Joseph. I'd have been wrong. When it ended, the Shit was lying on his bed, moaning.

I asked Joseph whether we shouldn't get help for him.

'How?'

'Call the guards.'

'And tell them what? That he wanted to bum you? You want to grass him up?'

It was obvious from the way he said this that I'd better not say yes, so I said I hadn't thought about it.

'He'll be all right.' He put his face right in the Shit's. 'Shut the fuck up or I'll give you something to moan about.'

When the lights came on next morning, the Shit's face was in a hell of a state. They took him to the infirmary and when he came back it was to another cell. One of the screws took me aside while I was lining up for breakfast and asked me if I knew what had happened but I said I didn't. Then he asked if I wanted to go into protective custody. Joseph had already warned me to avoid this. Everyone would think I was a nonce, I'd never have any exercise except in the company of people who really were nonces, people in the kitchen would piss in my food and when I went wherever I was going after my trial the fact that I was a nonce would go there with me. 'Stay out of there. You'll be looked after.'

And I was.

CHAPTER *36*

The trial didn't go smoothly.

When I was brought into the courtroom and put in the dock, I looked for the visitors' gallery. Poppy was right where she'd told me she'd be, in the front row. She smiled at me and I could see what it cost her to give that smile. She looked on the verge of tears.

The jury was mostly men. I asked Mister Mukherjee if that meant anything and he said, no, you couldn't read things into the sex of the jury. But he'd said earlier that we could do with some women on the jury because they'd be enraged by my mother's behaviour and the way I'd been brought up whereas men might think I should have been a bit harder. You couldn't say they would. They just might.

The prosecution really went into the force it must have taken to beat to death a fit man in the prime of life, which was what they said he'd been instead of the run down, smoke-kippered, booze-riddled waster he actually was. Then they put my mother on the stand. The prosecuting barrister asked her a few questions and that didn't go too badly. My mother said she'd only married the Creep to bring a father into the lives of her children, because children need a father's influence if they're to grow up decent. Especially boys. Then that barrister sat down and it was our turn.

Mister Mukherjee said, 'Missus McErlane, you referred to having married the deceased. Were you, in fact, married to him?'

My mother looked amazed. 'Of course. What are you suggesting? He was my husband.'

'You went through a marriage ceremony with him?'

'Not in a church, no. You don't need a church's blessing to be husband and wife.'

'In a registry office, then?'

'No.'

'So you weren't married to the deceased.'

'I regarded him as my husband. We were faithful to each other.'

'I see. But the deceased was not the accused's natural father?'

'No. But he treated him as…'

'Was the deceased the natural father of any of your six children?'

'Not as such. No.'

I saw some of the jurors smirk and I thought this was going the way we wanted it to. Mister Mukherjee said, 'Were you married to the accused's natural father?'

My mother looked furious. The judge told her she had to answer and she said, 'I can't remember.'

Well, Mister Mukherjee said, maybe he could help. He said, 'You haven't actually been married to anyone, have you?'

I really thought she was going to throw a wobbler, which I thought would be good for us. She was giving Mister Mukherjee a really savage look. 'What do you mean?'

'It's a simple question, Missus McErlane. Although that should really be Miss McErlane, shouldn't it? You've had six children and been intimate with more men than even you can probably count. Have you ever been through a marriage ceremony with anyone, in a church or a registry office or anywhere else?'

'Not as such,' she said again.

More smirks. Mister Mukherjee told me later that that wasn't necessarily a good thing because the jury might associate my morals with my mother's and that wouldn't help us. And, of course, we didn't know then what she was about to come out with.

'And even if you had been, you still wouldn't be able to say whether you'd been married to the natural father of your son, now would you, Miss McErlane?'

She was white now, and shaking. 'What do you mean?'

'You haven't the faintest idea who the father of your son really is. Have you? Like the rest of your children, he was conceived while you went about your work as a common prostitute.'

'How dare you?' She was screaming, and spit was spraying in all directions. She turned to the judge. 'Am I expected to answer to a fucking nigger?'

The jury was smiling and the people in court were laughing and the newspaper reporter was scribbling away. They must have been thinking this was better than *Big Brother.*

The judge said the court would take a short break and he would see both barristers in his room. He turned to the prosecuting counsel and said, 'In your case, after you've advised your witness of the standards of behaviour we expect in this court.'

I was taken to the basement cells. Mister Mukherjee came down to see me after he'd talked to the judge and before we went back into court. He told me the judge had warned him that I was on trial here and not my mother and he should be careful just how far he took things. He also said that the prosecuting barrister had asked the judge for permission to question my mother again because she had more evidence against me that she hadn't wanted to give but now was determined to.

'Do you know what that could be?'

I shook my head. I could see he was worried.

I was flabbergasted when my mother gave her "new evidence". She said I'd interfered with Leanne against Leanne's will. I looked up to the visitors' gallery and saw Poppy's face. She was furious. I thought if she could have hit my mother, she would have.

Mister Mukherjee immediately said he wanted Leanne called to give evidence herself. My mother said to the judge, 'She's ten. How can she come here? I won't allow it.'

The judge said it wasn't up to her to allow it or not allow it and if he had any more outbursts from her she'd be in contempt of court and she'd spend the night in the cells. Then he said they'd have another break while he saw the two barristers in his room again. So back I went to the cells.

When we all came back, the judge spoke to the jury. He said the evidence my mother had given was inadmissible and they were to put it from their minds. They were not to take it into account when they considered their verdict.

Soon after that we finished for the day. I asked Mister Mukherjee if the jury would be able to do that. He said, 'Could you? No, it's in their minds all right. You're a pervert who tried to diddle his ten-year-old sister.'

'She's twelve. And I didn't. My mother told me to and I refused.'

'Your mother told you to?'

I told him the whole story. He said he was going to have to think about it overnight. He said it was in the jury's mind and maybe he'd have to take it on. It would be a high risk strategy, but maybe he'd have to have a go.

* * *

Next morning, he told me he didn't think he had any choice. The jury had got something in their minds and he had to try to get it out.

First, the judge told the jury that he'd instructed them to forget evidence they'd heard yesterday, but now he was going to reverse that instruction because defence counsel wanted to deal with the matter. Then he handed over to Mister Mukherjee.

Mister Mukherjee started on my mother. Would she describe herself as a good mother? Yes, she said. She would. Wasn't it true, he asked, that I had usually had to go to school on foot and without any breakfast? She denied it. He warned her that he was in a position to call witnesses from school to say that I had. She said she'd always been there for me but I was a hot-blooded, strong-willed boy who refused to eat what was put in front of him or to take money from her when it was offered. So, he said, I had gone to school on foot and without any breakfast?

'That was his choice. He hates me. He's an unnatural son.'

'And as for this allegation that he interfered with your daughter, Leanne. That's pure fabrication, is it not?'

'What?'

'You made it up.'

'No.'

'Is it not true, Miss McErlane, that you told the defendant that his sister was turning into a most attractive young woman and he should consider himself lucky to be sharing a bedroom with her?'

'That's a lie. What kind of mother do you think I am?'

Then Mister Mukherjee produced a newspaper and told the Judge he wanted to offer it in evidence and to question my mother about it. The usher took it to the judge who looked at it and said that would be okay. They called it an exhibit and gave it a number and Mister Mukherjee said he'd brought copies for the jury. They were all given one and then Mister Mukherjee asked the usher to show the paper to the witness. He said, 'Do you recognise this, Miss McErlane?'

'Yes.'

'Did you write it?'

'Yes.'

'I'm going to ask that question again, Miss McErlane. Did you write that letter?'

'I dictated it, yes.'

'But you didn't write it.'

'He wrote it.' She pointed at me but didn't look at me. She hadn't looked at me for ages. I glanced up at Poppy and she was smiling.

'Your son Billy wrote it. Why didn't you write it yourself, Miss McErlane?'

'Will you stop calling me Miss! I'm a married woman.'

'We've been through that, Miss McErlane. We've established that you are no such thing. Why did you not write the letter yourself?'

My mother looked away. 'I don't write very well.'

'And your son does.'

'Better than me, anyway.'

'In fact, with all the difficulties you put in the way of his getting an education, your son won a prize for the best essay in the North of England.'

My mother said nothing.

'And he went on to place third in a national contest.'

Still nothing.

'You don't write very well. Can you read?'

My mother said something I couldn't hear and the judge told her to say it again, and speak up.

'Yes. I can read.'

'Good. Would you read the letter again now, please. To yourself, not aloud.'

We all watched my mother's lips move as she worked her way down the page.

'You say in this letter that your youngest daughter is eleven. That letter was written some months ago, yet yesterday you said she was ten. How old is she?'

'She's twelve.'

'I see. And you say she is growing fast and begins to look like a woman. Not the impression you wished to convey yesterday. You also describe the three children who shared a room as good children. That includes your son, Billy, does it not?'

The judge had to tell her she must answer. 'Yes,' she said.

'So at that time you regarded your son Billy as a good boy.'

'I suppose so. He hadn't killed anyone then.'

'Miss McErlane, will you tell the Court how your older daughter Chantal came to work, like you, as a prostitute?'

'That's a lie!'

'Miss McErlane, we will be calling witnesses who will say that you and your daughter, who was then fifteen, solicited for business in several public houses. And that the deceased, the man you call your husband though in fact he was not, pimped for you.'

'That is a lie!'

215

'Well, we shall wait until the jury has heard what those witnesses have to say and I have no doubt they will make up their own minds. It is true, though, is it not, that you encouraged your oldest son Billy to break in your younger daughter Leanne so that she could follow in the same career?'

'No!'

'And that he refused.'

'I won't listen to this. These are just filthy lies.'

'I put it to you that you regarded Leanne as no more than an asset in the family prostitution business. That, as your own attractions waned, you wished to establish yourself as a madam for your daughters.'

'How dare you?' But she couldn't go on because she had started to cry. The judge called a break in the proceedings and I was taken to the cells.

While I was there, Mister Mukherjee came to see me. I asked how he thought it was going.

'Hard to tell, Billy. I've been watching the jury. They're fascinated, but there's a risk they'll see you all as one. Especially after you take the stand and the other side tries to show you were running drugs. We want a manslaughter conviction and if they think you're no better than the others we may not get it.'

'What can we do?'

'Hope, Billy. A jury is twelve people. They all have their own experiences and their own views and you can never tell what they'll do till they've done it.'

When we resumed, Mister Mukherjee said he had no more questions for my mother.

Then it was my turn. The prosecuting barrister started out exactly as Mister Mukherjee had told me she would, by taking me through my story of how I'd killed the Creep. She didn't ask any awkward questions because they weren't interested in proving I hadn't done it – that would have been Mister Mukherjee's job if we'd wanted a Not Guilty verdict.

Then she sprang a surprise. 'You claim to have been overcome by rage when your stepfather said he wanted you to stop going to school and start helping him with his trading business.'

'Yes, Miss. Except it wasn't a...'

'But that isn't true, is it Billy? Your stepfather hadn't said any such thing. Had he?'

'Yes, Miss. He...'

'You were motivated by sexual jealousy. Weren't you?'

'Miss?'

'You suspected your stepfather of having designs on your younger sister, Leanne. Didn't you?'

'Well, I...'

'Yes or no, please. Did you or did you not believe your stepfather wanted to have sexual intercourse with Leanne?'

I looked at Mister Mukherjee. The judge told me I had to answer. I said, 'Yes, Miss. He did.'

'And Leanne was yours. Wasn't she?'

I could feel the blood red hot in my cheeks. My heart was beating so fast I thought I'd fall down. 'No,' I said. 'No. That's not how it was.'

The barrister looked at the jury. Then she looked at me. There was a nasty smile on her face. The jury couldn't see it, but I could.

She said, 'In that bedroom that you shared with a young girl just entering into the first bloom of womanhood, you conceived an unholy desire for her. Didn't you?'

217

'No, Miss.' I was horrified. 'No.'

'And anyone who looked at her was going to feel your wrath.'

'No.'

'You felt so strongly about Leanne, you'd kill anyone who tried to take her from you. In fact, you did.'

'No.'

She changed tack so quickly it took my breath away. 'Tell us about Regus Hunt.'

'Who?'

'Regus Hunt. You're not going to say you don't know him?'

'No. Of course not. He's my sister's boyfriend.'

'That's your older sister? Chantal?'

'Yes, Miss.'

'But that's not all he is. Is it? He's also your employer? You deliver drugs for him and collect the money?'

Mister Mukherjee was on his feet, but the judge made a calming gesture towards him. To the prosecuting barrister he said, 'Do you intend to call this Mister Hunt as a witness?'

'No, my Lord.'

'Is he a convicted drug dealer?'

'No, my Lord.'

'Then I have to remind you that we are here to try the case against the defendant. Mister Hunt is not on trial here. You will go no further down that track.'

'No, my Lord.' She bowed to the judge, but just for a fleeting moment the nasty smile was back.

The judge turned to the jury. 'Counsel has just behaved in a most improper way. As I am sure she knows. You must wipe from your minds and memories all trace of what has just been said.'

But I knew they wouldn't. As Mister Mukherjee had said, how could you? She'd done her job. I wasn't what the defence was trying to make me out as. I was a drug dealer who killed someone because he wanted to go to bed with an underage girl I regarded as my own.

We broke for lunch, but I was so roiled up I couldn't eat. When Mister Mukherjee came to see me, I said, 'How can she say those things? They're just not true.'

'Ah, Billy,' he said. 'This is a court of law. We're not here to get at the truth. We're here to find out which side has the best game plan.'

After lunch it was time for the defence. Mister Mukherjee went through a bunch of witnesses to establish that my mother and Chantal had been whores and that the Creep had been their pimp. Miss Taggart took the stand and said she'd seen me running to school almost every day and, when she'd asked why I didn't take the bus, I'd told her I didn't have any money. She also said I almost never brought any lunch and my mother hadn't got round to applying for free school meals for me, but she'd spoken to the Head and they'd agreed to feed me free of charge. She also said how hard I worked and what a pleasure it was to teach me.

That was it. That was the defence we'd planned. It had seemed fine when we'd talked about it but now it looked a bit thin, even to me. I looked at Poppy and she didn't seem very happy, either.

The judge said it was getting late and he'd leave the summing up till tomorrow.

Next morning, both barristers went through their cases for the jury. The prosecuting barrister said it was open and shut. I came from a family of undesirables and I was merely one more.

I was possessed by a desire that society had frowned on for thousands of years. When someone else wanted the girl I thought of as mine I had lured him to a quiet place and beaten him to death. That was premeditated murder, and the jury could bring in no other verdict.

Mister Mukherjee said the prosecution's closing arguments were a tissue of unsubstantiated assertions. He said I had not had any desire at all for Leanne. I had struggled to keep myself above the base instincts of my family and to find a better life through education, with no help from my mother. I had told the truth about the killing, it had been an act of sudden, insensate but perhaps justifiable rage when I saw someone attempting to close this escape route I had found. As soon as it was over I had deeply regretted the killing, which would stay with me for the rest of my life. It was right that I should be judged for what I had done, but there was no premeditation and the only reasonable judgement was not guilty of murder but guilty of manslaughter.

Then the judge talked to the jury. He said he had no guidance to give them, except to say that any judgement they returned must be unanimous and that their job was to decide whether the prosecution had established its case beyond any reasonable doubt. If they felt there was any doubt at all, they must acquit. He said the reason he had nothing more than that to say was that prosecution and defence had offered two starkly opposing versions and it was the jury's task to choose which they believed. Then he repeated what he had said about reasonable doubt and sent them off to choose a foreman and come to their verdict.

Doing that took them three days, which was as long as the trial had taken. Each morning I was taken from prison to the cells beneath the courtroom, and each evening I made the reverse journey. Mister Mukherjee didn't appear during that time. He was defending another case in another court.

I did a lot of thinking during those three days. One of the things I thought about was: had I been stitched up? I was taking the rap for Regus and I'd been told that I'd have the very best defence and everything would be done to make sure I got the best possible outcome. But had it? Regus had been kept out of it, that's for sure – but had they defended me to the best of their ability or hung me out to dry? I didn't know. I still don't.

And then Mister Mukherjee reappeared. The jury was ready to give its verdict. I was taken up to the courtroom, where the jurors had already taken their places. Poppy wasn't there, because we hadn't known when this would happen. The clerk told us to stand, the judge came in and sat down and so did everyone else, including me. The screw beside me told me to get back on my feet.

The clerk asked who the foreman of the jury was and a man stood up. The clerk asked if the jury had reached a verdict and the man said they had. The clerk asked if it was the verdict of them all and the man said it was. Then the clerk said he was going to put the charge and the foreman should answer "Guilty" or "Not Guilty". Just that. Nothing else. He would put the more serious charge first and then, if the verdict on that was Not Guilty, he would put the second charge.

Then he said, 'Do you find the accused, Zappa McErlane also known as Billy McErlane, guilty or not guilty of the charge of murder?'

CHAPTER 37

Guilty of Murder

Zappa Zapped; Killed Stepfather in Lust-Fuelled Rage

Zappa McErlane, 14, was convicted in Crown Court this morning of the premeditated murder of his common law stepfather, Antony Baker, 38.

The court heard that McErlane, who is also known as Billy McErlane, had conceived an illicit passion for his ten-year-old sister Leanne. Fearing that Baker planned to establish a sexual relationship with the girl, he lured him to a secluded place and beat him to death.

judge Merton told McErlane that the law allowed no ambiguity in sentencing in cases of premeditated murder. Because of his age, McErlane would be sentenced to be detained at Her Majesty's Pleasure, but he should be in no doubt that what this meant in his case was a sentence of life imprisonment. The judge said he would wait for psychiatric and social reports before deciding what tariff, or minimum sentence to be served, he should fix in this case.

Murderer's Mother Slams Son

Alice McErlane, mother of Zappa McErlane who was recently convicted of the murder of his stepfather, broke her silence today in an exclusive interview with this newspaper.

'He was an unnatural son,' she says. 'From his first days, he rejected the love he was given as the eldest male child.'

According to Alice, Zappa's stepfather tried everything he could to get close to the boy. 'Antony offered to help with his homework and tried to interest him in going to football matches together. He only wanted the best for the boy. But Zappa refused to have anything to do with him. It was like he'd closed his heart against him.'

Alice has no idea what made her son a murderer. 'He took the death of his father hard,' she says. 'They were very close. Maybe it was that. How can you tell?'

Alice burst into tears when I asked her about accusations made against her at the trial. 'It's a disgrace,' she said. 'How can a judge allow that? All sorts of lies were told about me to try to get Zappa off the hook and it isn't fair. I had no chance to tell them what lies it all was. Everyone around here knows the truth. That boy had love showered on him and look how he repays us.'

Can she ever forgive the killer of the man she loved? Amazingly, it seems she can. 'You can't fill your heart with hate,' she says. 'No-one is so bad, no soul is so black that a mother cannot forgive.'

Her harshest words she retains for the Council and Zappa's school. 'There are so many evil influences in this neighbourhood. We begged them to rehouse us so we could get away from all the things that were dragging Zappa down, but they didn't want to know.' As for his teachers, she says Zappa had great potential but none of them cared. 'He won a prize for an essay he wrote.

223

He loved reading and writing and we encouraged him all we could. He spent hours in the library and myself or his stepfather would go with him to help him find the books he needed and guide his work. But the teachers treated him like dirt.'

Alice says Zappa's girlfriend, Kylie, who she describes as "a sweet girl", is so devastated by what has happened that she refuses to speak to anyone. 'She won't even go to school. And she loves school.'

Chapter 38

I didn't see Mister Mukherjee again. Mister Henry came to see me right after the verdict. He wanted to know how I felt, but I couldn't tell him. I was too numb.

'It won't be so bad,' he said. 'The judge will set a short tariff. You'll see.'

That was almost the end of my time with Mister Henry. I only saw him once more.

I was taken straight to Young Offenders, with no time for a last visit from Poppy, and went through the stuff I've already described in the Induction Wing. Then the stuff with the psych and the probation officer started. They had to prepare reports for the judge.

I had hours with the psych. Hours. I couldn't have believed one person would spend so much time with me. It was obvious when I talked to other people that she didn't do that with everyone, so I asked her why.

She said, 'You're a fascinating case, Billy. I'll get a paper out of you, and possibly a book.'

Which was honest. I'd have to admit that.

But at least she was on my side. Or so I thought until the probation officer put me straight.

'You want to watch what you say to that psychiatrist,' he said.

'Miss Young? Why?'

'She's thinking you might be a psychopath.'

'Me?'

'You have some of the classic symptoms, according to her. If that's what her report says, they'll transfer you to Broadmoor.'

226

'Where's that?'

'It's a prison for the criminally insane, son. Get yourself in there, you'll never get out. And if you're not barmy when you go in, you damn soon will be. They have some of the most damaged minds in the country in that place. And that's just the staff.'

He was ex-Army, Mister Barnes, and proud of it. He didn't come out of what I'd started to see as the classic mould for people in his line of work. Although he did tell me there were a lot of old soldiers who'd gone into the probation service.

He said I'd have made a good soldier. He'd have been delighted to have me in his unit. 'Unfortunately, the Army doesn't recruit murderers. Which is odd when you consider killing's part of the job description.'

He went to visit my mother and my teachers. He wasn't impressed by my mother. 'Utter tart,' he said. 'Always a few like her hanging around a garrison, getting squaddies in trouble. You're well out of that, son.'

I suppose you'd call his the direct approach. Bracing. Tell it how it is.

He surprised me one day. He'd come back from the visits he was going to base his report on and he said, 'I know you're not going to tell me the truth, Billy. You can't. I understand that. So I'll tell you, shall I?'

I looked at him, wondering what was coming.

He said, 'You no more killed that man than I did.'

I didn't say anything.

He said, 'Don't worry. I'm not going to put that in my report. If they think you haven't accepted your guilt, you'll never get out.'

That was twice he'd used that expression, "you'll never get out". They weren't words I enjoyed hearing.

He said, 'Sandra Young's changing her mind about you, by the way. Thank God. You're not a psychopath now. You're a poor lost soul who had to grow up too fast and is riven by conflicting emotions. Do you feel riven, son?'

'I don't know what it means.'

'Not a word you hear often, I agree. Don't ask the delectable Sandra to translate. She'll know I've been talking to you. She is delectable, wouldn't you say?'

I nodded. You never really know what side someone's on. Mister Barnes could be genuinely friendly. He might really like me and want to do his best for me. Or it might be an act designed to get me to commit myself to something that would cause me pain. Even if I couldn't see what.

'Imagine those little titties shaking when you take her doggie style. Sight down her spine and slap her rosy arse for her. You didn't lust after your sister, either. I've seen Leanne and I just don't believe it. Miss Taggart pointed Poppy out to me. She's more your style.'

'How was she?' I asked.

'I didn't talk to her, son. But she looked okay. And Chantal had Kylie with her. Now there's a bit of jail bait. I do believe you shagged that, am I right?'

I made a movement that could have been a nod but could also have been a shake of the head.

'You'd better say yes, son. If you say no, I might start thinking you were mad and then where would you be?'

Then he said he was about done and he had enough to write his report. He held out his hand and I shook it. 'Good luck, Billy,' he said. 'You're due for a break. I hope you get it.'

* * *

Miss Young never told me what she'd said about me, but it can't have been bad because when Mister Henry came to see me for the last time he had good news.

'The judge has set a tariff of a year, Billy. That's as good as saying you shouldn't be locked up at all.' He must have seen the look on my face because he held his hand up, palm outwards, and said, 'That doesn't mean you'll get out in a year. It isn't the judge who decides, it's the parole board. You're a lifer. If the politicians at the Home Office think there are votes in keeping you locked up, you could still be inside in twenty years. But you won't be. Just keep your head down, don't cause trouble and don't let anyone cause it for you. Think you can do that?'

I nodded.

He shook hands, too.

CHAPTER 39

Looking back, I was taking a hell of a risk associating with that gang. But I wanted the pics. I went out with them three times, after which I had all I could use. I wish I hadn't gone along the fourth night.

You could tell, right from the start. They were always looking for trouble, but this time they had something special in mind.

It was two days later and I was cuddled in Wendy's arms. She was holding me tight and sometimes kissing me gently on the forehead. I liked being hugged. After a while, she said, 'If they were going to do something like that, why on earth would they do it in front of a photographer?'

I shook my head.

She kissed me on the lips. Then she started tugging at my belt. When she had me completely undressed, she did the same for herself. She lay down on top of me. 'You need a bit of TLC,' she said.

Melanie explained it to me. And she was right.

'You were the point, Billy. If they'd run across that poor girl without you, they might have done what they did or they might not. They pass girls all the time. What do they usually do?'

'Nothing,' I said. 'They might say something. Pretend to grab her. Call her a bad name. But not that.'

'They didn't run across this one, did they? They went looking for her. And you were with them. Did they know this was going to be your last time?'

'They knew I had the pics I wanted.'

'So this was their last chance.'

'To go to jail?'

'To be famous. That's what you offered, Billy. How would you describe them?'

'Animals.'

'How would *they* describe them?'

'Who knows?'

'You do. And so do I. They think they're outlaws, Billy. "Everybody hates us and we don't care". There are thousands just like them. They're frogspawn in a pond. Have you any idea what percentage of frogspawn gets to be frogs? But you could have made them special. Your pictures would have appeared somewhere and everyone would have known about them. Instead of which, you could have got yourself killed.'

I hadn't spent much of the money I'd earned, because I was mixing with students and students don't have a lot of money, but I had replaced my fixed lens camera with a lovely little micro four-thirds Olympus. That's what I was shooting with, but as soon as I'd realised what was going on, I'd pretended also to take pics on my mobile to cover the fact that I was picking out a text message to Wendy saying, "Call 999 and send police immediately to Farson Estate. Girl being attacked."

She called them right away and they got there fast but it was never going to be fast enough. The girl was screaming and resisting but they'd got her shoes off, they'd got her jeans off and any moment now they'd have her knickers off. Just looking at their faces made me feel ill. There was no humanity there. They looked like a pack of wild dogs that had brought their prey to ground. Hyenas, maybe, because they were laughing. Laughter without humour or compassion.

* * *

There wasn't any doubt about what they were planning to do and they *were* planning to do it. There were six of them and I didn't rate my chances in a six on one fight but I knew if I stood back and let it happen I'd be no better than them.

Kevin was as always the ringleader and he was planning to go first. He'd undone his belt and was pushing his pants down and that gave me whatever chance I might think I had. I shoved my camera into one pocket and the mobile into the other and stepped forward, over the heaving mass on the ground, to slam my fist into his chin.

He keeled over but didn't go down which suited me fine because it let me grab the back of his head, swing him over while he was still off balance and ram his face down hard onto the knee I bent below it. The Marquess of Queensbury wouldn't have liked it but it was effective. His nose broke, blood sprayed over my chinos and one of his teeth came out although I didn't realise that at the time. When I let go he went down, which gave me the chance to stamp on the side of his head. I'd hear no more from Kevin for the moment.

They'd all let go of the girl. If she'd had any sense she'd have run, which would have given me a chance to bolt, too, but that was too much to ask. She lay huddled on the ground.

Having dealt with the biggest first, I took the two smallest next, crashing their heads into each other with all the force I could muster. But I couldn't keep all of them in sight at the same time and someone behind me picked up a half brick and slammed it into the back of my head. I wanted to stay on my feet. I did everything I could to stay on my feet. But I couldn't. Black unconsciousness took over. I slipped to my knees and slumped forward.

That, thank God, was when the police arrived. Although, as with Kevin's tooth, I didn't know that at the time.

I was arrested with everyone else. I'd been there so I must be one of them. Then they put my name into their computer and realised who they'd caught in their net.

The detective sergeant running the case hadn't been allowed to speak to me until my head had been patched up and the doctor had satisfied himself there was no permanent damage. It didn't matter. He'd been happy to wait. I wasn't going anywhere.

They'd got me a duty solicitor. The DS said, 'You'll be put in front of a magistrate in the morning.'

I looked at the solicitor, but she didn't say anything. I said, 'On what charge?'

The sergeant smiled. He was enjoying himself. 'We'll be asking for revocation of your licence. And we'll get it.'

Still the solicitor's mouth remained closed. She looked as though she was watching a crime movie. I said. 'On what grounds?'

The DS looked at me as you might an insect you wanted to crush. 'Breach of the terms of your licence. What else?'

Again I looked at the solicitor. I wasn't going to get any help there. I said, 'It's against the terms of my licence to stop a girl being raped?'

'You shouldn't have been on that estate. You shouldn't have been mixing with those people.'

I turned to the woman sitting beside me. 'My licence says I can't go to Newcastle without permission for four years. Is there anything in it about any other places I can't go?'

There was a haunted look in her eyes, as though she was being asked to look at something she didn't want to look at. She didn't say anything. I said, 'You are a solicitor, right?'

She cleared her throat. 'Actually,' she said, 'I'm an articled clerk.'

'They cost less than solicitors,' said the DS. 'And it's the taxpayer picking up the bill. And there's no point spending more on you, because the outcome is inevitable. You're going back to jail where you belong. And this time you'll stay there.'

I said, still to the woman, 'What does it actually say in my licence?'

She said, 'I don't know. I haven't been given a copy.'

If there hadn't been so much at stake, I'd have laughed. 'Did you ask for one?'

'Let's not make a song and dance about it,' said the sergeant. 'You're also guilty of assaulting three men. One of whom I do believe is going to press charges against you.'

'I was preventing them from raping someone.'

'Assault is assault. Whatever excuse you might think you have.' He leaned forward across the table we were sitting at. 'I don't know what the do-gooders think they're doing, letting trash like you out on the street. You always end up back inside. Always.' He turned to the girl beside me. 'We're holding your client overnight,' he said. 'Unless there's anything you want to say?' He was standing up as he said this and the girl stood up with him.

'Just a minute,' I said, my head throbbing. 'Are you going to be representing me in court tomorrow? How are you going to do that if we don't talk about it?' She looked at the sergeant and he said, 'Tomorrow. You'll have five minutes with him before he's called.'

Then they both left and a uniformed sergeant led me to the cells.

* * *

So this was how it ended. The Lotus Estate did not let go that easily. It was a bog, a quicksand and it pulled you back and sucked you down whatever you might think you could do to escape.

I had a terrible headache and I was wondering how to go about getting some aspirin and a glass of water when the cell door opened and a copper said, 'You've got a visitor. Follow me.'

The visitor was Mister Howard. I asked how he'd known I was there and he said, 'Constable Doyle told us. He's really upset.'

The policeman who'd brought me here had stayed in the room. He was on a chair against the wall out of the way but he was listening. I made a little nodding movement in his direction, keeping my eyes on Mister Howard to warn him to be careful what he said but it was clear he didn't understand me. The copper did, though. He smiled. Not in a friendly way.

Mister Howard said, 'Tell me what you need us to do.'

I said, 'There's nothing you can do. I stopped a girl being raped and it seems that was breaking my licence. They're sending me back to prison. If I'd walked away and let them do it, I wouldn't be in trouble.' Then a thought struck me. 'You could ring Miss Brown.'

'The Education Officer?'

I nodded. 'They're supposed to give you one phone call when they arrest you but I haven't had it. Let her know what's happened, will you?'

'I will, Billy. And cheer up. It's always darkest before the dawn.'

Honestly. The things people say when they want to cheer you up. The stupid, ignorant things. I didn't suppose Mister Howard had ever been in trouble with the law. I would have laughed but the throbbing in my head was becoming almost unbearable. I said. 'You haven't got any aspirin, have you? My head's killing me.' He started to search his pockets but the copper said, 'You can't give anything to the prisoner, sir.' I said, 'I really need something for my head,' and the copper said, 'We'll get you something.' Then I said I was sorry but I needed to lie down, I didn't think I could take the pain in my head any longer and Mister Howard stood up and put his hand on my shoulder and told me again that everything would be all right and I said, 'Don't forget Miss Brown. Please.'

When the copper was taking me back to the cell I said, 'You won't forget my aspirin, will you?'

'As soon as the doctor says it's all right to give you some.'

I said, 'Is the doctor here?'

'He'll be in tomorrow.'

'Please. I just don't think I can wait that long. I've had my head caved in with a brick. Could you call him?'

'He'll be in tomorrow.' Then I was being pushed into my cell and the door was locked behind me.

I didn't sleep. I know people say, "I didn't sleep a wink" and although they really believe it the fact is that they've slept for hours, but I didn't sleep. My head hurt so much it felt as though it was still being hit regularly by a half brick every half minute and, anyway, all I could think of was jail and the fact that I was going back there and how all the luck I'd had to go with my hard work and other people's help had not been enough. I was angry and I was bitter but I was also giving up. Being nothing was what I had been born and raised to and I wasn't going to get away from that fate.

It was five in the morning when a faint light first appeared behind the thick glass bricks that did the job of windows in the cell and something had happened, I knew that, because suddenly there was a copper in my cell, a different copper, and he was handing me a glass of water and two tablets. Then another policeman came in with two slices of toast on a plate and said, 'Here, Billy, lad, eat these. You shouldn't take pain killers on an empty stomach.'

They both watched me eat the toast and swallow the tablets with the water. There was a lot of butter on the toast. Then one of them said, 'Smoking's not allowed in the cells, Billy. But we can take you out in the yard if you want a drag?'

I said, 'I don't smoke,' and the copper said, 'Oh. Okay. We don't get many people in here who don't smoke,' and I said, 'But thanks, anyway. Really, now that I've had those pills, I'd like to try to get some sleep?' and the copper said, 'Okay. Just shout if you want anything.' Then I said, 'What time am I going to court?' and the copper said, 'Oh, not today, probably,' and the other copper said, 'There's been a bit of a rethink on that,' and then I knew something had happened and I started to feel a whole lot easier about things.

When they went out, they didn't lock the door behind them. I lay down and pretty soon the pills started to do their work and I fell asleep.

I didn't wake till after nine and no-one tried to make me. It was only a minute or two after I opened my eyes that I heard someone say, 'He's awake,' and a couple of minutes after that the doctor who'd originally bandaged my head came in with two coppers and shone a light in my eyes. He asked some questions about how I felt, had I been sick, did I want to be sick and then he wrote a prescription and handed it to one of the cops who hurried off with it. 'Just heavy duty pain killers,' the doctor told me. 'There's no real damage done but a head that looks that messy on the outside can't feel very nice on the inside.'

Then the other policeman walked me through the cell block and into a lift and took me up to the fourth floor, which was the top floor. On the way a uniformed sergeant handed me some clean clothes. They were mine and when I looked surprised he said, 'Constable Doyle picked them up from your digs. You must be about ready for a change of clothes. Especially with all that blood on the ones you're wearing.'

The cop took me through a large office with a big desk at which no-one was sitting and showed me into a bathroom. There was a shower and a toilet and a washbasin and a mirror and two big, clean towels. Now, of course, I realise it was the private facility for whoever was the big cheese in that Station, but then I didn't have a clue what it might be. I was sure prisoners didn't usually get to use it, though. He put a sponge bag in my hand. It was my sponge bag with my razor and shaving gel and my toothbrush and toothpaste. 'No hurry,' he said. 'Get yourself good and clean, make yourself feel human and then there's someone waiting to see you. We'll give you breakfast while you talk to him. It'll just be a canteen breakfast, I'm afraid, but it's okay. We get fat on it.'

The someone waiting to see me introduced himself as Milan Kundashi. He was a lawyer and he explained that his firm and Mister Henry's worked together. 'And don't worry about our fee,' he said. 'Someone you know in Newcastle is paying.'

This conversation was not taking place in an interview room. We were at a table in the police canteen and I had a plate of bacon and eggs and sausage in front of me. Also two slices of toast and a mug of tea. There weren't many other people in the canteen, and those who were sat some distance away from us.

I said, 'They gave me a duty solicitor.'

'She's been told she won't be needed.'

'How did you know I was here?'

'Your Miss Brown was very busy yesterday evening. Her and your agent. Jessica something?' He opened his briefcase and took out a printout of the front page of a newspaper, which he handed to me. It was the *Newcastle Journal* and the headline read *Zero to Hero – and Back Again?* There was a picture of me, taken when I was at Jessica's gallery to receive my prize. I read the story closely.

Zero to Hero – and Back Again?

BL McErlane is no stranger to readers of this newspaper. As Billy McErlane he won first prize in an essay writing competition. As Zappa McErlane he was sentenced to imprisonment at Her Majesty's Pleasure for the murder of his stepfather, Antony Baker. And as BL McErlane he became Young Photographer of the Year and his work is increasingly sought after and steadily increasing in price. All this – and he hasn't finished his A levels yet.

And now, if police in Buckinghamshire have their way, he may never do so. Billy McErlane was arrested yesterday and is to be placed before a magistrate this morning with a view to having his licence revoked and his liberty curtailed. His crime? Single handedly preventing six violent hoodlums from raping a young girl.

In the course of this brave and praiseworthy action, McErlane's head was staved in with a brick, knocking him unconscious, but he held off the six thugs and kept the girl safe until police arrived. Police who had been summoned by Billy himself. His reward is to be sent back to jail.

Justification for locking McErlane up again is hard to find. The first reason advanced by the police was that "He should not have been there." We have read the terms of the licence releasing him very carefully. At no point does it limit his freedom of movement, provided only that he stays away from Newcastle until he is twenty. Faced with this, the police then said that they were taking their action because, in protecting the girl they wished to rape, McErlane had assaulted three of the gang. It seems that Buckinghamshire Police make no distinction between a person using what force is necessary to prevent a violent and obscene crime from taking place and those seeking to carry out that violent crime in the first place. Indeed, they informed us that one of the would-be rapists wished to bring a charge of assault against McErlane and that he would be afforded every assistance in doing so.

Late last night we were able to contact the Home Secretary as he left a party function. He assured us that he would be in touch with the Chief Constable of Buckinghamshire to ensure that McErlane's case would be thoroughly reviewed before any action that might later be considered questionable was taken.

As well as my photograph they had one of the Home Secretary. He looked as though he had eaten and drunk well before being doorstepped. I said, 'So what happens now?'

240

'This man will tell you.' He raised a finger towards a man sitting on the far side of the room. It was the detective sergeant who had arrested and questioned me the day before. The one who was so pleased by the prospect of getting my licence revoked. He came over and sat opposite me. As I finished eating my breakfast he said, 'Constable Doyle suggested I call inspector Walsh in Newcastle.'

'Sergeant Walsh?'

'Yes, well, he's an inspector now. You've behaved very stupidly. Twice.'

'Twice?'

'According to inspector Walsh, you let yourself be framed for a murder you didn't commit, which was the first very stupid thing. And then you consorted with this gang, which could have got your licence revoked and was stupid thing number two. We're going to release you. You can consider yourself lucky. I suggest you try to avoid doing a third stupid thing.'

'Yes. I mean, I will.'

'How did you know these people, anyway?'

I explained about the project and he said they'd need to examine my computer. I'd get it back, but they had to check whether I'd "unwittingly" taken pictures of any illegal activities.

Before I went home to hand over the PC, Milan Kundashi said he needed a few more moments with me. In private. The DS left us to get on with it.

Kundashi said, 'Don't let that sergeant's smile fool you. You've made yourself an enemy there. I suggest you give him no excuse at all to have a second bite at the cherry.'

'I won't.'

'He didn't call Newcastle because this Doyle fellow asked him to. He did it to cover his arse. I made him cough up the tape of your interview yesterday. He didn't caution you. He hadn't even arrested you. And if I'd made a transcript public he'd have been in a lot of trouble, just for his attitude.'

'Would you have done that?'

'I told him I would. And then there's the Press. As you will find out when we leave here. In the old days, the Police and the Home Secretary would have ignored any fuss the media stirred the public into making. Better hang an innocent man, as long as the innocent man didn't go to a good school, than undermine public faith in justice by admitting you'd made a mistake. Now, you get three old biddies with a PR mouthpiece who knows her stuff and the cops are falling over themselves to give the public what the police think the public thinks it wants. I don't know which is worse.

'Anyway, early this morning we managed to get the Deputy Assistant Chief Constable out of bed. He wasn't very happy. I offered him a deal and at first he told me to go to hell but after I'd explained the pain we were going to inflict on his Force and the certainty that we would have near one hundred per cent public support for the brave young man who'd seen off six would-be rapists at immense personal risk and now faced going to jail as a result he saw sense. He and I have done a deal. The deal is this. Any journalist asks how you feel about the Police, you feel great about them. They never threatened to take you to court and you can't imagine how the papers ever got hold of such an idea. They treated you like the hero you are. Yesterday they wanted to take you to hospital, but the A&E wards for miles around are full and patients are sleeping on trolleys in corridors. You said you felt too groggy to move so they offered you the blue light hotel. Comfortable room, looked a lot like a cell but the door was open, no-one bothering you but someone keeping an eye just in case.

They even fed you in the middle of the night when you felt hungry and they gave you a slap-up breakfast later. The doctor was watching over you so closely you probably got more medical attention here than you would have done in hospital.'

'That's rubbish!'

'It's the deal. You don't have to say it because I'll read a statement on your behalf on the steps of the police station when we leave, but any time you're asked you remember the deal we made. Okay?'

I nodded. 'If that's what it takes.'

'And whatever you think of that sergeant...'

'I don't even want to think about him.'

'...keep it to yourself.'

He was right about the Press. There were two television cameras and a whole bunch of photographers. They shouted questions while Kundashi read his statement and crowded round the police car that was going to take me home. Later, they were outside the hostel gates. I stayed home all day – didn't go to college, didn't see Wendy or Melanie. My head didn't hurt as much as it had, but it hurt. I slept for several hours. I didn't know when I'd get my PC back but I'd already decided to buy a new one, fitting to my status as celebrity photographer. I said a silent thank you to Joe Walker who'd hammered into me that I must always back my files up to an external drive.

When I woke, Missus Howard told me they'd saved lunch for me. Then she said Jessica had been calling and wanted me to call her back as soon as I was awake. And then she said the TV people had gone but the photographers were still outside and they were photographing everyone who went in and out and did I think I could possibly, *please*, give them all a joint interview in the garden so that they'd go away? Because people who lived in the hostel did not, by and large, want their photos in the paper. I said, yes, of course, but first I must ring Jessica.

'Pictures!' she screamed as soon as I called her. 'I need pictures and I need them *now*, Billy. You're so hot I could boil a fucking kettle on you.' Honestly, the mouth this woman had on her. I started to explain that I didn't think I had any that were quite ready to go public yet but Jessica wasn't buying that. 'Don't give me the temperamental fucking artist shit,' she yelled. 'Does Damien Hirst think he's an artist? No! Does Tracey Emin? Fuck me, I should certainly hope not. Real artists don't make a collage of their soiled knickers or turn shagging three hundred men into performance art. They're in the entertainment business, Billy. They're celebs. No different from Graham Norton and Lady Gaga. And that goes for you, too. We live in a celebrity culture. You can be the hottest thing on legs today and tomorrow nobody remembers who the fuck you ever were, so make your money while you can. Real artists can have all the talent in the world, but they starve in fucking garrets and no-one makes any money out of them till they've been dead fifty years. Is that what you want?'

It wasn't what I wanted, but when I tried to explain that I'd been working so hard on my project I hadn't had time for anything else she wouldn't let me finish. 'Your project is what I *want*, Billy. Right now, that's what you're famous for. You're the fucking hero who made a study of ghetto life and intervened to stop six pieces of shit from raping a girl. So give me pictures of the fucking ghetto. I'll double the price I've been charging. And I'll quadruple it if you've got any of the actual attack taking place.'

'Jessica, those men are going to trial. If we wreck it by selling pics of what they were up to before they've been tried I'll be back in prison before we've banked the money and this time I really won't get out.'

'So we save those until they've been sent down. And then we flog them to the *Sunday Times* as well as sticking them on punters' walls. But the ghetto, Billy. I must have ghetto pics.'

'It's a sink estate, Jessica. Like the one I grew up on. It's not a ghetto, for Heaven's sake.'

'Billy!'

I'd pushed her far enough. I promised she'd have fifty pictures good enough to sell by the end of the week. 'I'll start on them as soon as I've given this press interview.'

'Press interview? Wait, Billy! Wait till I'm there!'

But I knew what delay in getting rid of the hacks would do to the Howards, so I just said, 'I can't do that, Jessica,' and hung up. Then I went out and faced the Press.

I went to college as usual the next day. I was welcomed as a hero, the man who'd risked being maimed to save a girl from a fate worse than death. When I got back, Missus Howard said the police had been round and wanted me to go to the station as soon as I came in. I'd turned eighteen a week earlier and didn't need a responsible adult with me in the interview room, but Missus Howard said she'd sit with me if that's what I wanted, which it was. It wouldn't have been if I'd known what they wanted to talk to me about but I didn't. I assumed it was about turning the rapists in and she'd think what a hero I was.

The first thing the copper said was that Melanie had been arrested and questioned on suspicion of unlawful sex with a minor. Missus Howard came upright in her chair. I didn't want to look at her but I had to. She looked hurt, as though she'd trusted me to behave in a way she could respect and I had failed her. The policeman said they knew I'd been under age because the pics on my computer all had a Properties tab which showed when they'd last been saved or processed and the dates on many of what he called "the most interesting shots" were before I'd reached the age of sixteen. He said if Melanie had thought I was sixteen she probably wouldn't have been arrested, but she had access to my records and must have known how old I was. I gave a statement for the second time in three days and then we left.

Missus Howard drove into the Tesco car park. I went to get out of the car but she stopped me. 'I don't want to buy anything, Billy. I needed somewhere we can talk. Have you ever noticed there aren't any attractive places to park in this town?'

I said I hadn't.

'No, well. I suppose you have to be a driver to notice things like that.' She sat quietly for a while. Then she put her hand on my wrist. 'I'm sorry you had to go through that, Billy.'

'It was all right, Missus Howard. They were doing their job.'

She turned slowly to look at me, without removing her hand. 'I didn't mean the police. I meant what that woman did to you.'

'Oh. Yes.'

I could tell she was finding it hard. I said, 'What will happen to Melanie?'

'She'll lose her job. Of course.'

'Oh.'

'Billy. Actions have consequences. As you know as well as anyone.' She went on with some stuff I'd rather not have had to listen to. Stuff about how different the world would be if only people understood that pleasures had to be paid for and sometimes you had to ask yourself whether the gratification you'd get out of what you were thinking of doing would be worth the price you'd end up paying. 'What I've just said would describe eighty per cent of the people who go through our hands. Guy is unusual in that he's from a comfortable middle class background. You expect middle class people to have learned self-restraint. Mostly, what we get are people from where you're from.'

I was watching a woman taking raisins from a packet and feeding them to a toddler.

'Mister Howard and I have been interested in the way you and Guy have become friends,' Missus Howard said. 'You'd think you'd have more in common with the others. Why do you suppose that is?'

'I don't know'.

'Would you like to hear what I think?'

I grinned and she smiled back. She was a good sport, Missus Howard. Her theory was the obvious one, that I was good with words and so was Guy and I was quick on the uptake and so was Guy and none of the others were either of those things and so Guy and I sought each other out. I couldn't argue with any of that.

But the Melanie thing hadn't gone away and when Missus Howard asked why I was so gloomy when it wasn't me who'd done anything wrong, I said I had done something wrong. I'd kept pictures on my computer when I'd promised Melanie I hadn't and wouldn't and now it was going to cost her her job, and maybe a criminal record (though in fact, as it turned out a few months later, she was let off with a caution).

That gave Missus Howard a problem. She really had it in for Melanie, for exercising *droit de cuissage* on a helpless young boy who didn't dare say no to her, but she couldn't approve of breaking a promise.

(It was Guy who explained *droit de cuissage* to me. He said it was usually known as *droit de seigneur*, but *seigneur* meant Lord and he wasn't sure of the right word for Lady in this context. "Not that lady would be quite the word we're looking for. *Droit de putain*, perhaps." It's a good job I didn't understand what he was saying or I'd have dropped him. He said *cuissage* meant someone getting your legs apart and that was usually considered the chap's job and the thighs that had to be parted should belong to the girl and did I feel the slightest bit feminine when I was with her, old boy? I asked him if he'd like his teeth in his hand to play with and we went on with the snooker game we'd been playing before we got started on the French.)

And all this time I hadn't heard from Melanie.

But now I did.

'How could you do that to me?'

'I'm sorry.'

'You're sorry. You think that makes it all right?'

The mobile felt like a brick in my hand. Her ex was stepping in to look after her. He was going to take her away until the fuss died down. One of his conditions was that Melanie and I had no further contact. Ever. 'But you needn't think it's just him, Billy. You betrayed my trust. I don't want to see you or hear from you ever again. Do you understand?'

'What about our meetings? What about your reports?'

'There are no reports, Billy. I haven't needed to report on you for months. You're free. As long as you don't get into trouble, no-one will bother you.'

'Oh.' So why hadn't she told me that before? Just what exactly did she get out of having me believe my freedom from minute to minute depended on her?

'And you're *not* in trouble. I am. Thanks to you.'

'I'm sorry.'

'Just do me one last favour. Can you do that?'

'Of course.'

'When reporters bang on your door, say nothing to them. Will you do that for me?'

'Yes. Of course.'

Reporters? Oh, no.

But it did no good. Reporters came and although I didn't say anything to them about Melanie, not one word, they wrote their stories anyway.

One thing I hadn't expected came of all that. Although they knew I was out because they'd read it in the papers I had never told anyone at home where I was and now they knew. One afternoon as I was walking home a black BMW slowed down, the passenger side window opened and Marcus handed me a package. The window rolled up and the car drove on.

In the package were five thousand pounds and a note telling me not to put it in the bank because of money laundering rules. Regus had promised me a payoff when I got out and here it was.

And why hadn't I told Poppy? Because it was over between me and her and had been since before I was released on licence. The YOI was too far away for her to be able to visit easily but I'd written to her every week and she'd written back. She'd told me about her new home, and how much better life was when her mother only had one job and was home so much more, and what a good school she was at and how she'd got eight GCSEs and was confident of good enough A levels to get a university place. She wanted to read History. She also said how good it was that I might be able to do A levels, too, and how much she was looking forward to us being together again. After a while, though, that bit of her letters stopped being repeated. The letters themselves became shorter. Less informative. More like someone going through the motions.

I could hardly interrupt Melanie when she was sitting astride me with nothing on to ask her advice about the girl back home, but Dave Wilson could see that things weren't right and when he asked if anything was the matter I swore him to secrecy and then told him about Poppy. He was sympathetic but he held out no hope. 'Teenage relationships are difficult. And teenage relationships at a distance are impossible. She sees other young men every day and she's bound to fall for one. Everyone does. It isn't her fault. You can't go away from her the way you have and expect her to remain true. It isn't realistic. People aren't like that. She may look at some other guy and think, Well, he isn't Billy. But at least he's here. And you're not there, and there's nothing you can do about it.'

Listening to that was hard. It was worse than hard. It took three or four weeks – weeks during which I went on sending the same sort of letter I had been sending – before I could bring myself to write this one.

Dear Pops

I've had to steel myself to write this but I'm writing it in love and kindness and I hope you will read it in that light. I've had the sense for some time, when I read your letters, that you were writing out of duty and I don't want you to do that. If you are ready to move on I'd like you to say so. I still love you the way I always loved you but I can't be with you and maybe you need someone who can. If that's so, I won't stand in your way. And I really don't want to go on getting letters that you're writing in the time when you're not out with somebody else.

All my love for ever,

Billy

I looked at that letter when I'd written it and then I went for a shower. When I came back to my cell, I knew I couldn't send it. The mess we were in was my fault, not Poppy's. However much I loved her, I owed it to her to set her free without saddling her with feelings of guilt. I tore the letter up and wrote another one, which I did send.

Dear Pops

I'm sorry but it's time to be realistic. You're leading your life up there and I'm leading mine down here. I'd love to think that one day we'd be together again but in my heart I know that isn't so. Every time I write to you I feel miserable and every time I get a letter from you I feel worse, so I've reached a decision – I'm not going to write to you again and I'm asking you not to write to me.

Thank you for being the person you are,

Billy

When I sent that letter I felt really low – so low that I went out and talked to the other prisoners which was something I didn't normally do unless I had to. It was like I was putting myself on suicide watch. I did, though, feel a sneaky virtuousness at the idea that I'd sacrificed what I wanted to set the person I loved free. What the screw who censored the mail thought of my letter I don't like to think about even now.

CHAPTER 40

I'd never seen Wendy like this.

'I just want to know one thing, Billy. I'm sure I already know the answer, but I want to hear it from you. When you were sleeping with me, were you also still sleeping with that woman?'

Of course I had been. And that did it for me with Wendy. It took time for me to accept that – I couldn't take it in that what we had had was broken and couldn't be mended. A week after she'd ended our relationship, I turned up at the door of her granny flat. I said, 'Wendy, please. Can we talk?'

She stared at me as she might have at a mugger. 'We don't have anything to say to each other that hasn't already been said.'

'But I miss you so much.'

She didn't say a word. Just shut the door. I stood there for a while before I walked away. When I got back to the hostel, Guy asked if I'd been crying, and if so what about? I told him it must be hay fever.

'There's no pollen at this time of year, Billy.'

'Just mind your own business, will you?'

We both had to go on going to college because we had a target and we were going to meet it. Sometimes I'd turn and find Wendy watching me. She'd look away immediately, but the pain was there in her eyes.

We did have one more meeting, and what we discussed was choice of university. We'd already planned our applications so we'd have a chance of spending the next three years together and now Wendy didn't want that. So we agreed that, if we were both accepted by the same place and got our grades, one of us would turn it down. The one of us in question being me. Wendy said that was only fair.

As it happened, we needn't have bothered.

Jessica had sold all the pictures I'd entered in the competition. After matting and framing costs and her commission, I'd still cleared more than three thousand pounds. Then she sold all the pictures I sent her after I thought I was going back to prison and they brought in more than twice as much. I still had almost all of the money from the bargain range, which Jessica had invested for me. I was happy, but Jessica wanted more. 'We need to keep the momentum going, Billy. We need to hold an exhibition.'

The exhibition was a huge success. It was written up in the Sundays and the monthlies and everyone who was anyone came. I, the reclusive artist, stayed away.

Some people, though, I had to meet.

Jessica worked hard and she networked and she knew a lot of people. Norwich University of the Arts has a Fine Art BA course with a Printmaking & Photo Media option. Jessica said I should go there if I could. She invited some people from Norwich to the exhibition and they said they'd love to have me as long as I could draw as well as take pics, you have to be able to draw, it's an Art degree and not just photography, lots of art schools have given up on drawing but they weren't one of them. They said they'd seen the exhibition and that would more than count for my portfolio, but I would have to show them some of my drawings. So I did.

There was a bit of umming and aahing then, because although my drawing was better than most people's it wasn't by any means as good as the best they saw at Norwich. The word "amateur" was spoken. More than once. In the end, they offered me a place as long as I worked hard at drawing in my first year and showed some improvement.

Jessica said I'd have three years of lectures and teaching from some of the best artists in the world, some on the staff and some visiting. My mind would open. My horizons would expand. Most importantly, I'd learn everything I needed to know about printing.

Three days after arriving in Norwich I was on the bridge over the River Wensum, looking up at the St Georges Building with its four storeys of Victorian red-brick and pondering how best to frame it, when a man in a tracksuit spoke to me. 'Can you run?'

'I don't often need to.'

'No, but can you? We're short of a Centre and you look the right sort of build. But Centres need to be fast. Not as fast as Wings, but nippy for all that.'

He didn't sound like a lunatic. I said, 'Would you mind telling me what you're talking about?'

'You're not a rugby man?'

'No. No, I'm not a rugby man.'

'Would you like to be?'

And that is how I came to start playing rugby. As it turned out, he – the club coach – had made a good choice because, although pace is something a Centre needs, being able to give and take hits is even more important. As I'd told Missus Howard when we were at the arboretum and she asked me about being in care, I'd had the advantage then that I didn't care about being hurt. I had it still. For most of my first season, until I began to understand how the game was played, I was a liability tactically but right from the start I brought strength and power to the team and they welcomed me.

One Saturday morning when we were getting ready for a visit from a local club the captain took me and Chas Burley, our Fly Half, to one side. 'Watch out for their Number Six. He has a name for late tackles. You get the ball away, you're relaxed and not expecting anything, and then this guy hits you like a truck. Everybody knows about him but he gets away with it every time. He'll put you in hospital if he can.'

I could see why he'd warn Chas, fly halves get late hits all the time, but why me?

'Word's getting around,' he said. 'People are talking about you. You're a danger, so you're a target.'

I won't give all the details of the move here; I saw a T-shirt a while back that said, "The Older I Get, The Better I Was" and I think that's true for most ex-players. Of any sport. What I love to remember, especially if I have a glass of something in my hand, can only bore other people. I'll just say that it happened just as he'd said it would. I took evasive action, and the next time their Number Six and I were at close quarters I gave him a shot in the ribs he wasn't likely to forget, big though he was.

When the final whistle blew, we had won by one point. He was walking towards me with a grin pasted from one side of his face to the other. We shook hands and walked off the field side by side. After we'd showered, we met again in the bar and he bought me a beer. 'Any time you want to play serious rugby, come and join us.'

'You think college rugby isn't serious?'

He put his arm round my shoulder. 'You know what we think, when we come here? Usually? Fucking upstart college twats. That's what we think. Let's bring the fuckers down a bit. But you...you'd fit in anywhere, mate.'

In my second season they made me Vice-Captain. Year three, my final year at Norwich, I was Captain. I suppose I was surprised, but the coach said, 'You never raise your voice, and yet people do what you tell them to. In fact, you don't tell people, you ask them, and they don't say No. You're the best leader we've got.'

I wondered what Poppy would have said if she could have heard that. But then, I wondered a lot of things about Poppy. Most of all, I wondered how I could ever have been stupid enough to let her go.

Every Easter, we went on a rugby tour. Why a college in East Anglia should have chosen to tour in South Wales I have no idea, but they'd always done it and it was not to be questioned. We did the best we could, but it wasn't enough; Wales is rugby country in a way that England isn't and the young men we played against had grown up in the same village, playing with each other since they were eight years old. We weren't smashed in any of our three games, but we were beaten in every one of them.

On the last evening we were in a village of fewer than fifteen hundred people that has produced two Wales captains and Heaven knows how many players who've turned out for their country and the big Welsh and English clubs. That afternoon it had felt like we were playing every one of them. They'd laid on a spread in the clubhouse and we were drinking beer and eating.

After three years and three tours, I knew our opponents pretty well and they knew me. I was walking slowly along the clubhouse wall, looking at the shirts brought back from Australia, New Zealand, Argentina, France and the pictures of players who had exchanged them for their own club and country shirts at the final whistle. A young man a couple of years older than me put his hand on my arm. He had played at Inside Centre in each of my games here; we'd crashed into each other a few times. I said, 'Hello, Glyn.'

'Billy. You've met Ceri.' I had. Ceri and Glyn had married since our last visit and Ceri, a slim and beautiful Welsh girl when I had seen her the previous year, was still beautiful but now large in the way only impending motherhood could explain. 'Thing is, Billy, there's a favour we want to ask.'

I looked from one to the other. Ceri smiled and I thought it would be a hard man who could refuse a request from her. She said, 'We're having a baby.'

'Yes. I mean, I see that. I mean, congratulations.' We all laughed.

'What we wondered,' Ceri said, 'was whether you'd be godfather?'

'Me?'

'If you would.'

'But...I can't. It wouldn't be right.'

They looked disappointed. Ceri said, 'You don't have to be religious. It's not like that any more.'

'No, it's not that. It's...Ceri. Glyn. You'd be saddling your child with a convicted murderer for a godparent. I'm an ex-prisoner. I'm out on licence.'

'Oh, we know that,' said Glyn.

Ceri said, 'We do get newspapers in Wales, you know.'

Glyn said, 'Everybody here knows you're supposed to have killed someone.'

'And nobody thinks you did,' said Ceri. 'Or, if you did, he deserved what he got.'

'Thing is,' said Glyn, 'and the reason we picked you, you carry this lovely air of calm with you. Even on the rugby field. It's like you've been through terrible things no-one should have to endure and you haven't just survived, you've blossomed.'

'And that's what we want for our boy,' said Ceri. 'That example you can set him.'

'How do you know it's a boy?'

'A scan, Billy. So will you?'

Of course I said I would. That was the day I realised the old Billy was dead. I still recognised him and I always would, but he was invisible to anyone else.

My first girlfriend in Norwich was Amanda. I saw her looking at me almost from the moment we both arrived.

The old Billy would have done nothing about it and probably been surprised if she had made an advance – as surprised as I had been when Wendy wanted to go to the Ball with me. The new Billy, or at any rate the emerging Billy, did things differently.

She was in the union bar and I don't know whether I'd have approached her in the way I did if two pints of beer on an empty stomach had not given me courage. I said, 'My place or yours?' and she said 'My flatmates are out,' and took my hand.

I never did a poll and I can't be sure what percentage of first year students had sex but my guess would be: not as many as said they did. What I can be more certain of is that most of the sex wasn't very good. Not enough foreplay. All over too soon for both parties. These were young people, many of them doing it with a real person for the first time, and each as much in the dark as the other. I'd been taught by Melanie. The older woman of legend.

That first afternoon, when I raised my face from the junction of Amanda's thighs after bringing her to orgasm with my tongue, my face was spattered and fragrant with her juices and hers was a picture of ecstasy. 'Where,' she gasped, '*where* did you learn to do that?'

Of course I didn't tell her the truth. I was rolling a condom into place and she said, 'You don't need that. I'm on the Pill.'

'I'll use it anyway,' I said. 'Belt and braces.'

Except when she had her period, Amanda and I must have made love to each other every day for five weeks. Then it was over. What ended it, according to Amanda, was my selfishness.

'I'm on the Pill. The *Pill.* I can't get pregnant. You don't *need* a condom.'

'I won't make love without one. Sorry.'

'But *why?* You know it reduces my pleasure.'

'Oh? You don't enjoy it when we make love? You could have fooled me.'

'William. It's *my* body and *I* will control it. Not you. I don't suppose there's another man in this college who uses those things. Well. Apart from the gays. And you're not gay. I'll give you a written testimonial to that effect if you like. But if you won't stop using them, you and I are finished.'

She wouldn't give way and neither would I. We broke up. She found someone else and I found Cheryl. That lasted a few months and when it ended I found Katy. When Katy and I were through, Marcie turned up.

We met in the pub after rugby. Marcie was Australian and she said she had a thing about rugby players; they reminded her of home. Well, maybe. Marcie was the Queen of the Put-Down – she never used it on me but I saw her reduce girls to tears and men to silence with carefully directed scorn. I didn't like it and I realised after a while that I didn't like her, either, but she was wonderful in bed and we stayed together longer than maybe we should have.

The background to my time with all of these girlfriends was Poppy. In bed with them I did things I'd never dreamed of doing with her, but when I thought about love – the future – permanence – Poppy was who I thought about.

I held back from making contact because I didn't know where she was, what she was doing or who she was doing it with, but in the end I couldn't hold back any longer. I wrote her a letter telling her where I was and what I was up to and I addressed it to the flat in Gosforth with the request, which I hoped her mother would respect, to forward it to her. At the last moment I cut out and slipped in with the letter a picture from the back page of the *Eastern Daily Press* with the caption, *Billy McErlane goes over to score the try that gave the collegers unexpected victory over Elton Manor.* That felt like a good insight into my life.

I looked daily for Poppy's reply. It never came.

You're nineteen; you think you're fully formed; that the way you are is the way you're always going to be; but it isn't so. Actually, it's never so, but at the end of your teens it's even more not so. What would have happened if I'd known this when Regus told me what the deal was, I can't imagine. He'd have killed me, probably.

After I'd accepted that Poppy was not going to write back I had a couple more girlfriends but I didn't let any of it get serious. I learned to drive, because I thought it was long past time. And I enrolled in a rugby training camp, where I learned to be a better Centre than I had been.

When I graduated I spent one last evening at the rugby club and next morning I loaded my stuff into a rented car and set off on a four and a half hour drive from one side of the country to the other.

CHAPTER 41

When I was living with the Howards, Guy had talked a lot about where he went to school. One weekend we went by train to see it. I hardly said a word. If I had, I'd have given myself away.

The place Guy most wanted to show me was where the beautifully kept grounds of his school sloped down to the River Severn and the school boathouse. There was another boathouse just upstream from it and Guy said that was the town rowing club, as opposed to the school one. We weren't looking at it from the school side but from the opposite bank of the river. Just along from the two boathouses was a pub with a garden outside and then houses. Big houses, some of them converted into flats.

The point of this, the thing I'm keeping hidden in this description the way I hid my excitement from Guy, is that on this side of the Severn is a park. A big park, with people walking in it and riding bikes and doing the other things people do in parks, and some of them were families. I'm not going to suggest it was almost all families, because it wasn't, and I'm not going to say that everyone was happy and didn't shout at each other because some of them did. But there was a lot of that.

A lot of people who were happy and didn't do any shouting. And sometimes you'd see a father and a mother and a boy and a girl and sometimes there'd be a dog. And some of the people did have their arms around each other's waists and they talked to each other as they walked along and generally looked like people who like each other a lot. And sometimes a boy threw a stick for a dog, and sometimes a little girl twirled around on the path, watching her skirt be like a Catherine wheel.

It wasn't just the side of the park where the river was that had houses and flats overlooking it. The opposite side had gates that led right into the middle of the town, but the other two sides also had homes, one more than the other.

I took photographs of the park and the boathouses and the school grounds and the pub and the big houses some of which were divided into flats and later I printed some of them for Guy. I let him think I had taken them for him.

But I hadn't.

I took them because I knew one day I'd use them for what, in the weeks before leaving Norwich, I did use them for.

I was twenty-one, I wasn't short of cash and I knew there was more coming because I had a commission from the *Sunday Telegraph* and another from *La Stampa*. And Jessica had been selling my stuff quite regularly, and the prices had been going up.

So during my final term I explained to Jessica what I wanted and sent her some of the pics I'd taken on my visit with Guy and she talked to a couple of estate agents and found an apartment for sale overlooking the park. I hadn't even seen the place, just pictures of it, but I knew it was the flat of my dreams. The one I'd written about for the psychs while they were evaluating me. No-one would give me a mortgage because I didn't have a regular income, so Jessica raised one in her name, took money out of my account for the deposit and rented the flat to me. We agreed I'd pay off her loan and take ownership of the flat as soon as I had the money.

I might have a flat but I had no furniture, so I checked into a hotel while I set about making the flat what I wanted it to be. It took three weeks to get the walls stripped of paper and painted in the colours I wanted and curtains finished, furniture in place, kitchen and bathroom remodelled and all the pots, pans, cutlery, glassware and crockery I had chosen delivered. Jessica had told me we needed an extra twenty thousand on the mortgage to pay for all of this and I used every penny.

I had never had a place of my own before. I'd walk from one room to another, just for the sake of doing it. I'd touch the walls, the painted woodwork, the top of a sofa and the back of a chair. I'd stand for ages staring out of the windows, watching the people in the park.

I bought a food mixer with a dough hook and started making my own bread. I bought books on cookery and watched programmes on television and pretty soon I learned that you didn't need to follow recipes slavishly. If you were someone who liked food, and I am, what you needed to learn was techniques and not recipes and then you could do what you wanted. I bought a wine rack and filled it.

And then the tentacles of The Lotus Estate reached out and grabbed at my ankles.

CHAPTER 42

It was early morning when Jessica called me. 'Have you seen the papers?'

'I'm not up yet. What have you said this time?'

'This wasn't me. I'm sure someone will bring you a copy. Probably a journalist. They'll want a statement. Say nothing. Refer them to me. Understand?'

I showered, dressed and made breakfast, wondering what could possibly be causing so much fuss. I didn't have long to wait.

The woman on the doorstep said she was from the local paper but the one in her hand was a London tabloid. She wanted to come in.

'I'm sorry,' I said. 'It isn't convenient right now. Why don't you call my agent?'

'I can do that, of course. But I thought you might want to put your side of the story as soon as possible.'

'Story?'

'This story,' she said, waving the paper at me. 'Perhaps you haven't seen it yet.'

I took it from her hand, which was clearly not what she'd intended, and said 'Thank you.' As I walked into the sitting room I could hear her banging on the door, then shouting through the letterbox. I went back into the hall and said, 'Jessica Robinson is my agent. She'll be happy to talk to you.' Then I shut the sitting room door behind me to drown out her persistent voice. I sat down to read.

A Mother Sits and Waits

Photographer BL McErlane is riding high. Hanging one of his signed, limited edition prints on your wall will cost you. He shoots some of the glossiest high impact advertising around. For Sunday supplement assignments he earns serious money. Don't expect to see the man himself in the Sundays, though, or anywhere else. His agent Jessica Robinson chooses what he does with care and one of the things he doesn't do is interviews.

We should thank him. The world is full of celebrities who cannot bear to see a week go by without sharing their most ordinary thoughts. Who isn't pleased by a man who lets his work speak for itself?

But one person would love to hear from him – not just weekly but daily. His widowed mother.

She sits alone in a Newcastle flat, not far from the house in which she raised the artist and his five brothers and sisters. 'All gone now,' she says. 'That house was filled with laughter all day long and half the night. Now there's just me.'

Does no-one return to see her? 'My two oldest daughters are very good. They live near and I often look after my grandsons. Chantal has little Zappa, he's eight now, and Leanne's Dillon is four. But the boys? I don't even know where Tyler is, and I only hear about Billy when he's in the news.'

She always knew her son was born for greatness. 'His father died when Billy was still too young to remember him, but his stepfather treated him like his own. They used to sit there on the sofa together, making each other laugh. It was Antony who bought Billy his first camera.'

What message would she send her famous child? 'Just call me, son. A mother worries. Let me know you're all right.'

I rang Jessica. 'I've seen it. What do you think I should do?'

'Do? You should do nothing. It's publicity, and all publicity is good, but if you try to defend yourself you'll wreck it. Journos only have to go back through their files to see the gaps between what she's saying now and what came out at the trial. Leave it to them to do it. All we need from you is dignified silence. The woman who wrote that piece knew it was bullshit as she hit the keys.'

'Don't they care about the truth?'

'Grow up, Billy. Red tops don't worry about facts. All they're interested in is what will make the punter buy their rag instead of someone else's.'

'Okay,' I said. 'You're the boss.' I went to the window, the phone still in my hand. 'She's out there with a snapper. Did I tell you I bought a Mercedes convertible? They're shooting it.'

'Of course. They'll run their own follow-up. Picture of your mother's poverty-stricken flat; picture of your fancy car.'

'It's second hand,' I said. 'Will they have paid her?'

'Probably slipped her twenty quid.'

'Okay. I might hit the road for a while till things calm down.'

'Send me the pics.'

Hitting the road seemed like a good idea, and not just to avoid the Press. I had unfinished business and now could be the time to deal with it.

Poppy was in my mind and she wouldn't leave. I'd set up a Facebook account just to track her down but she didn't seem to be on it. Clearly, her mother had not passed on the letter I'd sent Poppy from Norwich. I wasn't going to leave it there, because I couldn't. I thought about her while I was awake and I dreamed about her when I slept.

I didn't have a satnav but I logged on to StreetMap and printed a map showing where Poppy's mother lived. I also typed Newcastle into Tripadvisor and booked a room in the Jesmond Dene Hotel. Then I put an overnight bag in the Merc's boot and set off for Gosforth.

I'd never met Missus Cannon. When she realised who I was, her face took on a very set look and I thought I'd been right – she hadn't wanted her daughter consorting with a murderer.

'Can I come in?'

'Close the door behind you.' She walked ahead of me into the sitting room. When I got there she was holding against her chest what looked like a framed picture that she had obviously taken off the wall. 'Sit down. Would you like a cup of tea?'

'That would be lovely.'

She took the picture away. I hadn't been able to see it but I guessed: Poppy's wedding photograph. My visit was in vain. I was too late. When she came back with a tray she said, 'You've got a nerve. Coming here after you broke my daughter's heart.'

'Me?'

'You. You said you didn't want to hear from her again. I've never seen a more heartless letter.'

'But…Missus Cannon…I wrote it for her. Because I loved her.'

She placed a mug of tea on a coaster in front of me and pushed a plate of chocolate biscuits in my direction. A memory came back to me: Poppy making tea and putting biscuits on a plate, the first time I went to her house. That day when she asked if she could be my girlfriend. The day after Regus had intervened on my side against the yobs. The day after I sold my future to the devil. She said, 'You dumped her because you loved her. I suppose that could make sense. If you were a halfwit.'

'It was obvious from her letters that she'd gone off me. I knew she was seeing someone else.'

The crack as she snapped a biscuit in half was violent. 'Listen to me. The only boy Poppy ever thought about was you. She never went with anyone else. And then you cast her off.'

'Oh.' My world was being violently rearranged. 'Is that why you didn't pass my letter on?'

'You think I open letters that aren't addressed to me? I didn't know who it was from till she told me.'

'Oh. So she got it.'

'She got it. If you've been blaming me because she didn't write back, you can stop.'

Of course, there was another side to that. If Poppy had got my letter, not replying had been her own decision.

'Is she with someone? Married?'

'I don't think that's your business.' I just didn't have an answer to that and I sat there and stared at her and then she said, 'Well, I suppose it might be your business. But I don't know if she'd want me to tell you.' When I still didn't say anything, she said, 'Look. Give me your address. I'll tell Poppy you called. She can decide whether she wants to be in touch. And don't let your tea go cold.'

I took out the notebook I used to record details of the pics I took, tore out a page and wrote down my address, email address, home phone number and mobile number. I added the URL of the blog Jessica paid someone to maintain in my name. Then I handed the page to Missus Cannon. Why I was doing this when I knew from the picture that Poppy was lost to me, I didn't know.

'Thank you. I'll send it to her. I'm not making any promises.'

'But you won't tell her not to get in touch.'

'Billy. You're in the news. You're obviously doing well. Why should I tell my daughter to have nothing to do with a man whose making money? But I warn you – Poppy is not a gold-digger and she won't want anyone to think she is. The fact that you're getting rich will be one more reason for her to want nothing to do with you.' She stood up. 'Wait there. Before you go there's something you can do for me.'

When she came back this time she was carrying the picture she'd taken away and I realised she was about to tell me how forlorn my hopes were. I saw how wrong I was when she turned it over and laid it on the table. It wasn't a wedding photo; it was one of my prints – the one Jessica had called *The Future*; the one she'd used to announce the Art for All series. I couldn't believe it was here. I just looked at it.

'Poppy gave me this. She knew I wanted something to put on that wall, over the fireplace.'

'It's one of mine.'

'I know it's one of yours. I'd like you to autograph it, please.'

I took out my pen once more and turned the print over so that I could release it from its frame. 'She didn't have to buy this. I'd have given it to her.'

'When I said she isn't a gold-digger, were you listening? She bought it because she's proud of you.' I looked up and smiled and she said, 'But don't read anything into that. You wrote to her. If she'd wanted to get together, she'd have written back.'

There was something she hadn't said. I didn't know what it was because you don't, you only know what people do say, not what they don't, but there was something. I could tell. And then, when I was at the door and about to be on the other side of it, she said it. 'It was that woman that did the damage.'

'That woman?'

'The older one. The one who lost her job over you.'

'Melanie.'

'Her. All the time you were away, Poppy kept herself decent for you. She had plenty of offers but she turned them all down. Even at college. I'm not saying she never went out with a boy because she did but she never...you know.'

I nodded. I did know.

'And then that got into the paper. While she'd been saving herself for you, what had you been doing? Well, we know what you'd been doing.' She put a hand on my sleeve. 'Poppy's a sensitive girl. And that's a lot to forgive.'

I didn't go straight home; I spent that night in the hotel room I'd booked and then I tootled slowly down B roads and roads that didn't qualify even as B, stopping in farm gateways to take pics and staying the night in pubs in out-of-the-way places.

When I got back to my flat, there was no sign of any journos. There was a lot of mail on the floor but none of it was from Poppy and nor was her voice one of those I heard when I dialled 1571.

I got on with my work but I was thinking all the time about Poppy. Processing pics, it came to me that I had none of her – I hadn't been a photographer when she and I had been an item. We'd never even gone into one of those little booths outside supermarkets where people get passport photos taken. I thought if I was never going to see her again, a photograph would at least be something to remind me of her. I wrote to her mother and asked if she had one she could spare.

When the phone rang next morning I picked it up and said "Billy McErlane."

'This is Poppy. Will you please leave Mam alone? She isn't why we're not together, and neither am I.'

I felt suddenly hot; sweat was standing on my skin; my heart was beating so loudly I could hear it. 'Poppy? Oh, Pops. I can't believe I'm speaking to you.'

'Nor can I. Not after the way you treated me. Listen. If you want to meet, we'll meet. As friends, Billy.'

'Where, Pops? Where?'

'I live closer to you than you probably think.'

I felt so excited I thought I might be sick. 'Tell me where and tell me when and I'll be there.'

'Do you know Birmingham?'

'I've been there. I wouldn't say I know it.'

'There's a Museum and Art Gallery in Chamberlain Street. I'll be having coffee there at eleven on Saturday. You can join me if you want to. But I want you to understand this, Billy. We'll be two old friends having a coffee together. No more than that.'

Of course I was there early. Since our phone call I hadn't been able to focus on anything else. I'd had emails from Jessica demanding to know what was going on.

When Poppy came in she smiled at me, the kind of smile you might give to someone you hardly knew, and queued at the counter. I went and stood beside her. 'Let me get this.'

272

'No, thank you. Go and sit down.'

When she joined me she had a scone and a cappuccino on a tray. She set them down carefully; just as carefully she buttered her scone and spread jam on it. She took a sip from her coffee cup. She looked at me. 'It's your meeting.'

I assumed that was to tell me to get on with it. 'It's lovely to see you.'

'Thank you.'

'Poppy...' I had come here knowing what I wanted to say. It deserted me. She waited for me to go on. 'I don't know where to start.'

'No?' She ate some scone and drank some coffee but she wasn't as distant as she wanted to appear. She put the cup down and reached across the table to take my hand in hers. 'Oh, Billy. What am I to do about you? Why did you dump me like that?'

'I'm sorry, Poppy.'

'I'm not asking whether you're sorry. I'm asking why you did it.'

'I thought you needed a chance at something better.'

'Wasn't that for me to decide?'

'And I thought you had someone else.'

She finished her scone and brushed her hands together, shaking off the crumbs. 'I gather Mam put you right on that.'

'She made me realise what I'd thrown away.'

'Billy. You know back then? At school? When I asked if I could be your girlfriend?'

'Yes?'

'I wasn't in love with you. I wanted to be your girlfriend because I wanted to be safe and I thought being with you would give me that.'

273

'I knew that, Pops.'

She took her hand away. 'That changed. When I realised what a special person you are. I came to see how lucky I was that you'd chosen me. Well, you hadn't, I'd chosen you, but that was what I told myself. That you'd chosen me. And I knew how lucky I was because I knew I didn't deserve you. You never pushed me, you never asked for what I didn't want to give, you talked to me as though I mattered.'

'You did matter. Do matter, I mean.'

'Do you understand how rare that was on the Lotus? Any other boy there – girls were objects. Sperm receptacles. Someone to slap when they were upset. Someone to hang on their every word, tell them how brilliant they were even though we knew they were dummies and never object when they made us feel small. The men are so horrible, it's a wonder every girl on the Lotus doesn't turn out a lesbian. But I had you. You were a dream, Billy. Except that you weren't, because you were flesh and blood. It didn't matter how long they kept you in; I'd wait for you. I'd work hard and go to uni and get a good degree and a good job so I could look after you and keep you when you were free. I imagined our life together – the children we'd have, the house we'd live in, the garden you'd keep while I was out being the breadwinner. Where we'd go for our holidays. I thought about you all the time. And then you wrote to me. You took all my dreams and broke them. Tore them into little pieces and stamped on them.'

'I'm sorry.'

'I swear if you say that again I'll smack you.'

'So what do we do now?'

She sat in silence for what seemed like ages. Then she shook her head. 'This wasn't supposed to happen. I was going to make you understand how you'd hurt me and leave you sitting there. After I'd given you this.' She reached into her bag and pulled out a photograph. Her, in her robes, at a university graduation ceremony. 'That was going to be your only reminder of me. For ever.'

'And now?'

'I don't know, Billy.'

'What do I have to do?'

'Mam likes to watch the old movies on TV. You know the ones.'

'I don't, actually.'

'No, I suppose not. Romances, I'm talking about. Where they never leap into bed together and the man woos the woman.'

'Woos?'

'Woos. You have heard the word, I suppose? Maybe it's just a librarian's word these days.'

'A librarian? Is that what you do?'

She nodded. 'Thanks to Mister Hunt and the deal you made with him I did everything I'd set out to do. I got my GCSEs, got my A levels, went to uni and got a Two-One in History. Then I looked for a job where I'd never have to meet people like the ones we were at school with. A library was perfect.' She reached across the table and laid her hand gently on mine. I felt like folding her in my arms but I didn't. It was far too soon for that. 'I'd like to be wooed, Billy. Nice and slowly, and with care. Mind, I'm not promising anything. You might be wooing for nothing.'

'I'll take my chances.'

'You can start today. Take me somewhere nice. Make me feel important.'

CHAPTER 43

I didn't deserve Poppy. If she'd been a vindictive person, the sort to make me pay for the hurt I'd inflicted, I couldn't have complained but she wasn't. She was someone who loved and I don't think she knew how not to do it.

The wooing did not take a long time. I think all she wanted was to know that I really was as sorry as I'd said I was and that I was still, underneath, the person she remembered. It was our third date. She'd never invited me to her place and she hadn't been to mine but that Saturday she had come to Shrewsbury and we were walking in the park. She said, 'Do you remember asking if I ever got a hug?'

I could feel myself going red. 'I wasn't trying it on.'

'I know you weren't. I think that was the first proper hug you'd ever had.'

'It was.'

'Thing is, Billy, I'd like it back.' She turned to face me and drew me close. She smoothed my chest with her hands. 'This is a nice jacket.'

'I bought it in Bruges. I gave myself a weekend there a few months ago. Lovely place.'

'Nice enough to go twice?'

'Oh, sure. It's…'

'We could go together, maybe.' Her arms wrapped themselves round me and I enfolded her in mine. Her face was tilted up, asking to be kissed, so I kissed her. We stayed like that, two people clasping each other, and I had that feeling I hadn't known since Wendy; had never felt with Amanda or Katie or Cheryl or Marcie. Or Melanie, for that matter. It's a physical thing, tenderness: the raising of hair on your skin; the warm closeness; the sense that you're with someone to whom you matter as much as they do. People went by us in both directions. They went on bikes and skateboards and roller skates and some just walking. People on their own, people with friends, couples, couples with children. There were squirrels running up and down trees and across the grass. All of that was going on; and Poppy and I just stood there and held each other.

She said, 'It's coffee time.'

'There's a Costa not far away.'

'Actually, I was thinking of your place.'

She walked round the flat looking at things while I made coffee. After she'd taken her first sip she said, 'It's decision time, Billy.'

'That makes me very nervous.'

'Oh, I've made mine. It's you, Billy – you're the one who has to decide. Is this for ever? Or just a nice interlude?'

My heart beat fast. 'It's for ever, Pops.'

She nodded. 'When you got out of prison, did they give you your condoms back?'

'Eh? Oh, I...'

'I'm asking if you'll keep me safe, Billy. I still don't want a baby.' Her eyes came up to hold mine. 'Not till I'm married.'

'I'll take care of you.'

'You'll be gentle, won't you?'

I wrapped my arms round her. I kissed her: on the forehead; on the cheek; on the throat; on the lips. She kissed me back. She eased herself out of my grasp, took my hand and led me towards the bedroom. Just before she gave herself to me she said, 'How much do you love me?'

'Up to the sky and down again, a million times.'

'You'd better, Billy Mac. You'd better.'

I was in a completely new world. How do you know you're in love? I've got a bird recognition book and when I'm looking out of the window if I see a bird I don't know I can check in the book and find out what it is but there isn't anything like that with men and women. There's no love recognition book that says things like, "If your heart beats faster when you think about her and if thinking about her is what you do all the time and if you're overcome with tenderness when you kiss her and touch her, oh, boy, better watch out my friend because you, sir, are in love." There's nothing like that.

That's how it was, though. I'd thought I was in love with Wendy, but I'd never had with her what I had now with Poppy. I *did* think about her all the time. I *was* filled with tenderness when I held her. She was the first person I'd ever met who was more important to me than I was. It wasn't sex, though sex with Poppy was far more important than it had ever been with anyone else. When I thought about my life and what I wanted to do with it, Poppy was the central element of every dream I had. I couldn't imagine a future without her.

One of the Sundays was running a series they called *Heritage Villages* and Jessica got me an assignment to take photographs of Cartmel. It's in Cumbria; I had to look it up to find that out. Poppy took a few days leave and we went there together. We arrived the Wednesday before a Bank Holiday weekend because Bank Holidays are when National Hunt race meetings take place in Cartmel and I wanted pics both of solitude and of the organised mayhem that surrounds a race meeting.

At six o'clock on that Thursday morning in May, the sky was blue and the sun was at exactly the right angle for landscape shots. I'd thought Poppy might like a little more time in bed, but she got up and walked with me, on my right because I held the camera in my left hand and we liked to touch.

We had to let go of each other when I wanted to photograph the church. It was a beautiful shot, ruined by the presence of two green waste bins and a blue plastic recycling box in front of the old stone wall. Poppy said, 'Shall I move those out of the way?'

'No need. I'll delete them when we get home.'

'How on earth will you do that?'

'It's one of the simplest things you can do. I'll just draw a ring round the bins and the box and tell Photoshop to do a contextual fill. The program will replace them with more wall. You'd know it had been played around with if you blew it up big enough to look at it pixel by pixel, but who's going to do that?'

'That's amazing.'

I got my pics and we walked into the church grounds, once more hand in hand. Poppy said, 'I must come back when it's open and pick up a leaflet. Find out how they held onto those beautiful stained glass windows.'

'Why would that have been difficult?'

'This is a huge church for a small village.'

'Yes, I can see that.'

'That's because it was a priory. There were monks here since the twelfth century. One prior and twelve monks. Like Christ and his apostles. Henry the Eighth hanged four of the monks and if it hadn't also been the villagers' church he'd have destroyed the priory and sold the land. A hundred and twenty years later, Cromwell and his maniacs would have seen the windows as papist. They'd have wanted to smash them. So how come they're still here?'

I was staring at her. How did she know all this?

'I googled the place before we came.'

'So did I. I didn't notice any of that.'

'My degree was in history, Billy.'

We left the church and walked through the square towards the race course. We'd be back here when the races were on, there would be crowds of people and this road to the car park would be closed because horses in some of the races would cross it, but right now there was only us and a man walking a Labrador that was too old to run very fast or very far.

'Would you like a dog, Billy?'

'A dog? I've never thought so. But if you do…'

'No, I don't want a dog. I just wondered about you. There's far more stuff I don't know about you than stuff I do.'

We talked about our childhood and I learned things about Poppy's family I'd never heard before. She wanted to know if I was in touch with my brothers and sisters and I said I wasn't, couldn't even say where some of them were. How about her? Yes, her mother was in touch with all her children, which meant Poppy was in touch with them, too.

'What about your father?'

She shook her head. 'He disappeared. Just cleared off. I have no idea where he is.'

'I don't think anyone ever knew who mine was.'

And then, I suppose inevitably, there was the big one. She turned me round to look straight at her and took hold of both my arms before she was ready to ask it. 'What about children, Billy?'

'Children? No. I'm pretty sure I don't have any children.'

She dug me in the ribs with her hand. 'I mean, do you *want* any?'

'Yes,' I said, and I knew that it was true. 'I want children. But I want to be married first.'

'Tell me why?'

'Because I want to end the cycle.'

She nodded. Her face was very close to mine. 'Okay. Do you have a particular bride in mind?'

I pulled away without answering. I turned from the track and we walked along a broad belt of grass with trees to the side until we came to a fence, at which point I had to get the camera in both hands again because beyond the fence was a group of buildings in an open field that said everything the editor paying for my trip wanted to know about how the past could exist harmoniously in the present. Poppy watched me as I framed my shots. 'You see things that I don't,' she said.

'And you know things that I don't.'

'We can learn from each other.'

'I already have. Learned from you, I mean.'

When I lowered the camera she hugged my arm. 'What? What have you learned?'

'I was with Wendy, and you know about that. I was also with Marcie, though I don't think you do know about that. There was whatever I had with Melanie. All of those times were good times but I was always still just me. This is different. I feel now like there's a new person called BillyandPoppy and I'm half of it.'

'Do you mean PoppyandBilly?'

'That too.'

'And which is best?'

'You know which is best.'

'Yes I do. But I want you to tell me.'

'Being half of PoppyandBilly will always be better than just being Billy.'

'That's how I feel. So why didn't you answer my question?'

'Your question? What was your question again?'

She slapped me on the arm. 'This marriage you want. Do you have anyone in particular in mind?'

'I suppose I do, yes.'

'Who, Billy?'

'You, my wonderful one. You.'

'Right answer, Billy Mac.' And she took my head in her hands and pulled it down and kissed me.

She looked at her watch. 'They'll be serving breakfast. Shall we go back to the hotel? And while we're eating, you can tell me about Marcie.'

Race day was another beautiful day. I'm not a gambler, but you don't have to bet to enjoy the colour and spectacle of a race meeting and the bravery of those small men (and two women) taking big horses over huge jumps was something to see.

Not all photographers were focused only on the racing.

Poppy stood close to me as I waited for a shot of galloping horses with a row of houses as background. She said, 'Those gardens come right down to the course.'

'I know. That's why I want these pics.'

'There's a gate in the fence of one of them. You could walk straight out of that garden onto the track.'

'I've seen it.'

'Do you suppose they lock it when the racing is on?'

'That's one of the things I'm going to have to find out.'

At that point, a man I'd never seen before stepped between us from behind and placed a black and white print in my hands and another in Poppy's. As we were looking at them, he put one arm round my shoulders and one round Poppy's and said, 'Over there.'

I could tell that Poppy had looked up, but she didn't realise who this was or what was happening and I did, and I tucked the photo I was holding of her and me hugging into my pocket and kept my head averted.

'Billy,' the man said. His tone was wheedling. 'You're a celeb. Everyone knows you. I'm just a poor guy trying to make my way in a tough world. Give me a break, eh?'

I thought about it, but I didn't have to think very long. I knew how lucky I'd been when Jeff Thomson broke into the prize ceremony at Jessica's gallery and turned me from an unknown into somebody. I also knew, because Jessica had told me, that the Press can turn against you just like that and if they do they can make your life a misery and your good fortune a thing of the past. I looked up, faced where I knew his photographer would be standing, and smiled.

'Thanks, Billy, mate.'

'How long have you been watching us?'

'Long enough. Have you got any news for our readers?'

'If we have an announcement to make, you'll hear it from my agent.'

'Of course. BL McErlane doesn't give interviews. Can I say that you and Poppy Cannon seem very happy together?'

'You're a journalist. I'm sure you'll say whatever you want. You can get another shot if you like, and then I have a job to get back to.'

'Lovely, Billy. Can I have the two of you turned in a bit? And talking to each other? Poppy, do you want to move a bit closer to Billy? That's lovely. Thanks, guys.' He put a card into my hand. 'Any time you want to give a struggling hack a hand up, call me. If I can do you a favour in return, I will.'

I caught his arm. 'Actually, we may have something for you.' I looked at Poppy. 'Is this okay?'

'You're the one the public knows, Billy. You call the shots.'

Without taking my eyes off her I said, 'I have asked Poppy to be my wife. I think she must be mad, but she has agreed.'

The journo was in close, pumping my hand and kissing Poppy on the cheek. I could see his photographer snapping away. 'Let me be the first to congratulate you,' he said. 'I *am* the first?'

'We won't tell anyone else for twenty-four hours. That should give you the time you need.'

'Thanks, Billy, mate, you're a star. What's your agent going to say?'

'She'll probably kill me for letting it out like this. You owe me.'

'Any time, Billy. Any time.'

'How did he know my name?' Poppy wanted to know when the journo and his snapper had gone.

'It's his job.'

'Will it always be like this?'

'You want to think again? About marrying me?'

'No, I don't want to think again.' She shrugged. 'I'll learn to put up with it. Billy?'

'Mhm?'

'This business of getting married?'

'Yes?'

'It won't just happen, you know. We have to plan it.'

'I suppose we do. No-one I know ever got married. I'm sure we can work it out, though.'

'You know you lied to that man?'

'Eh?'

'You said you'd asked me to marry you, and you hadn't. Haven't. I had to come damn close to asking you.'

'I'll call him back and tell him it was the other way round.'

'You will not.'

'I was teasing.'

'So ask me.'

'What?'

'*Ask* me. For God's sake, Billy, *propose!*'

I took a deep breath. Was this what I wanted? Yes. It was. 'Poppy. Will you marry me?'

'Well. I might.'

'What?'

'You don't get an answer to that question straight away, Billy. Jane Austen's leading men didn't, and you don't. You'll just have to wait.'

CHAPTER 44

In the car on the way home, Poppy said, 'Church or Register Office?'

'Eh?'

'The wedding, Billy. Where do you want it to be?'

'Oh. You've decided to accept then, have you?'

'Provisionally. If no better offer comes along.'

'That's very nice. Assuming you actually go through with it, I want what you want.'

'Church, then. So I can wear a nice white dress. With a veil and a tiara.'

'Okay.'

We drove on for a while, with Poppy fiddling with the collection of CDs I kept in the car. She put on *Blue is the Colour* by The Beautiful South. 'I love this one,' she said. At the very first track, she beamed. 'I'm glad you have the original album version, and not that one they made for radio.'

'I didn't know there was a difference.'

'Don't marry her, fuck me? The BBC won't play that, so their version says "take me" instead. And they wouldn't stand for "sweaty bollocks", either. They made them substitute "Sandra Bullock".'

'Who is Sandra Bullock?'

'She's an *actress*, Billy. *Demolition Man. Miss Congeniality.*'

'I don't go to the pictures.'

'We're going to have to change that. Didn't she win a Best Actress award? She did. She earns a fortune.'

'I'm very happy for her.'

'She was married to Jesse James.'

'Jesse James? Isn't he dead? That dirty little coward that shot Mister Howard has laid Jesse James in his grave.'

'Not that Jesse James. Let's shut up and listen to the music.'

When the CD finished, Poppy was still singing from that first track. 'I'll never grow so old and flabby, that could never be; don't marry her…'

I said, 'I hope you will grow old, and I hope you'll do it with me.' I was aware, though I didn't say so, that I'd interrupted at that point because I didn't want her to use the F word again. 'But I agree. You're too lovely ever to be flabby.'

'You're so sweet, Billy. Billy…When we were at school…did you mind when I wouldn't go to bed with you?'

'You never said you wouldn't go to bed with me.'

'I said I would if you wanted to. But you must have known I didn't want to and you must have known I was pleased when you said you didn't.'

I smiled. 'Yes, Pops, I did know that.'

There was no responding smile. She looked serious, as though this mattered a lot. For me it was in the past, a book I had closed, but it wasn't that way for her. 'So did you mind?'

'No. I didn't mind. And later on I was pleased.'

'Oh? Why?'

'Because Kylie had already given me a dose. I didn't find out till I got to Young Offenders and they gave me a medical, but if you and I had gone to bed together I'd have passed it on to you.'

I thought I'd gone too far. Poppy looked horrified. 'You had sex with Kylie?'

'Yes. I did.'

'*Kylie?* Billy, how *could* you?'

I shrugged.

'Jesus Christ.' She was shouting. 'Stop the car.'

'I can't, darling. It's a motorway.'

'Darling? *Darling*? You tell me you went to bed with Kylie and then you call me *darling*?'

I drove on. Listening to her saying nothing, I realised that that didn't happen often and I decided I didn't much like it. We must have covered ten miles before she spoke again. In a very quiet voice, she said, 'You are all right now?'

'Yes. Sorry, I didn't mean to shout. Yes. They treated me in prison and I'm clear. I haven't given you anything.'

She relaxed, though not a lot. Her body was turned away from me, to the extent she could do that in the passenger seat of a car. 'How did it happen? You and Kylie?'

When I'd told her the whole story, she had turned towards me again. She said, 'I'm disgusted.'

'I'm sorry, I…'

'Not by you. By Chantal.' She sighed. 'I never liked Chantal, but…' She looked at her lap, her fingers intertwined. Then she put a hand on my leg. 'How could they treat you like that?'

'Can I call you darling again?'

Her hand was still on my leg. 'Yes, darling. You can call me darling, darling.' She kissed her fingertips and placed them against my cheek.

We stopped at the next service station and got two coffees which we drank sitting quietly together, holding hands.

* * *

My escapade with Kylie was forgiven, because when we got back to Poppy's apartment where no-one could see us she wrapped her arms tight round me and held me close. She said, 'I want you to take all your clothes off and get into bed.' I did that very happily and she went to the bathroom and then joined me.

Afterwards – some time afterwards, to be frank – she got up and said, 'I'm cooking tonight.'

Poppy didn't have the same regard for food as I did and her cooking was a lot like Wendy's had been in the granny flat. We had grilled sausages, a grilled tomato, boiled potatoes and peas. There was lots of butter on the potatoes and HP Sauce on the sausages and I enjoyed it. While we were eating, the subject of marriage came up again.

'Who will you ask to be your Best Man?'

I hadn't thought about it, and said so. She sat back in her chair. 'You do want to marry me, Billy?'

'Poppy, you know I do.'

'Well, then, you need to think about these things.'

'I suppose the obvious person is Jessica.'

'No, Billy. I'm sorry, but no. Your Best Man cannot be a woman.'

I hadn't really been serious. I thought about Guy and rejected the idea. 'How about the last captain before me of my rugby team at college?'

Her eyes lit up. 'Perfect. Will he do it?'

'He will if I offer him enough free booze. Probably bring some of the other guys, too.'

'Which will be useful, because I don't see us having too many of your people there.'

I didn't, either.

There was another silence from Poppy. Then she said, 'I'm sorry, Billy.'

'Eh? What for?'

'I've seen other girls getting so bound up in their wedding plans they couldn't think or talk about anything else. I always swore I wouldn't be like that. I'll try to stop.'

'It's a big day,' I said. 'It's important.'

'The life we lead afterwards is more important than what colour gloves my bridesmaids wear.'

She was silent again for a while. Then she said, 'And that's another thing! Who am I going to have as bridesmaids?'

I looked at her. She was suppressing a grin, and then she wasn't suppressing it any more. She leaned over and kissed me on the forehead. 'I didn't know you were captain. Were you a good rugby player?'

Next morning, Jessica was on the phone.

'How many times in your life do you plan to get married, Billy?'

'Just once, I hope.'

'Really. All the more reason to handle it properly, then. You should have let me make the announcement. That's my job. Instead of which, I read about it in the paper. Now. The arrangements for the wedding. Do I talk about that to you or to her?'

'Her?'

'Your fiancée. Your bride. We'll need to set up an interview and I'll have to prepare her for it.'

'You'd better come here.'

Poppy had to go back to work and I was at my place, so we arranged to meet in Birmingham that Thursday evening.

* * *

Jessica kicked off by saying, 'I've talked to *Hello* and they'll pay for the whole thing. There'll be a cap, of course, it's not like Billy's a Premiership footballer or a singer or something, but it will be more than enough for a big spread. Poppy, I'm arranging for a designer to advise on the dress. Now. How far have you got with a guest list?'

Poppy said, 'Not far. But, then, it won't be a very long list. And there will be no *Hello.*'

'Poppy. Celebrity doesn't last for ever. If Billy has ten years of earning at his current level, he'll be doing well. He has to cash in while he can.'

'I'm not having my wedding turned into a circus. And I'll choose my own dress.' She put a hand on Jessica's arm. 'Let's not fight. I know how important you are to Billy. He couldn't have got where he is without you. But I hate those big vulgar football star weddings. We'll make a virtue of the fact that ours is quiet. Just close friends. You wouldn't be my chief bridesmaid, would you?'

Jessica had turned pink. 'I think at my age it had better be Maid of Honour,' she said. 'But I'd be delighted. I think you're on a good line here. Spurning the riches on offer to spend your big day quietly together and focus on the future. Yes, I think we could make that work. Especially if Billy makes a charitable donation on the day.'

Poppy said, 'You'd better decide who it should be to.'

I had been watching Poppy with something like awe. She was treating Jessica in a way that I would almost have guaranteed would result in open warfare between them, and Jessica was eating out of her hand. I'd never doubted that Poppy was the woman I wanted and needed to marry, but if I ever had I'd have stopped right now. The woman was brilliant.

'Do you have a date in mind?' asked Jessica. 'Only there's an assignment in the offing that Billy would be perfect for. It would lead to a book, he could make a lot of money and if the book came out around the time of the wedding he would make even more. His donation could be a percentage of the royalties.'

'Ah,' said Poppy. 'Well. I think it needs to be sooner rather than later.'

'That sounds intriguing.' As so often in my life, the third person in a conversation saw the point before I did.

'We both want to be married before children arrive. Which I'm afraid means we're on a deadline.'

After she'd said this, she sat there with no expression at all on her face. Nothing. Jessica, though, was smiling. Both of them were looking at me. Then Jessica laughed. 'He doesn't know, does he?'

Poppy said, 'I only confirmed it myself this morning. But there's no doubt.'

I said, 'Will someone please tell me what's going on?'

Jessica said, 'For a successful man, Billy, you can be very slow on the uptake.'

Poppy said, 'I'm pregnant, Billy. I didn't mean to be and I'm sorry, but…'

'Sorry?' I was on my feet; I was by her side; I was hugging her. I was laughing and on the verge of crying at the same time. With all the tenderness I could muster, I kissed her.

'I think Billy is telling you you don't need to be sorry,' said Jessica. 'Are you certain enough for me to tell the Press?'

'I'm certain,' Poppy said again. 'But just hold the announcement till Billy and I have been up to Newcastle and seen my mother, will you?'

* * *

When Poppy rang her, her mother wanted to know whether Poppy thought marrying a convicted murderer was a sensible move for a girl with a good degree. Poppy said we'd visit her as soon as possible, and we decided that had better be the very next weekend.

It went as well as I could have hoped. 'I suppose we can call that an armed truce,' said Poppy as we drove away two hours later. 'Conditional acceptance.'

And then we drove to the place neither of us wanted to see again.

The Lotus Estate had somehow diminished during my time away. The streets no longer seemed as long or as wide and the open spaces looked less generous. Considering how high unemployment was supposed to be, there weren't many people around. I said, 'My mother's moved. She's in a flat now. How are we going to find her?'

'We'll stop by that shop,' said Poppy. 'And ask.'

The shop was also a Post Office and it was where people collected their pension, their benefit or their dole. On the other hand, they might know where everyone lived but they weren't about to share the information with two strangers. Especially strangers who had a Mercedes sitting by the kerb. No-one round here with one of those could be up to any good. As we were walking out, a young woman with a child in a pushchair was going in. I didn't recognise her but she knew us. Poppy squeezed my hand. 'Hello, Shannon.' Shannon. Of course.

'You two,' the girl said. 'You stuck it out. Still together. Good for you.'

I smiled in silence while Poppy admired the child and chatted to Shannon as though they'd only seen each other the other day. Then she explained what we wanted.

'Billy's mam?' said Shannon, the tone of her voice changing slightly. 'Oh, aye. Ah know where she lives. Just wait while Ah buy me tabs and Ah'll show you.'

When Shannon came out of the shop, taking a cigarette from a packet of ten Lambert and Butlers, Poppy said, 'Is it far? Only…' and she gestured with her head towards the Merc.

'Is that your car? Eee, ya bugger. That's lovely, man, Poppy. No, it's just round the corner.' She stepped back into the shop. 'Mister Patel!' she shouted. 'Me friends are leaving their car here. You'll make sure nothing happens to it, won't you?'

'Aye, you're all right, pet,' said Mister Patel.

Reading the story about my poor widowed mother sitting at home waiting for me to call, you'd have pictured a miserable tower block with lifts that didn't work and the stink of urine on the stairs. It wasn't like that. She lived in a three storey building, each floor a separate flat. The Council kept the garden on two sides in good shape and the area at the back was asphalted for parking cars and to hold the wheelie bins. Against the other side was an identical building.

Shannon pointed at the door of the ground floor flat. 'If she's in, she's in there.' She looked at us both and smiled. 'I'm glad you're doing well.' Her eyes flickered towards my mother's door and came quickly back to us. 'Don't let anything spoil it.' She tossed the stub of her cigarette into a shrub in the apartment building's garden, took hold of the pushchair and wheeled it away.

I looked at Poppy. 'Shall we?'

'It's what we came for.'

My mother hobbled to the door on two sticks. She stared at us, her eyes going from one to the other and back. Was my mother short-sighted? Had she always been? At last she realised who she was looking at. 'What do you want?' she said. She turned away, dropped the sticks on the floor and walked unaided into her sitting room. I shut the door and we followed her. I said, 'What's with the sticks?'

'I'm disabled.'

'Oh. Right.' I started to laugh.

'If you've come to take the piss you can get out.'

A small boy was pressed against the wall, his eyes fixed on us. He had the most beautiful pale brown skin, tight curly hair and brown eyes and he must have been about four years old but he didn't say a word. Poppy knelt down in front of him. 'Are you Dillon?' she said. The boy's eyes flickered away towards my mother and back to Poppy but still he was silent. Poppy said, 'There's a bruise on his neck.'

My mother's face was red and angry. 'Listen, you,' she said. 'The last thing we need is somebody reporting us to the Social. We know how to bring children up.' Her head swayed in my direction. 'Look at him. He must be a millionaire now, which will be why you've got your claws into him, and he started out just like Dillon there.'

The sound of my mother's raised voice had Dillon cowering, pushing close to Poppy. She put her arms round him. I watched Dillon hold on to her as she pressed her lips to his cheek and he nuzzled close and it came to me. My career, Poppy, getting married – everything had come together. I had it all.

I looked back at my mother. 'Why did you tell that pack of lies to a journalist?'

'I didn't tell her anything. She came with her story ready. Did I do this and did we do that? She just wanted me to say Yes. So I did and she gave me forty quid and she went off happy.' Her eyes drifted away from me. 'If you want to know, you weren't the story I wanted to tell her. You've never been the story I wanted to tell. But no-one wants to hear about me.'

She was right, of course; nobody did. Including me. I was twenty-three years old and you don't get to twenty-three without knowing everything you need to know about your mother. Or so you think. 'I had ambitions,' she said. 'I was going to be a model. Or an actress. Your granny had a man at the time, he said I looked like Susannah York. He knew people. Agents. He was going to put me on a catwalk. But he put me on my back instead. By the time your granny found out I was too far gone. That's how I came to have Chantal.'

'And the man?'

'She kicked him out.' Her red and rheumy eyes fixed suddenly on mine. 'See? You want to know about the man. No-one wants to know about me.'

I'd never heard any of this before. She'd never talked about her past and the dreams she might have had – or, if she had, I hadn't heard her. I put out a hand to take hers, but she snatched it away. 'If you want to do something for Dillon, send us money.'

I took out my wallet and put five twenties on the table. My mother snatched them up without a word. 'Come on,' I said. 'We have to go.'

My mother didn't come to the door with us.

Outside, Poppy wiped a tear with the heel of her hand. She said, 'He's being beaten. You could see it under his shirt. A little tot like that and he's being beaten.'

'Why should he be any different?'

'And he's terrified. All the time we were there he didn't say a word. Did you notice that? And when your mam spoke, he shrank against the wall.'

'He's Leanne's son. He's going to need to be tough.'

'He isn't, though. Is he? Did you notice how he pressed up against me? He's a little sweetie.'

'Little sweeties don't hack it on the Lotus.'

'He'd blossom in the right sort of home.'

I didn't say anything. Poppy was looking at me. We walked for a minute or two before she spoke again. 'He'd be a lovely big brother to our baby.' She stopped, took my arm, made me look at her. 'We could adopt him, Billy. Give him the kind of home he needs.'

'What do you think Leanne would do then? She'd have another and then another and she'd expect us to adopt them all. And pay her for the privilege.' I started walking again, and Poppy followed.

'So we just leave him? Can we come back? Soon? Take him out and show him what life can be like?'

'Yes,' I said. 'Yes, we can come back and take him out.'

'And maybe he can come and stay with us sometimes?'

We came round the corner. A man on the other side of the road was peering into my Merc. He wore pink chinos, a pale blue rugby shirt, a scarlet jacket and a wide-brimmed yellow hat. We were in the middle of the road now, but a good pic won't wait. I took the Olympus from my pocket and framed him beside the car. Poppy exhaled. 'Will you look at the state of him? He looks like a mandrill's arse.'

She had a mischievous smile I'd never seen before. It captivated me. And I was glad something had turned up to relieve her sadness.

Then there was shouting, and swearing, and the sound of running feet. When it all came up in court Mister Patel gave his evidence and another witness gave hers and then the police traffic experts said what they thought had happened, but at the time all I was aware of was noise. People shouting. The witness said it was her shouting and us she was shouting at, telling us to for God's sake get out of the way, but I only realised what was happening when it was too late.

It seems three youths had parked a stolen Mondeo in front of our Merc. They'd come running out of Patel's Paper Shop with Mister Patel on their heels. Whether they saw us or not I don't know, because they weren't asked and they didn't say, but the place they aimed at, accelerating hard, was the very place where Poppy and I were standing. When I realised the threat I grabbed Poppy's arm and swung her towards the kerb but, as I said, I was too late. I felt an enormous jolt and we were flying. After that, nothing.

CHAPTER 45

I was unconscious for three days.

Once she knew I was out of danger, Jessica had me moved into a private room. The constant noise was muted where I lay and the movement that seemed to go on twenty-four hours a day passed me by in the corridor outside.

When you're in a hospital bed and you're really not very well, if you ask about another patient the nurse says, 'She's fine,' or, 'I don't know. I'll try to find out.' I wasn't fooled. The words can be okay but you only have to watch their eyes. So when Jessica came to see me it was the first question I asked. 'Poppy. Where's Poppy?'

'I'm sorry, Billy.' She started on the kind of soothing platitude Mister Howard had indulged in when I was under arrest and facing the loss of my licence and he told me it's darkest before the dawn, but I couldn't take it. I said I needed to sleep and could she come back tomorrow? My head was hurting and my back and legs felt as though a bus had driven over them. A nurse gave me some really heavy painkillers and, although I'd have said sleeping was the last thing I'd be able to do, I went out like a light and didn't wake again till the next morning.

A chaplain came to talk to me and if I'd been able to raise myself from the mattress I'd have punched his lights out and to hell with my licence. When Jessica came the next day she gave up after three unanswered sentences and went away again.

* * *

Jessica kept the papers from me as long as she could. That was sensible on her part because a photograph of me in my hospital bed appeared in half a dozen of them, but I only found out about that from one of the nurses. Jessica or the photographer or both of them together had stuck an oxygen mask on my face to make the pic more dramatic and the nursing staff were cross about that because the mask hadn't been fitted properly and it gave the impression that they (the nurses) didn't know what they were doing.

'Be grateful they didn't find any tracheal intubation equipment in the room,' one of the nurses told me. 'You'd probably be dead.'

'Or an insemination kit,' said the one helping make my bed. 'You'd be pregnant.'

'Poppy was pregnant.'

'Oh. I didn't know that. I'm sorry.' That was one thing that hadn't got out, then.

When I asked Jessica what she thought she'd been doing, she brushed it off. 'Never mind that. We have to get you out of here. Out of hospital and out of the country. Otherwise you're going to sit at home feeling sorry for yourself.' People's feelings were a nuisance to Jessica and she only went so far in pretending to accommodate them.

She talked about the commission she'd mentioned to me and Poppy. It really excited her. People think Route 66 is the longest Interstate in America but it isn't, and not only because it isn't actually an Interstate. Even if it were, it would still be five hundred miles shorter than the I-90. What Jessica and the publisher she'd sold the idea to wanted me to do was fly to Boston, rent a car there and drive the three thousand miles of the I-90 until it reached the west coast in Seattle. Along the way

I'd take the pics that would enable Jessica to put together a book. She'd call it *I90: Gateway to America*. With my high profile of the moment we'd sell to people who normally had no interest in photography and I'd make a fortune.

I didn't want to do it. I wasn't sure, after the pasting my body had taken, that I could drive three thousand miles. So I said no, not now, maybe in a few months.

'Well, think about it.'

'Okay. I'll think about it.'

'When you're ready to leave here, call me and I'll drive you home. The Police left your Mercedes outside the shop and someone stole it.'

I found out later that the Merc had been found in Wallsend, burnt out. It was a nice offer, considering that Shrewsbury wasn't exactly on Jessica's way home from Newcastle, but I said I'd be fine and I'd make my own arrangements. I didn't want to spend four hours in a car with Jessica. I knew she'd spend that time trying to persuade me to go to the States and do the I90 project and I didn't think I had the energy to resist.

Leanne came to see me. Me and my half-siblings didn't look like each other. Some of my mother's features have been shared around – Tyler and I both have noses a little bigger than most people would think necessary, for example – but you wouldn't look at us together and think, "Oh, yes. One family." It hadn't been clear to me the last time I saw her when she'd been twelve years old but it was now – whatever beauty had been on offer had gone to Leanne. Hair down to her shoulders, the deepest shade of black. Brown eyes slightly lengthened, the merest hint of an oriental inheritance, which she emphasised by lining them in black. A full, generous mouth. Flawless skin.

She'd got as far as saying she had a favour she wanted from me when a nurse came in with a security guard, who asked her to leave. Leanne fluttered her eyelashes at me. 'You want me to go, Billy?'

'Eh? No.'

'I had to sweet talk one of the male nurses to get in here. Apparently they have orders to keep me out.'

'They're imagining it, Leanne. Or you are.'

But they weren't, and she wasn't. The guard asked me to confirm that I was happy to have Leanne there and then he and the nurse left. Leanne explained the favour she wanted and I said no. She said she was sure I'd change my mind when I'd had time to think about it. Then she brushed her hair back from her face and kissed me. Not on the cheek; on the lips. At which point a flash popped behind her.

I had another visitor that day. 'I had your agent on the phone. She wanted me to delay burying Poppy until you were out of here. She wanted to have your picture taken standing at the graveside.'

'I'm sorry, Missus Cannon. She shouldn't have said that.'

'You didn't know she was going to call?'

I shook my head. 'I'd have told her not to.'

'Well. The funeral is tomorrow. I don't suppose you can be there.'

'No.'

After she'd gone, I turned on my side and stared at the wall. I cried and cried until I fell asleep.

When I woke up they brought me food, but I couldn't eat. I remembered how, as a boy, I'd run to school, imagining I was in a big important race. I wanted to run now, to run and never stop; to keep running until I came to the end of the world and still run, off the end of the world and into black nothingness.

A doctor came to see me and told me depression was not a physical illness; she said it was a chemical imbalance and she could give me pills that would make it easier to bear.

'And grief?' I said. 'Is that a chemical imbalance, too?'

She started talking about how little we understand of the connection between the body and the mind and how many people the pills had helped to get over loss that seemed unbearable.

'No,' I said. 'No pills.'

'Would you like us to arrange for a psychotherapist to talk to you?'

'No. No psychotherapist.'

'What can I do for you, then?'

'Nothing. You can't do anything for me.' I turned away from her, staring at the wall that had become my constant study. 'Actually, that isn't true. You can go away and leave me alone.'

That night, I dreamed of Poppy. I reached out to touch her, but she was too far away. I moved, but however far I moved she was still, always, just out of reach. There was no expression on her face. She was simply there, staring at me. I found out later that I'd been screaming, because two nurses came and they found my pillow so soaked with tears that they had to change it, not just the pillowcase but the whole pillow. They called for help and a doctor came and the two nurses held me while the doctor put a needle in my arm and injected me with something and then the blackness returned and I was falling into it and then there was nothing.

Jessica had returned to London but she was back the next morning, radiating fury. 'I gave clear instructions that that slut was not to be allowed near you.' She flung a newspaper onto the bed. 'Honestly, Billy, you're not safe to be left alone.'

I picked it up. The picture showed me and Leanne, her lips on mine.

Brotherly Love

BL McErlane enjoys a tender kiss with sister Leanne. The fashionable snapper, whose prints sell for stratospheric sums, was seriously injured nine days ago in a hit and run incident that left his girlfriend Poppy Cannon dead in the road. Three youths have been arrested for attempting to rob Patel's Papershop and stealing a Ford Mondeo; one has also been charged with causing death by dangerous driving and failing to stop after an accident.

Yesterday our photographer was on hand to capture a moment of touching intimacy when budding model Leanne McErlane visited her brother in his private hospital room in Newcastle.

BL McErlane first came to public attention at the age of fourteen when, as Zappa McErlane, he was sentenced to imprisonment during Her Majesty's Pleasure for the murder of his stepfather, Antony Baker. The court was told that the killer beat Baker to death to prevent him consummating with Leanne the sexual relationship he regarded as his own prerogative.

Friends of the couple said that Leanne and BL McErlane plan to set up home together in Shropshire. The identity of the father of the model's child, Dillon, is a secret she guards closely.

'Leanne's a model?' I said.

'She will be, thanks to you,' said Jessica. 'No-one had heard of her before yesterday but now she has a Twitter account and thousands following her. They set you up, Billy. Did you even know she had a photographer there?'

I shook my head.

'And now anyone who reads that is going to think Dillon is your son. Incest, Billy. People don't like it.'

'Who are these friends of the couple?' I said. 'I don't know anyone she knows.'

'Her, Billy. Leanne is the friends of the couple. Or her publicist is. Some PR jerk has got her into the papers on your back. Did you talk about setting up home together?'

'She asked if she could come and live with me for a while. Said our mam was driving her nuts.'

'And you said?'

'No.'

'I'll let it be known that no such plans exist. All we need from you is dignified silence. As always. We have to get you out of here, Billy.'

I nodded.

'The I90 gig is still available.'

'No.'

I wasn't going to commit to a trip to the States. I didn't know what I was going to do. And even as I write that, I know it isn't true. There was a way out. I'd known that when I found out that Poppy was dead; I'd known it when Missus Cannon came to see me; and now, as I thought about Leanne and what she had done I knew it even more strongly. There was a way out, and as soon as I got out of here I was going to take it.

CHAPTER *46*

It was three weeks after Poppy's death that I finally got home. Jessica wanted to arrange a carer for me but I said no. I didn't want anyone else in the flat. I didn't answer the phone, didn't read my mail, didn't open the door. I lived on sandwiches and tea. I looked at all the pictures I'd taken of Poppy: Poppy smiling; Poppy laughing; Poppy serious. Awake or asleep, I dreamed of her. I couldn't stop crying.

I've talked about how it felt to realise you're in love. How you think about the person all the time. The way that, when you think about the future, it has her at its centre. Now I had to face a future that didn't have her in it. I couldn't do it. And there was an alternative. It took me a few days to get there, sidling up to the thought and shrinking back, but I'd reached a conclusion and I knew what it was. PoppyandBilly was now just Billy again; and just Billy was not enough.

I googled suicide. I wanted to know the ways people did it, what could go wrong and what was foolproof.

After three days, I went for a walk in the park. I had the strangest feeling of being followed, but I didn't look round. I left the park on the other side and walked into town where I found a car rental firm and rented a Fiesta. I didn't need a big car for what I planned to do.

I parked outside the flat and waited till it began to get dark. At eight thirty I set off. It took me two and a half hours to reach the service station on the M48 near the Severn Bridge. Once again I had that feeling of being followed and from time to time I thought a car in the rear view mirror was one I'd seen before, but I knew I was probably mistaken.

I'd chosen this way out because my googling suggested that people who jumped off the Severn Bridge had a zero failure rate. The only drawback was that the currents carried bodies in unpredictable directions and many were never recovered, which meant that no-one could be sure you'd actually ended it. Or, if you had, that you'd meant to. I had dealt with that by leaving a note in the car.

I parked and began the walk to the bridge. The feeling of being followed was even stronger and it came to me that Poppy was with me. I had no idea whether anything came after death other than endless silence, but if Poppy was following me then clearly something did. She was there, beyond the grave, waiting for me. All I had to do was jump and we'd be together again.

There's a walkway the length of the bridge. It's meant for maintenance crews, but it was perfect for my purpose. I would have to walk some distance to get to a place that was well out over the river and not the rocks. As I walked I knew, this time for certain, that there was someone behind me – knew because I could hear footsteps. I didn't believe a ghost would make that sound. I turned to look. It was the journalist who had interrupted us at Cartmel. He was a hundred metres behind me but as I stood still he came closer. He held up a camera. 'You don't mind, do you, Billy? One last dramatic shot as you go over the side?'

'How long have you been following me?'

'Ever since you got out of hospital. I figured I owe you. I knocked on your door a couple of times; thought you might need someone just to sit with you for a while. Thought it might help if I told you about my brother. But you didn't answer. And now I see you've decided on a different way out, so I guess there's nothing I can do for you after all.'

'That's right. There isn't.'

'Something you can do for me, though. Editors will be queuing up for this one. Do you think you could throw your arms and legs out wide as you go? Like you were sky-diving, only without the parachute?'

'What kind of a shit are you?'

'Oh. Now that is a surprise. BL McErlane doesn't swear. Everyone knows that.'

'You'll be arrested.'

'Is it an offence not to prevent someone from topping themselves? I'm not sure. Anyway, it'll be worth it. I'll be famous. Put myself into an entirely new earnings bracket.'

I turned away and began to walk on. He followed me. 'Look at all these cars going past, Billy. Do you suppose any of them guess why we're both here? What you're planning to do? Do you think any of them would care if they did?'

I ignored him and kept walking.

'It's a good job Poppy's gone,' he said. 'I don't think she'd be very happy knowing what a coward you turned out to be.'

I turned on him. 'You know nothing about Poppy.'

'Oh, well, Billy, that's not entirely true. I've had a couple of very interesting chats with her mother. I believe you say "her mam" where you come from, is that right? She's told me a few things. Human interest stuff for my story. I understand Poppy was going to make you a father. That's a lovely little touch for my story.'

I started walking again. He stayed with me, not behind this time but by my side. He said, 'You know what the Welsh said about this bridge when it opened?'

I shook my head.

> 'Two lands at last connected
> Across the waters wide,
> And all the tolls collected
> On the English side.

Bloody Welsh, eh? Good rugby players, though.'

'What did you mean about your brother?'

'Cancer, Billy. I worshipped him. You do, with an older brother. I've never known grief like it. I wanted to tell you about that, see? Let you know you weren't alone. And that the pain eases.'

'You mean you wanted to sweet talk me.' I paused and looked over the edge.

'Do you mind if we go on a bit further, Billy? Only the light isn't too good here and I want to get the best shot I can. When I say the pain eases, I don't mean it goes away. It never does that. You'll feel it till the day you die. Well, that's not going to be long for you, obviously. But I didn't take that way out and it's five years since we lost my brother and I still feel the pain and the grief. People tell you to let it go, move on, but I think that's nonsense. Poppy was the most important person in your life and she deserves to have you mourn her for a long time. A very long time. Pity she's not going to get that. But there you are.'

I'd stopped again. My fists were bunched

He said, 'This is what life is, Billy. Isn't it? You can have some great times, if you're lucky. And you were lucky, because you had Poppy. I just had to look at you, that day in Cartmel. You don't see the real thing very often, but when you do you know what you're looking at. I did, anyway. But then life thinks, "Can't have this fellow getting above himself" and it kicks you right in the teeth. That's when the rest of the world finds out who you really are. The kind of man who can take the worst life hands you and spit right back in life's face? Or the sort that gives up? Takes the easy way out? Well, you've made your decision and I suppose that's your right. Light's not too bad here, Billy. You want to make this the spot?'

The tears were rolling down my cheeks. He stepped forward and put an arm round my shoulder. 'You want to jump, Billy?' His head was cocked as he looked at me. 'Or are you going to start acting like a man? Go home and accept what life has done to you and live with it?'

I said, 'You'll lose your story.'

'There'll be others. Make up your mind, though. It's cold out here. That's a harsh wind.'

He drove behind me all the way. It was four in the morning when we parked. An idea had been growing in my mind for the last fifty miles. I walked back to his car and he rolled his window down. I said, 'You haven't got a brother. Have you?'

'I've got three, Billy. There were four of us growing up. All boys. My mother kept trying because she wanted a girl to go shopping with and talk girl talk. It never happened. One of my brothers is a bit effeminate, if you want to know, but my mother won't talk to him about frocks and babies. She's an old-fashioned sort of woman in many ways.'

'Any of them dead?'

'All in the pink, mate, I'm pleased to say.'

I rested my hands on his car and looked at the ground. 'You lied.'

'In a good cause, Billy. And it cost me the scoop of my life. You going to offer me a cup of tea?'

We went in and I put the kettle on. Then I picked up the phone and rang Jessica. It took her a while to answer and when she heard my voice she said, 'Jesus *Christ*, Billy! What fucking time is it?'

I said, 'That 190 commission. Is it still available?'

CHAPTER 47

I couldn't go for three weeks because there were contractual issues to settle with the publisher, and because I wanted a visa. You can go to the States without one, if you have a British passport, but they can turn you away when you arrive and I had a criminal record. Jessica networked in her usual high powered way and someone in Grosvenor Square decided I was an okay guy and should be let in.

Also, there was something else I had to do. I rented another car and drove to Newcastle.

There wasn't a gravestone yet. Apparently it takes a while for those to be engraved and, anyway, they have to wait for the earth to settle. Standing beside that mound of earth, still freshly turned, brought my loss home to me as nothing else could have done. I knelt beside it. The gravel was hard on my knees but I didn't mind. What I wanted was to be able to hold her in my arms just once more. I couldn't do that. I'd never be able to do it again. I started to cry, but there was happiness as well as grief in the tears. At least I'd known her. Nothing could take that away.

I don't know how long I'd been there when I became aware that I wasn't alone. I stood up and brushed the dust off my pants. She said, 'Thanks for coming.'

'I'm sorry, Missus Cannon. I wish it had been me and not her.'

She looked at me in silence. Then she said, 'Your journalist friend was here. He said you'd wanted to kill yourself. That wouldn't have brought her back.'

'No.'

She looked at her watch. 'I'm going home for a cup of tea. If you've got your car you could give me a lift. Save me waiting for a bus.'

I did that, and Missus Cannon asked me in. She gave me tea and showed me photographs of Poppy from a time before I'd ever known her. I promised to send her prints of mine as soon as I got home. Then I left. I didn't visit my mother, near though she was. Perhaps there'd been a moment, when I'd offered her my hand only to have it rejected, when we could have started to put the past behind us. But it was not to be. She'd never wanted me, she didn't want me now, and I was going to leave it that way.

There were many times in those three weeks when I thought the memories and thoughts of Poppy would overpower me and I wished I'd taken my chance and stepped off the bridge, but I knew that was in the past as an option. I hadn't done it then and I wasn't going to do it now. I closed up the flat and checked in for my Virgin Atlantic flight to America. Front of the plane. Jessica wouldn't hear of my travelling any other way.

I didn't make the best start. In a seafood restaurant in Boston, with the whole of my trip before me, I was eating a bowl of clams with sliced chorizo and manchego in a saffron-flavoured garlicy-buttery sauce which I mopped up with an eight inch stick of garlic bread. Then the woman at the next table, like me a solitary diner, leaned towards me. 'If you like clams,' she said, 'I bet you'd love the taste of my pussy.'

Of course it was a commercial transaction she was offering and not a romantic overture but that wasn't the point. Poppy was gone and I could live with the hurt now but it hadn't gone away. I turned the woman down with more ferocity than was polite. In seconds a tall man with a boxer's chest and arms in a tight black T-shirt was between our two tables. He said, 'Is this man bothering you?'

The woman said something about gays, which created a problem for the man in the T-shirt because throwing an Englishman out of a Boston restaurant might be a popular thing to do but they didn't want a reputation for homophobia. Then the woman went outside to smoke a cigarette and I finished my meal quickly, settled the bill and left. I was shaking.

I joined the I-90 in my rented Buick, not to leave it till I reached the west coast in Seattle. That's when I found out what being a professional means. Life had no point without Poppy but I worked as though everything was fine. I did the job I'd said I'd do; I got my pictures and the people were as friendly and interesting as Americans always are. If I wasn't turned on, and I wasn't, I don't believe anyone looking at those early pictures would see that. But Jessica had known what she was doing when she got me out of England. You can't go through something so different, so exciting, so welcoming and stay wrapped in self-pity for ever. When I reached Sioux Falls in South Dakota I started to feel the trip the way she'd hoped I would. By the time I'd got to Montana, I was right into it.

People mock Americans because eighty-seven per cent or whatever it is have never had a passport, but why should they want to leave their own country? People there speak English, they have every kind of terrain, every kind of music and every kind of recreation.

And, of course, they have the people. For a project like mine it isn't enough to snap away at the scenery. You have to stop in a place a while, get to know people, find your way into their lives. Once you do, you realise America has some of the most unbuttoned, un-hung-up people in the world. Alvy Singer might have spent fifteen years in analysis but he is not the American norm. Most people just do their thing and if you don't like it that's your problem.

Take Dan and Vern in Buffalo, Wyoming. We met in the Occidental Saloon. Butch Cassidy and the Sundance Kid, Buffalo Bill and Calamity Jane all stayed at the Occidental and when you stand in the bar you can see twenty-three bullet holes in the ceiling. It brings back every Western you ever watched.

Dan and Vern and I got talking. The conversation turned to women. Dan and Vern liked women, but things had gone wrong. 'The design of women is flawed,' said Vern, who it turned out was a retired engineer.

'Flawed?'

'Well, sure. If you bought a house in that condition, you'd sue the plumber.'

'We've cracked it,' said Dan and Vern said, 'Yeah. My Sophie's a real doll.' They both cackled at that.

Dan and Vern had been friends for sixty years and they'd shared a home on Klondike Road for the past twenty. 'Out near the Willow Grove Cemetery,' Vern explained. 'We don't want to inconvenience folks too much when we go.'

Dan said it would be real polite of me if I'd step out to Klondike Road with them and meet their womenfolk. Naturally, I said yes.

* * *

It took three days before they'd agree to have their pictures taken and sign the release forms without which the publisher would never let them into print. When she'd finally overcome her scepticism and accepted that the pics were real and I hadn't set them up, Jessica said they were some of my best ever.

They kept these two dolls permanently inflated and sitting up in their tidy, spotless living room. Vern explained that Kerry was a Backdoor Baby because Dan sometimes liked to pack fudge but he, Vern, took his sex straight. On the other hand, he'd always liked big tits. I had to admit I'd rarely seen any bigger than Sophie's. Dan and Kerry had a two-seat sofa and Vern and Sophie had another at right angles to it. The television constituted the other side of this triangle. The four of them would sit up at night watching old movies, the men's arms around the women, the men eating corn chips, drinking beer and smoking. At the end of the evening, Dan and Vern would tidy the room, empty the ashtrays, drop chip packets into the pedal bin and fill the dishwasher. Then they'd pick the two girls up in their arms and carry them off to bed.

They had wardrobes of tarty underwear and slutty dresses, skirts and tops they bought on the Net and, once they'd decided to trust me, they went through a whole series of changes while I took photographs. I did not, thank God, get to watch them coupling with the dolls. Dan explained that they both needed Viagra now and, once they got started, it tended to last a very long time and, anyway, they preferred to do it in bed. 'We like a bit of privacy. We're not nuts, you know.'

Dan and Vern were odd, but no odder than some of their neighbours. In Framingham they'd probably have been locked up. By the time I got to Coeur d'Alene, Spokane and Moses Lake they seemed almost normal.

However hard the author works, books are sold on one or two incidents, one or two pictures. What people remember *190,*

Road to America for is Dan and Vern and their blow-up dolls, and the Church of Forgiveness.

I'd only been in Coeur d'Alene for two days and I was walking around getting my bearings when a man so fat you were surprised he could walk stopped me in the street. 'My son, we must talk, you and I.' He had a voice as deep as Paul Robeson's.

Normal people cross the road at this point and walk on. Photographers with paymasters looking for a freak show don't.

He held out a hand the size of a rugby ball. I shook it. 'The Reverend Humphrey Catalan.' Humphrey? He handed me a card; sure enough, that was the name he went by. His occupation: Pastor of the Church of Forgiveness. He wrapped a monstrous arm around my shoulder. 'Let us break bread together, son.'

We caused a bit of a stir in the coffee shop. It seemed the Reverend Humphrey had broken two of their chairs in the past and now he was only allowed on the bench that ran round the booth at the back, but this was already occupied by four teens.

'Stay cool,' said my new friend. 'We don't mind sharing.' With which words he eased himself through the entrance to the booth, sat on the bench and pushed effortlessly leftwards, sliding the four towards the end. I expected trouble. Instead, one of the youths stood up and raised his hands palm outwards. 'Okay, Reverend. You win.'

They filed out peaceably and took seats around a table. The Reverend Humphrey beamed at them. 'God bless you, William Kazsnowski. Tell your mother it's high time she made her confession.'

The waitress stood beside us, pad in hand. 'Making confession,' she murmured. 'Is that what they're calling it now?'

Humphrey ordered coffee and blueberry pie with ice cream and double whipped cream. I asked for coffee. Humphrey said, 'You should eat something, son.' I told him I'd had breakfast only an hour earlier. 'So did I, son. God's work requires that we keep up our strength.' He turned on me the same thousand watt beam he'd directed at the Kazsnowski boy. 'Introduce yourself, my son,' he boomed in a voice that might have been heard twenty miles away.

I handed him my own card. While he was reading it, I took the Olympus out of my pocket and shot him three times, bracketed for white balance. The fluorescent light was flashing and you never know what sort of light you're going to get. He tucked the card into his waistcoat pocket.

'So,' he bellowed. 'What's an English photographer doing in Coeur d'Alene?'

'Looking for the unusual,' I said.

'Looking for the unusual. Well, son, you sure came to the right place.' Lowering his voice to a decibel count that probably wouldn't carry more than two hundred metres, he said, 'You have the most terrible aura, son. You know that?'

'Aura?'

'That's why I spoke to you. You want to know what your aura says?'

'Maybe. I'm not sure how many people I want to share the information with.'

He looked blank. The waitress slapped down an enormous slice of pie and two coffees. 'He means he'd like it if you kept your voice down, Reverend.'

Humphrey began to open paper packets of sugar and empty them into his coffee. He looked at me. 'That true, son? You shy?'

Walking away, the waitress said, 'He's English,' as though that explained everything. Which, in Coeur d'Alene, possibly it did.

Humphrey shovelled pie into his mouth. When he had finished, he stood up, dropped some money on the table and made for the door. 'Let's go, son.'

I followed him out. 'Thanks for the coffee,' I said. He put his arm round my shoulder and began to walk. I had no option but to go with him.

'I'll give you a tour of the town,' he said. 'And while we walk we'll address the subject of your vengeful spirit.'

'What?'

'Unforgiving. I never saw a more remorseless, grudge-holding aura in my life. That's the City Park, by the way. You want to get a picture?'

'I'll come back for it. I don't hold grudges.'

'No?'

It's a strange place, Coeur d'Alene. Americans will tell you it didn't exist much more than a hundred years ago, which rather rudely ignores the Indians. Now it's a resort and you get lots of normal people, or people who can pass for normal in the northwest USA, and they have malls and restaurants and stuff to amuse themselves in. There's sailing in the summer and skiing in the winter and golf most of the time when it isn't actually snowing. Good old friendly USA.

But it started as a frontier trading post and went into mining and logging and gambling, and the people who did those things weren't clubbable. Coeur d'Alene was where you got off the steamboat to try your luck at prospecting for silver, and where you got back on the boat to go home, or more likely to drift on somewhere else, when you realised this was not the place you were going to make your strike. There was no welfare state and no safety net and if you didn't look after yourself in whatever way you could, you starved. It takes a certain kind of person to thrive in that environment and beneath the tourist polish all that independence and egoism is still there.

That was what I was looking for in Coeur d'Alene and *I90, Road to America* shows that I found it. I took a lot of photographs, far more than got into the book. I got to love the place. There aren't many places where I think, "I could live here," but Coeur d'Alene is one of them.

And I spent quite a lot of time with the Reverend Humphrey. He summed up the spirit of the place for me. 'Folks here will look after you if you need it, but we expect you to look after yourself first. Folks will pick up the slack if you can't hack it all the way. But folks ain't your first line of defence, son. Your first line of defence is you.'

I realised after a while that he was feeding me this stuff because I was British and he'd heard all about the British and what had happened to them. We were the brave little land that had helped John Wayne and Frank Sinatra win the war but now our hearts had been poisoned by socialism and we'd lost our self-reliance. This was the second time I'd been the brand someone was going to save from the burning, Melanie being the first someone, and I have sometimes wondered what it is about me that makes people want to rescue me like that.

When I showed Jessica my photographs of Humphrey, naturally I also told her about the man behind the pics. She said he wasn't really a priest, he was a psychotherapist. Or maybe just a dabbler in self-help psychobabble. Whatever, she said. Whatever turned your crank, or helped you survive in this jungle. She was going through a bad time just then. I got the feeling that someone she'd thought of as her long term partner had just gone, but she didn't talk about personal stuff to me and I couldn't even tell you whether that someone was likely to have been a man or a woman. That's how close we weren't. But she did tell me that life was precarious. She said the most any of us could hope for was to get through to the day we died without ourselves deciding to chuck it in before then. If we could stand there at that moment and say, "Well, I made it. I'm here. I got through to the end. And in a minute I'll be out of it," that would be success.

All of which I'd already worked out for myself. But I didn't say so. I might have questioned her tact, but Jessica didn't know I'd got so close to killing myself I'd actually walked out onto the Severn Bridge.

There was one pic I showed her that I certainly didn't show Humphrey, and it didn't make it into the book, either. We'd arranged to meet and walk into town where I was going to buy him lunch. There was no-one in the church and the door to Humphrey's house next door was open as it usually was. He'd told me many times just to walk in and that's what I did.

It was a two storey house but Humphrey lived most of his life on the ground floor because stairs caused him difficulty. He'd had a stairlift fitted but it had broken the first time he used it. If the sounds had been coming from upstairs I might still have gone up there to investigate, because there isn't much a photographer after a pic won't do. But they weren't coming from upstairs, they were coming from a room I'd never been in but which I knew was where Humphrey slept.

Of course I know I shouldn't have shot it. I probably shouldn't have shot two thirds of the pics I'm most proud of. But I did. The chance to immortalise the pastor's huge naked rump as it rose and fell with astonishing vigour was just too much to pass up. You can always delete a pic you've taken and wish you hadn't, but go back and grab the fleeting opportunity you missed first time around? Forget it.

Pictures capture what you can see. Good pictures also capture what you can feel. What I couldn't get was Humphrey's rhythmic grunting or the mewing sounds that were coming from beneath him. Who was doing the mewing, I couldn't see. Whoever it was was almost hidden by the Reverend's immense bulk and I remember worrying that she'd be suffocated. I could see from the position of her feet that she was face down, but her feet were all I *could* see.

Having got my picture, I went back to the front door, rang the bell and then slammed the door loudly as I re-entered the house. 'Humphrey?' I shouted. 'Are you here?'

There was a bellow which I'm pretty sure said, 'I'll just be two minutes' and I sat down to read one of the Church of Forgiveness's newsletters. After a little more than two minutes, a small, neat woman with flushed cheeks who I knew to be one of the Reverend's flock passed through the room, smiled shyly at me and departed. A few moments later, Humphrey arrived. He was pinker than usual and breathing quickly.

'I'm sorry, Reverend,' I said. 'I hadn't realised you were hearing confessions.'

He smiled, gestured me to my feet, placed his arm round my shoulder and led me into the street. 'Sustenance, son, I must have sustenance. I have quite an appetite today.'

I said I wasn't surprised. I also said God would provide for his hunger, just as he clearly provided for his other needs. I suppose it came out a bit sour. All right, I'd never been religious and never had the opportunity but I did have some idea of what priestly decorum was supposed to be and it didn't include banging the parishioners.

'Son, if the Almighty is opposed to men and women doing what He made us to do, He ain't never mentioned His opposition in my hearing.'

We had reached the door of a restaurant. I said, 'Mexican do you?'

'Sure, son,' he said as he followed me in. 'Mexican be fine.' Quality didn't matter to the Reverend. What mattered was quantity and he knew, as I knew, that he'd get that here.

All right, so the Reverend Humphrey Catalan wasn't everyone's idea of a priest. Coeur d'Alene has a lot of churchgoers and many would be likely to cross to the other side of the road when they saw him coming. There are four Baptist churches in town and he'd have been drummed out of all of them. The Catholics have got two and the Lutherans are also pretty big there and they, too, would have denounced Humphrey and all his works. He was a glutton and a lecher and he didn't say no to a drink when it was offered.

But he brought smiles to the faces of the women he rogered. He cared about people, he wanted to see them happy instead of sad and he had a very clear idea of how that was achieved. Sometimes he wasn't entirely serious and sometimes he was and he was never more in earnest than when he outlined to me the source of his Ministry.

'Thou shalt not avenge, nor bear any grudge against the children of thy people, but thou shalt love thy neighbour as thyself: I am the Lord. Leviticus nineteen verse eighteen. But that was an instruction to the Jewish people about the Jewish people. But then in verse thirty-four it goes on, But the stranger that dwelleth with you shall be unto you as one born among you, and thou shalt love him as thyself; for ye were strangers in the land of Egypt: I am the Lord your God. But then came our

Lord and the new dispensation, and when one of them who was a lawyer said unto Him, Master, which is the great commandment in the law? He answered him, Thou shalt love the Lord thy God with all thy heart, and with all thy soul, and with all thy mind. This is the first and great commandment. And the second is like unto it, Thou shalt love thy neighbour as thyself. On these two commandments hang all the law and the prophets. Matthew twenty-two, verses thirty-seven to forty.'

All of this delivered without a smile and in full majestic voice.

'And your neighbour doesn't just mean that sweet little thing with the big bazookas who lives next door, son.' He laid his hand on my shoulder. 'In this global village the Lord in His infinite wisdom and mercy has created, your neighbour is everyone and everyone is your neighbour. But what you need to take to heart, son, is Matthew eighteen, verses twenty-one to twenty-two. Then Peter came and said to Him, Lord, if another member of the church sins against me, how often should I forgive? As many as seven times? Jesus said to him, Not seven times, but, I tell you, seventy-seven times. You think that means seventy-seven times, son? It does not. It means you forgive without limit.'

'Why are you telling me this, Reverend?'

'Your aura, son.'

My aura. Of course. Sure. As long as you believed A that I had an aura and B that he could see it.

We had a lot of conversations, me and the Reverend Humphrey, and he got to know all about me and my childhood, me and Miss Maguire, me and my mother, me and Poppy, me and Melanie, me and Wendy. 'Seems to me, son,' he said, 'that if anyone has a beef with anyone it's Melanie and Wendy who have one with you.'

There was a cultural thing here. I'd been born with a few serious handicaps and, yes, I'd overcome them but there was still part of me that was ready to accept them as a crutch and what the Reverend Catalan wanted me to know was that that was not the American way. 'Other people were dealt shittier hands than you, son, and some of them did okay. Come to that, a lot of people got much better cards than you did and some of them are in jail, or bankrupt, or dead. Or maybe a combination of those things. When you come right down to it, it isn't the hand you're dealt that counts, it's how you play it. And what about that maths teacher? What about Regus? He believed you when he didn't have to. What about those teachers who gave up their time for you and didn't charge a cent for it? Where do you get off holding grudges?'

'I don't hold grudges.'

'What you have to do, son, you have to go through every single person you're holding a grudge against in your mind and you have to forgive them.'

'I don't hold grudges.'

'You believe that, huh? Forgiveness isn't for their sake, son. It's for yours. When you stand before the Lord on that last day He isn't going to ask whose fault it is. He's going to want to know what you did with what you were given. The parable of the talents, son. Matthew twenty-five, verses fourteen to thirty.'

I hadn't a clue what he was talking about. I said, 'Since you know Him so well, is God going to have anything else to say while He's got me standing there?'

'Sure is, son. He's going to point out how many people went out of their way to help you make something of your life and He's going to want to know what you did to give something back and who it was you gave it to. Not the people who helped you, 'cos by and large it sounds like those guys already got plenty. What you did for the people who couldn't ever have helped you 'cos they had nothing. What did you spread around, apart from shit? That's what your Creator is going to ask you on that fateful day.'

'He's got a pretty foul mouth on Him, then? For a creator?'

'Thou shalt not take the name of the Lord thy God in vain; for the Lord will not hold him guiltless that taketh His name in vain. Deuteronomy, son. Chapter five, verse eleven.'

CHAPTER *48*

When people heard my accent they wanted to talk and I let them, partly because I was sometimes lonely and partly because the next conversation just might be with another Dan and Vern or Reverend Catalan and put the finishing touch to my project. Increasingly, what people wanted to talk about was what was happening in my country rather than theirs. It was the summer of 2011 and Britain was engulfed in riots.

The mid-western states of the USA aren't a natural home for liberals and the opinion I heard most frequently was that this was what socialism brought you: take away from people the obligation to work to support their families, transfer that duty to the State and before you could turn round you'd have a nation of people who thought they had a right to what you believed was yours. They also said that if Obama was re-elected then by the time he left the White House he'd have brought the same disaster to America.

And then I saw my name in the paper. I was in Billings, Montana, eating a steak sandwich and reading the *Billings Gazette*, and there it was. Zappa McErlane, also known as Zappa Chung, also known as Zappa O'Leary. Amazing, that British news would appear in a Billings newspaper. I don't suppose the *Evening Chronicle* ever has any news from Billings.

I finished my meal, drank my coffee, paid and went back to my hotel room to log on to the Net and read English papers.

Youth and Aunt Arrested on Riot and Theft Charges

A young rioter and his aunt were each sentenced to seven years in jail at Newcastle Crown Court today. The court heard that Zappa Chung, also known as Zappa McErlane, also known as Tyrone Chung had broken into three stores on Northumberland Street and stolen goods including a 51 inch plasma TV, an eighteen carat lady's gold watch and women's silk underwear. Instructions on what to take came to him by text message on his mobile phone from his aunt, the model Leanne McErlane, and after each foray into a store he carried the stolen goods to a car parked in Ridley Place in which she was waiting.

Michael Bradshaw, defending for Leanne McErlane, said she had only gone along because Chung was determined to join in with the looting he had seen on television and she wanted to ensure his safety. She denied giving him instructions on what goods to steal. Although she accepted that the high end underwear Chung had returned with was her size, she said that was coincidence and it was in any case her intention to return the goods to the shops from which they had been stolen as soon as she could. She agreed that no goods had been returned when she was arrested five days after the burglary but attributed the fact that some of the underwear had been worn to worry over her nephew's future. She had become confused about which clothes were hers and which belonged to the store. As a model she was accustomed to wearing up-market clothes and did not at the moment of dressing distinguish one set from another. The reason she had been wearing a face mask was not to avoid recognition but because she had a cold and did not wish to risk infecting others. He asked the judge not to impose a custodial sentence as to do so would almost certainly destroy her burgeoning catwalk career.

Dennis Fisher, defending for Chung, said that the defendant was filled with remorse and realised the seriousness of the offences he had committed. Chung was the nephew of the photographer BL McErlane who was sentenced to imprisonment at Her Majesty's Pleasure for the murder of his stepfather and Chung had been fuelled by a feeling, which he now realised was misguided, that he would never match up to his uncle's reputation and had also been egged on by his aunt.

Judge James Martin said that Newcastle had been spared the excesses of the rioting that has scarred London, Birmingham and other cities and that he would have preferred this to continue. The sentences he was handing down were intended not only to punish the accused but also to discourage others from following in their footsteps. Although Zappa Chung is only thirteen years old, Judge Martin lifted reporting restrictions to allow publication of his name in view of the gravity of the offences. Chung has eighteen previous convictions including Actual Bodily Harm, Receiving Stolen Goods and Indecent Assault but this is his first prison sentence.

Chung's mother, Chantal McErlane also known as Chantal Chung, is serving a custodial sentence of one year after being found guilty of receiving stolen goods and fraud by misrepresentation.

My first instinct was that I had to do something. I squashed it. I'd signed a contract to finish my project and I would keep my word. I was going to get on with my job.

It was in bed that night that the doubt surfaced. I didn't care about my mother, didn't care about Leanne, didn't care about Zappa, didn't care about Chantal. They'd got themselves into this mess and they could get themselves out with no help from me. But what about Dillon?

I lay awake far into the night, talking to Poppy in my head. She had wanted to adopt Dillon. But she was no longer here. What would she want me to do?

I rang Jessica. 'You're not going to get involved, Billy?'

'I just want to send my mother some money for Dillon. She's been landed with him, she doesn't have much anyway and I don't want the kid to go short.'

'Okay. And that's definitely all? You won't get any deeper in than that? Because this child is not your responsibility, Billy.'

'Jessica. Please. Give my mother a hundred and fifty quid a week and tell her to buy food and clothes for Dillon. If she puts him in care the money stops.'

She grumbled a bit more but she agreed to do what I asked. I put Dillon out of my mind and got on with what I was doing, working my way towards the Pacific coast. Nine weeks later, I left Seattle sitting upstairs on a Northwest Airlines 747. I'd bought *Any Human Heart* in SeaTac Airport and by the time I reached Amsterdam I'd almost finished it. Dave Wilson had been right. Against that kind of competition, I'd never have made it as a writer.

When I got to Amsterdam I changed to a nice little KLM

Embraer and just over an hour later I landed at Birmingham. Jessica had arranged for a car to pick me up and she'd had my flat stocked with food. Thirteen hours after leaving Seattle I was making a pot of tea in my kitchen. An hour after that I was asleep.

CHAPTER 49

I spent five solid weeks, eight in the morning till six at night seven days a week, working on the pictures I'd taken. Then I asked Jessica to come up and take a look. She went into raptures. 'You're a genius, Billy. A fucking genius.'

I smiled, but she was not to be deflected. 'There's talent. There's hard work. There's competence and technical ability. You can find those things all over the place. And then there's the Angel of Genius going through the world and, every century or so, she taps someone on the shoulder and says, "It's You".'

'Like the Lottery ads.'

'Don't be flippant.'

"She." Of course. Important angels used to be male. Gabriel, for example. I don't know when it changed.

This was one of those theories, like the Governor's about Myra Hindley, where the person has said it so many times they have it down pat. Beethoven got the tap, apparently. So did Mozart. And, of course, there was Shakespeare. 'You know why people keep trying to prove Shakespeare didn't write his own plays? Because he wasn't suitable for his gift. That's what the Angel of Genius does. She taps the shoulders of people you'd never in a million years expect could be geniuses and she says, "It's you."'

So that was me put in my place. I was someone you wouldn't in a million years expect could be a genius. Not that I could argue with that.

We chose the pics she would show the publisher, I formatted them for her as tiff files, seven hundred dots to the inch, and she went off to London with them on two flash drives. Each drive had a thirty-two gig capacity and they were both almost full. Job done.

Then I bought a Saab to replace the burned-out Mercedes and drove to Newcastle.

The first thing that hit me was the smell – unwashed clothes, dirty floors, cigarettes. Dillon looked as though he hadn't been washed for ages. It was two in the afternoon and my mother was drunk. I went into the kitchen; dirty dishes filled the sink. When I opened the fridge I found half a carton of milk, mouldy cheese, some bacon and three eggs squashed behind nine cans of Harp and two bottles of Lambrini. On the table was a packet of CocoPops, a waxed wrapper half full of stale bread and a half-empty carton of Lambert & Butlers.

I walked back through the sitting room where my mother was lighting another cigarette with trembling fingers and into the smaller of the two bedrooms. Dillon followed me but only to the door, from where he watched with lifeless eyes. With a sinking feeling I faced what seemed obvious: my nephew wasn't the brightest. I looked in the drawers and the wardrobe. Then I went back to face my mother. 'When did Dillon last eat?'

'How should I know? He knows where stuff is.'

'He's four years old.' I knew I sounded censorious but I couldn't help it. I said, 'You've been getting a hundred and fifty pounds a week to feed him and clothe him. That's on top of whatever you get from the Social. Why haven't you bought him any clothes?'

She shrugged. 'I didn't want him, did I? I've done my bringing up children.'

I left the flat, slamming the door behind me. I have no idea where I walked. People spoke to me, some out of the Geordie's usual friendliness and some because they knew me; I didn't answer. I had my head down, my eyes staring sightlessly at the pavement. What the hell was I going to do?

I didn't want a child any more than my mother did. With Poppy, yes, but that was never going to happen now. I didn't want my sister's bastard. I didn't. But around my shoulders I could feel the Reverend Humphrey's huge arm, and in my ear I could hear his voice. "He's going to want to know what you did to give something back and who it was you gave it to." And there was Poppy. "Can we adopt him?" I'd have preferred a different route, maybe some anonymous charitable giving, but I knew I couldn't leave the kid here. I didn't know where it was because I'd never needed to, but there must be a school in Shrewsbury for children with learning difficulties. Whatever happened, he'd be better off with me than where he was.

I went back to my mother's flat.

'Dillon,' I said. 'You're coming with me. Get your toys together and let's go.'

He stared at me, seeming not to understand. I said, 'Toys?' and he shook his head. I looked at my mother. I said, 'Would you mind telling me what you're crying about?'

'I'm sorry, Billy.'

'What?'

'I'm on my own. Leanne's in jail, Chantal's in jail, I never see you. I meant to look after him. I did. But…' She waved a hand and fell silent, tears following each other slowly down her cheeks.

I wanted to shout at her; I wanted to tell her she was out of my life for ever; but I couldn't rid myself of the memory of the one time she'd unburdened herself. The story of her mother's man friend who said she looked like Susannah York. How he'd traded on her innocence. What he'd done to her. The birth of Chantal and the death of her dreams. Being stupid is unfortunate but it isn't a crime. I said, 'I'll go on sending you money. Try not to drink yourself to death.'

'Would anyone care if I did?'

Dillon fell asleep in the car. When he woke three hours later we were passing Chester Services on the M56. I didn't take him into the Gents' because somewhere on the road he'd wet himself, but I bought him a bar of chocolate. He ate it as though he hadn't eaten for a fortnight and then he started to cry. At six thirty we were home.

I hadn't a clue what I was doing. Dillon's face was covered in snot and tears and it had got onto his coat. I took him into the bathroom. How do you talk to a child?

'Do you know how to use the shower?'

He looked at me blankly.

I sighed and ran a bath, making sure it was not too hot. Then I turned to him. 'Do you want to take your clothes off and get in?'

He went on looking at me.

Maybe he was shy. Maybe Leanne had told him not to take his clothes off in front of men he didn't know. All kinds of stuff went on, you only had to read the papers. I went out of the bathroom and closed the door behind me but I stayed close, waiting for sounds of movement. Sounds of splashing.

There weren't any. After a couple of minutes I went back into the bathroom. Dillon hadn't moved. He looked at me with a sort of despair.

When I knelt down and got close enough to take his clothes off, I realised how bad he smelt. I lifted him into the bath. He looked up at me. His face was unreadable. Surprise? Fear? I couldn't tell.

I said, 'Can you wash yourself?' but he didn't answer. He hadn't said a single word in all the time I'd been with him. I picked up the soap.

There were marks all over him. Bruises, scratches, cuts. I soaped him as gently as I could. When I put the soap down, he picked it up again and held it to his nose, sniffing it. It smelt of lemons. Then it slipped out of his hands and into the water and as he tried to catch it it kept slipping away from him. He looked up at me again, and this time he smiled. Just for a second, but it was there.

What did a boy of four like to do? I had no idea. I'd loved reading, but not at that age. Maybe if there'd been books in the house, though. I might have then. But I didn't think anyone would have taught Dillon to read. Read? I'd never even heard him speak.

I could read to him, though. They'd read to me in my foster home and I'd loved it. The first foster home, when I was nine. Before I made it so they had to send me away.

I wrapped a fluffy towel round him and patted him dry. He wanted to keep hold of the towel, so I let him do that while I went off to put his dirty clothes in the pedal bin. Then I took them out again. He needed something to wear until I got him some more.

And then I thought, never mind what do boys of four like to do? What do they eat? And how do you ask questions of someone who can't talk?

* * *

339

I took Dillon into the kitchen and sat him at the table. Better keep it simple. There was a tin of baked beans in the store cupboard and I emptied it into a pan and lit the gas. I cut two slices of bread and toasted them, and poached an egg. I poured milk into a mug and set it on the table. Dillon emptied it. I poured him another. When the toast was done I buttered it, tipped the beans over the toast and put the poached egg on top of the beans.

Dillon didn't look very happy with the knife and fork, so I cut up the toast and egg and gave him a spoon. The meal disappeared inside him. I hadn't seen that single-minded ferocity in eating since I'd been in care. When it was gone, his hands and face were covered with butter, sauce and egg. He hadn't once looked up from the plate. I took him back into the bathroom and washed his hands and face. He made a move for the pan. Watching him pull his pants down and lever himself up on to it, I thanked God he'd learned to do something for himself.

Then I washed his hands again, and after that we got ready to go out. Cheryl who lived in the downstairs flat had seen us come in and when she saw us going out again she came to her door. 'Hello, Dillon,' she said. 'Have you come to live with Uncle Billy?'

Dillon didn't say a word. I said, 'How did you know his name, Cheryl?' and she said, 'Don't be daft, Billy. You've been all over the papers. And so has he.'

I wanted to go to Marks and Spencer, but it would be closed by now. Sainsbury's though, was open till eleven. We went up and down the aisles in a methodical way I never normally did and when we got to checkout the trolley was overflowing. It was like I'd got some atavistic thing going about providing for my family. Filling the cave.

Sainsbury's also do toys and I got him a little car that would fit in the palm of his hand. And I went to the clothes aisle and bought a pair of jeans, a vest, a shirt and a pair of underpants.

Then we went home again. Cheryl was lurking behind her curtains. She came to the door as we went past. She was holding out a bunch of thin paperback books.

'Stanley Bagshaw,' she said. 'We had them for when the grandchildren came, but they're too old for that now. You'll find them well thumbed, I'm afraid, but ours loved them.'

I said, 'Thanks, Cheryl. That's really kind.'

The flat had three bedrooms, but I'd taken one of those as my studio so it had my desk and computer and printer and books and stuff in it. I slept in the biggest bedroom. That left the guest bedroom which no guest had ever actually slept in so I'd never made the bed up.

Dillon followed me, car in hand, as I took the sheets into the bedroom. He must have known the bed was for him because when it was made he climbed up and lay down on it, the car pressed close to his chest. Then he sat up and laughed and this time I thought there was a bit more happiness in it than there had been before. Shortly after that I took his clothes off him and put him to bed with just his new underpants on in case of accidents. I dropped all the old stuff in the pedal bin.

Poppy came to me that night. I know how that sounds; grief-stricken man under stress finds his dead fiancée in bed with him. I'm not saying she was real and I'm not saying she wasn't. She *felt* real. Slipped into my bed while I was sleeping and wrapped her arms tight round me. There was nothing nasty about it. No cold flesh; no smells of yew trees and dead carnations. No sex either; none of that. Her lips were warm when she pressed them against my cheek, just as she'd once pressed them against Dillon's. She murmured, 'Thank you.'

Dillon slept till six the next morning. I dressed him and gave him poached egg on toast cut into pieces for breakfast. He still hadn't spoken and I was becoming reconciled to the idea that he couldn't. Dumb as well as thick. One more struggle I'd given myself. At nine we walked over the bridge and through the park into town. I'd written down the sizes on the labels in the clothes I'd taken off him, and because they were a bit tight I picked out things that were slightly bigger. I held them up in front of him to make sure they looked right. We got underpants and socks and jeans and shorts and T-shirts and tops. All stuff that was simple to put on. No buttons. As he realised that these things we were buying were for him, his face took on a stunned look that changed quite rapidly to excitement. You'd expect someone of that age to jump around and shout, but Dillon stayed very still and didn't make a sound. You could see it inside him, though. Like when you blow up a bicycle tyre very hard and you know it's full to bursting and one more stroke on the pump could see it ripping itself apart in a great explosion. He was like that. We also bought him a coat.

In Marks they don't have assistants to help choose shoes. I mean, they do have assistants, but they're more to tell you what they've got and what they haven't. I wanted someone who'd measure Dillon's feet and help me choose shoes that fitted him well, so I paid for what I'd bought and it was a pretty big bag it all went in and we went off to find a shoe shop. Dillon stayed pretty close to that bag. He was hopping along, looking at the bag and then up at me and then at the bag again and never taking his eyes off one or the other of us. He wasn't looking where he was going and he bumped into a couple of people so I put my free hand down and took hold of his. He grabbed mine and it felt like he was never going to let go. He still hadn't let go when we were in the shoe shop and going round the shelves. We were in there quite a while and when we came out the salesgirl seemed very happy. Although she was puzzled when Dillon wouldn't speak to her. 'His name's Dillon,' I said. 'He's shy.' I didn't want to say, "He can't speak and I think he may be retarded." I didn't want to be disloyal to the kid.

Although that was what I was thinking.

He did smile at her, though. She was young, sixteen or so, eighteen at the most and she was small and she probably felt more like another kid than an adult to him.

The reason the salesgirl was happy was that we'd bought three pairs of shoes. A nice smart leather pair with Velcro straps instead of laces. A pair of sandals, also with Velcro fastenings, that the girl said would be nice for him in this warm weather. And a pair that looked like trainers but had lights that flashed on and off, and in the heels there were little wheels.

I gave his old trainers to the girl and asked her to dump them. Then I asked Dillon which shoes he wanted to wear out of the shop. Really, I didn't expect an answer and I was just doing what I thought the girl expected before I made the choice for him, but Dillon surprised me by pointing at the trainers with the lights and wheels. The salesgirl smiled at me and we shared a together moment but what I was thinking was that he'd understood the question so he couldn't be completely retarded. There must be something there.

Because of the wheels, he had difficulty walking on the shoes at first and he held my hand tightly. Around this point I remembered he didn't have any night things so we went into BhS and got him two pairs of pyjamas. Then into Boots where we got him a toothbrush and a pot of Germolene.

I was exhausted. How women managed to combine a career with looking after children I couldn't understand. This was a full time job.

Before we left Boots I bought a tin of drinking chocolate and a couple of fruit bars. Then we went to a taxi rank and got a lift home.

Dillon sat beside me in the back of the car, looking around. He'd look up at me, then at our shopping, then outside at the other shoppers in the crowded streets, then back at me.

Cheryl was pulling up weeds when we got back. Dillon gave her a dazed smile. Then he pointed at his feet. 'Shoes,' he said.

We both stared at him. Then Cheryl said, 'They're beautiful shoes, Dillon. Did Uncle Billy buy them for you?'

After the effort of uttering, he seemed overcome by shyness. He pressed up against my leg and reached to hold my hand but he didn't say anything else.

I went into Dillon's room with him following and I laid all his new clothes on the bed. Then I picked out one of everything. Dillon realised what I was doing and started trying to get his clothes off. He was a lot better than his performance yesterday in the bathroom might have suggested, but getting his jeans off over his trainers defeated him. I helped him and then I dressed him in his new stuff. Then I made him some hot chocolate and sat him at the table and gave him one of the fruit bars. He favoured me with another smile. He had a strange smile. There was more doubt than happiness in it and it looked like something he didn't use very often.

I had bought myself a copy of *The Times* and now I sat down to read it while Dillon got on the floor with his car. There's a kind of floor covering, I don't know what it is but it looks just like a polished wood floor, it really takes you in, and the people I'd bought the flat from had had this stuff laid in every room. I'd liked it so I hadn't seen any need to cover it up. I'd had no idea at that time that there'd be a little boy wanting to roll a toy car around on it but as it turned out it was great for that.

I read my paper for a while and Dillon was engrossed in his game but then, and I don't know why because going out again was the last thing on my mind after the exertions we'd already had, I said, 'Would you like to go in the park?' Dillon nodded so I put my shoes on and then his and out we went. It was only as we were going down the stairs that it occurred to me that he'd understood the question and I began to wonder just how backward he really was. He didn't look backward, I'll say that. Not now that he'd eaten and slept and eaten again. I'd come across plenty of thick people while I was in care and he didn't look like that. His eyes were watchful and wary and cautious but they didn't look unintelligent. You'd say if you watched him that he worried a lot but you'd never say he didn't understand.

We walked along by the river and watched the ducks and a swan. Dillon was transfixed. When I was his age I'd probably had the attention span of a lop, suck the blood, bloat and move on and a lot of kids I was in care and at school with never got away from that but Dillon, he could concentrate all right when he wanted to. He just stared at those birds and then he'd glance up at me for a moment, almost like he was asking "Is this okay? Is this what you want?" and then he'd be back looking at the birds.

And then I felt his hand come into mine. It just crept in, like something that wanted to be there but didn't want to be noticed. It didn't go all the way, just lightly held the tips of my fingers as though it wasn't really there, honest, guv, and it could slip away again at the slightest sign that it wasn't welcome. When I looked down I saw that now he wasn't really looking at the ducks or me, he was glancing away like someone in a pantomime or a bad stage play as though his hand wasn't part of him and he had no idea what it was up to. I moved my hand to get a firm grip on his, get it right into the palm of my hand and then he did look at me, straight at me and, just for a moment, he smiled. He looked away then, but he didn't let go. He didn't let go all the way along the path and across the grass and up to where the trees were, and he was still holding on when we reached the children's playground.

We stood at the edge, watching the swings and roundabouts and the slide and all the kids in their bright clothes just like his, swinging and sliding and going round and round. And shouting and laughing, all of them.

And us on the edge, watching.

I said, 'Why don't you join in?'

He looked at me. I said, 'It's all right. I won't go away. I'll still be here.'

He looked round. Nearby were two benches at right angles to each other, facing the playground. What I assumed must be parents were sitting on the benches. One or two fathers, but mothers mostly. Dillon pointed at these benches. He didn't speak but his message was clear. "You sit there. And watch." So I did.

There was another boy, about Dillon's age and solitary like him. I watched them circle each other without seeming to.

Going about their own business but getting closer. Then the little boy said something and my heart soared when I saw Dillon say something back and the little boy laughed and so did Dillon and they ran away towards the steps of the slide. The little boy got there first and started to climb and when Dillon reached the bottom he looked over at me as if asking permission. I smiled and he started up the steps towards where the little boy was waiting, speaking to Dillon from the platform at the top. Then the little boy sat down, swung his legs forward onto the chute and pushed off.

I don't think Dillon had ever done this before. He looked awkward and unused as he copied the little boy's actions and very uncertain indeed as he began to slide but by the time he reached the bottom he was laughing. The little boy had waited for him and there was an animation about their chatter that made me wonder how I'd ever thought Dillon might be backward. He was scared. That's what he was. But backward? No. I remembered Poppy, scared that the person who made love to her would hurt her. Wendy had never seemed scared, or Melanie, and I wondered if fear was something we carried from the Lotus.

They ran back to the bottom of the steps and started to climb again, the little boy once more leading the way.

When the little boy got to the bottom of the chute this time there was a woman waiting for him. She grabbed him by the hand and dragged him away, protesting and looking back at Dillon, out of the playground and down the path. She was scolding the little boy furiously and as she passed me I heard the words "little nigger". I was meant to hear them.

Dillon stood motionless, watching his little friend go. What was going through his mind I don't know. Wondering what he'd done wrong, perhaps, or maybe just thinking how funny it was that life gave you these occasional nice times but mostly it was the same old shit and the one thing you could be sure of was that you had no power to change what happened.

A woman who'd been sitting on the bench, watching the whole thing, walked over to a little girl who looked like she might be about four years older than Dillon and spoke into her ear. The little girl looked uncertain but she went with her mother to where Dillon was standing. The mother knelt down and talked to Dillon and Dillon stared at her and then he stared at the little girl, and then the little girl took his hand and they ran off to the climbing frame. When the woman came back to her seat she sat down without looking at me. Her lips were set tight against each other. An angry expression.

I said, 'Thank you.'

She shook her head, just once.

Later on we were walking home and the flow started. I couldn't believe it. Dillon was talking to me. Not deep philosophical conversation, obviously. Or even joined up sentences. Just words, mostly. Pointing things out. Ducks. Grass. Dog. Like that. Then he said, 'Tired.' I swung him up and he put his arms round my neck and laid his face against my chest and in moments he was asleep. I'd never carried a child like that before and I wished so much that Poppy could see us. Be with us. He was hot and sweaty and he smelled a bit. I thought, the first thing you need when you wake up, my lad, is another bath.

But I knew that wasn't really his first need. It was important, yes. And so would be some Germolene on his abrasions, and cutting his toenails, and a proper pan and oven meal, and maybe a bit of Stanley Bagshaw, and then a good night's sleep.

But they weren't number one. What Dillon needed most of all was what my sister Chantal had once dreamed of. Dillon needed someone to love who'd love him back.

So do we all. Many people never find that someone, and I sometimes think every single thing wrong in the world comes from that failure.

But Dillon had found his.

AUTHOR'S NOTE

I hope you enjoyed this book. If you'd like to know more about my books (which include historical as well as contemporary fiction) you can find details on my blog at http://jlynchblog.com/.

One of the drawbacks to being a writer is that it's a very lonely occupation, and I love to hear from readers. If you have anything to say about *Zappa's Mam*, please feel free to email me at rjl@mandrillpress.com

ZAPPA'S MAM'S A SLAPPER

JOHN LYNCH

Lightning Source UK Ltd.
Milton Keynes UK
UKOW04f0852050415

249131UK00002B/16/P